Uriah Cummings

American Cements

Uriah Cummings

American Cements

ISBN/EAN: 9783337406271

Printed in Europe, USA, Canada, Australia, Japan

Cover: Foto ©Andreas Hilbeck / pixelio.de

More available books at **www.hansebooks.com**

Uriah Cummings

BY

Uriah Cummings.

BOSTON:
ROGERS & MANSON.
1898.

PREFACE.

In a subject so large as that to which the present treatise is devoted it will not be regarded as strange that there are controverted points and matters concerning which the authorities are not in harmony.

The multitude of facts which must be taken into consideration readily accounts for these divergences of opinion.

In that portion of the present work which has to do with the theoretical and chemical side of this very practical subject special reference is made, and special attention given, to such branches of the subject as are particularly matters of doubt, of conjecture, and of controversy.

A full and free discussion of such points has been thought desirable.

In the conclusions reached in the present treatise concerning the various silicates of which natural and other cements are made up, and in regard to matters wherein the present writer notes his dissent from the ordinarily accepted hypotheses, it is believed that the theories, if such they may be termed, which are here advanced, account for by far the greater proportion of those incontestable facts which come to the view of every investigator, and which must not be ignored, but rather accounted for, and accorded a place in any worthy system.

The chief motive, however, which has animated the present work, has been a desire to see adequate consideration paid to the claims and merits of American rock cements.

It has always seemed to the present writer that scant justice has been done to natural hydraulic cements, and that the tendency to regard artificial products as, in some mysterious manner, much superior to all others has no sufficient justification in the facts of the case, and that when all the evidence is heard it will be found and conceded, that for enduring qualities, for excellence in places of trial, for permanence, and for worth, no artificially made cement can be found to compare with that mixed in the moulds of nature.

The writer has not hoped to carry the assent of the reader at every step. He will feel amply repaid if any words of his find favor, or provoke sufficient discussion to lead to a much-needed inquiry along the lines which he has scarcely more than suggested. In this way much truth may be brought to light.

Aside, however, from the theoretical aspect of the subject, it has been thought to be a matter of great importance to bring to the attention of the reader, in some convenient form, much matter of a practical nature which has never found a place in any of the printed works.

Within these pages it is hoped that the manufacturer, and the practical every-day user of cements, who care little or nothing for the chemical nature of the product they handle, will find hints and aids which may be of value, and information which cannot readily be found elsewhere.

And finally, if a further word is necessary to justify the present attempt, attention is called to the fact, that since the publication of Gen. Q. A. Gillmore's most excellent book, written some thirty-five years ago, no work whatever has been produced which deals with the subject of American rock cements.

This period has been by far the most important in the history of the industry. The changes which have taken place during this time, the marked advances which have been made, the new processes which are being employed, and the marvellous growth of the trade, resulting from a rapid widening of the markets for the product, clearly present a profitable field for investigation and furnish many facts worthy of record.

URIAH CUMMINGS.

STAMFORD, CONN., 1898.

CONTENTS.

ILLUSTRATIONS.

AMERICAN CEMENTS.

CHAPTER I.

INTRODUCTORY — HISTORICAL — SMEATON AND HIS DISCOVERIES —
THE CEMENTS OF THE ANCIENTS — EUROPEAN CEMENTS —
AMERICAN CEMENTS.

In order to arrive at an understanding of the nature of American
rock cements, and to be able to judge accurately, or even approximately, as to the position these cements occupy in the world, and the
relations they bear to the natural and artificial cements of Europe,
together with the time of their first fabrication, and the uses that were
made of them, and to fairly comprehend the state of the art from its
earliest inception until the present time, it will be necessary to take a
glance at the history of this important building material, even though
it be a cursory one.

It seems to be conceded by all European authorities that John
Smeaton, C. E., of England, was the first to discover the source of
hydraulicity in certain limestones. The discovery was made in the
year 1756, while casting about for a reliable mortar to be used in
the construction of the Eddystone Lighthouse. It appears that prior
to that date nothing was known as to the hydraulic character of the
impure limestones of the blue lias formation which extends through
several counties in England.

In the year named, Smeaton discovered, during the course of
many experiments, that the cause of the hydraulicity of a limestone
was due to the presence of clay in the stone.

Pasley, in the preface to his work, dated Sept. 17, 1838, says of
Smeaton that " he was the first who discovered, in or soon after
the year 1756, that the real cause of the water-acting properties
of limes and cements consisted in a combination of clay with the carbonate of lime, in consequence of having ascertained by a very simple

sort of chemical analysis, that there was a proportion of the former ingredient in all the natural limestones which, on being calcined, developed that highly important quality, without which, walls exposed to water go to pieces, and those exposed to air and weather only are comparatively of inferior strength.

" By this memorable discovery, Smeaton overset the prejudices of more than two thousand years, adopted by all writers, from Vitruvius in ancient Rome to Belidor in France, and Semple in this country (England), who agreed in maintaining that the superiority of lime consisted in the hardness and whiteness of the stone, the former of which may or may not be accompanied by water-setting or powerful cementing properties, and the latter of which is absolutely incompatible with them.

" The new principle laid down by Smeaton, the truth of which has recently been admitted by the most enlightened chemists and engineers of Europe, was the basis of the attempts, by Dr. John at Berlin and M. Vicat (the engineer) in France, to form an artificial water lime or hydraulic lime in 1818, and of mine to form an artificial water cement at Chatham in 1826, to which I was led by the perusal of Smeaton's observations, without knowing anything of the previous labors of these gentlemen on the Continent, or of Mr. Frost, the acknowledged imitator of M. Vicat in this country."

In a work on "Hydraulic Mortars," published at Leipzig in 1869, by Dr. Michaelis, the following passage occurs: "A century has elapsed since the celebrated Smeaton completed the building of the Eddystone Lighthouse. Not only to sailors, but to the whole human race is the lighthouse a token of useful work, a light in a dark night.

" In a scientific point of view, it has illuminated the darkness of almost two thousand years. The errors which descended to us from the Romans, and which were made by such an excellent author as Belidor, were dispersed. The Eddystone Lighthouse is the foundation upon which our knowledge of hydraulic mortars has been erected, and it is the chief pillar of our architecture.

" Smeaton freed us from the fetters of tradition by showing us that the purest and hardest limestone is not the best, at least for hydraulic purposes, and that the cause of hydraulicity must be sought for in the argillaceous admixture.

"It was a long **time** before men of science confirmed this statement of the English engineer, or corrected the ideas on the hardening of hydraulic mortars, which were then necessarily confused on account of the imperfect state of chemistry at that time. **How** could **science** subsequently keep pace with practical progress? For even at **present,** though we have possessed for about half a century the most excellent hydraulic **mortars, the hardening** process is not yet completely **explained."**

These extracts from eminent authorities on hydraulic cement may be taken as substantial evidence that Smeaton **was the** first, not to discover, as claimed **by these and other writers, but** to re-discover the lost art of cement fabrication. There is no doubt whatever but that **the** ancients thoroughly understood **the value of** impure limestones **for** hydraulic cementing purposes.

The fact is, that the history of natural **rock cement reaches so far back into** the early ages, **that it is** impossible **to** learn precisely the date of its first fabrication. **But** we do know that the ancient **Egyptians made** natural **cement four** thousand years ago which **would set and harden under water. The** Romans over two thousand years **ago made most excellent natural** cement, and used it in enormous **quantities for sewers, water pipes,** bathing fountains, piers, break**waters, aqueducts, etc. Prior to** this time, an aqueduct over seventy **miles in length was built at the** ancient city of Carthage. **At one place it was** carried across a valley on arches over one hundred feet **high, and** there were one thousand arches in line. In its construction **an immense quantity of** natural hydraulic cement was used. Some of **these arches are still** standing. At one point where the arches were **highest a** single piece over **one** hundred feet in length **has** fallen from **the top** down upon the **rocks below. It** still lies there intact, un**broken, an** excellent **illustration of the toughness** and tenacity of natural rock cement.

In many places in Mexico and Peru natural rock cement was used **so long ago in stone masonry** that the stones themselves **are** worn away, leaving the cement mortar projecting **from** the joints. **During the winter of 1892,** while some excavations were being made in **the city of London,** England, for railway **purposes,** the workmen **came upon a heavy mass or natural** cement concrete **laid over eight** hundred **years ago.**

Owing to the proximity of buildings, it could not be blasted out, and men were set to work to cut it out with chisels and hammers, and the concrete was so hard as to turn the best steel that could be obtained.

Writers on the subject of hydraulic cements, used by the ancients, and especially that used by the Romans, have, without exception, asserted that their hydraulic cement was made by a mechanical mixture of fat lime and pozzuolana.

It is inconceivable that such an absurd fallacy could obtain and prevail throughout all the centuries from the time of Vitruvius, a Roman architect (who, it is asserted, served as a military engineer under Cæsar and Augustus), down to the time of Smeaton, in 1756, and still more absurd that it should be handed down from Smeaton's time to the present day without contradiction, when the experiments made by Smeaton, and published by him, utterly contradict such a theory.

G. R. Burnell, C. E., of London, in his work on "Limes, Cements, and Mortars, 1868," referring to Smeaton, says: "The results he arrived at were very remarkable, not only for their practical utility, but also as an illustration of the ease with which a very acute observer may stop short on this side of the attainment of a great truth. Smeaton found that the commonly received opinion that the hardest stones gave the best limes was only true as far as regarded each quality considered by itself. That is to say, that of limes not fit to be used as water cements, those made of the hardest stones were the best for certain uses in the air, but that, whether obtained from the hardest marbles or the softest chalk, such limes were equally useless when employed under water. He found that all the limes which could set under water were obtained from the calcination of such limestones as contained a large portion of clay in their composition.

"His experiments led him to use for the important work of the lighthouse a cement compounded of blue lias hydraulic lime from Aberthaw, and of pozzuolana brought from Civita Vecchia, near Rome.

"Even at the present day, it would be difficult to employ a better material than this, excepting that the price would insure a preference for the Roman cement, then unknown."

Smeaton, in his " Narrative of the Eddystone Lighthouse," says :
" It remains a curious question which I must leave to the learned
naturalist and chemist, why an intermediate mixture of clay in the
composition of limestone of any kind, either hard or soft, should
render it capable of setting in water in a manner no pure lime I have
yet seen, from any kind of stone whatsoever, has been capable of
doing. It is easy to add clay in any proportion to a pure lime, but it
produces no such effect; it is easy to add brick-dust, either finely or
coarsely powdered, to such lime in any proportion also ; but this seems
unattended with any other effect than what arises from other bodies
becoming porous and spongy, and therefore absorbent of water, as
already hinted, and excepting what may reasonably be attributed to
the irony particles that red brick-dust may contain. In short, I have
as yet found no treatment of pure calcareous lime that rendered it
more fit to set in water than it is by nature, except what is to be
derived from the admixture of trass, pozzuolana, and some ferrugi-
nous substance of a similar nature."

It would seem that this description by Smeaton, as to the action
of pure limes, coupled with his discovery as to the hydraulicity of
impure ones, ought to have annihilated the ancient fallacy, but it did
not.

Quoting again from Burnell : " Some curious facts might be
mentioned, not only to show the influence of a large body of masonry
in retarding the solidification of the mortar in the interior, but also of
the danger of using rich limes in cases where such masses are necessary. Amongst them we may mention a fact cited by Gen. Treus-
sart, who had occasion to demolish, in the year 1822, one of the
bastions erected by Vauban in the citadel of Strasburg in the year
1666.

" In the interior, the lime after these 156 years was found to be
as soft as though it were the first day on which it had been laid.
Dr. John mentions that in demolishing a pillar nine feet in diameter,
in the church of St. Peter at Berlin, which had been erected 80
years, the mortar was found to be perfectly soft in the interior. In
both cases the lime used had been prepared from pure limestone."

It is not known whether these lime mortars were made by an
admixture of sand, burnt clay, trass, or pozzuolana with the lime,
but, so far as results are concerned, they would have been the same,

for nothing is more certain than that pure lime, with or without admixture of any one or all of the materials named, cannot be induced
to harden by simple mechanical mixture of these substances whether
in air or water. It never has done so and never will. If fat lime
can be made to assume an hydraulic character, by its admixture with
pozzuolana, why did Smeaton seek further? He had the rich lime
and he had the pozzuolana. Why did he not use them if he believed
in the tradition that had been handed down through the centuries, —
that such a combination, although purely mechanical, would harden
under water?

If he believed that the Romans used this material in all their
wonderful hydraulic cement constructions, why did he hesitate for a
moment even? The answer is plain. Simply because he tried it in
every conceivable way, as he himself states, and found it was not
true, that such a mortar would harden under water. That is why he
sought further. And yet, all who write of Smeaton, on the subject
of his great discovery, while acknowledging that he found the ancient
theory false, insist that the public shall deem it true.

It is quite true, that rich lime, or even hydraulic lime, takes very
kindly to burnt and powdered clay, pulverized bricks, trass, or pozzuolana, all of which are substantially one and the same thing, the latter
two, however, being of volcanic origin. No one of them contains
inherent hydraulic qualities, and their mechanical incorporation with
rich lime can in no manner render the latter hydraulic.

Although Smeaton used pozzuolana with the Aberthaw hydraulic
lime in the construction of the Eddystone Lighthouse, yet it is doubtful if he would have done so had he not "fortunately found at
Plymouth (where he was cutting and fitting the stones for the lighthouse) a considerable quantity of this material which a merchant had
imported on speculation, expecting to sell it to the constructors of old
Westminster bridge."

Henry Reid, in his work on "Portland Cement," London, 1877,
states, "The Aberthaw lime in itself could have accomplished all he"
(Smeaton) "desired, for he had unlocked the mystery of hydraulicity,
and felt confident in the knowledge of its cause."

The composition of trass and pozzuolana will be found in the
table of analyses.

Although Smeaton had discovered during the winter of 1756–57 that certain strata in the blue lias formation would, after calcination, produce an excellent hydraulic lime, it appears that he only made use of layers containing clay in such proportion as to cause his manufactured lime to slake by hydration.

It is very probable that he calcined some of the lower layers, but, finding they did not slake readily, confined himself to the use of such layers as would do so.

The idea of pulverizing such layers as would not slake readily, then testing them, and forming thereby a very energetic hydraulic cement, did not occur to him; and this is probably the point referred to by Burnell, wherein he states, as already quoted, " An illustration of the ease with which a very acute observer may stop short on this side of the attainment of a great truth."

In 1786 De Saussure found that the lime of Chamouni set under water, and, like Smeaton, attributed this faculty to the presence of clay.

Mr. Parker, of London, in the year 1796, took out a patent for the manufacture of what he called " Roman " cement from the septaria, nodules of the London clay formation found in the Isle of Sheppy.

This septaria was natural cement rock, and after calcination it was reduced to powder in mills suited to the purpose. This was undoubtedly the beginning of the natural rock cement industry in modern times. Its introduction by Parker was soon followed by its manufacture from the blue lias formation, and it went into general use throughout England.

Reid says, in speaking of Parker's Roman cement, " The Thames tunnel could not have been made but for the advantages it secured, and many of the early railway tunnels were built with it as a cementing agent."

Burnell, as late as 1868, in his work on " Limes and Mortars," states in regard to Roman cement, " Almost all of the works executed in water in England at the present day are executed with it."

In 1802 natural cement was produced at Boulogne, France. The rock at Boulogne is in the form of septaria, and is sometimes called " Boulogne pebbles." Its proportions of clay and carbonate of lime are such that it is used for the production of natural Portland cement.

In 1810 Edgar Dobbs, of Southwark, London, obtained a patent for the manufacture of artificial hydraulic lime or cement, by mixing together in suitable proportions carbonate of lime and clay, and after drying, he moulded or cut it into pieces before burning. He then states that "the burning must be sufficient to expel the carbonic acid from the lime without vitrifying any of the substances."

This is the first record we have of the production of artificial cement, or, as it was then called, " artificial hydraulic lime."

From 1813 to 1818 the artificial hydraulic limes were produced in France by M. Vicat, and by Dr. John of Berlin, and Raucourt de Charleville in Russia.

In 1824 one Joseph Aspdin, of Leeds, England, obtained a patent for the manufacture of an artificial cement which, in his specifications, he designated as " Portland cement."

This being the first time the word " Portland " was ever coupled with, or in any way mentioned in connection with cement, whether natural or artificial, there is no doubt whatever that Mr. Aspdin is entitled to the doubtful distinction of inventing the term, for certainly it is a most absurd and meaningless word so far as it relates to hydraulic cement.

Mr. Parker, on the other hand, had ample justification for naming his product "Roman cement," for he had but reproduced a cement substantially identical to that used by the Romans 1800 years before, and it is to be deeply regretted that the title he then employed did not thereafter cling to the natural rock cements the world over.

In the year 1818, twenty-two years after Parker had patented his Roman cement, Canvass White of this country discovered and patented a similar cement found at or near Fayetteville, N. Y.

This cement was used in large quantities in the construction of locks, viaducts, and culverts on the Erie Canal, at that time in the course of construction. Subsequently the State of New York purchased the patent from Mr. White, paying him therefor the sum of $10,000, and made the discovery public property.

In 1824, the year in which Aspdin obtained a patent on his artificial Portland cement, natural cement rock was discovered at Williamsville, Erie County, N. Y., where a manufactory was established. This cement was used extensively in the construction of the locks on the Erie Canal at Lockport, N. Y.

In 1826 natural rock cement was produced at Kensington, Conn., and was continued for several years, the production amounting to about five hundred tons yearly. On account of unfavorable transportation facilities, the production ceased soon after the cements manufactured on the Hudson River were placed in the larger markets.

In 1828 a cement works was established at Rosendale, Ulster County, N. Y. The product of the factory was first used in the construction of the Delaware and Hudson Canal, then being built through the town of Rosendale.

Other cement works soon followed at this place. Owing to the general good quality of the cement rock, and its proximity to New York City, as well as the advantages afforded by cheap transportation on the Hudson River, this locality rapidly developed into the leading natural rock cement center of this country, a position it maintains to the present day. Its yearly production amounts to about two and three fourths million barrels.

In the year 1829 cement rock was discovered at Louisville, Ky., while excavations were being made for the Louisville and Portland Canal, and it was manufactured and used during that year in the canal walls and locks.

Here again the rock proved to be of excellent quality. This fact, taken in connection with the conveniences in the matter of transportation on the Ohio River, and the advantages resulting from a wide and uncontested field of trade, led to the rapid introduction of this cement, and made the locality the center of the cement industry beyond the Alleghenies, and in some seasons the production has been as great as one and three fourths million barrels, and is exceeded only by the production from the Rosendale district.

During the summer of 1831 excavations were made for a canal on the left bank of the Susquehanna River to connect Muncy and Lock Haven, Penn., at a point about ten miles west of Williamsport on land known then and now as "King's Farm." The excavations disclosed an enormous body of rock, which was ascertained by Mr. Robert Farries, chief engineer of the canal, to be hydraulic cement rock. Col. George Crane, a prominent man of his time, living in a stately stone mansion across the river directly opposite "King's Farm," was a contractor on the canal at the time, and at once set about constructing a cement works for the manufacture of cement from this deposit for use in the construction of the canal. He built five kilns with suitable facilities for grinding, and his cement was used in the construction of the locks, bridges, culverts, dams, and viaducts, the latter, in some places, being over three hundred feet in length.

When the canal was finished in 1834, the manufacture of the cement was discontinued, but the condition of the work done over sixty years ago with the product of this somewhat primitive plant gives promise to-day that the rocks themselves will endure no longer than the material which binds them together.

In 1836 the Cumberland Hydraulic Cement and Manufacturing Company established a natural rock cement works at Cumberland, Md., which has since been in continuous and successful operation. As a result of the excellent quality of this rock, other works were subsequently erected, and the yearly output has been large, and Cumberland cement bears a most excellent reputation.

In 1837 cement rock was discovered at Round Top on the left bank of the Potomac River, near Hancock, Md., by A. B. McFarlan, a contractor of Washington, D. C., who manufactured cement from this rock in the following year, and used it in the construction of the Chesapeake and Ohio Canal. The graceful viaducts along the line of this canal, with the mortar unimpaired, attest the enduring qualities of Round Top cement.

It was during 1838 that cement rock was discovered at Utica, Ill., and works were erected during that year by Norton & Steele to supply cement for the construction of the locks, culverts, and bridges of the Illinois and Michigan Canal, and the rock proving to be of most excellent quality, the manufacture, since that time, has been uninterrupted.

In 1845 this plant passed into the possession of Mr. James Clark of Utica, Ill., and was operated by him until 1888, at which time it was incorporated as the Utica Hydraulic Cement Company, and its capacity largely increased. This cement has always stood well in public favor. In the masonry laid with it over fifty-five years ago, the joints are as hard to-day as the stone itself.

In 1839 natural rock cement was first produced at Akron, N. Y. The rock proving of exceptionally fine quality, its manufacture has been continuous, and steadily increasing in volume. Some of the most important engineering works of the country have been constructed with it, and its enduring character is well established.

In 1848 cement works were established at Balcony Falls, Va., by H. O. Locher, and are known as the James River Cement Works. H. O. Locher & Co. are still the proprietors at Holcomb's Rock, Va. The cement from these works has always borne an excellent reputation.

In 1850 cement rock was found at Siegfried's Bridge in the Lehigh Valley, Penn., and cement was produced and used in the construction of the Lehigh Coal and Navigation Company Canal from Easton to Mauch Chunk. Its manufacture in the Lehigh Valley has been continuous, and has assumed large proportions, with a constantly increasing demand.

In 1850 cement rock was discovered at Cement, Ga., by Rev. Chas. W. Howard of Charleston, S. C., and the eminent chemist, St. Julien Ravenel, also of Charleston (and a personal friend of Prof. Agassiz), who analyzed the rock, found it to be of a high grade; and its manufacture was commenced by Mr. Howard and his son in the following year, and was prosecuted by them until the beginning of the late war, when they both volunteered in the Confederate service, and the cement factory was allowed to fall into disuse.

In 1867 Col. George H. Waring, then of Savannah, Ga., purchased the property, and again the plant was put in running condition, and has since been operated continuously as the Howard Hydraulic Cement Company, Geo. H. Waring, president.

The cement manufactured by this company probably has no superior in this or any other country. Used as an exterior plaster in 1852 by Dr. Ravenel on his house in Charleston, situated on the Battery, where the walls are exposed to the disintegrating influences of salt spray, the stucco still remains unimpaired, while the sandstone lintels of the windows have long since been worn away.

In 1867 hydraulic cement rock was first discovered at Fort Scott, Kan., and its manufacture was commenced in the following year, and since that time has been continued uninterruptedly, the works having, for several years, been controlled and operated by The C. A. Brockett Cement Company, of Kansas City, Mo. This company has some local advantages not enjoyed by others. An excellent vein of coal underlies the cement rock, being separated from it by a stratum of fine fire clay. This coal is used in the manufacture of the cement, which in its general characteristics greatly resembles that of Cement, Ga.

In 1869 the manufacture of natural rock cement was established at La Salle, Ill., on the line of the same cement rock formation running through Utica, Ill., and has since been in continuous and successful operation.

In 1870 a cement works was established at Howe's Cave, N. Y., and has been operated continuously since then, producing a cement of uniformly good quality, which has been used successfully in many very important public buildings and heavy masonry.

In 1874 the Buffalo Cement Company commenced the manufacture of natural rock cement at Buffalo, N. Y., and owing to the excellent quality of the cement rock, the manufactured product rapidly advanced in public favor.

In 1877 the works were rebuilt on a large scale, and the capacity greatly increased. With almost unequalled facilities for transportation, this company has been very successful, and now enjoys a large and increasing trade.

In 1875 the Milwaukee Cement Company entered upon the manufacture of natural rock cement near Milwaukee, Wis. The success of this company has been phenomenal. With rock of a uniform and reliable character, and with works equal, if not superior, to any in the country, and with splendid transportation facilities, this cement has gained an enviable position in the markets of the West.

In 1883 a large plant for the manufacture of natural rock cement was established at Mankato, Minn. The works are of stone, and present a fine and substantial appearance. The cement rock is of the very best quality, and the manufactured product has obtained a strong foothold in the markets of the Northwest. Mortar made from this cement becomes exceedingly hard and stone-like in character, whether above or below water, and withstands to a remarkable degree the disintegrating effects of alternate freezing and thawing.

In closing this brief and incomplete *résumé* of the rock cement industry in this and foreign lands, it may be well to emphasize the fact that in no other country of the world is there to be found cement rock formations which are at all to be compared with those so well distributed throughout the United States.

The principal source of rock cements in England is from the Liassic or upper and lower Blue Lias subdivision of the Jurassic rock formation, extending from Lyme Regis on the south coast in a northerly direction to Yorkshire on the north, and averaging some thirty miles in width.

From the Memoirs of the geological survey of the Jurassic rocks of Britain, and more especially the report on the Lias of England and Wales, by Horace B. Woodward, London, 1893, we glean certain facts regarding bed formations and the source of the Roman or rock cement supply in that country since the days of Parker to the present time, from which we can readily understand why the artificial production of cement was resorted to.

The Lower Lias, from which the rock cements are obtained, consists in its lower portion of layers of blue and gray limestones, more or less argillaceous. These layers occur sometimes in even and sometimes in irregular bands, often nodular and interrupted, and they alternate with blue and brown marls, clays, and shales. Nowhere in the Lower Lias is there any marked band of rock which can be traced continuously for any great distance. The higher portion of the Lower Lias consists of blue, more or less micaceous clays, shales, and marls, with occasional septaria nodules and bands of earthy and shelly limestones and sandy layers. There is no rigid plane of demarcation between them and the mass of limestones beneath, while the clays pass upward into the lower beds of the Middle Lias with no lithological break or divisional line.

There is no layer of the rock used for cement purposes which does not vary in its proportion of clay, ofttimes as much as twenty per cent in individual quarries; and we find that whereas one layer may contain eight per cent, the one next above or below may contain fifty per cent of clay.

Clearly it is not remarkable that a cement made from such an ill-assorted mass of material should lack uniformity. No rational man in America would dream of undertaking to produce a rock cement from such a jumble of clays, shales, marls, nodules, limestones, and cement stones. Is it then to be wondered at that artificial mixtures were employed in an endeavor to meet and overcome the dissatisfaction unavoidably growing out of the use of such natural rock cements?

Contrast these materials with our own massive cement rock deposits! Here we have immense beds of cement rock absolutely free from any extraneous substances, perfectly pure and clean, with layer upon layer, extending for thousands of feet, without an appreciable variation in the proportion of ingredients.

Cement rock quarries are worked in this country decade after decade without the necessity of discarding a pound of the material, and analyses taken during successive years show no marked changes in the constituent parts. Had England possessed such cement rock formations as are distributed throughout this country, it is extremely doubtful if the production of artificial cement would have been resorted to. Under such circumstances there would have been no occasion for it.

The magnitude and value of the work done with the rock cements of this country is almost beyond comprehension. They have been used in the largest buildings, tunnels, bridges, dams, and aqueducts constructed in America, and a failure has yet to be reported and recorded. More than seventy-seven million barrels have been so used during the past twelve years.

In subsequent chapters the various rock cement deposits of this country will be discussed in detail, with descriptions of the various plants, together with a mention of the important works executed with the various brands, the magnitude and permanence of which should set at rest all question and all doubts concerning the enduring qualities of American rock cements.

CHAPTER II.

Common Quicklime — Slightly Hydraulic Lime — Eminently Hydraulic Lime — Hydraulic Cements — Hints as to Methods of Cement Rock Calcination.

Nature has supplied this country with practically inexhaustible deposits of hydraulic limestones, and in almost endless variety of combinations.

In order to classify these varieties and reach intelligent conclusions concerning them, the following arrangement considered subsequent to calcination has been employed as fairly representative :—

1. Common quicklime.
2. Slightly hydraulic lime.
3. Eminently hydraulic lime.
4. Hydraulic cements.

The deposits from which all or nearly all of these classes may be obtained occur in nearly every State and Territory of the United States.

It is the presence of clay in greater or less proportions in these limestones which confers upon them their hydraulicity, or power to set and harden either in air or water.

The greater the proportion of clay in a limestone, up to a certain fixed limit, the greater will be its hydraulic activity.

COMMON QUICKLIME.

Pure lime of itself contains no setting properties whatever. It is a base which, if combined with an acid, like silica, loses its caustic properties, and takes a new form known as silicate of lime.

The latter, if composed of correct combining proportions, will, upon the application of water, commence to crystallize and harden, whether in air or water, and without an appreciable development of heat.

Pure lime alone when subjected to water will, in the process of hydration, develop heat as high as 300° F., but it will not crystallize, as has been stated so often by eminent writers.

That pure limestone occurs in massive crystalline form is due to its chemical combination with carbonic acid. It will also crystallize when combined with sulphuric acid, as in calcined gypsum, or plaster of Paris.

But with water alone, it will not crystallize. Mortars made from pure lime and sand will attain a certain degree of hardness when used above ground, due mostly to the process of drying out, and possibly a slight amount of reabsorption of carbonic acid.

This process is so slow, however, as to be inappreciable during an ordinary lifetime.

This is easily proven by placing in water a sample of the oldest lime mortar to be found. If the lime is approximately pure, the mortar will in a few days crumble into mud, and the lime will be taken up in solution in the water, and if the water is changed frequently the lime will entirely disappear, leaving the sand as clean as when in its native bed.

SLIGHTLY HYDRAULIC LIME.

Lime that contains sufficient clay to enable it to be classed as slightly hydraulic lime will contain ten to twelve per cent of clay. This amount of impurities will not prevent the lime from slaking, although it will slake more slowly than will a lime which is pure or nearly pure.

It will not appear as white as the latter, neither will it develop so high a degree of heat during hydration; but as a mortar-making material for brick or stone masonry it is vastly superior to that of pure lime, as it contains inherent setting and hardening properties amounting — with the proportion of clay mentioned — to about thirty per cent of silicates or active setting matter, i. e., hydraulic cement.

Such a lime, when made into mortar with the requisite amount of sand, will cement properly moistened bricks so firmly together that in a few years the bricks, rather than the mortar, will be disrupted when subjected to tensile strain.

EMINENTLY HYDRAULIC LIME.

A lime in which clay is present to the extent of eighteen to twenty-two per cent is classed as an eminently hydraulic lime. Containing about fifty per cent of hydraulic cement, it will, when properly calcined, reduced to powder, hydrated, and thoroughly mixed with sand, produce a mortar that, for enduring qualities, when exposed to the atmosphere, is superior to any known mortar-making material.

It is sufficiently hydraulic to be classed as a very slow-setting hydraulic cement.

Concrete made from such a mortar will require from sixty to ninety days to become sufficiently hardened to bear submersion.

This quality of lime has been used extensively in Europe for many years in the making of concrete blocks for sea-walls and general submarine masonry, — notably in France during the past sixty years.

Beckwith states that the hydraulic limestone quarries of Teil, France, have been worked for several centuries.

John Smeaton, C. E., of England, used an eminently hydraulic lime mortar in the construction of the Eddystone Lighthouse, in 1757.

There are tens of millions of tons of this class of hydraulic limestone in this country, which can be produced at a low cost and will be so produced, whenever our engineers and architects create a demand for it.

HYDRAULIC CEMENTS.

A limestone which, after calcination, is proven by analysis to contain thirty-eight to forty-two per cent of clay will produce an active-setting hydraulic cement.

Upward of one hundred and forty million barrels of this class of cements have been produced and consumed in the United States since its first production, in 1818.

During the last ten years ending Jan. 1, 1895, the production was 66,255,682 barrels.

Fully ninety-five per cent of all the great engineering and architectural work of this country has been done with this class of American rock cements.

The failures to do excellent work will not aggregate one hundredth of one per cent.

' Probably no country on the globe is more favored with such an abundance, and of such excellent quality, of natural cement rock, as is known to exist in a vast number of localities in this country.

In a few localities in France there are natural rock cement beds of first quality, but in England they occur very rarely.

In our classification of the impure limestones of the United States, we have defined the proportions of clay within certain narrow limits for the sake of a starting point, but the proportions of clay and lime vary in different localities, and the action of these ingredients is largely dependent on the proportions of the constituent parts of the clay, also when magnesia, to a greater or less extent, enters into the combination, all of which has an important bearing on the enduring qualities of a cement.

In nearly all natural cement rock formations, in all countries, it is found that the deposits consist of several layers or strata, and there is usually a slight variation in the proportion of ingredients as between the various layers.

As a rule the lower strata contain the greater proportion of clay, which gradually diminishes as we ascend in the series of layers.

All manufacturers of natural rock cement in this country fully appreciate the advantages to be gained by a thorough admixture of the several layers.

Whenever it is found that there is a considerable variation in the proportions of the clay and the carbonates, as between the upper and lower layers, and these are mixed together and subjected to calcination in the same kiln, it will follow, that with heat sufficient to expel the carbon dioxide from the upper layers, the lower ones will suffer somewhat from over-calcination, producing a variable quantity of light and friable clinker that has to be excluded as waste, being devoid of hydraulic energy.

By the calcination of the lower layers separately, and at such a temperature as will insure the leaving of one or two per cent of carbon dioxide in the product, and subsequently mixing this product thoroughly in the grinding with the upper layers of the series that shall have been calcined at a much higher temperature, a very perceptible improvement in the quality of the resultant cement is sure to follow, and the loss due to waste clinker will be obviated.

Fortunately the occasions for this precaution are exceedingly rare in this country; indeed, as a rule, the layers are so evenly balanced throughout that separate calcination is not practised, and the amount of loss by waste clinker is so slight as scarcely to be considered.

It remains true, however, that this matter of separate calcination, although it may at present seem trivial, will ultimately come into general practice with those manufacturers whose great ambition is to produce as nearly as possible a perfect cement, without regard to a slight advance in cost.

And in the present advanced state of the art, it is certainly along the lines indicated, namely, a classification and separation of the various layers into groups, and each group to be separately calcined at such temperature as will insure the best results, that any notable improvement in the quality of our American rock cements need be expected.

CHAPTER III.

SILICATES — THE EFFECT OF AN EXCESS OF ALUMINA, OF MAG-
NESIA, OF FREE LIME — ALKALIES — CHEMICAL COMBINATIONS.

There are two distinct classes of rock cements in this country,
although they are not distinguishable except by analysis.

The ordinary consumer will never note the difference, as the
action of both classes is the same under like circumstances.

They are classified as double (bi) and triple (tri) silicates, and
their compositions are known as

1. Silicate of lime and alumina.
2. Silicate of lime, magnesia, and alumina.

The combining proportions of these silicates differ materially, as
the former requires a greater percentage of silica than does the latter.

During the year 1894 the production of American rock cements
amounted to 7,595,676 barrels, and the proportions of the two classes
were as follows : —

1.	Bisilicates	.	.	.	.	.	2,557,464 barrels.
2.	Trisilicates	.	.	.	.	.	5,038,212 "
	Total	.	.	.	.	.	7,595,676 "

The percentages are approximately as follows : —

1. Bisilicates   33.67 ⎫
                           ⎬ = 100.
2. Trisilicates   66.33 ⎭

Although the terms " double " and " triple " silicates are used to
distinguish the two classes, it is not intended that the rule is at all
absolute.

On the contrary, it is wellnigh impossible to find a cement which
can rightfully be classed as a double silicate that does not contain a
small percentage of triple, and oftentimes a large percentage of single,
silicates ; therefore, the position of a cement in this classification is determined by the particular form of silicates which in its composition
predominates.

So far as durability and general excellence are concerned, no distinction can be drawn between these two classes of cements. They have been produced in this country for many years, the former since 1818, and the latter since 1824. The durability of either depends not as to whether it be a double or triple silicate, but rather upon the nearness with which it approaches true combining proportions. Whichever approximates this standard closest is, theoretically at least, the better cement; but, practically, it has been demonstrated by long-continued use that there may be an excess of the two bases, lime and magnesia, without detriment to the enduring qualities of the cements whether used in air or water.

A cement containing an excess of alumina will, when used below ground or in fresh water, remain stable and firm for an indefinite period, but is apt to disintegrate in masonry exposed to the atmosphere in a cold climate. Fortunately the rock cements of this country are not open to this objection, except to a very limited extent, as less than two per cent of the total output can fairly be so rated.

It is often stated by writers, especially those who advocate artificial or so-called Portland cements, that the rules governing chemically combining proportions must be strictly adhered to; that an excess of lime is not only objectionable, but positively dangerous.

If this be true, how are we to reconcile ourselves to its acceptance, while we have before us the unquestioned fact, that the natural rock hydraulic limes of France have been in use hundreds of years before Portland cement came into existence, and are in use to this day in vastly increasing quantities in sea water, in earth foundations, in masonry exposed to the atmosphere, in concrete blocks and arches, in monoliths, and in important works of every kind, and yet they contain not less than forty per cent of free lime?

Evidently there is a mistake somewhere; but rather than question unduly, hastily, or without apparent reason, the wisdom of so many of the eminent scientists who have persisted in this somewhat arbitrary view of the subject, we prefer to state such facts as are within the experience of those familiar with the use of cement, and at the same time, by quoting liberally from the works and statements of leading authorities, make clearly evident that the doctrine so maintained is without sound foundation. No cement, be it either natural rock or Portland, contains ingredients in exact combining proportions. There is usually a slight variation. Some contain an excess of clay, and others an excess of lime or magnesia. These variations are not so great, however, as to prevent prompt induration in air or water.

Much has been written by the advocates of artifical cements, of the importance of subjecting cements to a high degree of heat in calcination in order to bring out their best qualities.

According to these writers, cements that cannot sustain a high heat without injury are of a low grade, and, singularly enough, these writers are unanimous in the opinion that all American rock cements are calcined at a low heat, and, therefore, as a matter of course, are, by them, classed as low-grade cements.

It may be stated, in passing, that this is an error on the part of these writers.

There are many American rock cements that stand high in public favor that are calcined to a white heat, the same as that to which Portlands are subjected.

We will defer the discussion of this particular branch of the subject to future chapters, and confine ourselves to the elucidation of the various phases met with in a study of American rock cements.

A cement rock that produces the double silicates is a mechanical combination of two chemical compounds, viz., silicate of alumina (clay) and carbonate of lime, while that which produces the triple silicates is a mechanical combination of three chemical compounds, namely, silicate of alumina, carbonate of lime, and carbonate of magnesia.

The last two compounds named are combined in certain fixed proportions, while the clay is seldom so found, as the silica is usually in excess of true combining proportions with alumina.

These, with other compounds relative to the composition of hydraulic cements, will be found in the table of chemical combinations.

It does not follow that because a cement may contain ingredients the proportions of which are not in strict conformity to the law governing chemically combining proportions as ordinarily interpreted, it must necessarily contain an excess of one or more of the bases, for there may be, and often are, found triple, double, and single silicates in one and the same brand of cement; in fact, a cement is improved by diversifications of this character.

It may be taken as a truism that the essential constituents of a cement rock are carbonate of lime and silicate of alumina.

When undergoing calcination the lime becomes caustic by reason of the expulsion of the carbon dioxide, in which condition, and while at a high temperature, it attacks and disassociates the silicate of alumina, rendering the silica free as a silicic acid, the latter then combining in certain fixed ratios with the bases present, forms silicates.

This ratio is absolute. Any excess, whether of the acid or of the bases, must and does remain free and uncombined in the resultant cement.

Carbonate of magnesia acts in a similar manner to carbonate of lime, and when the two are present with a proportionate amount of silica, hydraulic energy, strength, and durability follow. And, as has been pointed out before, alumina, which is always present by reason of its combination with the only quality of silica obtainable, is not particularly objectionable unless it is in excess. It is not so good a base as lime or magnesia, and when in excess impairs the indurating value of the cement.

All cement rocks contain, in varying proportions, oxide of iron, soda, potash, etc., which are not objectionable if not in excess. The former gives color to a cement. One per cent will produce a yellowish cast, two per cent a drab, and four per cent produces a dark color. It has no effect whatever on the quality of a cement; it is simply an adulterant, and is usually in such limited amount as not to detract from, while it certainly does not add to, the value of a cement.

With the aid of the following table of chemical combinations, and the analyses of the various cements of this and other countries, it will not be a difficult matter to deduce conclusions which, it is hoped, may not be devoid of interest.

The alkalies, soda and potash, when present to the extent of three to five per cent, add much to the quality of a cement, as they have much to do as an aid to the caustic bases, lime and magnesia, in the conversion or reaction of silicate of alumina into silicic acid and alumina, or forming a silicate that is soluble in acids.

But the constituents, silicic acid, lime, magnesia, and alumina, being the essential ingredients in the formation of hydraulic cements, the non-essentials named will, for the sake of brevity and space, be omitted in our calculations.

CHEMICAL COMBINATIONS.

1. Oxygen   72.73 $\Big\} = CO_2$. Carbonic acid, or car-
     Carbon   27.27   bon dioxide.

2. Oxygen   28.57 $\Big\} = Ca\ O$. Lime.
     Calcium   71.43

3. Oxygen   40.04 $\Big\} = Mgo$. Magnesia.
     Magnesium 59.96

4. Oxygen   53.27 $\Big\} = Si\ O_2$. Silica.
     Silicon   46.73

5. Oxygen   47.00 $\Big\} = Al_2\ O_3$. Alumina.
     Aluminum 53.00

6. Carbonic Acid 52.40 $\Big\} = Mg\ CO_3$. Carbonate of mag-
     Magnesia   47.60   nesia.

7. Carbonic Acid 44.00 $\Big\} = Ca\ CO_3$. Carbonate of lime.
     Lime   56.00

8. Silica   63.83 $\Big\} = {}^{Al_2\ O_3\ +}_{3Si\ O_2}$ Silicate of alumina.
     Alumina   36.17

9. Silica   34.91 $\Big\} = 2CaO,SiO_2$. Silicate of lime.
     Lime   65.09

10. Silica   42.91 $\Big\} = 2MgO\ SiO_2$. Silicate of mag-
     Magnesia   57.09   nesia.

11. Silica   29.14
     Lime   54.34 $\Big\} = 100$ Bisilicate of lime and alumina.
     Alumina   16.52

12. Silica   28.33
     Lime   52.82 $\Big\} = 100$ Bisilicate of lime and mag-
     Magnesia   18.85   nesia.

13. Silica   24.41
     Lime   45.52 $\Big\} = 100$ Trisilicate of lime, mag-
     Magnesia   16.24   nesia, and alumina.
     Alumina   13.83

14. Silica   30.29 $\Big\} = SiO_2\ K_2\ CO_3$. Silicate of pot-
     Potash   69.71   ash.

15. Silica   36.15 $\Big\} = SiO_2\ Na_2\ CO_3$. Silicate of soda.
     Soda   63.85

CHAPTER IV.

TABLE OF ANALYSES. HYDRAULIC LIMES AND CEMENTS.

No.	Silica.	Alumina.	Iron oxide.	Lime.	Magnesia.	Potash and soda.	Sulphate of lime.	Carbonic-acid water and loss.
1	16.05	1.92	3.22	77.29	1.52			
2	24.33	3.73	....	71.94				
3	29.71	5.35	3.29	59.53	0.95	1.17		
4	20.57	1.13	....	77.76	0.54			
5	28.14	9.10	3.20	53.34	1.00	2.80		2.42
6	27.88	6.19	4.64	56.45	4.84			....
7	25.31	7.03	9.74	56.17	1.75			
8	44.50	15.00	12.00	8.80	4.70	5.50		9.50
9	48.94	18.75	11.92	6.40	2.42	3.93		7.64
10	19.75	7.48	5.01	60.71	1.28	0.75	1.64	3.38
11	24.90	8.00	3.22	59.38	0.38	0.50	1.46	2.16
12	20.42	12.00	1.87	63.13	0.58			2.00
13	23.36	8.07	4.83	58.93	1.00	0.50	0.85	2.46
14	22.74	7.74	3.70	56.68	0.57	0.63	1.66	6.28
15	21.11	11.30	3.36	58.03	2.93	0.71	0.51	2.05
16	24.30	2.61	6.20	39.45	6.16	5.30	....	15.23
17	34.66	5.10	1.00	30.24	18.00	6.16		4.84
18	23.16	6.33	1.71	36.08	20.38	5.27		7.07
19	26.40	6.28	1.00	45.22	9.00	4.24		7.86
20	25.28	7.85	1.43	44.65	9.50	4.25		7.04
21	30.50	6.84	2.42	34.38	18.00	3.98		3.78
22	29.98	6.88	2.50	33.23	17.80	7.10		3.13
23	30.84	7.75	2.11	34.49	17.77	4.00		3.04
24	27.30	7.14	1.80	35.98	18.00	6.80		2.98
25	27.98	7.28	1.70	37.59	15.00	7.96		2.49
26	28.38	11.71	2.29	43.97	2.21	9.00		2.44
27	19.90	5.92	1.14	46.75	16.00	8.02		2.27
28	22.62	7.44	1.40	40.68	22.00	2.23		3.63
29	26.69	7.21	1.30	43.12	19.55	1.13		1.00
30	24.34	8.56	2.08	61.62	0.40	2.00		0.80
31	22.91	8.00	1.90	61.76	2.70			2.63
32	23.32	6.99	5.97	53.96	7.76			2.00
33	22.10	15.00	3.21	55.98	0.37		3.34	....
34	24.94	9.00	1.16	63.64	1.26			....
35	27.60	10.60	0.80	33.04	7.26	7.42		2.00
36	33.42	10.04	6.00	32.79	9.59	0.50		7.66
37	22.58	7.23	3.35	48.18	15.00			3.66
38	22.44	6.70	2.00	32.73	0.67			35.46

No.	Silica.	Alumina.	Iron oxide.	Lime.	Magnesia.	Potash and soda.	Sulphate of lime.	Carbonic-acid water and loss.
39	28.43	6.71	1.94	36.31	23.89	1.80	....	.92
40	17.50	6.50	3.00	36.51	....	....	....	36.49
41	22.21	16.48	1.67	39.64	17.50	....	....	2.50
42	32.06	21.27	2.11	35.56	7.00	....	....	2.00
43	28.45	2.24	2.00	56.00	10.00	....	....	1.31
44	18.59	9.14	1.00	40.70	27.00	....	....	3.57
45	19.52	1.97	1.29	41.51	1.47	....	....	34.24
46	28.02	10.20	8.80	44.48	1.00	0.50	....	7.00
47	19.35	7.00	4.50	63.75	....	....	....	5.40
48	21.14	6.30	2.50	66.04	1.11	....	....	2.91
49	22.69	7.30	2.87	62.28	1.08	....	....	3.78
50	20.80	7.39	2.61	64.00	....	....	....	5.20
51	23.20	7.03	2.41	64.19	0.97	....	....	2.20
52	22.89	8.00	2.44	63.38	2.30	....	....	0.99
53	25.15	8.00	3.28	49.53	13.78	....	....	0.26

REFERENCE.

No. 1. Hydraulic Lime, Aberthaw, England, used in the construction of the Eddystone Lighthouse.

,, 2. Hydraulic Lime, Lyme Regis, England, used in the construction of the London docks.

,, 3. Eminently Hydraulic Lime, Holywell, Wales, used in the construction of the Liverpool docks.

,, 4. Hydraulic Lime, Teil, France.

,, 5. Hydraulic Cement, " King's Farm," on Susquehanna River, near Williamsport, Penn.

,, 6. Roman Cement, Rudersdorf, Germany.

,, 7. Roman Cement, Isle of Sheppy, England.

,, 8. Pozzuolana, near Rome, Italy.

,, 9. Trass, from the valley of the Rhine.

,, 10. English Portland Cement, " K., B. & S." brand.

,, 11. German   ,,   ,,   Alsen & Son.

,, 12. Natural   ,,   ,,   Boulogne, France.

,, 13. American   ,,   ,,   " Giant," Egypt, Penn.

,, 14. English   ,,   ,,   given by Reid as first quality.

,, 15. German   ,,   ,,   ,, ,, ,, ,, ,, ,,

,, 16. Buffalo Hydraulic ,,   Buffalo, N. Y.

,, 17. Utica   ,,   ,,   Utica, Ill.

No. 18. Milwaukee „ „ Milwaukee, Wis.
„ 19. Louisville „ „ " Fern Leaf," Louisville, Ky.
„ 20. Louisville „ „ " Hulme," Louisville, Ky.
„ 21. Rosendale „ „ " N. L. & C. Company," Rosendale, N. Y.
„ 22. „ „ „ " Rock Lock," Rosendale, N. Y.
„ 23. „ „ „ " N. Y. & R.," Rosendale, N. Y.
„ 24. „ „ „ " Hoffman," Rosendale, N. Y.
„ 25. „ „ „ " Norton High Falls," Rosendale, N. Y.
„ 26. Cumberland „ „ Cumberland, Md.
„ 27. Napanee „ „ Napanee, Ont.
„ 28. Akron „ „ " Newman," Akron, N. Y.
„ 29. „ „ „ " Cummings," Akron, N. Y.
„ 30. California „ „ South Riverside, Cal.
„ 31. American Portland „ " Saylor's," Coplay, Penn.
„ 32. Fort Scott Hydraulic „ " Brockett," Kansas City, Mo.
„ 33. Gate of France Hydraulic Cement, France.
„ 34. Vassy Hydraulic Cement, France.
„ 35. Utica „ „ La Salle, Ill.
„ 36. Shepherdstown Hydraulic Cement, Shepherdstown, Va.
„ 37. Howard Hydraulic Cement, Cement, Ga.
„ 38. Hydraulic Cement Rock on Platte River, Nebraska.
„ 39. Mankato Hydraulic Cement, Mankato, Minn.
„ 40. Hydraulic Cement Rock, near Salt Lake City, Utah.
„ 41. St. Louis Hydraulic Cement, near East Carondelet, Ill.
„ 42. Barnesville Hydraulic Cement, Barnesville, O.
„ 43. Warnock „ „ Warnock, O.
„ 44. Austin „ „ Austin, Minn.
„ 45. Hydraulic Cement Rock, Blacksburg, S. C.
„ 46. Round Top Hydraulic Cement, Hancock, Md.
„ 47. German Portland Cement, " Dyckerhoff " brand.
„ 48. „ „ „ " Germania " brand.
„ 49. „ „ „ " Porta " brand.
„ 50. American „ „ " Empire," Warners, N. Y.
„ 51. „ „ „ " Medusa," Sandusky, O.
„ 52. „ „ „ " Alpha," Phillipsburg, N. J.
„ 53. James River Hydraulic Cement, Balcony Falls, Va.

This table of analyses has been compiled with the utmost care, no labor having been spared to make it as perfect as possible.

Among the authorities consulted and relied upon are Beckwith, Bennett, Bode, Boynton, Cox, Davidson, DeSmedt, Dodge, Dorr, Miller, Newberry, Ogden, Reid, and Winchell, analysts and chemists of established reputation.

In many cases a selection has been made from several analyses of the same brand of cement, and in this, as in all other respects, great care has been exercised with a view to formulating a table which may be confidently relied upon.

CHAPTER V.

ANCIENT GREEK AND ROMAN MORTARS — CARBONATE OF LIME MORTARS — CONCRETE OF THE MOUND-BUILDERS — SULPHATE OF LIME MORTARS, ANCIENT AND MODERN.

A treatise on cements would hardly be complete without allusion to those cementing agencies which, although they can hardly be classed as hydraulic, as that term is now understood, were used in mortars and concretes centuries ago, and many specimens of which are still in a good state of preservation.

We refer to carbonate of lime and sulphate of lime, each of these being mixed with sand, clay, gravel, and finely broken stone. The latter having been used above, while the former was used both above and below ground. It is quite irreconcilable with our modern ideas as to the causes of the hardening of mortars, yet the fact remains that carbonate of lime has been made into a mortar by admixture with clay, sharp sand, and gravel, and after three thousand years is found to be as hard as a rock.

A paper by Dr. Wallace read before the Mechanics Institution, Glasgow, so completely covers this subject as to render a literal quotation desirable.

On Ancient Mortars. BY WILLIAM WALLACE, Ph. D., F. R. S. E, F. C. S. From the *London Chemical News, No. 281.*

" Having, by the·kindness of William Clarke, Esq., C. E., who has recently returned from the East, been supplied with specimens of mortars and plasters from well-known ancient buildings in Egypt, Greece, Italy, and the Island of Cyprus, I have submitted a number of them to analysis, with the object of determining several points of interest. The ages of the mortars vary from about sixteen hundred to upwards of three thousand years, thus dating back to the most ancient historical periods. I propose in the present notice to give the results of the analysis of such of the specimens as I have examined.

Mortar of the Great Pyramid. — Two specimens of mortar from the Pyramid of Cheops were examined, one being from the interior, and the other from the outside of the structure. That from the interior was from the great chamber or the passage leading to it. Both specimens present the same appearance, — that of a mixture of plaster of a slight pinkish color with crystalized selenite or gypsum. They do not appear to contain any sand, the silicic acid being evidently in combination with alumina as clay. Part of the selenite was probably burnt, and the result mixed up with burnt lime, ground chalk or marl, and coarsely ground selenite. The latter would act the part of sand in our mortars, *i.e.*, prevent undue contraction in drying. The quantity of water is almost exactly what is required to form the ordinary hydrate of sulphate of lime with two equivalents of water. The mortar is easily reduced to fragments, but possesses a moderate degree of tenacity. Prof. C. Piazzi Smyth, who is at present making explorations in the pyramid, and to whom I have communicated the results of my analysis, has informed me that large quantities of gypsum and alabaster are found in its vicinity; and that some enormous slabs of alabaster or selenite have been discovered lining the walls of a large tomb recently opened. The material of which the pyramid itself is constructed being limestone, there is no difficulty in accounting for the presence of the lime.

	INTERIOR.	EXTERIOR.
Sulphate of lime, hydrated	81.50 [1]	82.89 [1]
Carbonate of lime, (CO_2 calculated)	9.47	9.80
Carbonate of magnesia (do.)	.59	.79
Oxide of iron	.25	.21
Alumina	2.41	3.00
Silicic acid	5.30	4.30
	99.52	100.99

Ancient Phœnician Mortars from Cyprus. — Two specimens were obtained from Cyprus. The first is from the ruins of a temple near Larnaca, the highest stone of which at present remaining is five feet below the level of the ground, and the lowest about eighteen feet. Mr. Clarke supposes this to be the most ancient mortar in existence,

---

[1] Water by actual estimation, 16.66, 17.38.

and it certainly is one of the best I have ever seen. It is exceedingly hard and firm, and appears to have been made of a mixture of burnt lime, sharp sand, and gravel, some of the fragments being about half an inch diameter. On solution in hydrochloric acid, it gave a small quantity of soluble silica, amounting to .52 per cent.

The other specimen from Cyprus is a cement used for joining water pipes. These pipes were found near Larnaca, ten feet below the surface of the ground, and bear evidence of extreme antiquity; they are of red clay, about eleven inches in diameter, and are connected by spigot and faucet joints, the intervening spaces being filled with the cement, and afterwards coated with a black substance which was found to be bitumen. This mortar or cement is very hard and perfectly white in color. It will be observed that in both of these Phœnician mortars the lime is almost completely carbonated.

	TEMPLE.	CEMENT.
Lime	26.40	51.58
Magnesia	.97	.70
Sulphuric acid	.21	.82
Carbonic acid	20.23	40.60
Sesquioxide of iron	.99	—
Alumina	21.6	.40
Silicic acid and fine sand	16.20	.96
Coarse sand	3.37	—
Small stones	28.63	—
Organic matter	.56	.24
Water	.54	3.09
	100.26	98.39

Ancient Greek Mortars. — The first specimen is taken from a part of the Pnyx, the platform from which Demosthenes and Pericles delivered many of their orations. It has been long exposed to the action of the weather, is very hard, and of a grayish-white color. The other specimen is plaster from the interior of an ancient temple at Pentelicus, near Athens. It has not been exposed to the weather, the temple being in a cave; it is of a pale cream color, and moderately hard. The analytical results are the following:

	PNYX.	TEMPLE AT PENTELICUS.
Lime	45.70	49.65
Magnesia	1.00	1.09
Sulphuric acid	—	1.04
Carbonic acid	37.00	38.33
Sesquioxide of iron	.92	.82
Alumina	2.64	.98
Silicic acid and sand	12.06	3.90
Water	.36	3.07
	99.68	98.88

In the mortar from the Pnyx the carbonic acid is exactly the amount required by the lime and the magnesia, supposing both to be completely carbonated; in that from the temple the carbonating is nearly but not quite complete.

Ancient Roman Mortars. — These differ from those already mentioned in being evidently prepared by mixing with burnt lime, not sand, but puzzuolana, or what is commonly, although improperly, called volcanic ash. Of these, four specimens were examined, but two only of the analyses were completed, owing to deficiency of material. The first in the following table was taken from Adrian's Villa at Tivoli, near Rome; it is a tolerably hard and firm mortar, of a rather dark-gray color.

The second is plaster from the interior of a wall at Herculaneum; it is hard, evidently exposed on one side to the action of hot volcanic mud, and of a red tint. The third specimen is from the roof of the Latin tombs near Rome, of a pale reddish-brown color. The fourth is a cement or mortar from a mosaic forming the floor of the baths of Caracalla, Rome. All these mortars were hard and firm, and contained an appreciable amount of silicic acid in combination : —

	ADRIAN'S VILLA.	HERCULANEUM.	LATIN TOMBS.	MOSAIC.
Lime	15.30	29.88	19.71	25.19
Magnesia	.30	.25	.71	.90
Potash	1.01	3.40	not estimated.	
Soda	2.12	3.49	not estimated.	
Carbonic acid . . .	11.80	23.80	13.61	17.97
Peroxide of iron . .	4.92	2.32	1.23	3.67

	ADRIANS VILLA.	HERCULANEUM.	LATIN TOMBS.	MOSAIC.
Alumina	14.70	2.86	16.39	10.64
Silicic acid and sand .	41.10	33.36	36.26	30.24
Organic matter . . .	2.28	1.50	—	2.48
Water	5.20	1.00	8.20	5.50
	98.73	101.86		

General Remarks. — These analyses appear to show that the lime in mortars and plasters becomes, in the course of time, completely carbonated, and does not form a combination consisting of $CaO,HO + CaO, Co_2$, a conclusion that has been arrived at by some authorities. They also show that in all cases where the mortar is freely exposed to the weather a certain proportion of alkaline or earthy silicate is formed, which in all probability confers additional hardness, and that those mortars are the hardest which have been long below ground. It is well known to builders that those walls are strongest that are built during a rainy season, and that when mortar dries quickly it becomes crumbly and possesses little binding power. When kept wet for some time, a small proportion of silicate of lime will be formed, which will not only make the mortar itself harder, but will unite it more firmly with the stone. It is curious that the mortar which is probably the most ancient (the specimen from a Phœnician temple) is by far the hardest and firmest; in fact, like a piece of rock. It is a concrete, rather than a mortar, and its excellence seems to indicate that a large-grained sand is best for building purposes, and that even small gravel may, in certain cases, be used with advantage."

Prof. E. T. Cox, in his report of the geological survey of Indiana, renders an interesting, and, in view of the question of antiquity, a valuable acquisition to our knowledge of ancient mortars and concretes; and the question arises, was the old or the new world the first to produce from materials which to-day would be considered as useless for such a purpose, a mortar or concrete, which, being placed below ground, would become hard and stone-like in character and remain so throughout all the centuries that have elapsed since their first fabrication.

Prof. Cox says, " It is not alone in Europe that we find a well-founded claim of high antiquity for the art of making hard and durable stone by a mixture of clay, lime, sand, and fragments of stone; for I am satisfied that this art was possessed by a race of people who inhabited this continent at a period so remote that neither tradition nor history can furnish any account of them.

"They belonged to the Neolithic or polished stone age. They lived in towns and built mounds for sepulture and worship, and protected their homes by surrounding them with walls of earth and stone. In some of these mounds specimens of various kinds of pottery, in a perfect state of preservation, have from time to time been found, and fragments are so common that every student of archæology can have a bountiful supply.

"Some of these fragments indicate vessels of very great size. At the Saline Springs of Gallatin County, Ill., I picked up fragments that indicated, by their curvature, vessels five to six feet in diameter, and it is probable that they are fragments of artificial stone pans used to hold brine that was manufactured into salt by solar evaporation.

"Now, all the pottery belonging to the Mound-Builders' age which I have seen is composed of alluvial clay and sand or a mixture of the former with pulverized fresh water shells.

"A paste of such a mixture possesses in a high degree the properties of hydraulic pozzuolana and Portland cement, so that vessels formed of it hardened without being burnt, as is customary with modern pottery. The fragments of shells served the purpose of gravel or fragments of stone as at present used in connection with hydraulic lime in the manufacture of artificial stone.

"It will be seen by the following analysis of a piece of ancient pottery from the 'Bone Bank,' in Posey County, Indiana, that, so far as chemical constituents are concerned, it agrees very well with the composition of hydraulic stones.

"ANCIENT POTTERY, 'BONE BANK,' POSEY COUNTY, IND.

Moisture at 212° F.	1.00
Silica	36.00
Carbonate of lime	25.50
Carbonate of magnesia	3.20
Alumina	5.00

Peroxide of iron	5.50
Sulphuric acid	0.20
Organic matter, alkalies, and loss	23.60
Total	100.00

" It is my opinion, based upon the result of its analysis, that it is simply an artificial stone made from a mixture of river mud and pulverized fresh water shells. Instead of softening in water, as they would if made of clay alone, the shells give to the composition hydraulic properties, and vessels made of it harden on exposure to air and moisture. When filled with water and meat, pots made of this material could be placed over the fire and heated without fear of breaking them.

" Those ancient artisans must have been aware of the advantage derived from a thin body to resist breakage from expansion and contraction from the heat of the fire.

" I have a beautiful vessel from the ' Bone Bank,' made of artificial stone, which has ears, and is otherwise formed like an old-fashioned cast-iron dinner pot. It is five inches across the mouth, and seven inches in diameter at the bulge, five inches deep, and only one eighth of an inch thick. The bottom is smoked black, which goes to show that it was suspended over the fire for cooking purposes."

It will be noted that Prof. Cox describes the lime and magnesia as carbonates, and states that they are in the form of pulverized shells, and so used in the mixture, while Dr. Wallace takes the position that the lime was calcined and subsequently became carbonated.

By giving the carbonic acid its full equivalents of lime and magnesia to form carbonates of those bases, and the sulphuric acid its full equivalent of lime to form sulphate of lime, in the mortar from the temple at Pentelicus, as given by Dr. Wallace, it will be found that the excess of lime is so slight as to preclude the belief that the lime was calcined prior to its use, and that the position taken by Prof. Cox is the correct one, and it is not difficult to believe that in all these ancient mortars named, pulverized carbonate of lime was the cementing agent used.

The " Old Stone Mill " at Newport, Rhode Island, which, according to many learned antiquaries, was built by the Norsemen five hundred years before the landing of Columbus, was constructed with a mortar composed of pulverized shells, clay, sharp sand, and fine gravel.

The antiquity of this ancient structure has been a subject of much discussion.

J. P. MacLean, in *American Antiquarian*, stoutly maintains that it was built by or upon the lands of Gov. Benedict Arnold during the period of his residence at Newport, which was from 1653 until his death in 1678.

Mr. MacLean states that in the year 1848 some mortar taken from an old stone house in Spring Street, built by Henry Bull in 1639 (the year in which Newport was founded), some from the tomb of Governor Arnold, and some from various other buildings was compared with the mortar of the Old Mill, and found to be identical in quality and character.

Whether the Old Mill has been built more than nine hundred or only a little over two hundred years, the fact remains that the mortar with which it was constructed is composed of the materials as stated, and a careful examination of this structure, by the writer, during the summer of 1894, revealed some curious features which are not easily adjusted to modern ideas of stability.

The stones are mostly small and unshapen, and in many places the mortar joints are over an inch in thickness. Taken altogether, the work was carelessly done, and how such a wall could have been held in place for even two hundred years with such a mortar, and in such a climate, seems almost incredible. There are no indications of crumbling on the part of this curious mortar; on the contrary, it is hard and firm, and from present appearances is liable to remain so for centuries to come. The fact will not be overlooked that this mortar is composed of identically the same materials as are those mentioned by Prof. Cox as having been used by the Mound-Builders, which fact is rather damaging to the theory adduced by Mr. Mac-Lean in his attempt to overthrow the arguments advanced favoring the antiquity of the "Old Stone Mill."

It would be a rash man who, to-day, would build a structure of any importance with a mortar composed of pulverized shell-marl, clay, and sand; and yet, with the evidence before us of its having been so used in the "Old Stone Mill" in New England, where it has been subjected to alternate freezing and thawing through all these years, and even accepting Mr. MacLean's theory as to the time which has elapsed since its construction, it antedates by a full hundred years the time when Smeaton "lightened up the darkness surrounding the subject of mortars and their behavior under varied circumstances," and thus, it would seem that the permanence and durability of shell-lime, *i.e.*, carbonate of lime, mortar must be conceded.

But it is not at all clear how a mortar composed of such materials can, without calcination, become hard. It is quite true, as stated by Prof. Cox in his reference to the analysis of ancient pottery, that "so far as chemical constituents are concerned, it agrees very well with the composition of hydraulic stones;" yet this does not by any means constitute an hydraulic cement, which, it may be inferred, was meant by him where he states that "a paste made from such a mixture possesses in a high degree the properties of hydraulic pozzuolana and Portland cement, so that vessels formed of it hardened without being burnt, as is customary with modern pottery."

It is true that Portland cement is made by an admixture of clay and carbonate of lime ; yet, however thoroughly and intimately these two ingredients may be commingled, it is clear to every one who is at all familiar with the subject that this mixture, without further treatment beyond its mere mechanical incorporation, cannot be induced to harden beyond a natural moderate hardness due to the drying out of the clay.

By submersion it soon becomes plastic again. At such a stage, and in such a condition, there is no chemical affinity between these substances.

There are present two acids and two bases. Each of the former is chemically combined with one of the latter, in certain fixed proportions.

The lime is combined with 78.57 per cent. of its own weight of carbonic acid, which in hundred parts is lime 56, carbonic acid 44 = 100 carbonate of lime.

But clay is rarely found in true combining proportions, the silicic acid almost universally predominating. The latter combines with nearly 57 per cent. of its own weight of alumina.

The ratio in one hundred parts being silicic acid 63.83 and alumina 36.17 = 100 silicate of alumina.

In the analysis given by Prof. Cox, the silica is 36.00 and the alumina is 5.00. Therefore, as the 5.00 of alumina will combine with only 8.82 of the silica, forming clay 13.82, there must necessarily remain 27.18 of free and uncombined silicic acid, and this cannot combine with the lime, which already has its full equivalent of acid; and although the latter is volatile, it will not part from its combination with the lime, except through the agency of heat, even though the carbonate of lime is in intimate contact with free silicic acid through countless centuries, as is shown in the natural cement rocks throughout the world, nearly, if not all of which contain more silica than will combine with the alumina present, a fact which in no manner affects the relative proportions of the constituent parts of the carbonate of lime.

A suggestion that the ancients had succeeded in imitating Nature in her mode of hardening hydraulic cement stones is met with the familiar fact that such stones, if exposed to the weather in a climate where they are subjected to freezing and thawing, will crumble into gravel and mud — a result which does not seem to follow in similar mixtures compounded by the ancient Romans or by the Mound-Builders.

Prof. H. C. Bowen, of the School of Mines, Columbia College, New York City, in a correspondence with the author, advances an exceedingly plausible theory in regard to the hardening of the pottery belonging to the Mound-Builders' age.

He states that this pottery "is hard and unyielding, doubtless because of a slow cementing process brought about by infiltration and subsequent evaporation of water laden with calcium carbonate in solution.

"The same thing could be accomplished in a smaller way by taking a somewhat porous ball of dry clay, broken shells, limestone dust, or quartz grit and from time to time pouring upon it some water that is charged with calcium carbonate in solution; then to allow the ball to dry out, and to repeat this several weeks; at the end the ball, which at first was loose and without strength, will be found strong and very resisting.

"The calcium carbonate water spoken of above can be produced by putting amorphous limestone powder (impalpable) into a gallon bottle having about three quarts of rain water, and then charge the water and the space above it with clean carbon dioxide gas, and from time to time shaking the bottle vigorously, and also from time to time recharging the water with carbon dioxide.

" The explanation is somewhat simple, it being that the water carries calcium carbonate in solution and thus distributes it upon every portion of all the interior of the ball spoken of above. The water evaporating over the surface and crevices within the ball causes a slight incrustation, and in time pretty thoroughly fills up all the interior spaces, thus turning the mass into a solid structure. The manufacture of prehistoric pottery vessels involved probably a feeble baking process, baking being somewhat important."

Instances are often met with in nature where hardening is caused by infiltration of water charged with calcium carbonate, in various kinds of petrifactions, as in the turning of wood to stone. Sand sometimes becomes solidified by the action of carbonated sea waters, and it is extremely probable that by observing these facts in nature the Mound-Builders grasped the idea and applied it to the hardening of their kitchen utensils, which could have been done by the process described by Professor Bowen.

But it will be observed that, however true this theory may be as applied to the induration of the pottery produced by the Mound-Builders, it affords no explanation whatever for the hardness of the ancient masonry and concrete described by Dr. Wallace and the durability of the mortar in the " Old Stone Mill " at Newport.

SULPHATE OF LIME MORTARS.

The mortar of the great Pyramid of Cheops, as shown by Dr. Wallace, Mr. Cresy, and others, is composed of hydrated sulphate of lime (gypsum), carbonate of lime, and clay.

According to Strabo, the walls of Tyre were built of stone set in gypsum, a very common material, apparently, in Asia Minor and the center of the old Assyrian civilization.

The composition of pure gypsum is as follows:

Sulphuric acid	46.52
Lime	32.55
Water	20.93
Total	100.00

When heated to 230 degs. Fahr. gypsum will part with its water of crystallization. It then becomes sulphate of lime, its composition consisting of sulphuric acid 58.84, lime 41.16 = 100. If then pulverized and mixed with water into a paste, it will quickly harden to a solid mass, becoming crystallized again by recombining with its equivalent of water.

But should the heat be carried above 320 degs. Fahr. it will no longer harden by admixture with water. It will not crystallize. The naturally occurring anhydrite behaves in the same manner when reduced to powder. Although in rock form it has a crystallization, it is very different from that of gypsum.

One part of sulphate of lime will dissolve in 400 parts of water.

One part of slaked lime will dissolve in 760 parts of water.

Silicate of lime, the basis of hydraulic cement, will not dissolve in water.

Sulphate of lime was extensively used by the ancient inhabitants of Mexico, as well as those of Egypt, in their masonry; also for exterior as well as interior plastering, and history seems likely to repeat itself, in some respects, at least, in the use of this material.

In several places in the Western States, and notably in Kansas and Texas, beds of impure gypsum are found of a soft, mudlike consistency. The impurities consist chiefly of clay. Within the past few years some of these deposits have been developed, resulting in the building up of a new industry that bids fair to become quite extensive.

The material is taken from the beds and heated sufficiently to expel the water of crystallization contained in the gypsum, the same operation, of course, expelling the moisture from the clay, upon which the substance falls into an impalpable powder. It is then ready for the market, and is sold for purposes of plastering. It has many advantages over common quicklime for such a purpose, as it sets quickly, becoming dry and hard in a short time. It carries sand largely, quite equaling quicklime in that respect, and, unlike the latter, it requires no hair in plastering.

These gypseous-clay beds were probably a mixture of clay and carbonate of lime, and in the condition of natural hydraulic cement rock. Subsequently, these rocks were subjected to the action of sulphuric acid, which expelled the carbonic acid, and itself combined with the lime, forming gypsum. The presence of the clay, in intimate contact with the gypsum, prevented the latter from hardening, as would have been the case had the gypsum been pure. The sulphuric acid was undoubtedly produced by the oxidation of iron pyrites or by the oxidation of sulphuretted hydrogen from sulphur springs in the neighborhood of the deposits.

The manufacturers of this gypseous-clay cement claim that it sets much harder than ordinary plaster of Paris (calcined gypsum), and attribute to it many features of excellence which cannot be attained by any admixture of pure plaster of Paris and sand.

It is possible that the heated clay may act somewhat in the nature of a pozzuolana, and by reason of its finely comminuted condition, and its intimate contact with the sulphate of lime, effects may be produced that are not possible with a mixture of sulphate of lime and sand.

The Agatite Cement Plaster Company, of Kansas City, Missouri, controls a bed of this material at or near Dillon, Kansas, which is estimated to contain about six million tons.

Prof. Edwin Walters, in a report on this material, says : —

" Agatite is of a light ash-gray color. Its natural consistency is about that of hard plastic clay. When calcined it assumes a pulverized form. When mixed with water it sets as does hydraulic lime or cement. There seems to be ample time between the mixing and the setting for the mortar to be applied to its intended use.

" A sample of several weeks' setting broke under a tensile strain of 370 lbs. to the square inch. It may be safely said that in both tensile and compressive strength agatite is fully one half that of the very best Portland cement under the Neat test and equal under the part sand test. It is superior in strength to most of the hydraulic limes and ordinary cements. But, inasmuch as agatite is intended for interior work, it is not necessary that it should be of such great strength. It is very much stronger than lime and sand plaster, which is its principal competitor.

" Agatite does not differ widely in composition from the cement taken from the famous Cheops Pyramid of Egypt. The Egyptian cement runs higher in sulphate of lime and lower in oxide of iron.

" It is very probable that a cement that would stand in the climate of Egypt would also prove durable in the United States.

" I only make the comparison to show that if the agatite is kept reasonably protected from frosts and excessive moisture that it would last for ages. It has splendid adhesive qualities. It will stick to wood, stone, or brick without the aid of hair or any other substance.

" It is not decomposed by any of the basic acids, however strong they may be. Alkalies do not affect it.

" Besides being a choice material for plastering walls and ceilings, it is admirably adapted to all kinds of interior finish. When in the plastic state it may be embossed, stippled, drawn, or molded. Any design in bas-relief may be executed if prompt action is taken after mixing. The time allowed for execution is much greater than that for stucco, unless the stucco is mixed with glue or some retarder that is likely to cause decomposition.

"Another superiority over stucco is its hardness. Not only does it allow much more time for execution, but it is very much harder after it sets.

" Paper may be applied to either one or two coat work for a finish. It is probable that one coat will be the best method. Paints may be added to agatite mortar to give any desired color, when paper is not desired. If a white finish is wished, a putty or stucco coat may be applied on the surface of the agatite.

" This material is adapted for wainscoting, interior arches, and segments for the back-filling and setting of tiles, for statuettes, etc., etc."

There would seem to be no doubt that gypsum plaster will find an extended use in the near future, and in a measure supplant the use of quicklime as a plastering material in interior work of much importance and magnitude.

It is doubtful, however, if it can ever be used for exterior work in Northern latitudes until some means are discovered for rendering it proof against the action of alternate freezing and thawing.

The climates of Egypt and Mexico are such as to permit the use of this material for exterior work, and there is no doubt but that it could be so used with safety in our Southern States on brick, stone, or wooden structures, and very pleasing architectural effects thereby produced at a comparatively slight cost. Sulphate of lime as a cementing agent has not as yet received the consideration due to its merits in this country. Heretofore it has been extensively used in interior decoration and for similar purposes, but there seems to have been no advance made in the direction of permanent exterior work. It was used as an outside covering of the walls of the World's Fair Buildings at Chicago, which, however, were temporary structures.

By adding 26.47 per cent. of its own weight of water to this material, it becomes so hard and firm that, made into a briquette of one inch square cross section, and given one hour in air and twenty-three hours in water, it will sustain a tensile strain of 250 lbs. before fracture. It can be produced in this country in colors ranging from black to snowy white, and by the admixture of the various shades of sand or clay very pleasing effects can be produced.

There are immense deposits of gypsum in this country, notably in the States of New York, Virginia, Ohio, Michigan, Iowa, Kansas, Arizona, California, Texas, Colorado, and Utah.

The production from the various deposits amounts to about 255,000 tons yearly. Approximately, 63 per cent. of this amount is calcined into plaster of Paris, and 37 per cent. is ground and used as a fertilizer.

The importation of gypsum rock amounts to about 184,000 tons yearly. Could some cheap and effectual process be found to render this material practically frost-proof, its use in exterior ornamentation would rapidly assume immense proportions, and its value as a building material would be almost incalculable.

CHAPTER VI.

The Chemistry of Cements — Opinions of Leading Author-
ities — Practical Experiments to Demonstrate the
Truth or Falsity of Various Theories — Relative
Values of Limestones and Magnesian Limestones as a
Flux — Combining Ratios of the Various Silicates —
Analyzation of Analyses — Magnesian Cements —
Table of Atomic Weights — Method of Calculating
Chemical Combinations in Cements — Adulteration of
Artificial Cements — Effect of Increasing the Per-
centage of Lime — Becomes Brittle with Age — The
Toughness of Rock Cements Absent in the Artifical
Product.

The question has often arisen and has been discussed with a
greater or less degree of intelligence by writers during the past half
century concerning the effects of the presence of magnesia in a
cement.

The opinions are so various and contradictory as to lead to the
suspicion that very little is known about the subject,—a conclusion
difficult to disprove if investigation be confined to the purely hypothetical theories advanced.

It may be stated, however, that at the present time the prevailing
opinion is that, while magnesia may not be harmful in a natural
cement, even though present to the extent of 20 per cent. of the
total, yet more than 3 per cent. of the same material is dangerous in
an artificial cement.

This is the position taken by many leading authorities on the
subject. Others, however, qualify this statement, or, failing to determine the question, leave the subject in doubt and obscurity; while
still others maintain that magnesia is a valuable ingredient in a cement.

Prof. E. J. De Smedt, in his annual report to the Engineer Department, Washington, D. C., ending June 30, 1885, states in regard to the composition of a Portland cement : —

" Portland cement is composed of bi-basic silicate of lime and aluminate of lime ; sometimes it contains small quantities of magnesia as silicate or aluminate, some oxide of iron, alkali in small quantity, etc. Silicates and aluminates of lime are the principal constituents of Portland cement, the formulas of which to calculate with are as follows : —

$$2CaO. SiO^2 —\ Lime\ .\ .\ .\ .\ .\ .\ .\ .\ .\ 65.12$$
$$Silicic\ Acid\ .\ .\ .\ .\ .\ .\ .\ .\ .\ 34.88$$

$$100.00$$

$$2MGO. SiO^2 —\ Magnesia\ .\ .\ .\ .\ .\ 57.15$$
$$Silicic\ Acid\ .\ .\ .\ .\ .\ .\ .\ .\ .\ 42.85$$

$$100.00$$

$$CaO. Al_2O^3 —\ Lime\ .\ .\ .\ .\ .\ .\ .\ 67.33$$
$$Alumina\ .\ .\ .\ .\ .\ .\ .\ .\ .\ .\ 32.67$$

$$100.00$$

" The magnesia may be calculated as lime when found in small quantities.

" A limestone, such as dolomite, containing 46 per cent. of magnesia, has been pronounced unfit for making good cement, but when the percentage of magnesia is not too large it becomes in time just as hard as a cement containing no magnesia, with this difference, that it is somewhat slow in setting. In sea water containing magnesia such cement should be preferred, for the reason that it does not disintegrate in that water.

" After careful analyses, calculations, and comparative tests, I have found that the best results are obtained when the relative quantity of alumina is in the proportion of between one third and one fourth to the total amount of alumina and silica found by analysis. The quality of Portland cement is perfect in proportion as the above formulas are closely adhered to in its composition. Sulphuric acid in more than 1 per cent. is **detrimental,** and a small percentage **of** alkali, such as soda **or** potash, **adds very** much to the virtue of the cement.

" Now, it is not sufficient that the proportions should be correct; it is also necessary that calcination should be at the proper degree **of** heat and length of time, in order to produce the formation of bi-basic silicate of lime and aluminate of lime."

Prof. S. B. Newberry, a leading authority **on Portland** cement in **this country, in** a paper prepared for **the United States** Geological **Survey and** published in **Mineral Resources of the United States** for 1892, states : —

" Late experiments by Erdmenger and others seem to prove that magnesia is an inert material in cement mixtures, and that this constituent does not combine with silica and alumina after the manner of lime. The injurious effect of magnesia in Portland cement is ascribed to the very slow hydration and expansion of the free magnesia contained in the cement, causing cracking of the mass weeks or months after immersion in water. Magnesium carbonate calcined at low heat combines readily with water; that which has been heated to the temperature of the Portland cement kiln becomes hydrated only after the lapse of long periods of time. The harmlessness of magnesia in common hydraulic cement is doubtless due to the readiness and completeness with which it becomes hydrated on mixing the cement with water."

Prof. E. T. Cox, in his Geological Report for the State of Indiana, 1878, page 70, says : —

" For hydraulic purposes the **essential constituents of** a cement stone are carbonate of lime and silica. By calcination the carbonate of lime converts the silica into silicic acid, which forms a gelatinous mass with acids. Carbonate of magnesia acts in a similar manner to carbonate of lime, and when the two are present in the proper proportions hydraulic energy is uninterrupted, and a stone is formed, of great strength and durability, which consists of a double silicate of lime and magnesia. A portion of alumina is not objectionable in a cement stone in the presence of plenty of carbonate of lime and silica; it enters into combination as a hydrated silicate of lime and alumina. Sulphuric acid, or sulphate of lime, does not promote hardening or setting of the cement, and the same may be said of the oxide of iron.

Large quantities of these substances are therefore objectionable, and they may be looked upon as adulterations.

"Since carbonates of lime or magnesia, aided by alkalies, when present, are the active agents during the calcining of the cement stone in bringing about the decomposition of the silicates and forming a silicate that is soluble in acids, it will be interesting to present a tabular arrangement of the ratio of silica to the carbonates of lime and magnesia in the above, and some additional analyses of cement stones that are in common use: —

ANALYSIS.

	SILICATES.	CARBONATES.
Balcony Falls, Va.	100	149
Rosendale, N. Y.	100	248
Wabash County, Ind.	100	124
Cumberland, Md.	100	186
Beache's, Clark County, Ind.	100	262
Vassy, France	100	465
English	100	341
Bologne	100	311

"Between the silicates and carbonates, including the carbonates of lime, magnesia, and alkalies, when present, there is a wide variation in cement stones of good repute for hydraulic energy.

"It has already been stated that for hydraulic properties the essential constituents of a cement are silicic acid and caustic lime. The hardening under water is mainly due to the chemical combination of these two constituents *through the agency of water*, producing hydrated silicate of lime; where other bases are present, such as alumina and magnesia, double silicates are formed that become very hard and strong. In order to bring about this chemical change the silica must be brought to that condition which will enable it to form a gelatinous paste with acids. A portion of the silica may be in this condition naturally, but by far the larger portion remains unacted upon by acids until brought to a white heat in the presence of carbonate of lime."

Many years ago, M. Vicat, the famous French engineer, made the following statement: —

"Magnesia is a valuable ingredient in mortars to be immersed in sea water, and if it could be obtained at a cost that would permit of its application to such purposes the problem of making beton (concrete) unalterable by sea water would be solved.

" Without clay, that is to say, without silica, limes cannot be decidedly hydraulic.

" The different combinations I have tried, by mixing chalk and magnesia, have only produced limes susceptible of setting in the commencement, without any ulterior progress; but this solidification, imperfect though it be, denotes in the magnesia certain hydraulic properties which the alumina itself does not possess.

" If, then, some portions of clay be present, it might happen that a triple hydrate of lime, of alumina, and of magnesia might be formed which should possess all the conditions of hardness and of progression which characterize the best hydraulic limes.

" Two species of limestones which were found to contain respectively, before burning, as follows, viz.: —

Clay	4.00 and	5.50
Carbonate of lime	42.50 „	52.00
„ „ magnesia	53.50 „	42.50

yielded limes possessing the hydraulic character in an eminent degree."

M. Parandier stated that " a stone composed of 58 parts of carbonate of lime, 11 of clay, and 31 of carbonate of magnesia yields a very excellent hydraulic lime."

M. Dumas states that " if more than 10 per cent. of magnesia be present, hydraulic limes begin to become poor, and with 25 per cent. they become decidedly poor."

M. Berthier gives the analysis of a hydraulic lime obtained from a mixture of the stone of Villefranche, near Paris, with dissolved silica, in the proportions of 5 of the stone to 1 of the silica.

The analysis of the stone being : —

Carbonate of lime	60.90
„ „ magnesia	30.10
„ „ iron	3.00
„ „ manganese	6.00
Total	100.00

and the hydraulic lime thus obtained became much harder under water than any even of the natural hydraulic limes.

This mixture after calcination would exhibit by analysis the following : —

Silica	25.83
Lime	44.04
Magnesia	18.50
Oxide of iron	3.88
„ „ manganese	7.75
Total	100.00

And, as it contains the ingredients in proportions essential to a good hydraulic cement, it is not surprising that it became "harder under water than any even of the natural hydraulic limes."

Again, "when the magnesian limestones found nearer Paris are mixed with one fifth of their bulk of soluble siliceous matter they yield a lime still more energetic in its hydraulic properties than that above described, although the carbonate of magnesia is present in the proportion of 23 per cent."

Gen. Q. A. Gillmore in his "Treatise on Limes, Hydraulic Cements, and Mortars," ed. 1879, page 304, says: "Magnesia plays an important part in the setting of mortars derived from the argillo-magnesian limestones, such as those which furnish the Rosendale cements. The magnesia, like the lime, appears in the form of the carbonate ($MgO. CO_2$). During calcination the carbonic acid (CO_2) is driven off, leaving protoxide of magnesia ($MgO.$) which comports itself like lime in the presence of silica and alumina, by forming silicate of magnesia ($SiO_3, 3MgO$) and aluminate of magnesia ($Al_2O_3.$ $3MgO$). These compounds become hydrated in the presence of water, and are pronounced by both Vicat and Chatoney to furnish gangs which resist the dissolving action of sea water better than the silicate and aluminate of lime. This statement is doubtless correct, for we know that all of those compounds, whether in air or water, absorb carbonic acid and pass to the condition of sub-carbonates, and that the carbonate of lime is more soluble in water holding carbonic acid and certain organic acids of the soil in solution than carbonate of magnesia.

" At all events, whatever may be the cause of the superiority, it is pretty well established by experience that the cements derived from the argillo-magnesian limestones furnish a durable cement for constructions in the sea."

G. R. Burnell, C. E., of London, in his work on " Limes, Cements, and Mortars," 1868, page 17, makes the following remarkable statement : —

" In the actual state of our chemical knowledge, it is impossible to say whether there exist any definite proportions either of silica alone, of silica and alumina, or of silica and magnesia, etc., which are capable, when mixed with the same quantity of pure lime, of producing hydraulic limes of similar qualities. Indeed, the whole of this branch of chemistry, notwithstanding the important discoveries made in it of late years, is still very little understood.

" The action of the oxide of iron, for instance, quite escapes the attempts made to include it within any law. The action of the magnesia seems also involved in the same obscurity."

This being the true " state of the art " as late in the history of cements as 1868, it is not difficult to understand and appreciate the conflicting opinions of the leading authorities rendered prior to the date named, as well as those expressed subsequently, and it may truthfully be said that even at the present time the art of cement fabrication is but little understood. In fact, but a slight and scarcely visible abrasion has been made on the surface of the subject, and, considering the limited number of scientists who take any special interest in the subject, it may safely be predicted that any advance in the art is destined to be of slow growth ; and that many years will have elapsed before it can truthfully be claimed that the chemistry of cements is at last freed from the fetters of tradition and rests securely on a solid and permanent foundation.

And when it is considered how vastly important the subject is, in view of the fact that over 30,000,000 barrels of cement enter yearly into the works of construction in Europe and America, it is to be regretted that our universities and institutes of technology do not embrace in their curriculums a systematic study of the chemistry of cements.

So largely does this material enter into the construction of all engineering and architectural works, and so rapidly does the field for its use widen, that it is becoming a necessity that this subject should receive the attention its importance merits.

As already stated, the discussion concerning the effects of the presence of magnesia in a cement has extended over a long period of years, and, unfortunately, many conclusions have been drawn which are purely hypothetical, and, lacking in practical proof, are not only useless, but, by being misleading, become harmful. An error of this character is afforded in the passage quoted from Gillmore.

Silicates are not decomposed in the manner stated. The only portion of a cement that could be thus acted upon by carbonic acid is the lime and magnesia that may be in excess of true combining proportions with the silica present.

Practical experience has demonstrated that any cement which contains an excess of either lime or magnesia, if not thoroughly hydrated prior to its application, is attended with the danger of expansion. And any cement deficient in these bases is subject to shrinkage. An excess of lime in a cement, whether natural or artificial, without thorough hydration, as already stated, will surely expand to a greater or less extent. And, as the process of hydration as usually practised consists in the mere spreading of the manufactured cement on a floor and by repeated turnings with shovels, exposing the body of the cement to the atmosphere, the caustic lime takes up the moisture in the air, and produces a hydrate of lime which is thereby rendered non-expansive. And its influence on the resultant mortar is the same as when a given percentage of thoroughly slaked quicklime is added to a harsh or quick setting cement, rendering it less active and imparting a pasty consistency to the mortar. An excess of lime in a cement, whether inherent in the cement or added subsequently, if the hydration has been conducted thoroughly and conscientiously, cannot be considered as harmful; on the contrary, it may be, on the whole, beneficial. The only danger attending its use arises from the extreme liability of an imperfect hydration.

The often expressed opinion that any excess of lime or magnesia will ultimately dissolve out of the masonry, leaving the mortar porous, and thereby lead to disintegration, is not borne out by the facts. Teil hydraulic lime, containing thirty-four to forty per cent. of free lime, has been used in enormous quantities for centuries, and certainly in sea water since 1832, and the free lime which it contains shows no signs of dissolving out, whether used in air or water.

In the manufacture of artificial cements, which invariably contain an excess of lime, the question of thorough hydration presents in the case of large and extensive works quite a serious problem, one which enters quite seriously into the cost of manufacture.

The large floor space necessary for the purpose and the time required for thorough hydration, the large stock to be carried and the labor involved in turning, enter into the cost of production, and, as in these days of close and severe competition the strictest economy in manufacture becomes imperative, it is evident that the process of hydration is oftentimes hurried and imperfectly done.

The author has never, in a long series of trials, been able to find an artificial cement of foreign or domestic production which, when made into grout and poured into bottles, would not sooner or later fracture every bottle.

The only significance to be attached to these trials consists in the fact that none of the brands tried contained magnesia in excess of the empiric limit of three per cent.

The expansion, therefore, could not be charged to that source, and the only conclusion to be drawn was that the process of hydration had been improperly conducted, and caustic lime had been permitted to remain in the cement when packed for the market.

Neither lime nor magnesia will expand in a cement if combined with silicic acid or when in a free and uncombined condition, if thoroughly hydrated.

There are no known cements which would be damaged in quality should they contain magnesia up to the combining limit.

We have shown that magnesia combines with silica in certain fixed proportions, and that when lime enters into the composition the proportions as between silica and magnesia are changed, but in either case the proportions are fixed and constant. A true silicate of magnesia will attain a hardness equal, if not superior, to that of silicate of lime.

The former contains a larger percentage of silica, as will be seen from the following table.

Silicate of Magnesia.

Silica, 42.92

Magnesia, 57.08

Totals 100.00

Silicate of Lime.

Silica, 34.91

Lime, 65.09

100.00

If there is any advantage in the inherent hardness of the constituent parts considered separately, the advantage would seem to be in favor of the silicate of magnesia, as silica is harder than either of the bases named, and, while it requires but 760 parts of water to dissolve one part of lime, magnesia is practically insoluble in water.

An illustration is afforded in the large number of shell-marl beds found in many portions of this country (nearly all of which are formed by animal secretion in the waters of former lakes or ponds). Although the surrounding or adjacent rocks are in most instances magnesian limestones, from which by infiltration the ponds became supplied with calcium carbonate in solution, and from which the shells were secreted, it is very rarely that the shells are found to contain even three per cent. of magnesium carbonate — being practically pure calcium carbonate.

Several years ago, the author, in searching for a reason for this general belief in the dangerous qualities of magnesia in a cement when exceeding the time-honored limit of three per cent., instituted a series of experiments.

Magnesian limestones were secured which varied in their proportions of carbonate of magnesia from five to fifteen per cent. These were marked and treated separately, by grinding the samples to impalpable powder, to which was added clay in an equally fine condition, in such proportions as are prescribed as the correct formulæ for Portland cements, and, after a thorough admixture of these ingredients, the samples were moistened and formed into balls and cakes, which were then calcined with coke to the point of incipient vitrifaction, after which the samples were finely pulverized, the powder thoroughly hydrated, formed into patties, balls, and briquettes, and given the usual time in air and water.

The tests extended from one day to one year. The weight and tests were fully up to the standard for the best artificial cements. Some of the samples are now nine years old ; they have been kept in both fresh and salt water, and they show no signs of expansion or checking, and are exceedingly hard.

Following in this line to determine if it were possible that a good cement could be produced, should the lime be replaced entirely by magnesia, many experiments were conducted with various substances known as silicates of magnesia, with varying success, until a trial of serpentine (Mg_3 Si_2 O_7 + $_2H_2$ O) was reached.

In the experiments with this material much difficulty was experienced, owing to the varying qualities of this rock. It was found that verd-antique, a mixture of serpentine and calcium carbonate, and many samples mottled or otherwise not uniform in color or texture gave results that were not entirely satisfactory. But the dark green varieties which were uniform in color and fine in texture gave results that were most surprising.

Samples of this class from near Philadelphia, Penn., near New Haven, Conn., and Marquette, Mich., yielded an hydraulic cement that equaled in hardness and toughness the best natural or artificial cements.

In the calcination of this cement the heat required is not so great as that necessary for ordinary cements. With the latter the heat must be high enough to at least expel the carbon dioxide from the carbonates, which requires above 2700° Fahr., while serpentine, which has parted with its carbon dioxide through metamorphic action, requires a heat but little above that necessary to expel the water of crystallization to render it suitable for grinding, after which it becomes practically an hydraulic cement.

The samples tested were slow in setting, requiring one day in air before submersion. Neither shrinkage nor expansion was detected. Samples of this cement have now been kept in both fresh and sea water for seven years, and, except by analysis, they cannot be recognized as other than ordinary cement of the finest quality.

The theory that more than 3 per cent. of magnesia is harmful in an artifical cement has not been sustained, except by the single argument that it remains free or uncombined in the cement, and, owing to the high temperature to which that cement is subjected during calcination, slowly hydrates, and expands after the lapse of many days and, perhaps, months.

Whenever it can be shown that magnesia does not combine with the silica, then the truth of the theory will have to be admitted.

But to establish the theory as a fact it must first be shown that silica and magnesia do not combine, as in Serpentine ($Mg_3 Si_2O_7 +_2 H_2O$), Talc ($Si_5 O_{14} Mg_4$), Sepiolite ($Si_3 O_8 Mg_2 +_2 H_2 O$), or in Olivine ($Mg_2 Si O_4$), and among the silicates of magnesia and lime, as in asbestos, the augites, hornblendes, and pyroxene.

How can these be admitted as chemical combinations of silica, lime, and magnesia, without admitting a similar combination in cements?

The theory has not the slightest foundation, in fact. Its absurdity has been demonstrated daily since the foundation of the cement industry in this country.

But in an endeavor to account for the expansion of some of the artifical cements, this theory has been advanced by many leading authorities, principally in Germany, who, it may be noted, have never advertised for an adverse opinion, and among the imitators of those authorities in this country the theory has passed current as sound doctrine. But the untenableness of this doctrine seems not to have occurred to its advocates, even when they find checking and expansion taking place among artificial cements containing but a trace of magnesia.

When a cement containing an excess of lime has been calcined at an extreme high temperature, the free lime will be much slower to hydrate than would be the case were the cement calcined at a lower temperature, and herein may be found the reason for checking, which, to account for, has been attributed to the presence of magnesia.

As instances of this character, the foundation of the Bartholdi statue in New York Harbor may be cited. After this work had been laid several months, the surface became covered with innumerable checks and cracks.

The landing of the main entrance of the Capitol Building, Washington, D. C., fronting Pennsylvania Avenue, was so literally covered with checks and cracks that a dime dropped upon it would rest on a check or crack, and it was found necessary to cover it with asphalt.

Both of the cases cited were done with a German Portland cement having a reputation second to none in this country, and the analysis of which shows but a trace of magnesia.

The only conclusion, therefore, to be drawn is that the checking resulted from a lack of thorough hydration of the lime that was present in excess of true combining proportions.

Had American rock cement been used in the work cited, and had the same results followed, it is extremely probable that the engineer and contractor would have been censured for not having used Portland cement.

The question of hydration is one which demands careful consideration. It is a question which rarely enters into the calculations of engineers and architects, who rely almost wholly on short time tensile tests, which rarely extend beyond thirty days.

A cement which needs hydration will, when this operation is but partially effected, test higher during the time mentioned than when thoroughly hydrated. Yet at the end of six months or a year the benefits of thorough hydration will appear in the tests.

These results follow, whether the cement contains more or less magnesia, not in excess of its true combining proportions.

The author has had a practical experience of many years with the cement which is represented in the table of analyses as No. 29, by which it may be seen that it contains a large percentage of magnesia.

The rock from which this cement is produced, when calcined, at the temperature employed in Portland cement making, i. e., sintered, then ground and hydrated, will weigh, without compacting, 85 lbs. per cube foot, which is equivalent to 106 lbs. per struck bushel.

It will test 100 lbs. tensile strain per square inch at one day, 250 lbs. at seven days, 400 lbs. at one month, 700 lbs. at six months, and at one year a major portion of the briquettes cannot be broken on a 1,000 lb. testing machine.

Commencing in 1883, and continued yearly since that time until the present, briquettes made from this material have been placed in running water, and kept there, and they neither expand, check, nor shrink, but are infinitely harder than the rock from which they were produced.

The motive for presenting this particular instance is because of its direct bearing on the question of the presence and influence of magnesia in a cement.

Practical experiences of this kind completely dispose of many of the fallacies by which the consideration of this subject is complicated.

If the tendency to expand is greater in magnesia than in lime, it ought to exhibit such tendency in the common building lime. Of the more than sixty millions of barrels of this material which is produced yearly in this country, not less than two thirds of it is produced from magnesian limestone, the proportion of magnesia ranging from 10 per cent. up to a percentage rendering the material dolomitic in character.

The heat required for the calcination of this rock is fully as high as that used in the production of Portland cement.

It is generally used immediately after slaking. Yet it does not expand and rupture brickwork and stone masonry, although the magnesia is absolutely free. It is not chemically combined with the lime; neither does it so combine subsequently with the gangue with which it is made into mortar or concrete, its deportment being the same as that of the lime with which it is associated.

If magnesia does not expand in work where it is beyond all question in a free or uncombined condition, it certainly cannot do so when it is converted into silicates, as in an hydraulic cement, whether the latter is a natural or artificial product.

Evidence of a most conclusive character bearing on this question of the formation of magnesian silicates in a cement, whether natural or artifical, is furnished in the carefully ascertained values of the various limestones and magnesian limestones when used as a flux in the smelting of iron ores.

It is familiarly known that the silica contained in iron ores is removed by combining it with lime, or lime and magnesia (dependent on the character of the stone used), the resultant product being a silicate of those bases in the form of clinker or slag.

The value of this fluxing material is measured by its capacity for taking up the silica contained in the ore.

It is evident, therefore, that these values diminish in direct ratio with the increase in the percentages of silica, clay, and other impurities contained in the stone.

Thus we find that if a magnesian limestone contains 15 per cent. of impurities, 12 parts of which are silica, as in No. 8 of the following table, the fluxing value of the stone falls to less than one half the value of that of a practically pure magnesian limestone, like No. 1 in the table.

This decrease in values is due to the silica found in the stone, which takes up its equivalent of lime and magnesia, leaving only the excess of those bases to combine with the silica in the ore.

A study of the table, which is compiled with unusual care and exactness, should serve to dissipate all doubt, and place beyond further controversy the evident fact that magnesia combines with silica, and when for that purpose, it is used as a flux, it has even a greater value than lime.

In all respects the law holds good in the fabrication of hydraulic cements, as the clinker or slag from smelting furnaces is simply an unground hydraulic cement.

Should the stone used be of an impure variety, the resultant slag is a mixture of natural and artificial hydraulic cement, although of such varying proportions as between the acid and the bases as to be practically valueless for that purpose.

Nevertheless, it is largely used as an adulterant by unscrupulous European manufacturers of artificial cements.

If we are to believe the printed reports of the transactions of the societies of English, German, and Belgian Portland cement manufacturers, it would seem that those organizations are utterly powerless to suppress the dishonest practises of many of their members.

TABLE OF RELATIVE VALUES OF LIMESTONES AND MAGNESIAN
LIMESTONES AS A FLUX.

(Nos. 2, 4, 7, and 10 Limestones. 1, 3, 5, 6, 8, and 9, Magnesian Limestones.)

No.	Lime.	Magnesia.	Carbon dioxide.	Silica.	Alumina oxide of iron, etc.	Totals.	Flux Totals.	Flux Values.
1	37.00	16.00	46.68	0.32	....	100	53.00	1.000
2	56.00	.....	44.00	.....	....	100	56.00	.937
3	45.00	8.00	44.17	1.00	1.83	100	53.00	.922
4	53.00	.....	41.66	3.00	2.34	100	53.00	.797
5	36.00	16.00	45.89	2.00	0.11	100	52.00	.906
6	44.00	8.00	43.38	2.00	2.62	100	52.00	.828
7	52.00	.....	40.87	4.00	3.13	100	52.00	.750
8	31.00	14.00	39.76	12.00	3.24	100	45.00	.484
9	39.00	6.00	37.25	12.00	5.75	100	45.00	.406
10	45.00	.....	35.37	15.00	4.63	100	45.00	.219

The question of the presence of alumina in a cement, its action and influence on the quality, and its mode of combination, has also been the source of much discussion by the authorities. The presence of alumina is due to the fact that silica, without which hydraulic cement has not been produced, is not found in quantities sufficiently fine except in combination with alumina, *i. e.*, in clay. And so it may be said to be an unwelcome accompaniment to silica in the composition of an artificial cement, while in natural cement it is inherent in the cement rock, being combined with the silica.

It is both basic and acidic in its character. In its combination with silica, as in clay, its action is purely that of a base. In this condition of silicate of alumina it is not decomposed by heat, as is demonstrated in the production of fire-brick from that material.

Taken in a pure state, alumina will combine with lime, forming aluminate of lime, thus proving its acidic character.

Its combining proportions with silica and lime, considered separately, are as follows:

Silica	63.83	Alumina	32.67
Alumina	36.17	Lime	67.33
Totals	100.00		100.00

The author has been furnished some beautiful specimens of aluminate of lime by Prof. S. B. Newberry, who produced them in his laboratory, and states that " they were practically fused at a bright yellow heat. A low temperature compared with that required to produce Portland cement."

The basic character of alumina exceeds the acidic, but it is so feeble that it is not capable of forming salts with weak acids, while its acidic character is also feeble and can only form compounds with strong bases.

These peculiar characteristics of alumina have led to a variety of opinions concerning its true position in an hydraulic cement composition.

Many excellent authorities assert that in a cement both silicate and aluminate of lime are formed. While others maintain that silica combines with both bases, lime and alumina, forming bi-silicate of lime and alumina.

Some of the advocates of each of these theories claim that magnesia, if present, remains inert in the cement, that is, free and uncombined. While others maintain that it combines only with the silica and lime; while still others maintain that it combines with the silica, lime, and alumina, forming a triple silicate.

It has also been stated by some eminent chemists that after calcination all the constituents, silica, alumina, lime, and magnesia, are
in a free condition, and that it is only by the application of water
that silicates are formed, some claiming that silicate of lime and
aluminate of lime are thus formed; and by others that by the application of water the silica combines with all the bases present in
certain fixed proportions; but in neither of these last two mentioned
cases is it admitted that water combines with and causes the crystallization of silicates already formed by the agency of heat.

While the analytical side of the cement question seems to be
fairly well understood, it is apparent that the synthetical side has
been neglected.

That neither magnesia nor alumina is absolutely essential to
the fabrication of an hydraulic cement has been well demonstrated;
but each is present, in greater or less proportion, in all cements, and
it is interesting to note the theories advanced by our leading
authorities in regard to the perplexing problems attending the presence of these two bases and their mode of combination.

The views of Prof. DeSmedt on this question, also those of
Prof. Cox, are clearly expressed in the quotations already given,
from their writings.

Leonard F. Beckwith, C. E., New York, in his report on the
"Hydraulic Lime of Teil," page 23, says: "The method of manufacture strongly influences the composition of limes and cements.
At a high temperature, silicate of lime and the double silicate of
lime and alumina are formed. At a low heat, the double silicate is
not formed, and the alumina, acting towards the lime the part of an
acid, produces aluminate of lime," and that "the latter is weak and
the first element to become decomposed in sea-water."

Henry Reid, C. E., London, in his work on " Portland Cements,"
ed. 1877, page 151, says: "Alumina, when in excess in a clay, impairs the indurating value of the cement in the making of which it
is used. Aluminate of lime possesses excellent hydraulic properties,
but the temperature necessary for its formation is much higher than
that at which silicate of lime is produced.

" If, therefore, a clay contains an excess of alumina, part of the
silicate of lime will be overburnt before the whole of the alumina
can enter into combination with the lime."

Prof. S. B. Newberry in "Mineral Resources of the United States, 1892," page 746, says: "Cement possessing hydraulic properties is always obtained when a mixture of carbonate of lime and clay, in proper proportions, is strongly heated. Although this operation appears very simple, yet the chemical reactions which take place in the burning and hardening of cement, and the chemical nature of the cement itself, are still more or less obscure. Le Chatelier has shown, perhaps conclusively, that the essential constituent of Portland cement, burned at high temperature, is a compound of silica and lime, probably of the formula $3CaO.SiO_2$. The alumina and oxide of iron of the clay appear, therefore, to play an unimportant part in the hardening of cement. Nevertheless, Le Chatelier failed to obtain the trisilicate on heating lime and silica together, a mixture of lower silicates (bisilicate) and free lime being always obtained. It is evident, therefore, that in order to produce complete combination of the silica and lime at the temperature of the cement kiln, some other substance, such as alumina or iron oxide, must be present to act as a flux. By fusion with the oxyhydrogen blowpipe, however, the writer has lately succeeded in bringing pure silica and lime into combination in the proportion required by Le Chatelier's formula, obtaining a product which showed all the qualities of good cement. It appears, therefore, that the possibility of making cement from silica and lime alone is only a question of temperature. As to the part played by the alumina and iron oxide of the clay, it is interesting to recall that Dr. Schott long ago found that the alumina in cement mixtures can be completely replaced by oxide of iron, or the oxide of iron by alumina, without injury to the resulting product. He thus obtained cements containing only silica, lime, and alumina, and equally good cements containing only silica, lime, and iron oxide, showing that alumina and oxide of iron act in a precisely similar manner.

"The exact way in which the alumina acts in promoting the combination of silica and lime is, however, still more or less uncertain. Le Chatelier considers that in the burning of cement the silica and alumina first combine with a small amount of lime, forming a fusible glass, and that this gradually takes up more lime, becoming more and more basic, and at the same time less fusible, until finally the all-important trisilicate, which is the essential constituent of cement, is produced. Le Chatelier has, however, shown that alumina and lime form exceedingly fusible aluminates, especially when the lime is present in large proportion. In view of this fact, it seems to the writer much more probable that a fusible aluminate is first produced, and that this is then gradually decomposed by the silica with the formation of the trisilicate, the alumina finally remaining in combination with a comparatively small proportion of lime. Substantially the same view has already been advanced by Michaelis. Experiments now in progress under the writer's direction are expected to throw light on this interesting question. . . . .

"It is well known that in making Portland cement the proportions of basic and acid constituents (lime and clay) must be almost absolutely constant, the best results being obtained with from 2.8 to 3 parts of lime to 1 part of silica. In natural rock cement, if the magnesia be disregarded, the clay will generally be found to be very greatly in excess, the proportion of lime to silica not usually exceeding 1½ or 2 to 1. At the low temperature at which the natural rock cement must of necessity be burned, it is probable that the chief reaction which takes place is the combination of the alumina with the lime, and that most of the silica remains uncombined. The quick setting properties of hydraulic cement accord closely with the behavior of calcium aluminate, and indicate that the latter is the active constituent in cement made from natural rock. The progressive hardening of this cement under water and the great strength which it often ultimately attains may be explained by the gradual action of the amorphous silica present on the aluminate, an action similar to that known to take place between the silica of pozzuolana, slag, etc., and slaked lime."

In the American Cyclopædia, Vol. IV., page 185, the following singular theory will be found attributed to MM. Rivet and Chatoney: "Where cements are calcined at a high heat, silicate of alumina and silicate of lime are formed, which on the addition of water undergo decomposition with the formation of aluminate and silicate of lime, containing each three instead of six equivalents of water, which is the case when a heat only sufficient to drive off the carbonic acid of the carbonate of lime is employed; and the decomposition which must take place before the final hydration also explains the slow setting."

We thus have here a variety of opinions which to the lay mind must give rise to conjecture, at least, and to those who take a deep interest in the subject, and who desire to arrive at the truth, must certainly open a wide field for research and experiment.

With a view to the acquirement of some knowledge of a practical nature in regard to this question of chemical combinations, the author instituted a series of experiments, which, being entirely mechanical, except as to the analyses, were more or less crude.

One of these consisted in pouring three quarts of rain water, in a gallon bottle into which were gradually sifted a few ounces of natural rock cement which had been calcined to an unvitrified clinker and ground exceedingly fine.

The bottle was shaken vigorously and continuously for several minutes, thus giving the water ample time to act on the powder before the latter was allowed to settle. This operation was repeated at frequent intervals to avoid a setting of the cement, as would have been the case if left undisturbed. The following day the water was poured off, and a new supply used. After the third washing the cement was dried and submitted for analysis.

Previous to the experiment the cement had been carefully analyzed. The following table gives the analyses. No. 1 before, and No. 2 after, washing.

	No. 1.	No. 2.
Silica	24.30	26.01
Alumina	6.62	7.07
Oxide of Iron	2.41	2.16
Lime	52.35	51.97
Magnesia	6.16	6.52
Potash and Soda	5.30	2.77
Carbondioxide	2.10	2.26
Loss	.76	1.24
Totals	100.00	100.00

The constituents which show an increase in percentages are those which sustained no loss in the washing, while those which show a decrease lost a portion in the operation, which becomes more noticeable when illustrated by ratios.

	No. 1.	No. 2.
Ratio of silicic acid to lime, as	10 to 21.5	10 to 19.9
,, ,, ,, ,, ,, alkalies, as . . .	10 to 2.17	10 to 1.06

The ratios as between silicic acid and the magnesia and alumina are practically constant.

It is not contended that this experiment is at all conclusive, but it furnishes evidence that magnesia and alumina were chemically combined with the silica, else they certainly would have been washed out, or at least partially so.

The loss of 7.45 per cent. in the lime amounts practically to the excess above its true combining ratio with silicic acid, which is as 10 to 18.6.

The prime object of this experiment was to determine the truth or falsity of the theory so often advanced, that the magnesia and alumina are inert substances in a cement, and the results demonstrate that, by a careful system of washing, all inert or uncombined matter may be removed.

The fact that neither magnesia nor alumina are separated from the silica except by the use of acids, as in analysis, should be a sufficient refutation of the idea that either of those constituents are free and inert in a cement.

The difficulties in the way of a settled theory concerning the fabrication of a cement are furnished by the almost interminable variations in the percentages of the constituents, silica, alumina, lime, and magnesia.

A study of the table of analyses will disclose the fact that no two cements are alike in this respect, and every change from some fixed standard, with the varying action due to that divergence to be accounted for, involves the subject in doubt, and opens the way to endless discussion among those who make a study of the chemistry of cements; while engineers, architects, and others who are in a position to determine the brand of cement to be used, are guided by practical experience in the use of the various brands, paying but little regard to the chemical side of the question.

They find that for some purposes one brand of cement answers, while for another class of work some other brand is preferred. It matters little to them whether one brand contains a greater or less amount of magnesia or alumina than the other. They desire a satisfactory result, and, as a rule, are far less prejudiced than any other class connected with the art.

A cement manufacturer who does not fully and unequivocally

believe his own production to be in every conceivable way superior to all others is yet to be found.

It is a fact familiar to all who are interested in the subject of hydraulic cements, that the question of quality is ordinarily determined by tensile strain test. It is a convenient method of reaching conclusions as to the relative values of different brands of cements.

That slight attention is given to the analysis of a cement is due to the fact that a mere analysis, as it appears in a table, does not convey to the average mind any definite meaning.

And when several analyses are compiled in one table, there is a confusion of ideas as to the significance of the almost endless variety of compositions that exist; and it is not difficult, therefore, to account for the almost universal use of the tensile-strain testing machines.

It should be understood that an analysis stands mainly as a basis for further calculations. That it is but the statement of a problem, the conclusions of which, when worked out, will disclose the percentages of silicates or active setting matter in the cement, and, consequently, the percentages of inert substances; for that the constituents, silica, lime, magnesia, and alumina do combine chemically in fixed proportions, is a fact established beyond all controversy.

If all cements were found to contain these constituents in true combining proportions there would be but little left to be said on the subject. But as such conditions are rarely, if ever, met with, the most that can be done toward arriving at actual values is to determine, from a given analysis, the amount of silicates, and the amount and kind of inert matter present.

When a system for so doing is clearly understood, a long step will have been taken toward a clearer and better understanding of the actual merits of a cement.

It will then be discovered how utterly unreliable and misleading are the readings of a testing machine, unless held in strict subserviency to a superior knowledge, gained only by a thorough study of the chemistry of cements.

As a simple method for calculating the percentages of silicates in an hydraulic cement, the analysis of which may be given, we have prepared the following formulæ, which will be found to serve the purpose.

COMBINING RATIO OF THE VARIOUS SILICATES.

SILICATE OF LIME.

	A.			B.	
Silica	1.000		Lime	1.000
Lime	1.864		Silica	.536

SILICATE OF MAGNESIA.

	C.			D.	
Silica	1.000		Magnesia	1.000
Magnesia	1.330		Silica	.752

SILICATE OF ALUMINA.

	E.			F.	
Silica	1.000		Alumina	1.000
Alumina	.566		Silica	1.764

BISILICATE OF LIME AND ALUMINA.

G.		H.		I.	
Silica	1.000	Lime	1.000	Alumina	1.000
Lime	1.864	Alumina	.304	Silica	1.765
Alumina	.566	Silica	.536	Lime	3.291

BISILICATE OF LIME AND MAGNESIA.

J.		K.		L.	
Silica	1.000	Lime	1.000	Magnesia	1.000
Lime	1.864	Magnesia	.356	Silica	1.503
Magnesia	.665	Silica	.536	Lime	2.803

TRISILICATE OF LIME, MAGNESIA, AND ALUMINA.

M.		N.		O.		P.	
Silica	1.000	Lime	1.000	Magnesia	1.000	Alumina	1.000
Lime	1.864	Magnesia	.356	Alumina	.852	Silica	1.765
Magnesia	.665	Alumina	.304	Silica	1.503	Lime	3.291
Alumina	.566	Silica	.536	Lime	2.803	Magnesia	1.172

Although the formulæ which are headed by silica are all that are really essential for a correct determination of the percentages of silicates, yet for the sake of simplifying the work, and rendering it an easy task to calculate the percentages of silicates or active setting matter, and thus to readily determine the correct amount as well as the kind of inert substances in a cement, the other formulæ have been given.

To determine which formula to use, it is only necessary to note which of the component parts is the least in any given analysis, then use the formula which is headed by that ingredient, care being taken to note the number of bases under consideration, as the ratio is not the same for all classes of silicates.

To illustrate the use to which these formulæ may be put, a few of such numbers in the table of analyses as will best serve the purpose of employing the greatest number of the formulæ will be selected.

ANALYZATION OF ANALYSES.

No.	1	2	3	4	5
Silica	24.33 —	6.58 =	17.75 —	17.75 =	00.00
Alumina	3.73 —	3.73 =	0.00 —	0.00 =	0.00
Lime	71.94 —	12.27 =	59.67 —	33.08 =	26.59
Totals	100.00	22.58		50.83	26.59

Bisilicate of lime and alumina	22.58
Silicate of lime	50.83
Free uncombined lime	26.59
Total	100.00

Column No. 1 gives the analysis as shown in No. 2 of the table of analyses.

Column No. 2 shows the percentage of bisilicates contained in the cement, which is obtained by using the formula I, in which it will be seen that 1.000 alumina combines with 1.764 silica.

Therefore alumina $3.73 \times 1.764 = 6.58$ silica, and by the same formula it will be seen that 1.000 alumina in a bisilicate is combined with lime 3.289, therefore $3.73 \times 3.289 = 12.27$ lime.

The new column No. 2 is now formed by placing the three constituents opposite their respective names, and the footing shows that the total percentage of bisilicate of lime and alumina is 22.58, which being subtracted from column No. 1 leaves silica 17.75 and lime 59.67, column No. 3.

Now by referring to formula A, it will be found that 1.000 silica combines with 1.864 lime, therefore silica 17.75 × 1.864 = 33.08 lime.

This gives silicate of lime 50.83 as found in column No. 4. Column No. 5 shows the amount of uncombined material, which in this case is 26.59 free lime.

For a second illustration No. 5 of the table of analyses will be used.

No.	1	2	3
Silica	28.14	28.14	30.73
Alumina	9.10	9.10	9.94
Oxide of iron	3.20		
Lime	53.34	53.34	58.24
Magnesia	1.00	1.00	1.09
Potash and soda	2.80		
Loss	2.42		
Totals	100.00	91.58	100.00

The first column contains the analysis of No. 5 in full. The second column contains such numbers of the first as constitute the essential constituents or active setting matter of an hydraulic cement, and is reduced to hundreds, as shown in the third column, by dividing each number by the total 91.58, as, for instance, silica 28.14 ÷ 91.58 = 30.73, which is the percentage of the silica, as shown in the third column, along with the percentages of alumina, lime, and magnesia, which in the following table will be found under No. 1.

No.	1	2	3	4	5	6	7
Silica .	30.73 —	1.64 =	29.09 —	15.90 =	13.19 —	13.19 =	0.00
Lime .	58.24 —	3.05 =	55.19 —	29.65 =	25.54 —	24.58 =	0.96
Magnesia	1.09 —	1.09 =	0.00 —	0.00 =	0.00 —	0.00 =	0.00
Alumina	9.94 —	.93 =	9.01 —	9.01 =	0.00 —	0.00 =	0.00
Totals	100.00	6.71		54.56		37.77	0.96

Trisilicate of lime, magnesia, and alumina	6.71
Bisilicate of lime and alumina	54.56
Silicate of lime	37.77
	= 99.04
Uncombined base (lime)	0.96
Totals	100.00

There being three bases in this cement, it is evident that the first formula to be used will be found under the head of trisilicates, and the magnesia being the lesser in quantity, formula O is used as follows : —

Magnesia 1.09 × 1.503 = 1.64 silica, which is placed in column 2 opposite silica.

Again, magnesia 1.09 × 2.803 = 3.05 lime, which is placed in column 2 opposite lime.

And lastly, magnesia 1.09 × .852 = .93 alumina, which being placed in column 2 opposite alumina, and the total magnesia also being placed in column 2, completes the column, the footing of which shows that the total amount of trisilicate in the cement is 6.71.

By subtracting column 2 from column 1, the remainder is shown in column 3, and as there are now but two bases, lime and alumina, in this column, it is clear that the proper formula will be found under the head of bisilicate of lime and alumina, and as the alumina is the lesser in quantity, formula I is used in the same manner as in the previous analyzation, which in this analysis forms column 4, showing 54.56 bisilicate of lime and alumina. The remainder, in column 5, shows but one base, and as it is slightly in excess of the remaining silica, formula A is used, the same as in the previous table, resulting in column 6, which shows 37.77 silicate of lime.

Column 7 exhibits the total remaining uncombined matter in the cement, which is found to be less than one per cent.

Number 15 of the table of analyses is selected for the next illustration.

As in the preceding table the inert matter is deducted, and the active ingredients are calculated to hundred parts, and placed in column No. 1.

No.	1	2	3	4	5	6	7
Silica . .	22.61 —	4.72 =	17.89 —	16.63 =	1.26 —	1.26 =	0.00
Lime . .	62.15 —	8.80 =	53.35 —	31.00 =	22.35 —	2.35 =	20.00
Magnesia	3.14 —	3.14 =	0.00 —	0.00 =	0.00 —	0.00 =	0.00
Alumina .	12.10 —	2.68 =	9.42 —	9.42 =	0.00 —	0.00 =	0.00
Totals .	100.00	19.34		57.05		3.61	20.00

Trisilicate of lime, magnesia, and alumina 19.34
Bisilicate of lime and alumina 57.05
Silicate of lime 3.61

Percentage of silicates 80.00
    „   „ uncombined base 20.00
    Total 100.00

The following is an analyzation of analysis No. 20 of the table of analyses.

The non-essentials being discarded, the analysis in hundred parts appears in column No. 1.

No.	1	2	3	4	5	6	7
Silica	28.96	—15.87	=13.09	—00.54	=12.55	—11.03	=1.52
Lime	51.16	—29.58	=21.58	—01.00	=20.58	—20.58	=0.00
Magnesia . . .	10.89	—10.53	=00.36	— 0.36	= 0.00	— 0.00	=0.00
Alumina . . .	8.99	— 8.99	= 0.00	— 0.00	= 0.00	— 0.00	=0.00
Totals . .	100.00	64.97		1.90		31.61	1.52

Trisilicate of lime, magnesia, and alumina 64.97
Bisilicate of lime and alumina 1.90
Silicate of lime 31.61
Percentage of silicates 98.48
    „   „ uncombined matter 1.52
    Total 100.00

The analysis of a raw cement stone being given, and it being desired to reduce it to the percentages of silicates, which would appear after calcination, the following will be found an easy method for making the calculation.

Analysis No. 40 in the table is that of a raw cement stone, as will be seen in the reference table. The carbon dioxide was subtracted from the calcium carbonate for the sake of convenience in placing it in the table. The analysis of the stone is given in column No. 1 in the following table.

No.	1	2	3
Silica	17.50	17.50	28.92
Carbonate of lime . . .	65.20 (lime)	36.51	60.34

Alumina	6.50	6.50	10.74
Oxide of iron	3.00		
Water and loss.	7.80		
Totals	100.00	60.51	100.00

Column 2 contains the essential constituents, the carbonate of lime being reduced to lime. By reference to the table of chemical combinations, it will be seen that carbonate of lime is composed of lime, 56, carbon dioxide, 44; therefore $65.20 \times 56 = 36.51$ lime.

The essential constituents, as shown in column 2, are reduced to **hundreds** in column 3, and is shown in column 1 of the following table.

No.	1	2	3	4	5
Silica	28.92 —	18.95 =	9.97 —	9.97 =	0.00
Lime	60.34 —	35.34 =	25.00 —	18.58 =	6.42
Alumina . . .	10.74 —	10.74 =	0.00 —	0.00 =	0.00
Totals . . .	100.00	65.03		28.55	6.42

Bisilicate of lime and **alumina** 65.03
Silicate of **lime** 28.55

Percentage of silicates 93.58
      „   „ uncombined 6.42

Total. 100.00

Should carbonate of magnesia appear in the analysis of a cement stone, the amount of magnesia will be found by multiplying the carbonate by .476, as shown in the table of chemical combinations, and the product is placed in the column of constituent parts, as was done with the lime in the preceding table.

The following analyzations are taken from **the** corresponding numbers in the table of analyses, and reduced to hundred parts, the analysis appearing **in column No. 1.**

No. 47.

No.	1	2	3	4	5
Silica	21.48 —	13.71 =	7.77 —	7.77 =	0.00
Lime	70.75 —	25.57 =	45.18 —	14.48 =	30.70

Alumina	. . . . .	7.77 —	7.77 =	0.00 —	0.00 =	0.00

Totals	. . . . .	100.00	47.05		22.25	30.70

Bisilicate of lime and alumina	47.05
Silicate of lime	22.25
Total silicates	69.30
Free lime	30.70
Total	100.00

No. 48.

No.	1	2	3	4	5	6	7
Silica .	22.35 —	1.76 =	20.59 —	9.99 =	10.60 —	10.60 =	0.00
Lime .	69.82 —	3.28 =	66.54 —	18.63 =	47.91 —	19.76 =	28.15
Magnesia	1.17 —	1.17 =	0.00 —	0.00 —	0.00 —	0.00 —	0.00
Alumina	6.66 —	1.00 =	5.66 —	5.66 =	0.00 —	0.00 =	0.00
Totals	100.00	7.21		34.28		30.36	28.15

Silicate of lime, magnesia, and alumina	7.21
Silicate of lime and alumina	34.28
Silicate of lime	30.36
Percentage of silicates	71.85
„ „ free base	28.15
Total	100.00

No. 50.

No.	1	2	3	4	5
Silica	22.56 —	14.15 =	8.41 —	8.41 =	0.00
Lime	69.42 —	26.39 =	43.03 —	15.68 =	27.37
Alumina	8.02 —	8.02 =	0.00 —	0.00 =	0.00
Totals	100.00	48.56		24.09	27.37

Silicate of lime and alumina	48.56
Silicate of lime	24.09
Percentage of silicates	72.65
Free lime	27.35
Total	100.00

No. 52.

No.	1	2		3		4		5		6		7
Silica .	23.70	— 3.58	=	20.12	—	11.05	=	9.07	—	9.07	=	0.00
Lime .	65.63	— 6.67	=	58.96	—	20.60	=	38.36	—	16.91	=	21.45
Magnesia	2.38	— 2.38	=	0.00	—	0.00	=	0.00	—	0.00	=	0.00
Alumina	8.29	— 2.03	=	6.26	—	6.26	=	0.00	—	0.00	=	0.00
Totals	100.00	14.66		37.91				25.98				21.45

Silicate of lime, magnesia, and alumina 14.66
Silicate of lime and alumina 37.91
Silicate of lime 25.98

Percentage of silicates 78.55
Percentage free base 21.45

Total 100.00

The foregoing calculations sufficiently illustrate the system of calculating the percentages of silicates or active setting matter in a cement, or cement rock, from such analyses as are usually rendered by chemists and analysts. They also determine the classes of silicates which may be present and their percentages.

In a cement containing the three bases, lime, magnesia, and alumina, there may be found the three classes, namely, triple, double, and single silicates.

As has already been stated, a cement containing two or three silicates is superior in quality to that which contains but one.

To illustrate, let us suppose a cement to contain silica, lime, and alumina in exact combining proportions and forming a double silicate of lime and alumina, as in the following : —

Silica 29.14
Lime 54.34
Alumina 16.52

Total 100.00

Now if we take 8.00 from the alumina, and add an equal amount to the silica and lime in the proportions of 2.80 to the silica and 5.20 to the lime = 8.00, the new table will be formed as shown in column

No. 1 below, and the double and single silicates will appear in the second and third columns respectively.

No.	1	2	3
Silica	31.94 —	15.04 =	16.90
Lime	59.54 —	28.04 =	31.50
Alumina	8.52 —	8.52 =	0.00
Totals	100.00	51.60	48.40
Bisilicate of lime and alumina . .			51.60
Silicate of lime			48.40
Total			100.00

There can be no question whatever that a cement formed with the two classes of silicates, as shown in the latter table, will be superior in quality to that shown in the preceding table, which is due to the fact that in a cement, whether natural or artificial, lime is superior to alumina as a base, in the mortar of masonry or concrete, used either above or below water, and especially is this true in regard to masonry or concrete submerged in sea water.

No better demonstration of this fact is afforded than in the use of Tiel hydraulic lime, which contains less than 2 per cent. of alumina. Although this material contains a large percentage of uncombined lime, it has never been surpassed in its ability to resist the action of sea water, and those cements which have failed in sea water, whether natural or artificial, are found to contain a large proportion of alumina. Therefore, as shown in the last two tables, the alumina may vary 50 per cent. in amount, and still remain within the limits of true combining proportions, yet it is extremely probable, and, indeed, it may be stated as an absolute certainty, that as between the two compositions referred to, the latter would, while the former would not, sustain continued immersion in sea water.

It seems desirable that some explanation be made or reason given for the position taken in regard to the combining ratio of the various silicates. To make a concise statement of the conflicting opinions concerning this vexed question, it is best to give them in the order of their popularity.

First. Hydraulic cement is produced by the formation of silicate and aluminate of lime during **calcination.** Magnesia, if **present,** is inert or uncombined.

Second. **By the** formation of bisilicate of lime and **alumina** during calcination, magnesia, if present, forms silicate and aluminate of magnesia.

Third. The formation of silicate of lime during calcination, the alumina and magnesia remaining **uncombined, or** playing **an** unimportant part.

Fourth. That **after calcination** the constituents, silica, and whatever bases may be present, exist in a free state, and that by the application of water, a silicate is formed combining all the bases present in certain proportions; the excess, **if any, is** uncombined.

Fifth. Whether the material **is natural** cement rock or **is** artificially compounded, the formation, during calcination of triple, double, and single silicates occurs (dependent on the number of bases **present),** in certain **fixed proportions,** any excess, whether of silica or **the** bases, remaining uncombined.

The preceding chapters, the table of chemical combinations, and that of combining ratios, **are sufficient** evidence of our belief in the correctness of the fifth proposition, and it is but just and **proper to** state that we are substantially alone in this **belief.**

The nearest approach to it is the opinion of Professor Cox, who, **however, as shown** by his writings, inclines to the fourth proposition.

Without wishing to arrogate any special knowledge of the art, or to attempt the building up of a new theory in relation to the chemical combinations existing in a cement, or contradictorily oppose the views of others on this subject, yet it is due to state that we find it impossible to accept many of the opinions given, such, for example, as that both silicate of lime and aluminate of **lime are** formed in a **cement.**

While it is true that **aluminate of lime can be, and is, formed by the** action of heat when **these constituents are treated separately, that it can** so form when in the presence of silica and lime, **we do not believe.**

We have already shown that alumina has both a basic **and** acidic character, although **both are** comparatively weak; and **we** believe that its acidic character entirely disappears when in the presence of the much more powerful silicic acid, and **that** when in

the presence of that acid it can only assume the properties due to
its basic character, and it therefore combines with silica in certain
fixed proportions with lime and magnesia; and therefore when these
three bases are present, with silicic acid, a combination is formed by
the acid and the three bases in fixed and unalterable proportions, in
accordance with the law of atomic weights.

There can be no doubt that if a mixture should be compounded
which contained a small amount of silica and a large amount of
lime and alumina, the excess of the two bases over and above their
equivalents of silica would combine, forming aluminate of lime.

But inasmuch as there are no known cements, whether natural
or artificial, which contain alumina in excess of its combining ratio
with the silica and lime present, it is needless to pursue this subject
further.

That magnesia can remain uncombined, when present with
silicic acid and lime, or lime and alumina, is a theory which has been
so often disproved, that it seems incredible that advocates of this
fallacy should be found among the higher authorities, who claim
that in an artificial cement more than three per cent. is not to be
tolerated, while in natural rock cements it is uncombined, and therefore inert.

The Rosendale cements, which, in quality and general excellence, stand in the front rank among American rock cements, contain from 15 to 18 per cent. of magnesia. These cements are never
hydrated, being packed at the mill-spout as fast as ground; and
when used, are taken from the packages and mixed with sand and
water, and immediately applied in masonry or concrete.

If the magnesia in these cements is in a free and uncombined
state, as claimed by many writers, it must certainly follow that in the
subsequent hydration, expansion and disruption of the masonry is
inevitable. And so, if these cements are kept in packages any length
of time, say three or four months, as often occurs in the hands of
dealers in cements, the hydration of the free magnesia would certainly expand the packages and burst the hoops. And yet this dis-
tension of packages never occurs, and the idea of a disruption of
masonry through the use of Rosendale cement is simply absurd.
Millions of barrels of this brand of cement are used in many of the
greatest engineering and architectural works in the country, such as

the high bridge over the Harlem, the New York and Brooklyn suspension bridge, the Croton aqueducts, the tallest buildings in lower Broadway,— in short, it may be said that New York and Boston are built with this cement,— and furthermore, the Akron, Milwaukee, Utica, and Mankato brands of cement, all contain practically as much magnesia as do the Rosendale brands; and yet there is no known instance of any of these brands ever expanding in masonry, and magnesian cements are used in this country to the extent of nearly five million barrels yearly. These facts alone stand as a complete refutation of the absurd theory that magnesia is free in these cements.

It is as quick to combine with silica as is lime. During calcination it parts with its carbon dioxide at a lower heat than is required for the expulsion of that acid from the lime, and becoming caustic in advance of the lime, is the first to attack the silica, freeing the latter from its combination with alumina, thus rendering the silica as free silicic acid, and if the high heat is continued, a reaction takes place, and chemical combination ensues between the acid and the three bases, in accordance with their atomic weights, as fully illustrated in the table of combining ratios.

A simple illustration of the fact that the reaction follows the separation of the alumina from the silica, and a chemical combination with the acid and all the bases takes place, is afforded by the following experiment: —

First. Take a piece of magnesian cement rock and from it secure two pieces weighing one or two pounds each, and after they have been gradually dried out, to prevent what is known by kiln men as "popping," which is caused by a bursting into small pieces through the sudden conversion of the moisture contained in the rock into steam, place both these pieces in a smith's forge and rapidly drive them up to nearly a white heat, then suddenly withdraw one of the pieces from the forge, and as quickly as possible crush it to powder while hot.

Second. Continue the heat with the other piece for half an hour or so, then stop the blower and allow the piece to cool gradually, keeping it covered in the forge until it is cold, then crush to powder.

Third. Keep the two samples separate and wet them into balls,

patties, or briquettes, and note the **difference in the action of the
two.** The **first will** heat, expand, and check, and **if placed** under
water will become of a mud-like consistency, and if in air, **it will**
crumble into dust-like ashes ; while the second sample will not heat,
will not expand or check, and after an hour in air will sustain sub-
mersion and become hard.

The first sample was withdrawn from the heat after the expulsion
of the carbon dioxide, and before it had time for the reaction and
formation of silicates, and the constituents were in a free condition,
as shown by the heat and expansion when hydrated, while the second
sample was accorded the necessary time for such reaction and **chemi-**
cal combination ; thus proving the **truth of our assertion, that when-**
ever present with silica and lime, and under high and continued heat,
both magnesia and alumina combine with the silicic acid in precisely
the same manner as lime combines, in certain **fixed** proportions,
according to the law of atomic weights.

A table **of** the atomic weights of such elements as are found in
hydraulic cements is herewith given. The numbers indicate **the**
relative weights of the atoms constituting the elements.

ELEMENTS.	SYMBOL.	ATOMIC WEIGHT.
Aluminum	Al.	27.
Calcium	Ca.	39.9
Carbon	C.	11.97
Hydrogen	H.	1.
Iron	Fe.	55.9
Magnesium	Mg.	23.9
Manganese	Mn.	54.8
Oxygen	O.	15.96
Kalium (Potassium)	K.	39.03
Sulphur	S.	31.98
Silicon	Si.	28.
Sodium (Natrium)	Na.	22.99

Although the system employed in calculating the percentages of
the various chemical combinations which occur in hydraulic cements
is familiar to many, yet a desire has been expressed that it be illustrated in a plain and practical manner, which may be readily under-

stood by those who have little time to devote to such study, and for this reason a place is given to the following calculations.

SILICATE OF LIME.

Silica (SiO_2) is a chemical combination of silicon and oxygen in the proportion of one atom of silicon (Si) to two atoms of oxygen (O).

By reference to the table, it will be seen that the atomic weight of silicon is 28., and that of oxygen is 15.96. Two atoms of oxygen will therefore weigh 31.92.

Thus, 28. + 31.92 = 59.92 = silica. By dividing each number by 59.92 we get the percentage of each.

28.00 ÷ 59.92 = Silicon 46.73 $\Big\}$ = 100 Silica (SiO_2).
31.92 ÷ 59.92 = Oxygen 53.27

Employing the same method with reference to lime (CaO) we find that the atomic weight of calcium is 39.90, which, being added to one oxygen 15.96 = 55.86 = lime.

Therefore $\quad$ 39.90 ÷ 55.86 = Calcium 71.43 $\Big\}$ = 100 lime (CaO).
$\qquad$ 15.96 ÷ 55.86 = Oxygen 28.57

Silicate of lime is formed by a combination of silica and lime in the proportion of one part of the former to two parts of the latter, the combining numbers of which are as already given.

1 Silica = 59.92 $\qquad \Big\}$ = 171.64.
2 Lime (55.86 × 2) 111.72

59.92 ÷ 171.64 = Silica 34.91 $\Big\}$ = 100 Silicate of Lime (2CaO,
111.72 ÷ 171.64 = Lime 65.09 $\qquad$ SiO_2).

CARBONIC ACID.

Carbon (C) 11.97 $\qquad \Big\}$ = 43.89.
2 Oxygen (O) 31.92

Carbon 11.97 ÷ 43.89 = Carbon 27.27 $\Big\}$ = 100 Carbonic Acid (CO_2).
Oxygen 31.92 ÷ 43.89 = Oxygen 72.73

CARBONATE OF LIME.

Lime 55.86 $\qquad \Big\}$ = 99.75.
Carbonic Acid 43.89

55.86 ÷ 99.75 = Lime 56 $\qquad \Big\}$ = 100 Carbonate of Lime
43.89 ÷ 99.75 = Carbonic Acid 44 $\qquad$ (CaO, CO_2).

SILICATE OF MAGNESIA.

$$\left.\begin{array}{l}\text{Magnesium } 23.9 \\ \text{Oxygen } \quad 15.96\end{array}\right\} = 39.86 \text{ Magnesia (MgO)}.$$

$$\left.\begin{array}{ll}1 \text{ Silica} & 59.96 \\ 2 \text{ Magnesia } (39.86 \times 2) & 79.72\end{array}\right\} = 139.68$$

$$\left.\begin{array}{l}59.96 \div 139.68 = \text{Silica} \quad\quad 42.92 \\ 79.72 \div 139.68 = \text{Magnesia } 57.08\end{array}\right\} = \begin{array}{l}\text{Silicate of Magnesia } (2\text{MgO}. \\ \quad\quad SiO_2).\end{array}$$

Among the manufacturers of artificial cements during the past twenty years or so there has been a constantly growing ambition to increase the number of pounds of tensile strain their cement will sustain, expecting thereby to improve the quality of their respective brands.

Goaded on by the universal preference for the brands showing the highest tests, they are striving by every means at their command to attain still higher results.

Many experiments were tried by adding foreign substances in varying percentages, among which may be mentioned sulphate of lime, which still obtains among nearly all the producers of Portland cement.

It is not denied by the manufacturers that by its use much higher short time tests are possible, and they justify its use by their assurance to the public that they do not use too much of it, thereby admitting its harmful character, which is so great that the German society of Portland cement manufacturers publicly advertise that the members of that society are not permitted to use more than three per cent. of this material in their cements.

No one will claim that a mixture of sulphate of lime in a cement is beneficial; on the contrary, it is well known to be harmful, and that a cement is better without it, even though it may not test so high by a few pounds in one-day or seven-day tests.

Its use simply illustrates the unreasoning desire to reach a little higher mark in testing.

Several years ago it was discovered that an addition of lime beyond its equivalent of silica would permit of a higher heat in calcination, which in turn gave a cement the quality of sustaining higher short time tests; and the manufacturers were not slow in availing themselves of this apparent advantage.

And thus the proportion of lime has been gradually increased until to-day there will be found in all brands of Portland cement, as has already been stated, from 2.7 to to 3.2 parts of lime to 1 part of silica.

Although it was learned that by increasing the proportion of lime higher short time testing results followed, yet it became evident that such a cement must necessarily contain a large proportion of free lime, which was not considered a desirable result; and to overcome this unpleasant difficulty, some of the leading authorities asserted that the excess of lime was taken up and combined with the alumina, forming aluminate of lime, as shown in the tables quoted from Professor De Smedt, who, it will be observed, gives the combining proportions as silica 34.88 and lime 65.12, the ratio being silica 1, lime 1.86, and the ratio of alumina 1 and lime 2, to form aluminate of lime.

But as the percentage of lime has been gradually increased, it has been found necessary to establish a new ratio as between the silica and lime, the German authorities taking the lead in this new departure; and it is now gravely asserted that 1 molecule of silica combines with 3 molecules of lime, making the ratio 1 of the former to 2.79 of the latter.

As the modern Portland contains from 2.80 to 3.25 of lime to 1 of silica, the lime, which is in excess of the new ratio, is conveniently taken up by the alumina, forming aluminate of lime.

Thus for the present, at least, the authorities on Portland cement seem to have the ratio satisfactorily adjusted.

It is probable, however, that some way would be found to show conclusively that 1 part of silica combined with 4 or more parts of lime, should some genius discover a way to produce higher testing results by such a manipulation of proportions.

To show the tendency toward increasing the proportion of lime, which is done solely for the purpose of gaining higher short time tests, it is only necessary to take as an illustration the analysis of one of the foremost brands of English Portland cements; a cement which, twenty years or so ago, commanded the largest sale, and the highest price of any cement in the American markets.

The analysis was carefully conducted by the painstaking and conscientious chemist, Prof. E. T. Cox, while he was State geologist of Indiana.

The constituent parts of this cement, after discarding the non-essentials, will be found in column No. 1 of the following table, and the percentage of silicates appears in the succeeding columns.

No.	1	2	3	4	5	6	7
Silica .	30.89 —	1.65 =	29.24 —	17.44 =	11.80 —	11.57 =	00.23
Alumina	10.82 —	0.94 =	9.88 —	9.88 =	0.00 —	0.00 =	0.00
Lime .	57.19 —	3.08 =	54.11 —	32.52 =	21.59 —	21.59 =	00.00
Magnesia	1.10 —	1.10 =	0.00 —	0.00 =	0.00 —	0.00 =	0.00
Totals	100.00	6.77		59.84		33.16	00.23

Silicate of lime, magnesia, and alumina	6.77
Silicate of lime and alumina	59.84
Silicate of lime	33.16
Total silicates	99.77
Uncombined silica	00.23
Total	100.00

It will be observed that, in the matter of proportions, this cement was as nearly perfect as it was possible to be made. It was tested frequently by the author for many years, and it was never known to check or expand, and it became exceedingly hard and permanent in masonry, and was used in sidewalks and similar work, almost to the exclusion of all other brands, and yet it would rarely exceed 250 lbs. in a seven days' test. Neither did it become glassy and brittle with age, like the modern Portland cements, a result due entirely to the demand for higher short time tests; a demand which, to the detriment of its quality, has compelled the manufacturers of the brand in question to increase the proportion of lime, as may be seen by reference to No. 10 of the table of analyses, in which it will be observed that the ratio of silica to lime is as 1 to 3.07, while the ratio in the earlier analysis as herein given is 1 to 1.85+, which is practically the true combining ratio, *i. e.*, 1 to 1.86+.

The new ratio which is sought to be established is best shown by the formula $3CaO.SiO_2$, while that for the long accepted ratio is $2CaO.SiO_2$. These two formulæ, reduced to percentages, are given in the order named.

Silica	.	.	.	.	26.38
Lime	.	.	.	.	73.62
Totals	.	.	100.00		

Silica	.	.	.	.	34.91
Lime	.	.	.	.	65.09
			100.00		

There is no simpler way to demonstrate by practical experiment which of the two formulæ comes the nearest to actual facts, than by mixing together clay and gypsum, with the latter in excess, and calcining to a white heat. The amount of sulphate of lime remaining will determine the amount of lime that has combined with a given amount of silica.

Such experiments made under the direction of the author demonstrated very clearly that the correct ratio is not in accord with the modern theory that 3 molecules of lime combine with 1 of silica.

It is well known that if we calcine 100 pounds of gypsum to a white heat, the only change which is effected is the expulsion of the water of crystallization, amounting to 20.93 per cent. of the total weight, leaving 79.07 sulphate of lime, which is composed of lime 32.55 and sulphuric acid 46.52.

If, however, the 100 pounds of pure gypsum are finely ground and thoroughly mixed with 23.27 pounds of dry clay, composed of silica 17.45 and alumina 5.82 = 23.27 clay, the composition in hundred parts will be as follows:—

Sulphuric acid	37.74	
Lime	26.40	= 81.12 gypsum.
Water	16.98	
Silica	14.15	
Alumina	4.73	
Total	100.00	

If this mixture is then calcined to a white heat, the water of the gypsum will first be expelled, and when the high heat is reached, the silicic acid will expel the sulphuric acid and itself combine with the lime and alumina, forming an hydraulic cement pure and simple, the analysis of which will appear in column No. 1 of the following table, the succeeding columns exhibiting the amount and kind of silicates contained therein.

No.	1	2	3	4	5
Silica	31.25 —	18.44 =	12.81 —	12.81 =	00.00
Lime	58.30 —	34.39 =	23.91 —	23.88 =	00.03
Alumina	10.45 —	10.45 =	00.00 —	00.00 =	00.00
Totals	100.00	63.28		36.69	00.03

Silicate of lime and alumina	63.28
Silicate of lime	36.69

Total silicates	99.97
Total free base	0.03
Total	100.00

It will here be seen that, the silica being present in full combining proportions with the lime, the sulphuric acid was all expelled. Whereas, had there been an excess of lime, it would have retained its equivalent of sulphuric acid in combination as sulphate of lime.

Now if we deduct 4 from the silica, thus leaving the lime in excess, the analysis before calcination would appear as in the following table.

Sulphuric Acid	39.00
Lime	27.29 } = 83.84 gypsum.
Water	17.55
Silica	11.28
Alumina	4.88
Total	100.00

After calcination at white heat, the analysis, reduced to hundreds, will appear as shown in column No. 1 of the following table, the succeeding columns showing the kind and amount of silicates and sulphates in the cement.

No.	1	2	3	4	5
Sulphuric Acid . . .	17.10	.	.	.	17.10
Lime . . . . =	52.07 —	30.64 =	21.43 —	9.48 =	11.95
Silica	21.52 —	16.43 =	5.09 —	5.09 =	0.00

Alumina	9.31 —	9.31 =	0.00 —	0.00 =	0.00
Totals	100.00	56.38		14.57	29.05

Silicate of lime and alumina 56.38
Silicate of lime 14.57

Total silicates 70.95
Sulphate of lime 29.05

Total 100.00

Since the days when it became the rule to add an excess of lime for the purposes stated, there have been no artificial cements produced which do not become brittle and glassy with age.

While such a cement is being used, and while under the eye of the engineer, and until the work is finished and has passed inspection, and an occasional examination thereafter, it seems to have acted in a most admirable and satisfactory manner. It has set hard, as was expected, and the matter soon becomes ancient history with the engineer or architect, whose attention is required by things present. And yet this cement is not laid away as though dead. It is not by any means inactive.

Its crystallization is rapid, as evidenced by its prompt induration, and it is this rapid crystallization which inevitably results in rendering the mortar brittle, and thereby liable to subsequent disintegration, a result which does not follow in the use of well-balanced American rock cements, which, although they do not in the earlier days subsequent to their use exhibit the hardness common with the artificial cements, nevertheless, at a later period, reach the same degree of solidity, and exhibit a toughness and tenacity of cohesion unknown among the modern artificial cements.

Evidence is fast accumulating which tends to prove that all cements, whether artificial or natural, which become brittle and glassy with age, contain little or no magnesia, while those which are tough and stonelike in character do contain it; and the toughness is found to be in direct ratio with the amount of magnesia present.

CHAPTER VII.

Various Methods of Testing — Rock Cements Improved by
Seasoning — Specifications by U. S. Engineers and
Others — Report of Committee to A. S. C. E. on Uni-
form System for Tests — Cement Testing by Cecil B.
Smith before the C. S. C. E. — Prof. Porter on Cement
Testing and Varying Results by Different Testers
— Testing Machines — Opinions Based on Short Time
Tests Often Deceptive — Briquettes become Brittle
with Age — Prediction as to Future Specifications —
Absurd System of Averages — The Color Whim.

Early in the present century, several mechanical contrivances
were introduced, designed for the purpose of measuring the values
of cements.

Conclusions were sought to be reached by subjecting samples of
cement, mortar, and concrete to various tests, among which may be
named the needle or penetration test, the transverse, adhesive, compressive, torsional, and tensile strain tests, and in later years came
the boiling and freezing tests.

The needle test, invented by M. Vicat, was perhaps one of the
earliest, if not the earliest, method employed.

General Totten employed the needle test at Fort Adams, Newport, R. I., for several years prior to 1830, and soon thereafter employed the transverse test.

It may be stated that the needle test was practised to determine
the time in setting, and the relative hardness attained at stated
intervals during the process of hardening of the cement samples.

As this test did not indicate the ultimate strength of a cement,
or a cement mortar, it soon gave place to the transverse and the adhesive tests.

General Gillmore employed the needle, the transverse, the tensile, and the adhesive tests prior to 1860.

Briefly, these tests may be described as follows: —

The relative hardness of the samples at stated intervals during and after the process of setting was measured by the penetration of a steel point or needle impelled by the impact of a falling body.

The transverse test consisted in the molding of cement or cement mortar into prisms or bars usually 2 ins. by 2 ins. by 8 ins., under pressure, which, after setting, were placed in water, and after a specified number of days had elapsed were broken by being placed on supports 4 ins. apart, and a pressure brought to bear midway between the supports.

The adhesive properties of a cement were measured by cementing bricks and blocks of stone together in pairs under pressure during the time of setting, and afterwards drawing them apart by a force applied at right angles to the plane of the joint.

The tensile test was practically the same as that now in vogue; the form of the briquettes, and the machines for conducting the tests named, have changed considerably, but the principles involved are practically unaltered.

The transverse and compressive tests are still occasionally resorted to, but the torsional and adhesive tests are no longer practised to any extent.

Between 1850 and 1860, the mode of testing cements by means of the tensile-strain testing machines gained largely in public favor in France, and was soon followed by a like tendency in England.

It was adopted by the Metropolitan Board of Works in London in 1859, and under the supervision of Engineers Grant, Bazalgette, Colson, Mann and others, soon became considered as a valuable adjunct in the determination of the qualities of the various cements offered on that work.

From that time until the present, the tensile-strain method of testing cements has constantly grown in public favor, and has become the universal practise among engineers, architects, and manufacturers.

Why this mode of testing the strength of cements and cement mortars survived almost to the exclusion of the others, it is hard to determine.

It certainly cannot compare with the transverse test for simplicity of machinery or accuracy of results.

In the formation of the samples to be tested for the transverse tests, the prisms, being straight, uniform bodies, could be readily subjected to any predetermined pressure, and the density of the prisms be gaged to a degree of uniformity unattainable in the modern briquette.

Cement testing, although practised now much more than formerly, is still far from being reduced to any fixed system of rules.

Each engineer or architect is a law unto himself, and United States engineers even, do not seem to be governed by any one standard, and it would be difficult to find a brand of cement which could fulfil all the requirements of the various specifications which are from time to time given out to the manufacturers.

Thus, for example, one set of specifications states that " the cement must be freshly burned," but, " must not take less than twenty-five minutes to bear the light wire, that is, a weight of four ounces on a wire one twelfth of an inch in diameter."

Now nearly all of our best brands of rock cements will bear the light wire in about one half of the time specified, if tested when fresh, but will fulfil the requirements if they have had time to season.

Much also depends on the amount of water used, as the initial set can be retarded by a trifling addition of water, or hastened by using just enough to enable the cement to be molded.

But in this, as in many other matters connected with the testing of a cement, the manufacturer has nothing to say. He is at the mercy of the engineer, and engineers who are willing to accept suggestions from the manufacturers are not as thick as autumn leaves in Vallombrosa.

It is certain that all the best brands of rock cements in this country are improved by one or two months of seasoning, and all this that we read about, to the effect that rock cements must be used immediately after manufacture, lest deterioration may set in, is arrant nonsense.

The author is familiar with every brand of rock cement produced in this country, and he does not know of one brand that is not improved by one to two months' exposure.

The manufacturers understand this, for, to learn the value of seasoning, they have **but to set aside** a tightly closed **package** filled fresh from the mill spout, and take some from the **same** grinding and spread it in a dry place where the air has free access to it, and at the end of thirty or sixty days test both samples.

And yet they are daily confronted with specifications stipulating that the cement must be freshly burned.

Some of the very best brands of rock cements in this country are vastly improved by four months' exposure, if kept on floors high enough from the ground to preclude the possibility of the absorption of moisture from below.

A rock cement which is not improved by an exposure of **from thirty to sixty** days can hardly **be** considered a strictly first-class cement.

There. are several of our best brands of rock cements that are naturally moderate in setting when given even a brief exposure, yet when tested fresh, will take a rapid surface hardening and give every appearance of being naturally quick setting ; but an examination of the fracture of briquettes made from such cements will disclose the fact that at twenty-four hours crystallization has barely commenced, thus giving evidence of not too rapid setting. Still the superficial hardening, due to freshness, will cause them to bear the light wire too soon to bring them within the specifications.

In this way it oftentimes happens that a really first-class cement may be rejected because it sustains the light wire too soon.

The author has seen a fresh cement rejected because it bore the wire too soon, and the sample set aside, and after a few days had elapsed, tested again from mere curiosity, and found to be slow enough to come within the specifications.

During the few days of exposure the peculiarity noted had entirely disappeared.

Specifications governing cement tests, derived from various authentic sources, are herewith given : —

U. S. Engineer Office,

Portland, Maine, Feb. 14, 1893.

Peter C. Hains, Lieut.-Col. of Engineers.

The cement is to be hydraulic, uniform in quality, fresh, dry, finely ground, free from lumps, and put up in good sound barrels, each barrel of cement to weigh not less than 300 lbs. net. A sample is to be submitted for test, and the entire quantity delivered must be fully up to the sample.

The cement must not set within twenty minutes. Briquettes made of neat cement, mixed with a proper proportion of water, must show a tensile strength per square inch of not less than 60 lbs. after exposure to the air for twenty-four hours; kept one day in air and six in water, not less than 100 lbs.; and kept one day in air and twenty-seven in water, not less than 180 lbs.

At least 90 per cent. must pass through a sieve of 2,500 meshes to the square inch.

The cement will be subjected to such other tests as the engineer may deem necessary.

U. S. ENGINEER OFFICE,
ARMY BUILDING, 39 WHITEHALL STREET,
NEW YORK, N. Y., Jan. 25, 1893.

G. L. GILLESPIE, LIEUT.-COL. CORPS OF ENGINEERS.

The cement will be of first quality American cement, fresh, dry, full weight, finely ground, free from lumps, and put up in good sound barrels.

The bids will state the special brand proposed to be furnished, and the bidder will deliver a sample barrel upon Pier 3, East River, for test, at least ten days before the opening of the bids.

The cement will be expected to stand the following tests: Cement neat must be set in about thirty minutes, and have tensile strength per square inch as follows: —

Samples which have been kept in air and broken at twenty-four hours after setting, 70 lbs.; at seven days, 125 lbs.; at fourteen days, 170 lbs.; and at thirty days, 225 lbs.

Samples which have been kept twenty-four hours in air and then in water until broken: at twenty-four hours, 70 lbs.; at seven days, 90 lbs.; at fourteen days, 120 lbs.; and at thirty days, 150 lbs.

Cement one part, sand two parts, tensile strength per square inch, samples kept in air until broken: at twenty-four hours, 15 lbs.; at seven days, 35 lbs.; at fourteen days, 50 lbs.; and at thirty days, 65 lbs.; and immersed in water twenty-four hours after setting: at twenty-four hours, 15 lbs.; **at seven** days, 30 lbs.; at fourteen **days, 45** lbs.; and at thirty days, 65 **lbs.**

U. S. ENGINEER OFFICE,
CUSTOM HOUSE, PITTSBURGH, PENN., July 31, 1894.
CAPT. R. L. HOXIE, CORPS OF ENGINEERS, U. S. A.

AMERICAN HYDRAULIC CEMENT.

INSPECTION.— Ten **per cent.** of the packages in each car-load, and no more, will be selected for weighing **and** testing. The **weight and** quality of all cement in each car-load will be determined by weighing and testing these **selected packages.** The average net weight **of all** packages in **each car-load lot will be** the average net weight **of** all the selected **packages.** The failure of any one of **the** selected packages to **stand the required tests will be** sufficient reason **for** rejecting this **car-load lot, excepting only those** packages which **may have stood the test.** Rejected cement will be immediately re-shipped to the **contractor at his expense, and the cost of** all handling of same will be charged against his **account.**

FINENESS.— Ninety-five per cent. by weight must pass through a cement wire sieve having **2,500 meshes per square inch, and made** of **No. 35** wire, Stubb's W. G.

PREPARATION OF TEST BRIQUETTES.— Cement will be mixed neat, **with** enough water only to thoroughly moisten and **make it** coherent, and will be pressed into the mold with a spatula. Temperature not below 60°.

SETTING.— The surface must yield to the pressure of a wire $\frac{1}{24}$ in. diameter, carrying a weight of 1 lb. thirty minutes after completion of briquette.

TENSILE STRENGTH PER SQUARE INCH OF CROSS-SECTION. — This will be for each package the average strength of five briquettes. These will be kept in air **until set,** and then immersed in water until they are put into the clips of the testing machine, **being** tested **wet.** After twenty-four hours' immersion in water, the tensile strength must be **70 lbs., and after** seven days' immersion, 125 lbs.

CHECKING AND CRACKING.—When made into a thin cake, allowed to set in air, and immersed in water, no checking or cracking **must be shown.**

Specifications for the cement used in the masonry of the depressed Harlem Railroad tracks in New York City.

The cement must be of the best quality of freshly burned and ground hydraulic cement. It will be subject to test made by the engineer or his appointed inspector, and must stand a proof tensile test of 50 lbs. per square inch of sectional area on specimens mixed to a stiff paste and allowed a set of thirty minutes in air and twenty-four hours under water; and of 90 lbs. on specimens allowed a set of seven days under water, and shall be 90 per cent. fine when tried with a sieve of 2,500 meshes to the square inch.

It must take not less than twenty-five minutes to bear the light wire — that is, a weight of 4 ozs. on a wire one twelfth of an inch in diameter.

The following specifications for hydraulic cement were drawn by a United States engineer who advertised for a large amount of cement and received but one bid.

The cement must possess the following requisites : —

FIRST.— It must be fresh, slow setting, and so finely ground that 85 per cent. of it shall pass through a sieve of 2,500 meshes per square inch.

SECOND.— After being mixed neat and filled into a glass bottle, or similar vessel, and struck level with the top, it must not crack the vessel in setting, nor rise out of it, nor become loose in it by shrinkage.

THIRD.— When mixed neat and made up into briquettes, and given one hour in air, then twenty-three hours in water, the cement must be capable of withstanding a tensile strain of 35 lbs. per square inch before it is fractured; and after seven days in water, succeeding the first hour in air, it must sustain a tensile strain of 125 lbs. per square inch.

FOURTH.— Its initial setting shall not take place in less than thirty minutes from the time it is mixed neat into a paste.

FIFTH.— The cement must possess reliable uniformity of all these qualities.

It will be noted that these specifications state that "the cement must be fresh," and yet, "the initial set must not take place in less than thirty minutes."

It is doubtful if any brand of rock cement could fulfil all the requirements.

The following letter is in reply to an inquiry by the author : —

TREASURY DEPARTMENT,

OFFICE OF THE SUPERVISING ARCHITECT,

WASHINGTON, D. C., May 14, 1896.

Sir : — Replying to your letter of the 11th inst., you are informed that the requirements of cement to be used under this office are as follows : —

Hydraulic cement, mixed neat, one day in air and six days in water, should stand a tensile strain of 90 lbs. per square inch.

Portland cement, mixed neat, one day in air and six days in water, should stand a tensile strain of 350 lbs. per square inch.

This office has no printed forms governing the making of mortars and concretes ; specifications for this class of work vary according to circumstances.

Respectfully yours,

(Signed)

WM. M. AIKEN,

Supervising Architect.

1895.

DEPARTMENT OF PUBLIC WORKS,

PEORIA, ILLINOIS.

ALMON D. THOMPSON, CITY ENGINEER.

All cement for concrete foundations shall be what is commonly known as American Natural Hydraulic Cement, of quality equal to the best obtainable in the markets. All Portland cement used on the work shall be the best obtainable in the markets. They will be subjected to rigid inspection, and that rejected shall be immediately removed by the contractor.

The contractor must submit the cement for inspection and testing at least ten days before using, and such inspection and tests will be made only from samples obtained by the inspector from cement delivered on the work.

The inspector shall be notified of each delivery of cement. All cement must stand the following tests: —

Two cakes, 3 ins. in diameter and ½ in. thick, with thin edges, will be made.

One of these cakes as soon as set will be placed in water and examined from day to day. If the cake exhibits checks, cracks, or contortions, the cement will be rejected. The other cake described will be used for setting and color tests.

The time will be noted when the cake has become hard enough to sustain a wire $\frac{1}{12}$ in. in diameter loaded with ¼ lb.

When the wire is sustained, the cement has begun to set, and this time shall not be less than ten minutes for natural cement, nor less than forty-five minutes for Portland cement.

When the cake will sustain a wire $\frac{1}{24}$ in. in diameter loaded with 1 lb., the set is complete, and this time must not be less than one hour nor more than three hours for natural cement, nor less than two hours nor more than six hours for Portland cement.

The cake used for setting test will be preserved, and when examined from day to day must be of uniform color, exhibiting no blotches or discolorations.

The cement must be evenly ground, and, when tested with the following standard sieves, must pass at least the following percentages: —

	Natural.	Portland.
No. 20 sieve, having 20 meshes per lineal inch .	100%	
No. 50 sieve, having 50 meshes per lineal inch .	90%	98%
No. 74 sieve, having 74 meshes per lineal inch .	80%	94%
No. 100 sieve, having 100 meshes per lineal inch .		90%

The diameter of wire for sieves being respectively: —

For No. 20 sieve, No. 28 Stubb's wire gauge.
For No. 50 sieve, No. 35 Stubb's wire gauge.
For No. 74 sieve, No. 37 Stubb's wire gauge.
For No. 100 sieve, No. 40 Stubb's wire gauge.

All cement for test briquettes will be mixed with barely sufficient water to make a stiff mortar.

The neat briquettes to be pressed into the molds **by hand and** the sand briquettes to be compacted by light tapping.

The sand for cement tests will be crushed quartzite of such fineness that all will pass a sieve of 20 meshes per lineal inch, and none of it a sieve of 30 meshes per lineal inch.

The required tensile strength **per** square inch shall be as follows :—

Neat Cement.   Natural. Portland.

One day, till set in air, remainder of time in **water** .   60 lbs. 150 lbs.
One week, one day in air, six days in **water** . . . 150 lbs. 400 lbs.

CEMENT ONE PART AND SAND TWO PARTS.

One week — one day in air, **six days in water** . . 75 lbs.

CEMENT ONE PART AND SAND ONE AND ONE HALF PARTS.

One week — one day in air, **six days in water** . . 85 lbs.

CEMENT ONE PART AND SAND THREE PARTS.

One week — one day in air, six days in water . . . . . 140 lbs.

Briquettes for the seven-day tests shall be covered for the first twenty-four hours with a damp cloth.

The specifications covering the use of cement on the new Croton aqueduct for New York City, and drawn by the chief engineer, Benj. S. Church, 1884, were as follows : —

" The greater part of the masonry **is to be laid in** American **cement mortar,** but Portland cement is to be used whenever directed.

" **The American** cement must be equal in **quality to** the best **Rosendale cement** ; it must be made by manufacturers of established reputation ; **must** be fresh and very fine ground, **and in** well-made **casks.**

" The Portland cement must **be of** a brand equal in **quality to the** best English Portland cement.

" To insure its good quality, all **the** cement furnished **by** the contractor will be subject to inspection and rigorous tests ; and if found of **improper quality** will be branded, and must be immediately removed from the work; the character of the tests to be determined by the engineer.

"The contractor shall at all times keep in store, at some convenient point in the vicinity of the work, a sufficient quantity of cement to allow ample time for the tests to be made without delay to the work of construction.

"The engineer shall be notified at once of each delivery of cement. It shall be stored in a tight building, and each cask must be raised several inches above the ground by blocking or otherwise."

The tests employed on the line of the aqueduct were those recommended by the American Society of Civil Engineers, which are herewith given.

AMERICAN SOCIETY OF CIVIL ENGINEERS.

REPORT OF THE COMMITTEE ON A UNIFORM SYSTEM FOR TESTS OF

CEMENT.

PRESENTED AT THE ANNUAL MEETING, JAN. 21, 1885.

To the American Society of Civil Engineers: —

Your committee, appointed to devise a uniform system for tests of hydraulic cement, has the honor to submit this final report. Those portions of the preliminary report presented at the annual meeting held Jan. 16, 1884, which are not embodied herein, are superseded.

A uniform system of testing cement, in order to be practical, must be simple, rapid, and easy of application, and should, of course, be reasonably accurate. Between the very careful tests of the laboratory, which consume much time and involve considerable expense, and the rough and unsatisfactory trials often resorted to from necessity, there is a middle ground, which it has been the endeavor of the committee to occupy. The system proposed is by no means a perfect one — such has not yet been discovered — but it is hoped that it will be useful in eliminating many of the inaccuracies of the usual methods, and by making the system uniform, enable the experiments of the various members of the profession, in different parts of the country, and others interested in the subject of cement testing, to be satisfactorily compared.

The testing of cement is not so simple a process as it is sometimes thought to be. No small degree of experience is necessary before one can manipulate the materials so as to obtain even approximately accurate results.

The first test of inexperienced, though intelligent and careful persons, are usually very contradictory and inaccurate, and no amount of experience can eliminate the variations introduced by the personal equations of the most conscientious observers. Many things, apparently of minor importance, exert such a marked influence upon the results, that it is only by the greatest care in every particular, aided by experience and intelligence, that trustworthy tests can be made.

The test for tensile strength on a sectional area of one square inch is recommended, because, all things considered, it seems best for general use. In the small briquette there is less danger of air bubbles, the amount of material to be handled is smaller, and the machine for breaking may be lighter and less costly.

The tensile test, if properly made, is a good, though not a perfect indication of the value of a cement. The time requisite for making this test, whether applied to either the natural * or the Portland cements, is considerable (at least seven days, if a reasonably reliable indication is to be obtained), and as work is usually carried on, is frequently impracticable. For this reason short time tests are allowable in cases of necessity, though the most that can be done in such testing is to determine if the brand of cement is of its average quality. It is believed, however, that if a neat cement stands the one-day tensile test, and the tests for checking and for fineness, its safety for use will be sufficiently indicated in the case of a brand of good reputation; for, it being proved to be of average quality, it is fair to suppose that its subsequent condition will be what former experiments, to which it owes its reputation, indicate that it should be. It cannot be said that a new and untried cement will by the same tests be proved to be satisfactory; only a series of tests for a considerable period, and with a full dose of sand, will show the full value of any cement; and it would be safer to use a trustworthy brand, without applying any tests whatever, than to accept a new article which had been tested only as neat cement and for but one day.

The test for compressive strength is a very valuable one in point of fact, but the appliances for crushing are usually somewhat cumbersome and expensive, so much so that it seems undesirable that both tests should be embodied in a uniform method proposed for general adoption. Where great interests are at stake, however, and large contracts for cement depend on the decision of an engineer as to quality, both tests should be used if the requisite appliances for making them are within reach. After the

---

* Where the word "natural" is used in this connection, it is to be understood as being applied to the lightly burned natural American or foreign cements, in contradistinction to the more heavily burned Portland cement, either natural or artificial.

tensile strength has been obtained, the ends of the broken briquettes, reduced to one-inch cubes by grinding and rubbing, should be used to obtain the compressive strength.

The adhesive test being in a large measure variable and uncertain, and, therefore, untrustworthy, is not recommended.

FINENESS.

The strength of a cement depends greatly upon the fineness to which it is ground, especially when mixed with a large dose of sand. It is, therefore, recommended that the test be made with cement that has passed through a No. 100 sieve (10,000 meshes to the square inch), made of No. 40 wire, Stubbs's wire gauge. The results thus obtained will indicate the grade which the cement can attain, under the condition that it is finely ground, but it does not show whether or not a given cement offered for sale shall be accepted and used. The determination of this question requires that the tests should also be applied to the cement as found in the market. Its quality may be so high that it will stand the tests even if very coarse and granular, and, on the other hand, it may be so low that no amount of pulverization can redeem it. In other words, fineness is no sure indication of the value of a cement, although all cements are improved by fine grinding. Cement of the better grades is now usually ground so fine that only from 5 to 10 per cent. is rejected by a sieve of 2,500 meshes per square inch, and it has been so fine that only from 3 to 10 per cent. is rejected by a sieve of 32,000 meshes per square inch. The finer the cement, if otherwise good, the larger dose of sand it will take, and the greater its value.

CHECKING OR CRACKING.

The test for checking or cracking is an important one, and, though simple, should never be omitted. It is as follows:—

Make two cakes of neat cement 2 or 3 ins. in diameter, about ½ in. thick, with thin edges. Note the time in minutes that these cakes, when mixed with water to the consistency of a stiff plastic mortar, take to set hard enough to stand the wire test recommended by General Gilmore, $\frac{1}{12}$ in. diameter wire loaded with ¼ of a lb., and $\frac{1}{21}$ in. loaded with 1 lb. One of these cakes, when hard enough, should be put in water, and examined from day to day to see if it becomes contorted, or if cracks show themselves at the edges, such contortions or cracks indicating that the cement is unfit for use at that time. In some cases the tendency to crack, if caused by the presence of too much unslacked lime, will disappear with age. The remaining cake should be kept in the air and its color observed, which for a good cement should be uniform throughout, yellowish blotches indicating a poor quality; the Portland cements being of a bluish gray, and the natural cements being light or dark, according to the character of the rock of which they are made. The color of the cements when left in the air indicates the quality much better than when they are put in water.

TESTS RECOMMENDED.

It is recommended that tests for hydraulic cement be confined to methods for determining fineness, liability to checking or cracking, and tensile strength; and for the latter, for tests of seven days and upward, that a mixture of 1 part of cement to 1 part of sand for natural cements, and 3 parts of sand for Portland cements, be used, in addition to trials of the neat cement. The quantities used in the mixture should be determined by weight.

The tests should be applied to the cements as offered for sale. If satisfactory results are obtained with a full dose of sand, the trials need go no further. If not, the coarser particles should first be excluded by using a No. 100 sieve, in order to determine approximately the grade the cement would take if ground fine, for fineness is always attainable, while inherent merit may not be.

MIXING, ETC.

The proportions of cement, sand, and water should be carefully determined by weight, the sand and cement mixed dry, and all the water added at once. The mixing must be rapid and thorough, and the mortar, which should be stiff and plastic, should be firmly pressed into the molds with the trowel, without ramming, and struck off level; the molds in each instance, while being charged and manipulated, to be laid directly on glass, slate, or some other non-absorbent material. The molding must be completed before incipient setting begins. As soon as the briquettes are hard enough to bear it, they should be taken from the molds and be kept covered with a damp cloth until they are immersed. For the sake of uniformity, the briquettes, both of neat cement and those containing sand, should be immersed in water at the end of twenty-four hours, except in the case of one-day tests.

Ordinary fresh, clean water, having a temperature between 60 and 70 degrees F., should be used for the water of mixture and immersion of samples.

The proportion of water required varies with the fineness, age, or other conditions of the cement, and the temperature of the air, but is approximately as follows : —

For briquettes of neat cement : Portland, about 25 per cent.; natural, about 30 per cent.

For briquettes of 1 part cement, 1 part sand; about 15 per cent. of total weight of sand and cement.

For briquettes of 1 part cement, 3 parts sand; about 12 per cent. of total weight of sand and cement.

The object is to produce the plasticity of rather stiff plasterer's mortar.

An average of five briquettes may be made for each test, only those breaking at the smallest section to be taken. The briquettes should always be put in the testing machine and broken immediately after being taken out of the water, and the temperature of the briquettes and of the testing room should be constant between 60 and 70 degrees F.

The stress should be applied to each briquette at a uniform rate of about 400 lbs. per minute, starting each time at o. With a weak mixture one half the speed is recommended.

WEIGHT.

The relation of the weight of cement to its tensile strength is an uncertain one. In practical work, if used alone, it is of little value as a test, while in connection with the other tests recommended it is unnecessary, except when the relative bulk of equal weights of cement is desired.

We recommend that the cubic foot be substituted for the bushel as the standard unit, whenever it is thought best to use this test.

SETTING.

The rapidity with which a cement sets or loses its plasticity furnishes no indication of its ultimate strength. It simply shows its initial hydraulic activity.

For purposes of nomenclature, the various cements may be divided arbitrarily into two classes, namely: quick-setting, or those that set in less than half an hour; and slow-setting, or those requiring half an hour or more to set. The cement must be adapted to the work required, as no one cement is equally good for all purposes. In submarine work a quick-setting cement is often imperatively demanded, and no other will answer, while for work above the water-line less hydraulic activity will usually be preferred. Each individual case demands special treatment. The slow-setting natural elements should not become warm while setting, but the quick-setting ones may, to a moderate extent, within the degree producing cracks. Cracks in Portland cement indicate too much carbonate of lime, and in the Vicat cements too much lime in the original mixture.

NOTE.— Your committee thinks it useful to insert here a table showing the average minimum and maximum tensile strength per square inch which some good cements have attained when tested under the conditions specified elsewhere in this report. Within the limits given in the following table, the value of a cement varies closely with the tensile strength when tested with the full dose of sand.

American natural cement, neat : —

1 day, 1 hour or until set in air, the rest of the 24 hours in water, **from 40 lbs. to 80 lbs.**
1 week, 1 day in air, 6 days in water, from 60 lbs. to 100 lbs.
1 month (28 days), 1 day in air, 27 days in water, from 100 lbs. **to** 150 lbs.
1 year, 1 day in air, the remainder in water, from 300 lbs. to 400 lbs.
American and foreign Portland cements, neat : —
1 day, 1 hour, or until set, in air, the rest of **the 24 hours in water, from** 100 lbs. to 140 lbs.

1 week, 1 day in air, 6 days in water, from 250 lbs. to 550 lbs.
1 month (28 days), 1 day in air, 27 days in water, from 350 lbs. to 700 lbs.
1 year, 1 day in air, the remainder in water, from 450 lbs. to 800 lbs.
American natural cement, 1 part of cement to 1 part of sand : —
1 week, 1 day in air, 6 days in water, from 30 lbs. to 50 lbs.
1 month (28 days), 1 day in air, 27 days in water, from 50 lbs. to 80 lbs.
1 year, 1 day in air, the remainder in water, from 200 lbs. to 300 lbs.
American and foreign Portland cements, 1 part of cement to 3 parts of sand : —
1 week, 1 day in air, 6 days in water, from 80 lbs. to 125 lbs.
1 month (28 days), 1 day in air, 27 days in water, from 100 lbs. to 200 lbs.
1 year, 1 day in air, the remainder in water, from 200 lbs. to 350 lbs.

Standards of minimum fineness and tensile strength for Portland cement, as given below, have been adopted in some foreign countries.

In Germany, by Berlin Society of Architects, Society of Manufacturers of Bricks, Lime, and Cement, Society of Contractors, and Society of German Cement Makers.

STANDARD OF 1877.

Fineness, not **more than** 25 per cent. to be left on sieve of 5,806 meshes per square inch.
Tensile strength, **1 part** cement, **3** parts sand, 1 day in air, 27 days in water, 113.78 lbs. per square inch.

STANDARD OF 1878.

Fineness, not more than 20 per cent. to be left on sieve, as above.
Tensile strength, same mixture and time as above, 142.23 lbs. per square inch.
In Austria, by Austrian Association of Engineers and Architects.

STANDARD OF 1878.

Fineness, same as German of 1878.
Tensile strength, same mixture as above, 7 days, 1 day in air, 6 days in water, 113.78 lbs. per square inch.
28 days, 1 day in air, 27 days in water, 170.68 lbs. per square inch.

In Austria a standard for the minimum fineness and tensile **strength of Roman cement** was established and generally accepted, as follows : —

STANDARD OF 1878.

Fineness, same as Portland.
Tensile strength (1 part of cement, 3 **parts of sand), for**
Quick setting cement (taking 15 **minutes or less to set**): —
7 days, 1 day in air, 6 days in water, 23 lbs. per square inch.
28 days, 1 day in air, 27 days in water, 56.9 lbs. per square inch.
Slow setting cement (taking more than 15 minutes to set): —
7 days, 1 day in air, 6 days in **water,** 42.6 lbs. per square **inch.**

28 days, 1 day in air, 27 days in water, 85.3 lbs. per square inch.

The Roman cements correspond to those classified in this report under the head of natural cements.

Standards have been adopted also in Sweden and Russia.

SAMPLING.

There is no uniformity of practise among engineers as to the sampling of the cement to be tested, some testing every tenth barrel, others every fifth, and others still every barrel delivered. Usually, where cement has a good reputation, and is used in large masses, such as concrete in heavy foundations, or in the backing or hearting of thick walls, the testing of every fifth barrel seems to be sufficient; but in very important work, where the strength of each barrel may in a great measure determine the strength of that portion of the work where it is used, or in the thin walls of sewers, etc., etc., every barrel should be tested, one briquette being made from it.

In selecting cement for experimental purposes, take the samples from the interior of the original packages, at sufficient depth to insure a fair exponent of the quality, and store the same in tightly closed receptacles impervious to light or dampness until required for manipulation, when each sample of cement should be so thoroughly mixed, by sifting or otherwise, that it shall be uniform in character throughout its mass.

SIEVES.

For ascertaining the fineness of cement it will be convenient to use three sieves, viz. : —

No. 50 (2,500 meshes to the square inch), wire to be of No. 35 Stubb's wire gauge.

No. 74 (5,476 meshes to the square inch), wire to be of No. 37 Stubb's wire gauge.

No. 100 (10,000 meshes to the square inch), wire to be of No. 40 Stubb's wire gauge.

The object is to determine by weight the percentage of each sample that is rejected by these sieves, with a view not only of furnishing the means of comparison between tests made of different cements by different observers, but indicating to the manufacturer the capacity of his cement for improvement in a direction always and easily within his reach. As already suggested in another connection, the tests for tensile strength should be applied to the cement as offered in the market, as well as to that portion of it which passes the No. 100 sieve.

For sand, two sieves are recommended, viz. : —

No. 20 (400 meshes to the square inch), wire to be of No. 28 Stubb's wire gauge.

No. 30 (900 meshes to the square inch), **wire to be of No. 31** Stubb's wire gauge.

These sieves can **be furnished** in sets as follows, an arrangement having been made with a manufacturer of such articles, by which he agrees to furnish them of the best quality of brass wire cloth, set in metal frames, the cloth to be as true to count as it is possible to make it, and the wire to be of the required gauge. Each set will be enclosed in a box, the sieves being nested.

Set A, three cement sieves, to **cost $4.80.**

No. 100	7 **ins.** diameter.
No. 74	6½ „ „
No. 50	6 „ „

Set B, **two sand sieves, to cost $4.**

No. 30	8 **ins. diameter.**
No. 20	7½ „ „

STANDARD SAND.

The question of a standard sand seems one of great importance, for **it has** been found that sands looking alike and sifted through **the same** sieves give results varying within rather wide limits.

The material that seems likely to give the best results is **the crushed** quartz used in the manufacture of sandpaper. It is a commercial product, made in large quantities and of standard grades, and can be furnished **of** a fairly uniform **quality. It is clean and sharp, and** although the present price is somewhat excessive (3 cents per pound), it is believed that it can be furnished in quantity for about $5 per barrel of 300 lbs. As it would be used for test only, for purposes of comparison with the local sands, and **with** tests of different cements, not much of it **would be** required. The price of the German standard sand is about $1.25 per 112 lbs., but the article being washed river sand is probably inferior to crushed quartz. Crushed granite could be furnished at a somewhat less rate than quartz, and crushed trap for about the same as granite, but no satisfactory estimate has been obtained for either of these.

The use of crushed quartz is recommended by your committee, the degree of **fineness to be such** that it will all pass a No. 20 sieve and be **caught on a No. 30 sieve.** Of the regular grade, from 15 to 37 per cent. **of crushed quartz** No. 3 passes a No. 30 sieve, and none of it passes a **No. 50 sieve.** As at present furnished, it would need resifting to bring it **to the standard** size, but if there were sufficient demand to warrant it, it could undoubtedly be furnished of the size of grain required at little, if any, extra expense.

A bed of uniform, clean sand of the proper size of grain has not been found, and it is believed that to wash, dry, and sift any of the available sands would so greatly increase its cost that the product would not be much cheaper than the crushed quartz, and would be much inferior to it in sharpness and uniform hardness of particles.

MOLDS.

The molds furnished are usually of iron or brass, the price of the former being $2, and of the latter $3 each. Wooden molds, if well oiled to prevent their absorbing water, answer a good purpose for temporary use, but speedily become unfit for accurate work. A cheap, durable, accurate, and non-corrodible mold is much to be desired, but is not yet upon the market. Plates Nos. XLIV. and XLV. show the form of briquette and of metal mold recommended. It may be added that your committee are not in entire accord with respect to the merits of this form of briquette, its principal defect being that the rupture must take place at the neck or smallest section, whether the strain be one of extension only or otherwise. With a briquette of such form that oblique strains would usually produce rupture in oblique directions, the trials taking this character would be rejected, and the accuracy of the results correspondingly increased thereby.

CLIPS.

In using the clips recommended in the preliminary report, it was found in some instances that the specimens were broken at one of the points where they were held. This was undoubtedly caused by the insufficient surface of the clip, which, forming a blunt point, forced out the material. Where the specimens were sufficiently soft to allow this point to be imbedded, they broke at the smallest section, but when hard enough to resist such imbedding they showed a wedge-shaped fracture at the clips To remedy this the point should be slightly flattened so as to allow of more metal surface in contact with the briquette. Clips made in this way have been used, and good results obtained.

To adapt the 1 in. clips of the Riehle machine only a slight amount of work is necessary; the ends being rounded, as shown in Plate No. XLVI., will admit the proposed new form of briquette, and yet not prevent the use of the old one, thus allowing comparative tests of the two forms to be made without changing the clips.

There should be a strengthening rib upon the outside of the clips, as shown in Plate No. XLVI., to prevent them from bending or breaking when the specimens are very strong.

The clips should be hung on pivots, so as to avoid, as much as possible, cross strain upon the briquettes.

MACHINES.

No special machine has been recommended, as those in common use are of good form for accurate work, if properly used, though in some cases they are needlessly strong and expensive. Machines with spring balances are to be avoided, as more liable to error than others.

It is by no means certain that there exists any great difference in well-made machines of the standard forms given.

The experiments of the committee do not seem to justify an expression of preference for any one machine. Plates Nos. XLVII. and XLVIII. show three American machines, with the prices obtained from the manufacturers.

AMOUNT OF MATERIAL.

The amount of material needed for making five briquettes of the standard size recommended is, for the neat cements, about 1⅔ lbs., and for those with sand, in the proportion of 3 parts of sand to 1 of cement, about 1¼ lbs. of sand, and 6⅔ ozs. of cement.

All of which is respectively submitted.

Q. A. GILLMORE,
Chairman.

D. J. WHITTEMORE.
J. HERBERT SHEDD.
ELIOT C. CLARKE.
ALFRED NOBLE.
F. O. NORTON.
W. W. MACLAY.
LEONARD F. BECKWITH.
THOS. C. McCOLLOM.

In February, 1895, Cecil B. Smith, Ma. E., M., Can. Soc. C. E. Assistant Professor of Civil Engineering, McGill University, Montreal, delivered before the Canadian Society of Civil Engineers the following exhaustive dissertation on the TESTING OF CEMENTS, which, through his courtesy and the courtesy of the society named, we are permitted to publish in full : —

TABLE I.—STANDARD CEMENT TESTS.

Nationality.	Date of Standard.	Authority of Standard.	Weight per Bushel or C. F.	Specific Gravity.	Chemical Analysis.	Residues or Fineness.	P. c. of Water in Mixing.	Constancy of Vol. or Blowing Test.
Canadian.	1894	Recommended by the C.S.C.E. Committee and of little value.	Considered to be indefinite	3.12 to 3.25 } Portland.	Not more than 2% Sul. Acid. Not more than 5% Magnesia. Portland. Natural. Lime 60.05 Lime 37.18 Silica 24.31 Silica 28.11 Al₂O₃ 10.84 Al₂O₃ 27.62 Mag. 3.00 Mag. 7.09 Alkalies 1.60	Less than 5% on 50 sieve No. 35 Stubbs gauge.	Standard consistency, and 27 days in ordinary water or 60 lbs. to nearly penetrate mortar in a box 3" diar. 1½" high.	24 hours in water at 120° F. 4" diar. water test, 24 hours after setting in boiling water.
English.	1893	Practise no. Standard Regulations.	About 112 lbs. per bushel for Portland.	Not less than 3.10 for fresh or 3.07 for 3 months old (dried 15 minutes).	Recommended to be made.	5% on 50 sieve 12% on 100 ", 25% on 150 ", 30% on 180 ", wire mesh.	Approximately 25% Neat. 1.2% 3 to 1, Faija mixer.	Same as above, of which this is the original.
United States.	1885	Recommended by A. S. C. E. generally used and adopted.	(Authority of Clark.) French Port 60 per CF. English Port 78 to 87 per CF, American Port 95 per CF.	Not specified.	ditto	5 to 10% on 50 sieve down to 3 to 10% on 176 sieve.	Approximately 25% Neat Port., 30%, of discoloring, Natural, 15% to 1 stiff mortar.	1 pat in air 1 month for signs Neat pat in air till set, then 1 month in water for checking.
German.	1893	Government Regulations.	370 lbs. per barrel net.	3.12 to 3.25 } for Portlands, increase with age.	ditto	10% on 76 sieve wire ½ of mesh.	Same as the Canadian, which is a copy of this one.	Submerged 28 days in water at ordinary temperature, no checking.
French.	1884 or later.	Government Regulations.	1 litre to weigh within 3½ ozs. of heaviest cement from same factory, all sifted through No. 100 sieve.		Not more than 1% Sul. Acid. Not more than 4% Fe O₂. When Si. and Al. are less than 44% of lime.	None specified, argued that fine grinding gives high strength in periods of tests chiefly, which disappears with later on.	Sea water, standard consistency round ball dropped 20 on slab to retain its general form without cracks.	Pat in sea water (?) days, no cracking or bulging.
Austrian.								

Tensile Strength			Compressive Strength			Setting Quality	
Neat	1 to 1	3 to 1	Neat	1 to 1	3 to 1	How determined.	How defined.
Not yet specified, to be reported on 1 year later.			reported on 1			Gilmore's needles incipient set to bear 1/8" diar. 1/4 lb. full set to bear 3/4" diar. 1 lb.	
1 week 300-400 1 month 450-650		3 days 110 1 week 120-220 1 month 200-350				Vicat's needles incipient set to bear, 66 lbs. to not quite penetrate, full set to bear up same setting.	2 hours or more slow less time quick same setting.
Natural 1 day 40-80 1 week 60-100 1 month 100-150 1 year 300-400 Portland 1 day 100-140 1 week 250-550 1 month 150-700 1 year 450-800	Natural 1 week 30-50 1 month 50-80 1 year 200-300	Portland 1 week 80-125 1 month 100-200 1 year 200-350				Gilmore's needles.	
		1 month 227½			1 month 2275	Vicat's needles	Same as English.
Minimum. 1 week 285 1 month 498 3 months 640; to show 25% increase 1 week to 1 month.		Minimum. 1 week 114 1 month 213 3 months 256				Vicat's needles.	Incipient to be not less than 30' full set to be not less than 3 hours or more than 12 hours.
		1 week 114 1 month 171					

TABLE 1.—STANDARD CEMENT TESTS.—Continued.

Kind of sand used.	How put in Molds.	Rate of loading in tensile tests.	Time in air before immersion.	No. of tests used for Averages.	Time of Mixing.	Wearing Qualities.	Adhesive Qualities.
Standard crushed quartz to all pass No. 20 sieve all caught on No. 30 sieve.	10 lbs. per square inch steady pressure.	200 lbs. per minute.	24 hours.	Not stated, probably 5	1 minute for quick setting. 2 minutes for slow setting, mechanical mixer.		
ditto.	10 lbs. on briquette for 5 minutes, or shaken in molds or beaten with trowel for 1 minute.	400 lbs. per minute.	24 hours.	5	1 minute or more, mechanical mixer.		Mr. Mann. 1 week 57, 1 month 78, 3 months 98 } ground glass. Fineness has great effect.
ditto.	Pressed in with trowel without ramming.	ditto.	24 hours.	Smallest section only.	1 minute or more, hand or mechanical mixing.		
Standard crushed quartz, ½ to pass 20, ½ caught on 30. ½ to pass 30, caught on 38 sieves.	Bohmes' apparatus. 150 blows with trip hammer weighing 4.4 lbs.	15 lbs. per minute.	24 hours.	10	1 minute for quick setting, 3 minutes for slow setting cements.	1 to 1 and 2 to 1 give higher results still than neat or 3 to 1 tough at 7 days as at 20 days.	Advised to be investigated, reported on and to be made on ground glass.
Crushed Cherbourg quartz pass No. 20, caught on No. 30 sieves.	Filled in and tamped with rammer weighing 3 0 7 ozs. till water stands on surface.	Not specified.	24 hours then in sea water of 59° to 64° F.	6 Mean of 3 highest taken.	5 minutes by hand on a slab, temperature of air 59° to 64° F.		
				10 Mean of 6 highest taken.			

CEMENT TESTING.

This subject has so often been written on, and is being so continually and persistently investigated, that it forms, as it were, an inexhaustible mine.

But this very feature shows how very important and yet how little understood it is, for when investigators continue to disagree, the presumption is, that there is either a lack of agreement as to the basis on which the investigations are made, or else a failure, up to the present, to solve all the intricate mazes of the problem, or indeed a combination of the two.

To illustrate the first point, a tabular synopsis (Table I.) is presented, giving the present standard tests in use, in various countries, according to the latest obtainable information. The variations, in many cases, are too great to be reconciled, in others trifling; but it is evidently difficult to compare results obtained in different countries, and a hopeless task to ever bring them to a uniform standard. What it behooves us, as Canadian engineers, to do is to take such sensible and immediate action on the subject as will commend itself to the good graces of all of us, if possible, or, if not, of a great majority of those who test the manufactured article.

However, before proposing a mode of conducting such tests as will (according to the author's experience) be of practical utility to practical men, the following Table (Table II.) is presented to the society as embodying results which have been obtained during the last two sessions, in making ordinary commercial, private, and student tests (chiefly commercial and private).

Many results have been discarded as being inaccurate, and only those are recorded here which are believed to be very close to the truth, much closer than is ordinarily obtained.

These results have been classified according to country of manufacture, and somewhat on a scale of increasing tensile strength.

Let us consider the various qualities given in their tabular order.

(a) *Specific Gravity*.
The average of Canadian Portlands = 3.11.
The average of English Portlands = 3.10.
The average of Belgian Portlands = 3.055.
The average of all Portlands (16) = 3.09.

TABLE II.
CONDENSED TABLE OF CEMENT TESTS. 1893–1894.

Designation of Origin	No. in Table	Obtained from	Specific Gravity	Per cent water for standard consistency	Residue per cent on Sieve No. 20	No. 50	No. 80	No. 120	Blowing test result	Time of setting in air Incipient	Full	Neat Cement 3 dys.	1 wk.	2 wks.	3 wks.	4 wks.	2 mos.	3 mos.	4 mos.	6 mos.	1 yr.
Canadian N	1	Dealer	3.01	33⅓	0	7.2	12.5	18.3	very good	4°00′	7°45′	78	71			124	226				
Canadian N	2	Maker	2.96	33½	0	2.9	11.7	21.4	good	0°45′	2°45′	99	150			268	377	448	478	492	
Canadian P	3	Maker	3.12	25½	0	1.1	14.2	31.2	good	5°00′	20°00′	125	210			356					
Canadian P	4	Maker	3.12	26	0	0.8	2.7	6.7	good	0°37′	3°10′	335	388			525					
Canadian P	5	Maker	3.09	25	0	0.6	5.5	13.2	good	1°00′	5°00′	278	399			459					
Canadian P	6	Maker	3.12	24	0	0.9	6.4	13.2	good	4°30′	6°00′	438	558			674					
Canadian P	6a	Dealer		24	0	3.0	13.6	20.7	very good	2°00′	6°30′	312	531			611					
Canadian P	6b	Dealer		24	0	2.3	27.0	40.7	fair			300	307								
Canadian P	6c	Dealer		23	0	31.1	52.2	61.2	bad			253	264								
English P	7	Dealer	3.09	33	0	10.5	21.6	39.5	good	3°20′	6°30′	160	230			331					
English P	8	Dealer	3.09	25	0	14.0	28.4	22.9	good	13′	2°00′	390	414			528					
English P	9	Dealer	3.10	26	0	1.4	12.8	26.5	good	25′	50′	250	420	372		453					
English P	10	Dealer	3.08	23½	0	6.7	19.2	23.1	good	30′	1°00′	336	386	396		552					
English P	11	Dealer	3.41	23	0	4.0	14.2	28.5	good	2′	3°00′	244	477			504	560	637	627	644	
English P	12	Dealer	3.13	24	0	4.2	19.5	26.3	bad	20′	2°30′	335	362	444		547					
English P	13	Dealer	3.13	24½	0	4.5	17.3	12.9	very good	20′	4°00′		344	350		422					
English P	14	Dealer	3.12	24	0	0.25	5.0	30.5	bad	27′	2°30′	387	387			495					
English P	14a	Dealer	3.05	23	0	5.6	20.9	30.1	some bad	27′	2°30′	343	343			469					
English P	14b	Dealer		23	0	5.3	19.7					304	309			410					
Belgian N	15	Dealer	2.97	30	0	7.7	15.4	19.4	very good	1°00′	2°00′	154	210			285 Fl'd					
Belgian P	16	Dealer	3.03	26½	0	2.2	12.4	20.6	good	5°00′	12°00′	232	332								
Belgian P	17	Dealer	3.02	26	0	3.1	12.9	20.1	bad	5°10′	5°00′	328	394			457					
Belgian P	18	Dealer	3.09	27	0	0.3	2.8	9.4	good	1°20′	4°50′	255	390			492					
Belgian	19	Agent	3.08	25	0	0.9	6.2	15.8	good	2°40′	7°00′	452	536			525					
	20			25	0	4.0	10.8						152	450	463	485					533
	21			25									345	459		545					648
	22																				606
	23																				593
Total																					

AVERAGE TENSILE STRENGTH IN POUNDS PER SQUARE INCH.

	1 to 1.							1 1-2 to 1.	2 to 1.						3 to 1.						
	1 wk.	2 wks.	4 wks.	2 mos.	3 mos.	4 mos.	6 mos.	1 month	1 wk.	4 wks.	2 mos.	3 mos.	4 mos.	6 mos.	1 wk.	2 wks.	4 wks.	2 mos.	3 mos.	4 mos.	6 mos.
	68		102	125	162	137	163	132							30		72				
	76		115	151											49		75				
															43		92				
															100		126				
	232	345	316	245	253	257	531		151	198	189	106	189	271	55		136				
	192		204						48	77					95		115				
									126	207					72		96	104			
															60	79	102				
			195												54	64	90				
	134														34						
															133		154				

TABLE II.— *Continued.*

CONDENSED TABLE OF CEMENT TESTS. 1893–1894.

	Neat Cement.						1 to 1.			2 to 1.				3 to 1.		Neat 1″ x 1″ broken on 6″ centers.					No. of Tests.		
	1 wk.	2 wks.	3 wks.	4 wks.	2 mos.	1 year.	1 wk.	4 wks.	2 mos.	1 wk.	4 wks.	2 mos.	1 wk.	1 wk.	wks.	1 wk.	2 wks.	3 wks.	4 wks.	1 year.	Tensile.	Comp.	Trans.
																					27	1	0
	1285			2255	1600		900	1350													100	8	0
																				33	3	0
				2492																	33	4	0
	1362				4975									42	475	205					30	7	1
	3025													99	4212	392					35	0	0
																					15	0	2
															1025						6	0	0
														54							10	0	0
	1502			1720										54							10	5	2
	1967			2650										73					84		30	2	5
					4500														99		40	1	0
																					29	1	0
								3325													105	0	0
								2826	3200			800							112		44	0	2
																					14	0	0
																					30	0	0
																					30	0	0
																					93	0	0
	1250			1950						743	953		718		900						35	8	0
																					10	0	0
																		86			13	0	0
	2970			4350																	50	0	0
																					24	6	0
	1200	1555	5310	2566		6391														113	12	10	2
						4826													59	4	17	3	2
		3000		4400		5066														60(?)	13	9	2
																					6	2	1
																					894	83	19

NOTE.—The sand briquettes were lightly tamped with a small iron rammer.

It would seem advisable, therefore, to specify a minimum for Portlands of 3.10.

The samples were not dried or prepared in any way; if they were dried for fifteen minutes, according to English practise, it is probable they would go somewhat higher.

It will be noticed that the only two Portlands (?) whose specific gravities were low (Belgians Nos. 16 and 17) were both poor cements. One, No. 16, sets slowly, and the briquettes made for 4 week tests, and immersed in water after 24 hours were found sloughed down in the tanks, and had evidently run and set over again! They would not give any test to speak of. Evidently the hydraulic property, in 24 hours, was not enough to hold them together, while the other one (No. 17) failed in the blowing test. Altogether, it is doubtful whether these cements are Portlands or naturals, although sold as the former, owing to their color being gray.

It will be noticed, with satisfaction, that Canadian Portlands stand at the top in specific gravity, judging by the samples tested, which were, however, all received from manufacturers.

The specific gravity of natural cements might be placed at 2.95, although it is not so likely to be under-run, owing to the ease with which this can be obtained.

(b) *Water required for standard consistency.*

This is considered by many to be very important; but many tests have demonstrated to the writer that what is especially needed is that there shall be sufficient to make good briquettes; to err, say, 1 per cent. in adding water is fatal if too little, while if too much, it does not seem to affect the strength of briquettes at 1 week, certainly not at 4 weeks. This is contrary to statements often made regarding the increased strength given by a minimum amount of water; but probably what is referred to is an excess of water sufficient to make a thin batter or soup. Undoubtedly, such an amount not only makes the briquettes shrink and crack in drying, but will seriously affect the early strength.

A very peculiar effect was met with in two Canadian and one English Portlands. They were evidently fresh, and when mixed with a normal amount of water would work into a good plastic mass, but in about one or two minutes after the water was added, they would suddenly set so hard that it was useless to attempt to put them in the molds.

By increasing the per cent. of water to about thirty, a thin batter was made, which could be got into the molds before this action took place; of course this amount of water made the set very slow, and deadened the indurating action in 1 week tests.

When tests were made, several weeks later, on these cements, this effect had disappeared; perhaps some one connected with the industry can explain the cause of this action.

(c) *Residues or Fineness.*

The variation is enormous, as the following statement shows: —

Residue on No. 50 Sieve. Per Cent.		Residue on No. 80 Sieve. Per Cent.	Residue on No. 120 Sieve Per Cent.
Coarsest	31.4	52.2	61.2
Finest	0.25	2.7	6.7

The English Portlands are generally very coarse, as will be seen, and the selected Canadian ones fine.

It is not putting it too severely to say that specifying a certain residue on No. 50 sieve is a direct premium on coarse grinding and so, in fact, are neat tensile tests.

For instance, English brands, Nos. 10, 11, 12, 13, and Nos. 14 A, 14 B, are all evidently ground to pass a specification of 5 per cent. residue on No. 50 sieve, and are all very coarse when sifted on finer ones, thus plainly showing the failure of the specification to obtain as good a product as possible.

The author would urge the severest requirements for fineness.

Various papers read and the statements of manufacturers themselves go to show that the increased cost is very slight, not more than ten cents per barrel between ordinary and fine grinding,

10 per cent. residue on No. 80 sieve ⎫
20 per cent. residue on No. 120 sieve ⎭ as maximums are not too

high for present facilities for fine grinding; this would let in three out of four Canadian Portlands tested, one out of ten English Portlands tested, two out of four Belgian Portlands tested, or in all six out of eighteen brands. There are signs, however, that the English manufacturers are waking up to finer grinding, and will soon fall into line; there is no reason why educating influences should not bring grinding down much finer still for ordinary brands, but for the present, too much severity would defeat the object in view. (For tests on the effect of fine grinding, see Series I. of Experiments.)

(*d*) The time of incipient and final set, as found by Gillmore's needles, does not seem to affect the strength, except for very short tests, when the slow settings are generally stronger. Good cements may be either the one or the other; but ordinarily, unless for tidal work, a slow setting one has the desirable feature of allowing masons to mix and use good-sized batches of mortar, without constant tempering, which is the practise with quick-setting ones, much to their own hurt.

(*e*) The blowing test advised by Faija has detected a " blowey " tendency in several instances; but much late evidence seems to throw some discredit on blowing tests, whether made with hot or boiling water, on the ground that manufacturers can, by the addition of sulphate of lime, cause the cement to be so slow setting and set so strongly as to resist the blowing tendency of so much as 3 per cent. of free lime added after the cement had been burnt. If this is a fact, chemical analysis will need to be resorted to more frequently, to detect this dangerous adulteration, which is fatal in sea-water and bad in any case, as the great strength which it gives to cements at early dates is apt to decrease at longer periods. Belgian No. 19 cement tested gave higher results at 1 week than at 4 weeks; this looks a little suspicious.

Cements have been tested usually neat; the Germans have reached the stage of three to one mixtures as the deciding test, and this would seem to be the only rational way of testing a cement, *i. e.*, in the same condition as it is used.

The difficulty, however — and it is a very serious one — has been to get anything like uniform results in sand tests. The variation in putting the mortar in the molds has been so much more than the variation in the cementing value of the cement that the tests were valueless, so that most testers have clung to neat tests as being simple and a fair index of cementing qualities. That this view is in fault and misleading, every tester will admit, and it is only partly avoiding the difficulty to specify a certain fineness, strength, and specific gravity in combination, as even then the results are not definite, because each cement is different in cementiecous value. However, for those who have facilities for testing cement neat only, — and these will probably be in the majority for some time to come,— it would seem that 350 lbs. at 1 week neat and 450 lbs. at 4 weeks neat are easily obtained, and quite enough to specify. Eleven brands tested would give this much strength and stand the blowing test, and of these there are six brands fine enough for 10 per cent. residue on 80 sieve and 20 per cent. residue on 120 sieve, with a specific gravity varying from 308 to 313, while the six brands which are not strong enough are also too coarse.

The tests on natural cements are not extensive enough to form a good basis, but it would seem easy to get 100 lbs. neat at 1 week and 200 lbs. neat at 4 weeks, and a fineness the same as for Portlands.

The tests on No. 2 natural and No. 11 Portland were carried on for 6 months, and show the natural to be gaining on the Portland, although each has evidently nearly reached a maximum. This would seem to bear out the idea which many people yet have, that, in time, a natural cement, not being so brittle, will catch up to a Portland. Long time tests are very much needed on this subject.

Natural cements being underburnt (usually) have very much less combining power with sand ; the one to one natural is not as strong as two to one Portland, according to tests made last year as per Table II. in which the mixtures were made with 15 per cent. of water for one to one, and 12 per cent. of water for three to one mixtures, the mortars being lightly tamped into the mold with an iron rammer ; the tests made this year, however, by means of a uniform pressure, give much higher results for one to one naturals, when 20 per cent. of water is used, which would seem to be nearer to the amount used in practise, making a soft plastic mortar. (See pressure tests.)

Natural cement has many uses. It is being passed aside in many quarters. Why ? because *if immersed in water* for 1 week or 4 weeks, it will give low tensile tests. That terror of the present day, the testing machine, condemns it.

Now there are many occasions where it would not be wise to use anything but the best Portlands — such as laying mortar in extreme frost, or where great immediate strength is required, or for subaqueous work generally; but, on the other hand, no one doubts the *durability* of good natural cement. Works in Europe hundreds of years old, and all the work done in the United States and Canada previous to thirty years ago, are built with such mortars, and stand as witnesses of their lasting qualities.

Moreover, tests made on No. 1 natural cement (see Series III., frost tests) show that while it cannot be immediately exposed to extreme cold, yet when it is exposed, after it has set, it will resist frost thoroughly, and become stronger than if immersed in water at an ordinary temperature. There are thousands of situations where natural cement mortar, 1 cement, 2 sand, will be found amply strong for the purposes required, in which case it will be found cheaper than Portland mortar, 1 cement, 3 sand. Referring ahead to Series III. (frost), it will be seen that if mortars are tested in open air, the Portlands are weaker and naturals stronger than if the briquettes had been under water. This is a point of much importance, because if work is to be done which will not usually be submerged, as in damp foundations, abutments on land, culverts, etc., then tests made in open air will give results more favorable to naturals. In so many words our standard tests say: "Let us test all hydraulic cements under water; whether the mortar as used will be so or not, we will be on the safe side." This, as a generality, is doubtless best; but if we consider what a large propor-

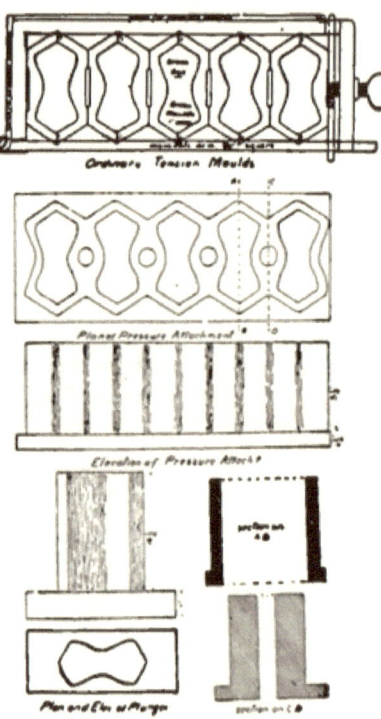

TABLE III.

Tested in tension.   Pressure sand tests.

Brand.	Mixture.	Per cent of water.	Pressure per square inch.	1 week tests, 1 air, 6 water.							4 week tests, 1 air, 27 water.						
				High-est.	Low-est.	Aver-age.	Weight when tested in ounces.	Weight after two days' evaporation.	Per cent. of eva-poration.	Product col. 3 x col. 6.	High-est.	Low-est.	Aver-age.	Weight when tested in ounces.	Weight after two days' eva-poration.	Per cent of eva-poration.	Product col. 3 x col. 6.
No. 2	1 to 1	15	10	45	23	32½	4.56	3.98	12.63	410.4	71	39	59	4.64	4.01	13.49	795.9
		17½	10	105	106	136	5.26	4.84	7.98	1085.3	282	205	239½	5.32	4.95	7.03	1683.7
		20	10	130	94	117	5.56	5.08	8.62	1008.6	292	239	265½	5.52	5.17	6.34	1683.2
		22½	10	123	106	113½	5.54	4.99	9.88	1124.4	258	200	235	5.49	5.12	6.74	1583.9
No. 2	4 to 1	15	20	47	42	43½	4.79	4.05	15.52	675.1	95	70	84	4.99	4.22	15.40	1293.6
		17½	20	144	111	126½	5.37	4.92	8.38	1060.0	218	160	176½	5.27	4.83	8.35	1473.7
		20	20	157	90	114	5.07	5.13	9.63	1097.8	297	212	264	5.62	5.28	6.12	1615.6
		22½	20	126	110	119	5.54	5.03	9.28	1104.3	295	234	262	5.56	5.21	6.29	1648.0
No. 15	1 to 1	15	10	86	40	62½	4.92	4.42	10.46	653.7	112	98	104	5.04	4.41	12.50	1300.0
		17½	10	60	37	52	5.14	4.60	10.50	540.0							
		20	10	149	108	133	5.60	5.12	8.46	1125.1							
		22½	10	129	120	125	5.68	5.19	8.76	1095.1							
No. 15	1 to 1	15	20	49	42	45	4.94	4.18	15.46	695.7							
		17½	20	184	145	160½	5.62	5.28	6.61	1100.5							
		20	20	146	114	135½	5.63	5.17	8.20	1114.1							
		22½	20	130	108	118	5.72	5.25	8.22	970.0							
No. 15	3 to 1	15	10	20	14	16½	4.75	4.03	15.21	251.0	35	19	28	4.61	3.88	15.88	444.6
		17½	10	12	5	7	4.59	3.92	14.66	102.6	48	32	40	4.66	4.15	11.03	441.2
		20	10	13	7	11	4.73	4.17	11.79	129.7	23	5	15	4.86	4.24	12.75	191.2

Brand	Mixture	Per cent. of water	Pressure per square inch	1 week tests, 1 air, 6 water — Lbs. per sq. in. Highest	Lowest	Average	Weight when tested in ounces	Weight after two days' evaporation	Per cent. of evaporation	Product col. 3 x col. 6	4 week tests, 1 air, 27 water — Lbs. per sq. in. Highest	Lowest	Average	Weight when tested in ounces	Weight after two days' evaporation	Per cent. of evaporation	Product col. 3 x col. 6
No. 15	3 to 1	15	20	23	9	16	4.64	3.97	14.48	231.7	55	28	38	4.56	4.01	12.15	**461.7**
		17½	20	7	2	5	....	....	....	....	40	25	31½	4.74	4.23	10.80	**361.8**
		20	20	17	8	12½	4.85	4.28	11.75	146.9	28	19	24	4.89	4.36	10.80	**259.3**
No. 9	3 to 1	15	10	25	14	19	4.37	3.81	12.77	242.6	71	58	63	4.54	3.89	14.24	897.1
		17½	10	35	18	27	4.49	4.07	9.35	252.4	106	92	96	4.72	4.24	10.17	976.3
		20	10	27	20	23½	4.68	4.08	12.01	303.4	134	101	120	4.65	4.18	10.14	1218.8
		22½	10	27	22	24½	4.85	4.23	12.86	315.1	88	74	79	4.70	4.16	11.49	907.7
		25		11	8	10	4.81	4.13	14.13	141.3	53	33	46½	4.73	4.11	13.18	612.9
No. 9	3 to 1	15	20	37	33	[34]	4.66	4.95	13.22	459.5	86	62	71½	4.69	4.15	12.22	873.7
		17½	20	33	20	27½	4.53	4.10	9.54	262.3	124	103	114½	4.75	4.27	10.15	1162.1
		20	20	29	25	26½	4.8	4.19	12.78	338.7	143	109	127	4.69	4.26	9.17	1164.5
		22½	20	25	22	23	4.86	4.27	12.06	277.4	103	87	95½	4.81	4.28	11.02	1052.4
		25		27	22	[25]	4.80	4.18	12.89	374.4	53	44	49	4.70	4.09	12.94	634.1
No. 10	3 to 1	15	10	37	30	34½	4.70	4.18	11.07	384.9	59	54	55½	4.77	4.18	12.27	681.0
		17½	10	48	22	31½	4.67	4.12	11.69	368.2	87	63	70	4.84	4.35	10.05	703.5
		20	10	48	32	37½	4.79	4.24	11.41	427.8	65	62	63½	4.89	4.32	11.68	741.6
		22½	10	34	27	30	4.95	4.33	12.45	373.5	50	38	44½	4.88	4.22	13.48	609.0
		25		33	15	23½	4.92	4.27	13.14	308.7	34	23	28½	4.86	4.15	12.94	368.8
No. 10	3 to 1	15	20	44	27	33½	4.68	4.11	12.18	408.0	67	54	64	4.95	4.40	11.04	673.4
		17½	20	37	16	27	4.65	4.08	12.13	327.5	88	47	68	4.84	4.31	10.96	745.3
		20	20	42	31	35	4.82	4.24	11.96	424.5	84	56	71	4.97	4.42	11.03	283.1
		22½	20	36	23	29½	4.90	4.28	12.65	373.1	85	70	75	4.90	4.35	11.23	842.2
		25		33	27	31	5.00	4.35	13.06	403.0	58	34	48	4.85	4.27	11.92	572.3

tion of cement is used in situations usually not submerged, it would seem more rational to test cements under conditions similar to those under which they are to be used in each case, be it in water *or air*.

As before mentioned, all the sand tests given in the Table (Table II.) were made by tamping the mortar lightly into the molds with an iron rammer weighing about ½ lb. and ½ in. square section.

This has been done in as nearly a uniform manner as possible. About three layers were tamped, and then a fourth layer smoothed off with a spatula. Every effort was directed toward uniformity in method, and, doubtless, some degree of accuracy was obtained; but it was felt that the best possible would only enable comparisons to be made in this laboratory, it would not enable any to be made with results obtained elsewhere.

The Cement Committee of the Society (of which the writer was made a member, by invitation) advised that tests should be made under a pressure of 10 lbs. per square inch. It was not defined at the time whether this applied to sand tests only or to neat tests also; but the necessity for pressure is not so great in neat tests, because any one with ordinary skill and practise can make a good neat briquette, and a light pressure will not affect the result much, as will be shown farther on.

In November last the molds for applying pressure (see drawings), which were from a design of the writer's, modified by Mr. Withycombe, were completed, and since then several hundred briquettes have been made with them. It would seem a simple matter to mix up mortar, put it under a plunger, and by putting on 10 lbs. per square inch, make briquettes; but theory and practise must be fellow-laborers. Now, 12 per cent. of water is considered the correct thing in 3 to 1 mixtures, but with this amount, the mortar would not pack at all in a closed mold under so light a dead pressure, and it is light dead pressure that is wanted; even 20 lbs. per square inch was of no greater effect; then 15 per cent. of water was tried, with very little better results.

It was finally concluded to try several series with different percentages of water, and thereby determine the best per cent. for making a good briquette.

These series (see Table III.) ran from 15 per cent. to 25 per cent. of water, and were for 10 lbs. and 20 lbs. pressure per square

TABLE IV.

CONDENSED SUMMARY OF PRESSURE SAND TESTS.

Put in molds with 20% water, 20 lbs. per square inch.

Brand	Mixture	Lbs. per sq. in. Highest	Lowest	Average	Weight when tested	Weight after two days' evaporation	Per cent of evaporation	Product col. 8 x col. 6.	Lbs. per sq. in. Highest	Lowest	Average	Weight when tested	Weight after two days' evaporation	Per cent of evaporation	Product col. 8 x col. 6.	Remarks. Temp. of air.
		1 week tests, 1 air, 6 water.							4 week tests, 1 air, 27 days water.							
No. 1	1 to 1	75	46	58	5.25	4.55	13.33	773.1	102	80	93	5.32	4.70	11.73	1090.9	60° F.
No. 2	1 to 1	157	90	114	5.67	5.13	9.63	1097.8	297	212	264	5.62	5.28	6.12	1615.6	60° F.
No. 15	1 to 1	146	114	135½	5.63	5.17	8.29	1111.1								61° F. (1)(2)
No. 15	3 to 1	17	8	12½	4.85	4.28	11.75	146.9	28	19	24	4.89	4.36	10.80	259.3	60° F.
No. 3	3 to 1	19	8	13	4.74	4.17	12.06	156.8	52	37	47	4.48	3.89	13.20	620.0	60° F.
No. 9	3 to 1	29	25	26½	4.80	4.19	12.78	338.7	143	109	127	4.69	4.26	9.17	1164.5	63° F. (1)(2)
No. 10	3 to 1	42	31	35	4.82	4.24	11.96	424.5	84	56	71	4.97	4.42	11.03	783.2	65° F.
No. 8	3 to 1	34	25	30½	4.78	4.12	13.70	191.8	85	75	80	4.99	4.41	11.55	924.0	58° F. (1)(2)
No. 5	3 to 1	15	12	14	4.94	4.37	11.58	457.4	58	41	50	5.13	4.36	15.01	750.0	68° F.
No. 4	3 to 1	52	30	39½	4.79	4.09	14.61	1015.3	118	83	103	5.02	4.49	10.56	1087.7	59° F.
No. 19	3 to 1	77	58	69½	4.77	3.97	16.84	1313.5	143	101	129	4.88				54° F.
No. 6	3 to 1	83	74	78	4.56	4.13	9.54	180.7	139	118	128	4.90	4.28	12.65	1619.2	74° F.
No. 11	3 to 1	25	15	19	4.69				46	37	41½	4.85	4.18	13.90	576.8	48° F.
No. 14A	3 to 1	15	8	10½					36	24	30	4.88	4.16	14.76	442.8	53° F.

inch for 1 week and 4 weeks, and each result tabulated is the average of 5 briquettes, and the whole table the result of 77 experiments, or 385 briquettes.

The result, to the author's mind, is definite; 20 per cent. of water is just sufficient to make a plastic mortar, so that a good briquette can be formed while more water tends to drown the cement, and make it weaker at both the 1 week and 4 week tests, although longer tests would probably show a recovery in this respect.

This 20 per cent. applies to 1 to 1 and 3 to 1 mixtures, and will probably be about right for 2 to 1 also, if it is desired to make such tests. It is conclusive from the table that if any standard test under light pressure is to be adopted for sand tests, 20 per cent. of water must be prescribed as a definite part of the test, and in this way perfect uniformity obtained. It is understood that the sand used is standard sand dry and sharp, a finer or rounder sand would allow less water to be used. This amount of water, while greater than that usually given by authorities whose method of making sand briquettes is by some severe hammering process (e. g., German) is still close to the amount used in practise.

Even at the risk of repetition, it is worth saying again, that plastic mortar made with 20 per cent. of water is close to practise, and will give regular and accurate tests if put into molds under light pressure. The amount of this pressure does not seem to be of such great importance, but 20 lbs. per square inch gives rather sharper-edged briquettes, with about the same variation in uniformity and the same tensile strength per square inch. This is equivalent to 20 feet of masonry, which, of course, is more than practise would give; but the tests do not vary to any extent when compared with those made with 10 lbs. per square inch. Therefore, it is not deemed of sufficient importance to sacrifice good manual results. Therefore, 20 lbs. per square inch pressure and 20 per cent. water was adopted about 1 month ago, and the following results obtained (Table IV.).

Whether the future will bring sand tests to greater uniformity than this remains to be seen; but it is believed that, in this way, the sand-combining qualities of cements can be compared with accuracy with one another, and in future such will be the method adopted in the cement laboratory at McGill, subject to the modifications of our cement committee.

It is earnestly to be desired that a code of tests be formulated at once, and all members urged to test under this **code.** Let all cements **stand or fall** under it.

COMPRESSIVE TESTS.

These are doubtless more valuable than tensile ones, **in** the sense that we use mortar usually **in compression.** There are several reasons, however, why such tests are **not really** needed : —

1.   Because the **strong machinery needed** would not be generally available.

2.   Because the **compressive strength, after all,** varies quite regularly with the tensile, being 5 to 6 times as great at 1 week or 4 weeks and gradually increasing to 9 to 10 times as great at a year, because by this time the cement is becoming brittle, and has attained its maximum tensile strength. This is more particularly true of Portland cements, as naturals do not get so brittle.

3.   Because the compressive strength of cement **mortar is so** great that we **need** seldom **concern** ourselves with it, but should rather know the adhesive **and tensile strengths, should they ever** be called into play, **and, moreover,** the strength of **mortar in thin joints** is much **greater than in cubes.** Tests on **cubes always go higher for small cubes than for large ones.** (See also series [IV*a*] tests of mortar joints in brick piers.)

TRANSVERSE TESTS

Have often been advocated, **and the machinery** needed may be quite simple; but **there are** two **objections which would** preclude there being any great value in such tests : —

1.   Because the coefficients of rupture in **transverse testing are** known to be at fault in not really indicating **the tensile strength of the outer layer or fiber.** This could possibly be **avoided by determining** certain corrections, **as a thesis** paper to the *Engineering News* pointed out : —

2.   The main **objection is** that **a flaw of a** very slight **amount** may be objectionable in such **tests if** situated near the tension face. Any **cement tester** knows that bubbles will occur. They may be very minute, or **if of** any size may be **deducted in** tensile tests, while in **transverse tests,** who could determine **the correction** to be made?

Also tests made show that if tested upside down from position molded, the results are higher than when tested as molded. Altogether, this method of testing does not seem to commend itself to general use.

To conclude the subject of ordinary testing for commercial purposes, and with the addition of chemical analysis, where available, for scientific ones also, the following seems to be a good basis to work on, that 4 tests should be made in combination : —

1.   Specific gravity 3.10 for Portlands, 2.95 for naturals.

2.   Blowing test.   In the absence of really final knowledge on the subject to continue to specify pats in steam at 115°F. for four hours, in water at 115°F. for twenty hours, at which time if the pats are stuck tight to the ground glass, the cement may be considered safe, while if it has loosened from the plate but has not yet cracked or warped, it may be immersed again for twenty-four hours at 115°F., or else placed in water of ordinary temperature for four weeks, after which, if no further signs have developed, the cement may be considered safe.

(3) Fineness : —

10 p. c. residue on No. 80 sieve $\Big\}$ as maximum.
and 20 p. c.   ,,   ,,   ,, 120   ,,

(4) Tensile strength :—

		Portland.	Naturals.
Minimum neat	3 days	250	75
,, ,,	1 week	350	100
,, ,,	4 weeks	450	200

1 to 1 and 3 to 1 sand tests with 20 p. c. water, and 20 lbs. per square inch pressure to be determined by tests made and results furnished within the next year.

SERIES I.

SPECIAL TESTS.

On the effect of fine grinding : —

(a) 2 oz. cement passing No. 120 sieve   .   .   Cement
    2 oz.   ,,   caught on No. 120 sieve $\Big\}$.   .   Sand
    2 oz.   ,,   ,,   ,, No. 80 sieve
    2 oz. sand

tested at 4 weeks gave 165 lbs., while

2 oz. cement passing No. 120 sieve . . . Cement
6 oz. sand . . . . Sand

gave 121 lbs. tested at the same age.

Thus, if in the first instance we consider all but the finest as sand, then our result is only 35 per cent. higher than the 2d mixture, showing of how little value the coarser particles were.

(*b*) No. 8 English Portland (very coarse) gave in ordinary test 414 lbs. 1 week neat, 528 lbs. 4 weeks neat; but when all the particles caught on No. 80 sieve were rejected, the results were 393 lbs. in 1 week, 484 lbs. in 4 weeks, demonstrating the well-known fact that neat tests of Portlands operate against fine grinding, and therefore should be considered only in connection with fineness and specific gravity.

(*c*) Equal portions (same brand) of residues on No. 50 and No. 80 sieve were mixed with 22 ½ per cent. water, and gave 262 lbs. in 1 week and 324 lbs. in 4 weeks, which is very surprising, and can only be accounted for on the ground that the dust of cement clinging onto the coarse particles was sufficient to hold them together, or else that the mechanical action of mixing the mortar broke up many coarse particles into finer ones.

(*d*) To show the superior value of fine cement in sand mixtures, the following results have been obtained : —

	1 to 1.		2 to 1.		3 to 1.	
	Ordinary.	Fine on 120 Sieve.	Ordinary.	Fine on 120 Sieve.	Ordinary.	Fine on 120 Sieve.
No. 2 Natural 1 week 20% water 20 lbs. pressure.	114	190				
No. 2 Natural 4 week 15% water tamped..... ...	98	65				
No. 2 Natural 4 week 15% water tamped.........	145	123				
No. 15 Natural 1 week 20% water 20 lbs. pressure	166	229				
No. 15 Natural 4 week 14% water tamped........			77	125		
Brand A Natural 4 week 20% water tamped......	31	39				
No. 3 Portland 4 week 12% water tamped........					72	121
No. 3 Portland 4 week 20% water 20 lbs. pressure.					47	100
No. 9 Portland 4 week 20% water 20 lbs. pressure.					49	109
No. 5 Portland 4 week 12% water tamped........					82	102
No. 6 Portland 4 week 12% water tamped........					126	188

These results should be a convincing argument to users of Portland cement that fine grinding is worth paying for, because the finer the same cement the greater its sand-carrying value is.

The only partial exception in the above results is No. 2 natural

This is either erratic, being, however, duplicated, or if not, is easily accounted for. An underburnt cement is easily ground, and therefore is not apt to be *well* ground ; very easy grinding will make it fine enough, and the better burnt particles being a little *better* burnt are, therefore, harder and escape grinding ; but these particles, not being very hard, are probably bruised up in mixing, and form the best part of the cementing substance ; therefore, when those are sifted out, the underburnt fine particle has not as great a cementing value as the mixture would have unsifted. On the other hand, the coarse particles in Portland cement are much harder, and are always a detriment in a sand mixture.

SERIES II.

HOT WATER TESTS.

(*a*) No. 1 Natural cement neat, 2 months old, gave when tested the following results : —

(1) Water at temperature 52° F., 226 lbs. average.
(2) „ „ „ 122° F., 250 lbs. average.

(*b*) No. 1 Natural cement 1 to 1, 2 months old, gave when tested the following results : —

(1) Water at temperature 47° F., 125 lbs. average.
(2) „ „ „ 118° F., 129 lbs. average.

(*c*) No. 4 Portland, neat, 1 month old, gave when tested the following results : —

(1) Water at temperature 65° F., 533 lbs. average.
(2) „ „ „ 118° F., 616 lbs. average.
(3) „ „ „ 186° F., 556 lbs. average.

(*d*) No. 4 Portland, 3 to 1, 1 month old, gave when tested the following results : —

(1) Water at temperature 66° F., 81 lbs. average.
(2) „ „ „ 183° F., 81 lbs. average.

These tests, which are very uniform, indicate that for either natural or Portland cements tested neat or with sand, there is a slight gain in strength, by using hot water in mixing.

The *advantage* being that for exposure to frost the cement will set quicker and resist the frost action better. By referring ahead to frost tests, it will be seen that cements exposed at about same temperature (natural cement only tested with hot water in frost) gave much higher results when mixed with hot water, being in ratio, 94 to o for neat cement No. 1 Natural, and 117 to 44 for 1 to 1 cement No. 1 Natural.

SERIES III.

FROST OR EXPOSURE TESTS.

This series consisted of various investigations into the strength of mortars when mixed with different conditions of water and under different exposures, reference being particularly made to frost. All tests were made in quadruplicate.

The first set was submerged, after 24 hours, in water of laboratory tanks.

The second set was kept on damp boards in a closed tank for the whole period, and never allowed to dry out.

The third set was allowed to set in the laboratory, and then exposed to the severe frost and left in open air for the whole period.

The fourth set was exposed in from 8 to 10 minutes to the

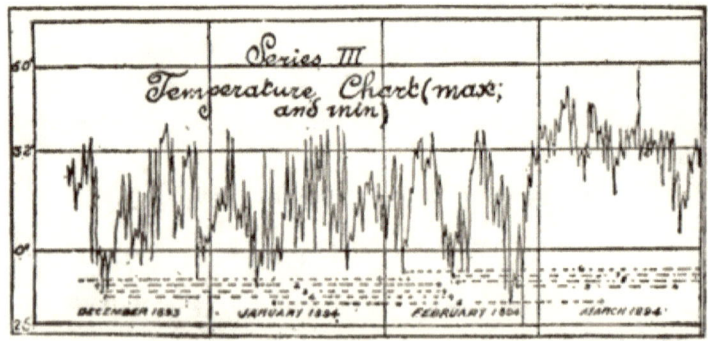

severe frost, and left there for the whole period, except to take them out of the molds when they were set or frozen.

Table V is here given, showing the results obtained, and accompanying it is a temperature chart showing the weather to which these mixtures were exposed during their whole period.

TABLE V.
FROST OR EXPOSURE TESTS. SERIES III.

Mixture	Age	Tensile Strength Water test (1)	Damp air test (2)	Exposure after setting (3)	Exposure before setting (4)	Compressive Strength 1	2	3	4	Dates of Exposure	Temperature of Exposure for 3	Temperature of Exposure for 4	Time from mixing till exposure	Natural time of set	No. of tests	REMARKS
No. 11. Portland Neat.	2 mos.	602	471	282	334	3200	1780	1600	1900	Dec. 6th to Feb. 6th.	+23° F.	+22° F.	30′(3) 12′(4)	25′	16	
1 to 1.	"	377	276	194	233					Dec. 11th to Feb. 11th.	+5° F.	+3½° F.	40′(3) 8′(4)	35′	20	
2 to 1.	"	168	150	105	111	800	720	660	440	Dec. 12th to Feb. 12th.	−½° F.	0° F.	40′(3) 10′(4)	37′	24	
3 to 1.	"	104	85	92	97	300	520	230	300	Dec. 13th to Feb. 13th.	−5° F.	−6° F.	1°27′(3) 10′(4)	1°25′	24	Nos. 3 and 4 showed irregular and injured fractures.
No. 1. Natural Neat.	"	226	221	349	0	1600	1500	2300	1390	Jan. 12th to Mar. 12th.	+2° F.	+5° F.	4°15′(3) 11′(4)	4°15′	24	No. 4 tension completely blown in fragments.
1 to 1.	"	125	229	187	44	2800	2000	0	800	Feb. 5th to April 5th.	+8° F.	+6° F.	8°0′(3) 10′(4)	8°00′	22	Some of No. 4 tension injured and No. 3 compression.
Neat.	"	250	281	159	94	1500		3300		Feb. 13th to April 13th.	+13° F.	+5° F.	6°0′(3) 10′(4)	6′0′	24	Mixed with water at temperature 122° F.
1 to 1.	"	129	170	80	117					Feb. 14th to April 14th.	+9° F.	0° F.	3°0′(3) 8′(4)	2°50′	20	Mixed with water at temperature 118° F.
Neat.	1 mo.	155	278	217	249					Feb. 26th to Mar. 26th.	+17° F.	+7½° F.	7°0′(3) 9′(4)	7°0′	20	Mixed with 2% brine.

It will be noticed that these tests were purposely made in cold snaps so as to make the tests as severe as possible.

It would appear improbable that mortar immediately exposed to severe frost would become stronger than that allowed to set in a warm atmosphere, but the results of all the Portland cement tests, both in tension and compression (with one exception) assert it ; and also that those allowed to set in the laboratory, and then exposed continually, are the weakest of all the four conditions treated of. This would go far to dispute the advisability of covering up mortar laid in frosty weather.

The next deduction from the Portland cement tests is that laboratory tests made with briquettes submerged give higher results than can be expected in open-air work, and therefore that engineers should add this to the various other degenerating contingencies, such as bad mixing, dirty sand, etc. A deduction not much evidenced in the table is that it is not safe to lay Portland cement mortar below 0° F. because the third and fourth series of 3 to 1 Portland exposed at —6° F. gave ocular evidence that their structure was injured, and the test-pieces broke most irregularly, while the other exposures at about 0° F. gave no evidence of any injury at all. Coming to the natural cement mortar in the fifth and sixth lines, we find much different results. The first one is decisive, and is that this particular cement mortar cannot be laid in zero weather. The first set were all blown to pieces (except the cube), which surprisingly stood 1,390 lbs. while the second set, although not quite blown to pieces, all showed extreme injury.

The most peculiar result is that this same cement, neat, if given a few hours to set in the temperate air, will on exposure to the frost attain a strength highest of the 4 conditions ; this is quite remarkable, that while the Portland cement was strongest when submerged, the natural cement was stronger in damp air and strongest in frost.

Indeed, the Portland cement, in air, for 1 to 1 mixtures, was very little stronger than the 1 to 1 natural.

All of the natural cement specimens exposed to frost showed a disintegrated layer on the outside about ⅛ in. thick; underneath this the structure was quite sound, and doubtless much of the variations in tests is due not so much to a weakening through the whole mass as to a reduced sectional area.

The last series made with 2 per cent. brine in mild weather for 1 month (exposed at + 7½° F.) showed that salt increased the strength, making them as strong as others were at 2 months when mixed with fresh water, and also again emphasized the advantage to this natural cement of open-air tests.

It would seem that either hot water or salt are therefore very strengthening in their effect.

SERIES IV.

SHEARING TESTS.

This series of experiments was carried out with a view of obtaining more information on the shearing strength of mortar. The method adopted was as follows : —

Three bricks placed as shown in sketch were cemented together, and tested at the end of one month. It was found that by placing pieces of soft wood at *A*, *A*, *A*, an action as nearly as possible a shear was obtained, and gave very satisfactory results, the pressure being practically concentrated along the two mortar joints. No side pressure was applied, because the desire was to obtain minimum results where friction was not assisting.

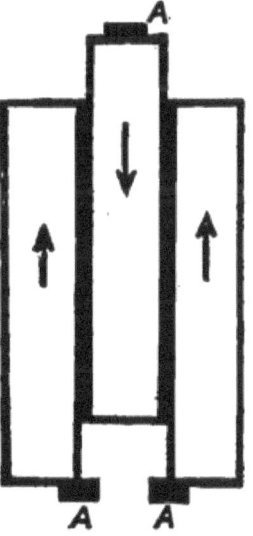

The combined effect of adhesion and friction can easily be computed if the adhesion and superimposed load are known.

The results are divided into lime-mortar, natural cement mortar, and Portland cement mortar, also into ¼ in. and ½ in. joints, also into flat common unkeyed bricks and pressed Laprairie brick keyed on one side. (1) The lime mortar was mixed 1 lime to 3 of standard quartz sand, by weight ; (2) natural cement mortar was mixed, 1 of No. 2 natural cement to 1½ standard sand ; (3) Portland cement mortar was mixed, 1 of No. 5 Portland cement to 3 standard sand. The test pieces were chiefly allowed to stand in the laboratory at a temperature of 55 to 65 degs. Fahr., but one set of natural cement mortar and two of Portland cement mortar were duplicated by immersing in water for 29 days, after setting in air 24 hours before submersion.

These results point out many interesting facts: (*a*) the first fact noticeable is that the results are independent of the *thickness* of joint; this is true of lime and cement mortars. (*b*) The next one is not evidenced to any extent in the table, but was quite apparent in the testing, viz., that the adhesion of the mortar to the brick was greatest when the mortar was put on very soft, and least when the mortar was dry. This will largely uphold the use of soft mortars by masons, albeit their reason is a purely selfish one, the mortar being easy to handle. The tensile tests of cements made *very* soft are lower than when the mixture has the minimum amount of water for standard consistency. But for adhesive tests the case is evidently the reverse. It may be here mentioned that in these tests all bricks were thoroughly soaked with water before the joints were laid. (*c*) Coming now to the tests on lime mortar, the shears were through the mortar, except in the fourth experiment, and therefore they are quite independent of the key of the pressed brick on the surface of adhesion. This would point out the fact that keyed brick are superfluous in lime mortar joints, and the shearing strength per square inch averages about $10\frac{1}{2}$ lbs. per square inch. The tensile strength of the same mixture at the same age was 30 lbs. per square inch, and the compressive strength 102 lbs. per square inch. (*d*) The natural cement mortar showed distinctly that its adhesive strength was not as great as its shearing strength, which is the reverse of the lime mortar tests. It also showed that the keyed brick aided in some unknown way, for the results on them are three times as great as with the common flat brick. Of course this may have been, and probably was, partly due to the different surface of adhesion. In five tests out of twenty-one made on the natural cement mortar, the mortar sheared through, and the average of these five was 97 lbs. per square inch, which gives the shearing strength proper, while the average adhesive strength of the thirteen tests in air which came loose from the bricks was 26 lbs. per square inch in common brick, 48 lbs. per square inch on Laprairie pressed brick, and 38 lbs. per square inch on Laprairie pressed brick for three tests submerged in water for the whole period.

This would show that the adhesive strength is nearly twice as great on pressed brick as common brick, and that submersion in water had a rather harmful effect than otherwise on the adhesive strength, and was certainly of no benefit.

TABLE VI.

TABLE OF SHEARING TESTS, OR MORTAR ADHESION TO BRICK SURFACES (in shear.)

Series IV.

Kind of Mortar.	Joint.	Brick.	No. of tests.	How indurated.	Shear in lbs. per square inch.			REMARKS.
					Average.	Least.	Greatest.	
Lime 1. Sand 3.	¼"	A	5	in air.	9.7	8.4	11.9	All sheared through the mortar.
Lime 1. Sand 3.	½"	A	4	in air.	12.1	6.1	19.8	All sheared through the mortar.
Lime 1. Sand 3.	¼"	B	5	in air.	12.0	9.1	15.5	All sheared through the mortar.
Lime 1. Sand 3.	½"	B	5	in air.	8.0	5.5	11.0	All came away from brick (mortar dry).
No. 2.								
Natural Cement 1 Sand 1½.	¼"	A	5	in air.	22.3	8.0	32.1	All came away from brick.
Natural Cement 1 Sand 1½.	½"	A	5	in air.	29.0	24.0	33.0	All came away from brick.
Natural Cement 1 Sand 1½.	¼"	B	5	in air.	75.0	25.0	118.0	Two came away from brick, three sheared.
Natural Cement 1 Sand 1½.	½"	B	3	in air.	85.0	43.0	118.0	One came away from brick, two sheared.
Natural Cement 1 Sand 1½.	½"	B	3	in water.	38.0	34.0	42.0	All came away from brick.
No. 5.								
Portland Cement 1 Sand 3.	¼"	A	3	in air.	10.6	10.2	11.6	All came away from brick. } The brick which was on top in the original laying, always sheared first and at a less load than that of lower one, which, of course, set under twice as much load or pressure.
Portland Cement 1 Sand 3.	¼"	A	3	in water.	13.0	10.2	16.4	All came away from brick.
Portland Cement 1 Sand 3.	¼"	B	3	in air.	16.5	9.2	24.2	All came away from brick.
Portland Cement 1 Sand 3.	¼"	B	3	in water.	27.1	20.2	36.9	All came away from brick.

A. Common, flat, unkeyed, salmon brick.
B. Laprairie pressed brick, key on one side.

The tensile strength of the same mortar at the same age was 132 lbs. per square inch; the compressive strength was not obtained, but would have been about 1,000 lbs. per square inch. The hints to be taken from these tests are that pressed brick keyed on both sides will give much higher results than flat common bricks, and would probably place the shearing strength of such joints at 100 lbs. per square inch, and make it largely independent of the consistency of the mortar. Also that the shearing strength is very much higher in proportion to the tensile strength than was the lime mortar shearing strength to its tensile strength, but about the same proportion to its compressive strength, *i. e.*, 10 to 1.

It becoming evident that the thickness of joint had no appreciable effect, the Portland cement mortar tests were made all ¼ in. thick. The results are surprisingly low. The adhesion on the common brick is about the same for air drying or submersion in water, and is slightly less than one half that of natural cement mortar tests of 1½ to 1. This is a significant fact, for while a neat tensile test of No. 2 natural cement 4 weeks old is 268 lbs., the No. 5 Portland is 459 lbs. for the same age, and a 3 to 1 No. 5 Portland is 82 lbs. for same age. (See table of general laboratory results.) Thus while any test of this cement would show that a 3 to 1 mixture of the latter would be nearly equal to a 1½ to 1 test on the former, yet in their adhesive properties to common brick the heavily dosed sand mixture was only half as strong as the natural cement mortar with a smaller dose of sand. We might easily have expected this; but the main point is: is it taken account of, in considering the comparative values of these mixtures, that the adhesive strength of a Portland cement mortar heavily dosed with sand is low as compared with a weaker but richer mixture of natural cement mortar? The shearing of Portland mortar shows that the adhesion to pressed brick is greater than to common brick, but not in such proportion as in natural cements, being 1½ or 2 to 1 in place of 3 to 1 in the latter. But here again comes out the advantage given to Portland cements by testing them under water; the submerged specimens are stronger than open air ones, while in natural cements the reverse is the case.

Table VI. summarizes the results obtained.

TABLE VII.

MORTAR JOINTS IN COMMON BUILDING BRICK PIERS.

Composition of Mortar.	Age of Test.	Thickness of Joints.	Dimensions of Brick Pier.	Per cent. water in mortar.	Loads in lbs. per square inch.				Compression per foot under a total load of		
					1st signs of failure in mortar.	1st signs of failure in brick.	Bricks falling rapidly.	Maximum load.	5,000	20,000	35,000
No. 1. 1 Lime. 5 Building sand.	1 week.	$\frac{3}{8}''$	7.80" by 7.85", 16.57" high. 6 bricks. 61.2 sq. in. area.	37 (?)	245	327	980	1,143	.015"	.08"	.13"
No. 2. 1 Lime. 5 Building sand.	3 weeks.	$\frac{3}{8}''$	8.0" by 8.0". 11.16" high. 4 bricks. 64.0 sq. ins.	37	469	563	1,406	1,553	.007"	.043"	.075"
No. 3. 1 Lime. 5 Building sand.	3 weeks.	$\frac{3}{8}''$	7.9" by 7.9." 24.50" high. 9 bricks. 62.4 sq. ins.	37	400	689	897	1,282	.005"	.053"	.094"
No. 4. 1 Lime. 3 Laboratory sand.	1 week.	$\frac{1}{4}''$	7.75" by 7.85." 11.42" high. 4 bricks. 60.84 sq. ins.	34	287	575	....	1,117	.032"	.133"	.158"
No. 5. 1 of No. 2 Natural cement. 1½ Lab'tory sand.	1 week.	$\frac{1}{8}''$	7.80" by 7.90". 11.15" high. 4 bricks. 62.01 sq. ins.	22½	968	1,190	1,403	1,984	.009"	.027"	.054"

No. 6. 1 of No. 5 Portland cement. 3 Laboratory sand.	1 week.	¼"	800" by 7.95". 11.30" high. 4 bricks. 63.60 sq. ins. area.	20	755	959	1,305	1,564	.007"	.007"	.019"
No. 7. 1 No. 5 Portland. 1½ Lab'tory sand. Common building bricks.	1 week.	¼"	8.00" by 8.00". 11.5" high. 4 bricks. 64.0 sq. ins. area.	20	1,125	1,563	....	1,734	.000"	.0045"	.011"
No. 8. 1 No. 11 Portland. 1 Lab'tory sand. Laprairie pressed brick.	12 days.	¼"	8.3" by 8.3". 11.8" high. 4 bricks. 68.9 sq. ins. area.	....	1,679	1,800	1,930	1,960	.001"	.006"	.011"
No. 9. **1 Lime.** **3 Lab'tory sand.** **Laprairie** pressed **brick.**	4 weeks.	¼"	8.2" by 8.2". 11.5" high. 4 bricks. 67.2 sq. ins. area.	35	260	853	....	1,263	.048"	.115"	.156"
No. 10. 1 No. 2 Natural. 1½ Lab'tory sand. Laprairie pressed brick.	4 weeks.	¼"	8.4" by 8.4". 11.0" high. 4 bricks. 70.6 sq. ins. area.	22½	1,345	1,629	1,746	1,983	.000"	.0027"	.005"
No. 11. 1 No. 5 Portland. 3 Lab'tory sand. Laprairie pressed brick.	4 weeks.	¼"	8.4" by 8.4". 11.1" high. 4 bricks. 70.6 sq. ins. area.	20	1,204	1,600	1,629	1,785	.002"	.011"	.016"

NOTE:— These results were obtained after the publication of the paper, and are the additional pier tests promised in the text.

SERIES IV. (*A*)

THE STRENGTH OF MORTAR IN COMPRESSION IN BRICK MASONRY.

All engineers realize that the strength of mortar is much less tested in cubes than in thin layers, but just what proportion they bear to one another is not very well known. The following experi-

ments have been made with a view of obtaining this information, (See table VII.).

At the same time that these tests were made, mortar was also made into test pieces, and tested at the same age. We are thus enabled to form an idea of the relative strengths of mortar in thin joints and in cubes, and also to form an intelligent opinion of the comparative strengths of lime mortar, natural cement mortar, and Portland cement mortar. The mortars of the fourth, fifth, and sixth tests are identical with the mortars of the *shearing* tests, and show the same clear superiority of the natural cement 1 ½ to 1 over the Portland cement 3 to 1 when used in this manner. Table VIII. summarizes the results obtained.

Roughly speaking, the lime mortar at 1 week 5 to 1 is 6 times as strong; the lime mortar at 1 week 3 to 1 is 14 times as strong; the natural cement mortar at 1 week 1 ½ to 1 is 4 times as strong; the Portland cement mortar at 1 week 3 to 1 is twice as strong as the same mortar tested in cubes at the same age.

Referring to the amount of compression in Table VII., it will be seen that the amount of compression per foot is much less according as this ratio is less; *i. e.*, the less yielding the mortar, the nearer does the strength in cubes approach to the strength in joints. This is to be expected, because the more yielding substances will be at a

TABLE VIII.

	Strength of Mortar per square inch.			Loads released at 17,500 lbs., set observed per lineal foot.	
	In joints.	In cubes.	In tens'n.		
(1)	245	40	17	....	1 week old, mortar, 1 lime, 5 sand.
(2)	469	57	20	.01″	3 weeks old, mortar, 1 lime, 5 sand.
(3)	400	57	20	.03″	3 weeks old, mortar, 1 lime, 5 sand.
(4)	287	21	....	.08″	1 week old, mortar, 1 lime, 3 sand.
(5)	968	250	....	....	1 week old, mortar, 1 Natural Cement, 1 ½ sand.
(6)	755	341	43	.00	1 week old, mortar, 1 Portland Cement, 3 sand.

much greater disadvantage when unsupported at the sides than if enclosed in a thin masonry joint.

In the second, third, fourth, and sixth tests at 17,500 lbs., the load was released, and the permanent set observed was as given in the fifth column of the preceding table.

It seems probable from this, therefore, that the lime mortars must have yielded to an injurious extent before there were any external signs. But whether this was the case or not, it is impossible to say, because the compression was quite uniform up to and in many cases much past the points of evident failure.

It seems fair to suppose that 1 week and 3 weeks are about the minimum and average times which would elapse before the maximum load might be put on a brick wall, and when it is remembered that these joints were less than ¼ in. thick, the amount of compression in a high brick wall under a load of 80 or 90 lbs. per square inch is seen to be very great, and under a load of 300 to 400 lbs. per square inch, a brick wall 50 ft. high in lime mortar would not only fail, but compress from 2 to 6 ins. in doing so — the compression practically all taking place in the mortar, as in the unyielding Portland cement mortar the compression is seen to be very small.

The second part of this paper will contain tests made on piers built with pressed brick, in which the mortar has had longer time to harden, and interesting results are looked for.

The brick in this case was, as mentioned in Table VII., common building brick. The photograph given illustrates the method of testing and the interesting manner of failure of fifth test, in which the lines of least resistance are clearly defined.

SERIES V.

EVAPORATION AND CRUSHING TESTS AND EVAPORATION AND TENSILE TESTS.

(a) *Evaporation and crushing tests.*

This series had for its first intention, information on the comparative and actual amount of evaporation of moisture from different mortars made with different cements, but it soon developed into an endeavor to obtain some relation between crushing strength and evaporation. Any law on the matter, if there is any general law, will of course take years to demonstrate; but enough has been done to show that any investigations on this subject will be fruitful of results. The method of procedure was as follows: Mixtures were kept in damp air 30 days, then immersed 2 days in water of ordinary temperature, then taken out and weighed; they were then kept in the warm dry air of the laboratory at a temperature of about 65 degs. Fahr. exactly 2 days, when they were again weighed and immediately crushed. The experiments recorded in Table IX. were all made on 2 in. cubes, and 2 days was established, because it was found that at that time the evaporation was practically complete. Other experiments (not recorded) made on 3 in. cubes gave less evaporation per cent. and also less strength. Attached to this are three diagrams; the first two show strength and evaporation in different mixtures and with five brands of cement. The third diagram is the

product of the other two, and is quite worthy of inspection, because **it** would appear from it that it would be possible to estimate fairly and accurately, without actually crushing a specimen, what load it would bear.

TABLE IX.

EVAPORATION AND CRUSHING TESTS.

No. 11 — PORTLAND.

SERIES V.

Mixture.	Evap. per cent. in 2 days.	Crushing strength per square inch.	Product.	Max. wt. of 2 inch Cube.	$\left(\sqrt[2]{\dfrac{2}{\text{wt.}}} \right)$	Column 4 divided by column 6.
				oz.		
Neat.	1.48	3925	5809	10.43	22.16	262.1
1 to 1	3.41	2211	7539	10.12	21.71	347.3
2 to 1	6.20	1031	6492	9.39	20.66	314.2
3 to 1	10.39	544	5652	9.14	20.30	278.4
4 to 1	11.49	431	4952	8.92	19.97	247.9

No. 10 — PORTLAND.

Mixture.	Evap. per cent. in 2 days.	Crushing strength per square inch.	Product.	wt.	$\left(\sqrt[2]{\dfrac{2}{\text{wt.}}} \right)$	Column 4 divided by column 6.
Neat.	0.97	4367	4231	9.84	21.31	199.0
1 to 1	2.20	3062	6736	10.23	21.87	308.0
2 to 1	5.59	1079	6032	9.43	20.72	291.1
3 to 1	8.61	*940	8093	9.15	20.31	398.4
4 to 1	11.68	504	5886	8.86	19.87	296.2

* One day older than others.

No. 3 — PORTLAND.

Mixture.	Evap. per cent. in 2 days.	Crushing strength per square inch.	Product.	wt.		
Neat.	4.65	1863	8662	10.00	21.62	400.7
1 to 1	4.10	1875	7687	10.12	21.71	354.1
2 to 1	5.67	1417	8034	9.60	20.97	383.1
3 to 1	8.11	687	5572	8.95	20.01	276.2
4 to 1	12.56	412	5176	8.88	19.90	260.0

No. 15 — NATURAL.

Mixture.	Evap. per cent. in 2 days.	Crushing strength per square inch.	Product.	wt.		
Neat.	6.76	1888	12762	9.40	20.67	617.4
1 to 1	5.08	1437	7300	9.65	21.02	347.3
2 to 1	6.12	988	6046	9.32	20.57	293.9
3 to 1	8.34	575	4796	9.05	20.16	237.9

No. 2 — NATURAL.

Mixture.	Evap. per cent, in 2days.	Crushing strength per. square inch.	Product.	wt.		
Neat.	5.93	2575	15720	9.43	2072	758.
1 to 1	10.32	703	7254	9.06	2016	359.9
2 to 1	8.93	810	7233	9.28	2057	352.6

Reference to the table and diagrams will show that the evaporation increases and the strength diminishes with the increase of sand in the mixture. This is, of course, almost self-evident, but the striking difference in the amount of evaporation for different cements neat is unaccountable. This difference disappears as the admixture of sand increases, and we are led, therefore, to conclude that there is something inherent in the cement itself, which aids it more or less in holding particles of water in suspension. The natural

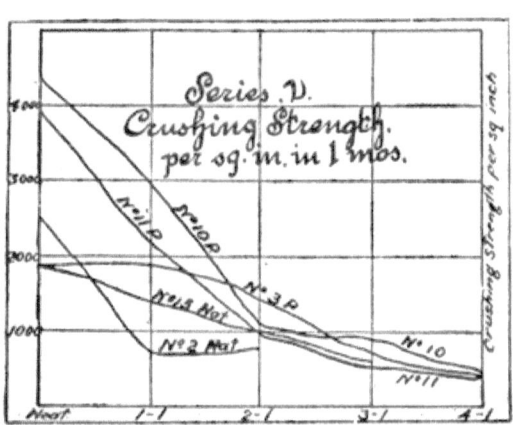

cements show high evaporation neat, so also does the No. 3 Portland, which has a high specific gravity (see general tables), and the cubes

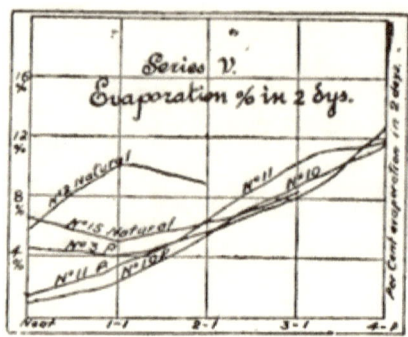

of which weighed more than those of the No. 10, which evaporated least. We cannot account for it on the ground of Portland and natural, but one thing is evident, that that same quality which enables it to hold water in suspension also aids it in holding particles of sand together, but not particles of itself. The third diagram showing the convergence of lines on the 1 to 1 mixture is very striking. The *product* of the *crushing strength of a* 1 *to* 1 *mixture* and the *evaporation per cent.* under conditions named is practically CONSTANT. This is for one condition only, namely, 32 days, with access of water and 2 days' drying. This means in plain words that we may possibly be able to test with a balance instead of a crushing machine.

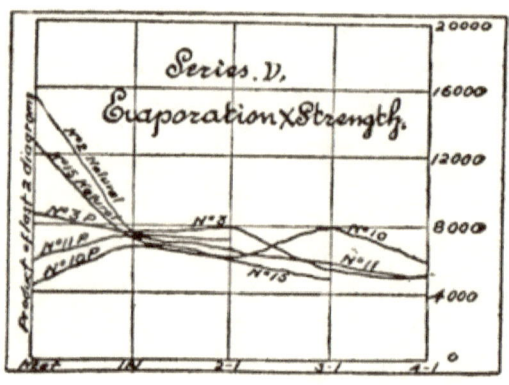

It is probable that the microscope would reveal a decided difference of structure in various cements. It is, of course, well known that the underburnt natural cements have softer, rounder, and more easily pulverized grains than that produced by the highly burnt clinker of the Portland. It is possible, therefore, that the evaporation qualities of a neat cement would indicate more closely than anything else the degree of burning practised, independent of the fineness. It will be noticed by Table II. that the residues on sieves afford no clue to the density of the mixture, and no guide to determine beforehand the evaporation. Neither does the weight of the specimens vary at all regularly either with the crushing strength or evaporation.

It would seem that the coarse, angular laboratory sand had its interstices just about filled up with a 1 to 1 mixture, and the strength of the mixture depended directly on the amount of evaporation, in an inverse ratio. The Evaporation diagram No. 4 is the same as No. 3,

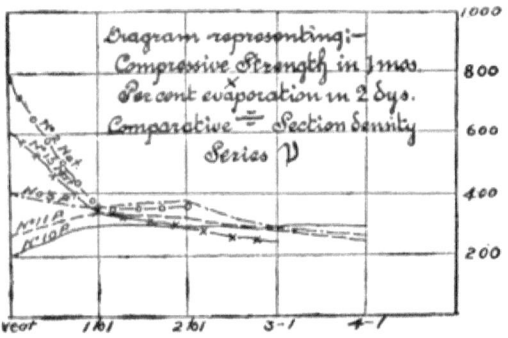

except that this product is referred to a uniform section density (*i. e.*) $\left(\sqrt[3]{\dfrac{2}{weight}}\right)^2$; the diagram is practically the same, showing that the variation in weight of test pieces made practically no differ-

(*b*) *Evaporation and tension tests.*

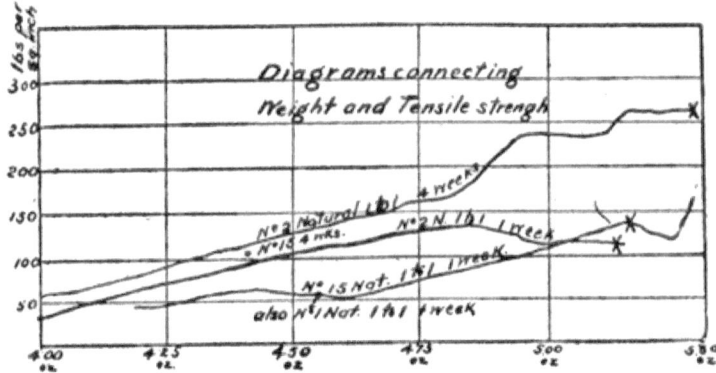

ence in the results, *i. e.*, the per cent. of evaporation determines the strength in 1 to 1 mixtures, but is no criterion in neat ones.

In Table III. and Table IV. the per cent. of evaporation in 2 days is again given, and diagrams are plotted showing the relation between the tensile strength and the weight of the dried briquettes in the pressure tests, and also other diagrams showing the product of tensile strength and evaporation plotted on a base of weights of briquettes.

The × marks in the diagrams show the positions of tests made

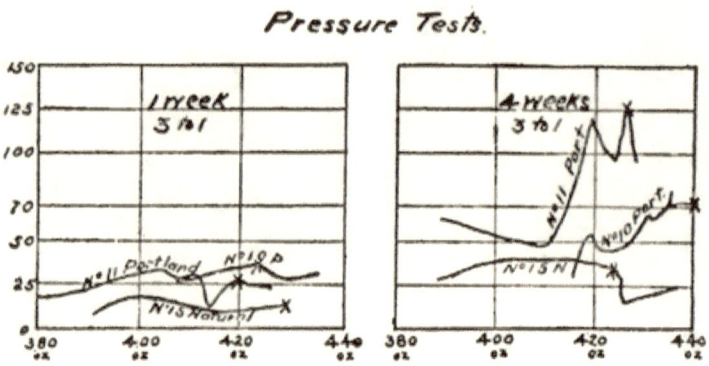

with 20 lbs. pressure and 20 per cent. of water, and they are seen to stand at prominent and usually maximum points on the diagrams, proving that this is the best point to select of all the tests made.

It will be seen in these diagrams as in those of crushing tests,

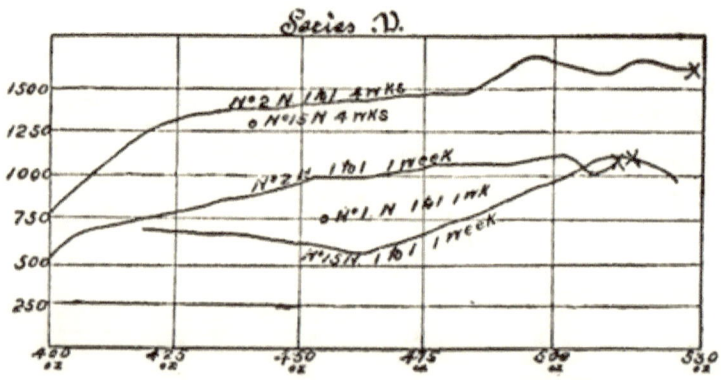

that in 1 to 1 mixtures the variation of evaporation and strength combined is not very great, but not so close as in the former tests.

The 3 to 1 tests are very erratic, as might have been expected with different per cents. of water and different amounts of

pressure. It is evident that each cement has distinctive qualities of
its own, because with the same weight of briquette the strengths
vary, and this brings up the important point that in sand tests the
strength ought to be referred to some basis of weight of briquette,
because a slight variation in weight seems, from Table IV., to affect

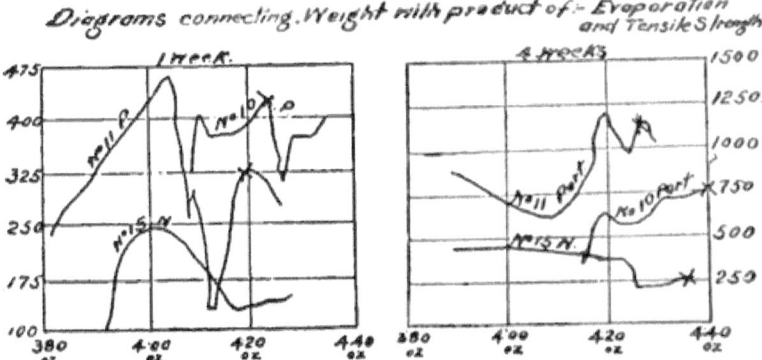

the strength very much. It would not take much evidence to
determine the average weight, and all tests could be reduced to this
by multiplying by $\left(\sqrt[3]{\frac{1}{weight}}\right)^2$ which would change the section
density to a standard.

SERIES VI.

SUGAR TESTS.

Sucrate of lime is soluble in water, and it was chiefly a matter
of interest to see the effect of sugar on cements in weakening them,
because it has been asserted by several writers that the reverse is
the case; one investigator several years ago showed by tests that
from ½ to 1 per cent. of sugar would in 4 to 6 months give a gain
in strength.

Sugar, in these tests, 2 per cent. of the amount of cement (by
weight), was used, and the diagrams attached sufficiently indicate
the results. In the Portland cement the strength ranges closely at
50 per cent. of the ordinary strength as far as 6 months, while with
the natural cements, the sugar effect was overpowering. After 1
week's immersion the briquettes showed signs of cracking, and as
time went on became completely checked, and expanded so much as

to give practically no tests. This is further evidenced by the upper surface, which was protected by a coating of iron deposited from Montreal water, being intact, while the checking was greatest on the bottom where the water had free access.

The lime mixtures, kept in open air, showed encouraging results for 2 months, and seemed to prove that the use of sugar, in lime, as practised in India, was beneficial; but the 3, 4, and 6 months' tests disprove it. Altogether, it seems evident that this much or more sugar would be damaging in its effects on any kind of mortar in any

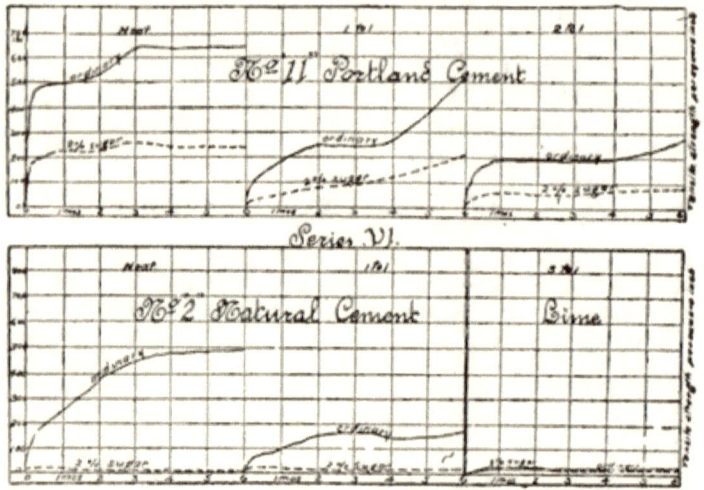

situation, and it is extremely doubtful whether any sugar whatever would have other than a weakening effect.

In concluding this paper, the author cannot but help feeling that he is, as it were, dipping just on the surface of a vast subject, and that the more one finds out, the larger the unknown fields beyond appear.

In any efforts that have been made, the frequent manual aid and more frequent sound practical advice of Mr. J. G. Kerry have been of much service, and here is the place to acknowledge it.

The endeavor has been to find out anything of practical use to the engineering profession; and if any points raised here will fulfil this desire, the object of this paper will be, in the main, accomplished.

PAPER II.

FROST TESTS.

IN a previous paper, read before the society, the writer promised to place before its members the results of certain frost tests which were being made at that time.

They are now given, in hope that they may be of some interest to those engineers who are contemplating the building of cement mortar masonry, or cement concrete in cold weather.

Method of procedure. — The briquettes were all made in the same manner, the 1 to 1 mixtures having 18 per cent. of water, and the 3 to 1 mixtures 15 per cent., being purposely greater than the amount used in ordinary laboratory tests, so as to get the mortar softer, and resembling more closely the condition in which masons use mortar in ordinary construction, as the effect of frost may be greater on soft mortars than on dry ones.

The briquettes were all rammed into the molds in 3 layers, and the briquettes to be subjected to frost tests were immediately put outside on a window-sill. In a few hours, after the briquettes were frozen hard, they were removed from the molds, and left exposed on the window-sills for two, three, or four months, care being taken to keep the snow swept off so as to allow the frost to have its full effect.

The tables, given, speak for themselves, and probably each engineer will draw special conclusions of his own ; the writer will only mention a few points that seem obvious to him.

I. FOUR MONTHS TESTS.

It would appear, from these tests, that it is quite safe to build masonry work in November, in Montreal climate, when the materials are mixed and exposed to the air at about the freezing point. The proportion which the strength of the frost tests bears to the submerged ones is about that which would be obtained under the most favorable circumstances. The briquettes were all firm, smooth, and hard on the surface, and although subjected to 4 months of severe frost in an exposed position, they did not seem to have been at all damaged.

II. THREE MONTHS TESTS.

These were all made in December, and the coldest days were purposely selected. Yet the only briquettes which were blown in pieces

FOUR MONTH TESTS.

BRIQUETTES MADE DURING MONTH OF NOVEMBER, 1894.

Date of Exposure.	No. of Brand. (See Paper L.)	Ordinary time of setting. Initial.	Full.	Mixture.	Temperature at time of mixing. Lab. air.	Water.	Materials.	Temp. of outside air.	Time elapsed from mixing to time of exposure.	Tensile Strength. Lab. Tests.	Exposed specimens.
Nov. 14	1	6°00'	12°00'	3 to 1	59°	56°	59°	36½°	10'	321	236
16	2	5°30'		1 to 1	64°	60°	64°	53°	7'	302	229
2	2	45'	2°45'	1 to 1	65°	58°	60°	60°	10'	484	250
1	15	1°00'	2°30'	1 to 1	65°	62°	64°	66°	10'	541	237
	Averages				63°	59°	62°	51°	9½'	412	236
Nov. 5	3	5°00'	20°00'	3 to 1	68°	65°	65°	37°	12'	141	147
26	4	37'	3 to 10	3 to 1	64°	58°	57°	29°	7'	256	200
27	5	1°00'	5°00'	3 to 1	61°	62°	56°	36°	7'	237	183
28	6a	2°00'	6°00'	3 to 1	68°	64°	63°	28°	8'	222	128
6	8	3°20'	6°30'	3 to 1	63°	59°	60°	42°	11'	172	114
9	9	13'	2°00'	3 to 1	57°	57°	61°	35°	11½'	194	182
13	10	25'	90'	3 to 1	62°	55°	57°	34°	8'	174	176
19	11	30'		3 to 1	60°	55°	57°	35°	7½'	153	141
21	12	25'		3 to 1	60°	52°	58°	34°	9½'	155	162
20	14	20'		3 to 1	61°	54°	58°	39°	9'	119	102
22	19	2°40'	7°40'	3 to 1	58°	54°	56°	37°	7'	253	387
	Averages				58°	58°	61°	34°	8½'	185	171

REMARKS CONCERNING EXPOSED SPECIMENS.

All these were of natural cements. They were brought in and kept 2 or 3 hours before testing, and allowed to warm so as to drive out the frost, and insure a test not being made on a frozen specimen. There were no external signs of any effect produced by 4 months' exposure.

All these were of Portland cement. They were, when necessary, brought into the laboratory and kept there for 2 or 3 hours before being tested, so as to insure that no tests were made on frozen briquettes. No signs of the effect of frost were visible on any of the specimens.

THREE MONTH TESTS.

BRIQUETTES MADE DURING THE MONTH OF DECEMBER, 1894.

Date of Exposure.	No. of Brand (see Paper I.)	Ordinary time of setting. Initial.	Final.	Mixture.	Temperature at time of mixing. Lab. air.	Water.	Material.	Temp. of outside air.	Time elapsed from mixing to time of exposure.	Tensile Strength. Lab. Test.	Exposed specimens.	REMARKS CONCERNING EXPOSED SPECIMENS.
Dec. 26	1	6°00'	12°00'	1 to 1	62°	60°	58°	+7°	5'	247	0	Briquettes frozen long before set could take place, all blown to pieces by frost.
Dec. 24	(old) 2	5°30'	2°45'	1 to 1	66°	52°	53°	+10½°	5'	198	0	ditto
	2	45'		1 to 1	65°	60°	60°	+19½°	8'	190	233	Seemingly quite sound, but broke irregularly as to loads and position of fractures.
Dec. 1	15	1°00'	2°30'	1 to 1	61°	56°	56°	+16°	7½'	484	311	Practically sound, some slight cracks on the surface.
										337	272	About 1·16″ on the surface, disintegrated, the remainder quite sound.

Average of No. 2 and No. 15

Date of Exposure.	No. of Brand.	Initial.	Final.	Mixture.	Lab. air.	Water.	Material.	Temp. outside air.	Time.	Lab. Test.	Exposed.	REMARKS.
Dec. 3	3	5°00'	20°00'	3 to 1	60°	60°	56°	+17°	7'	108	101	ditto
Dec. 31	4	37'	3°10'	3 to 1	60°	56°	56°	+19°	6'	204	85	ditto
Dec. 31	5	1°00'	5°00'	3 to 1	48°	45°	46°	+14½°	6'	218	111	Three of these disintegrated for 1·16″ on outside, the other two injured to the very center, average of three being (72).
Dec. 31	6½	2°00'	6°30'	3 to 1	5-	48°	49°	+8½°	6½'	247	47	Seemed perfectly sound and solid.
Dec. 8	8	3°20'	6°30'	3 to 1	69°	63°	63°	+21°	6½'	191	163	These during a warm spell of three days remained quite soft, not setting at all; when tested, they showed a slight weathering on the top surface.
Dec. 10	9	13'	2°00'	3 to 1	68°	64°	64°	+14°	8'	151	113	Seemed perfectly sound and solid.
Dec. 18	10	25'	50'	3 to 1	57°	53°	53°	+18½°	7½'	132	154	Disintegrated for ⅛″ on top and sides, remainder solid looking.
Dec. 27	11	30'	1°00'	3 to 1	70°	65°	65°	+7°	7'	107	59	Disintegrated for ¼″ on top and sides, remainder solid looking.
Dec. 28	12	25'	3°00'	3 to 1	61°	55°	59°	+9°	6'	89	23	ditto
Dec. 31	14	20'	2°30'	3 to 1	50°	50°	54°	-7°	7'	131	49	Only 1 briquette was disintegrated on the surface, but all were weak and brittle, crumbling if rubbed with the fingers.
Dec. 29	19	2°40'	7°40'	3 to 1	65°	61°	61°	-6°	6'	223	87	
Averages					60°	53°	54°	+10½°	6⅔'	164	90	

TWO MONTH TESTS.
(With cold water.)
BRIQUETTES MADE DURING THE MONTH OF JANUARY, 1895.

Date of Exposure.	No. of Brand. (See Paper I.)	Ordinary time of setting. Initial.	Full.	Mixture.	Lab. air.	Water.	Materials.	Temp. of mixture just before exposure.	Temp. of outside air.	Time elapsed from mixing to time of exposure.	Tensile Strength. Lab. Tests.	Exposed specimens.	REMARKS CONCERNING EXPOSED SPECIMENS.
Jan. 14	2	45'	2°45'	1 to 1	61°	32°	+19°	40°	+18°	6'	295	21	Practically all blown to pieces, the solid core of two briquettes giving 10½ lbs. = 21 lbs. average.
Jan. 5	15	1°00'	2°30'	1 to 2	57°	36°	+26°	38°	— 3°	6'	330	87	All the exterior blown to pieces, interior solid.
		Averages			59°	34°	+22½°	39°	+ 7½°	6'	312	54	
Jan. 21	3	5°00'	20°00'	3 to 1	63°	32°	+14°	34°	+13°	6½'	86	0	All soft and crumbling. **No strength** at all.
Jan. 24	8	3°30'	6°30'	3 to 1	57°	32°	+ 5°	36°	+ 5°	9'	214	5	Cement frozen when mixed 6', mixed by hand, a very severe test; briquettes appeared firm on surface, but crumbled when touched.
Feb. 29	9	13'	2°00'	3 to 1	60°	32°	+20°	37°	+18°	6½'	133	92	Disintegrated on top for 1-16''; remainder solid.
Feb. 5	10	25'	50'	3 to 1	55°	34°	—1°	30°	—1°	6'	+15	39	This mortar frozen when mixed, mixed by hand on table; a very severe test, briquettes appeared firm on surface, but weakened all through.
		Averages			59°	32½°	+ 7°	34°	+ 6°	7'	144	34	
Average of Nos. 3, 8, and 9					60°	32°	+13°	36°	+12°	7'	144	32	

TWO MONTH TESTS.

(With hot water.)

BRIQUETTES MADE DURING THE MONTH OF JANUARY, 1895.

Date of Exposure	No. of Brand. (See Paper I.)	Ordinary time of setting. Initial	Final	Mixture.	Lab. air.	Water.	Mater-ials.	Temp. of mixt're just before exposure.	Temp. of outside air.	Time elapsed from mixing to time of exposure.	Lab. tests.	Exposed specimens.	REMARKS ON EXPOSED SPECIMENS.
Jan. 18	2	45'	2°45'	1 to 1	64°	125°	35°	68°	+11°	6'	428	109	Badly blown on exterior for ⅛", but interior still solid.
5	15	1°00'	2°30'	1 to 1	57°	126°	30°	65°	+3°	6'	250	23	Top surface blown off for ¼", interior solid looking.
			Averages		60½°	125½°	32½°	66½°	+7°	6'	339	66	
Jan 21	3	5°00'	20°0'	3 to 1	63°	125°	18°	61°	+15°	6'	85	0	All soft and crumbling, no consistency at all.
23	8	3°20'	6°30'	3 to 1	64°	110°	20°	59°	+20°	6½'	99	47	Set very slowly in laboratory, those exposed were neither frozen nor set after 4 hours.
30 Feb.	9	13'	2°00'	3 to 1	63°	119°	18°	59°	+18°	5½'	109	88	Disintegrated for about ½" on top, remainder solid.
5	10	25'	50'	3 to 1	55°	115°	−11°	54°	−11°	7'	132	21	Slightly disintegrated on top, and weakened all through.
			Averages		61°	117°	+11°	58°	+10½°	6'	106	39	
Average of Nos. 3, 8, and 9					64°	118°	+19°	60°	+18°	6'	98	45	

TWO MONTH TESTS.

(With 2 per cent. of salt in the water.)

BRIQUETTES MADE DURING THE MONTH OF JANUARY, 1895.

Date of Exposure.	No. of Brand. (See Paper I.)	Ordinary time of setting.		Mixture.	Temperature at time of mixing.			Temp. of mixture just before exposure.	Temp. of outside air.	Time elapsed from mixing to time of exposure.	Tensile Strength.		REMARKS ON EXPOSED SPECIMENS.
		Initial.	Full.		Lab. air.	Water.	Materials.				Lab. Test. specimen.	Exposed specimen.	
Jan. 18	2	45'	2'45"	1 to 1	64°	33°	22°	41°	11°	6'	320	73	Blown on surface for about ⅛", interior solid.
9	15	1°00'	2°30'	1 to 1	58°	40°	9°	42°	9°	6'	280	143	Slightly blown on bottom, other fine cracks on top, otherwise solid.
Averages					61	36°	15½°	41½°	+10°	6'	300	108	
Jan. 21	3	5'00'	20'00'	3 to 1	65°	29°	25°	39°	25°	6'	101	39	Exterior worn with loose sand, but interior hard and firm, water was slushy at time of mixing.
28	8	3°20'	6°30'	3 to 1	56°	30°	13°	30°	12°	6½'	183	224	In perfect condition, water was slushy at time of mixing.
31	9	13'	2°00'	3 to 1	57°	30°	17°	30°	19°	6'	195	92	One briquette badly affected, and others quite sound. No. 10 is not tested.
Average of (5)					59°	30°	18°	33°	17°		118	130	

NOTE.— Each test recorded in this table is the average of 5 briquettes, all briquettes rammed moderately, in 3 layers, with an iron hammer having ⅜" square end, and weighing about ½ lb.

were those made from two very inert, slow-setting, poor Canadian natural cements. The two other natural cements (one Canadian, the other Belgian) were quicker setting, and stood the test well. With the Portland cements, the diminution in strength is more apparent than real, the proportion of 90 to 164, which is the average of 11 brands, is really between briquettes ¾ to ⅞ in. square, and briquettes 1 in. square, the frost specimens being weathered off.

It is reasonable, however, that a briquette 1 in. square, exposed on 3 sides to the direct action of the frost, is rather more severely tested than mortar would be if placed in a wall, even the bottoms of the briquettes resting freely on the stone window-sills were largely uninjured, and the centers of all the briquettes appeared uninjured. As a result of these experiments, the writer would feel perfectly safe in laying cement mortar in December, with Portland or active natural cements, in weather 10 to 15 degs. above zero, and in the most exposed situations, expecting in the spring, to find ¼ to ½ ins. disintegrated at exposed joints, and needing re-pointing, or better still, the pointing could be left till spring, and done once for all.

III. TWO MONTHS TESTS.

These tests were much more severe in their nature, the sand and cement were exposed for hours in the open air, in small quantities, until they were absolutely down to the temperature of the outer air, and in the cold water and salt water series the water was also exposed, until it was, in three cases, actually below the freezing point, being in a slushy condition.

These materials were put together in the laboratory, as rapidly as possible, and exposed again at once, the usual interval being about 6 minutes, and the actual temperature of the mortar just before exposure having reached about 33 or 34 degs. F., while in the hot water tests the mixture rose, on an average, to 58 or 60 degs., just before exposure, which was just about laboratory temperature.

The experiments are hardly extensive enough to be fully conclusive, being made only on 7 brands of cement, but they point clearly to the advantage of the use of salt. Those briquettes made with salt showed good strength and little injury; although made with materials, at low temperatures exposed in severe cold, they seemed to be chiefly affected only on the surface.

On the other hand, the use of hot water does not seem to be of any advantage, particularly in Portland cements; a reason advanced by one writer for this fact was, that the bringing together of materials in a mortar, at widely divergent temperatures, exerted a prejudicial effect on the cement, hindering proper crystallization, and that the use of materials, at, as nearly as possible, the same temperatures would produce more rapid and stronger action. The effect of hot water on natural cements is not so disappointing, but does not show much increase over the strength of similar specimens made with cold water.

The general result of these experiments, to the writer's mind, points to the idea that in any weather, in winter, not extremely cold, say not lower than + 15 degs. F., masonry work can be laid with cold sand, cold cement, and cold water, provided the natural time of set of the cement is not more than 5 or 6 hours, and that by the addition of about 2 or 3 per cent. of salt to the water, the same work may be done in weather down as low as zero, which is as cold as men will work. The disintegration will not extend probably deeper than ¼ to ½ ins.—the remainder of the mass being quite sound.

By what process cement sets, after it has, in a few minutes, been frozen solid, and remains frozen for months, the writer will leave to others to explain, but set it certainly does, without ever having been thawed out.

———

The following able and complete paper makes clear many of the points of the subject under discussion, and we are confident will be appreciated by engineers and cement testers generally.

By the courtesy of its author we are permitted to print it in full, together with drawings of his automatic cement testing machine, which, from its excellent construction, seems to leave little room for improvement.

REQUIREMENTS FOR TENSILE STRENGTH IN CEMENT SPECIFICATIONS.

BY J. M. PORTER, ASSOC. M. AM. SOC. C. E., PROFESSOR OF CIVIL ENGINEERING, LAFAYETTE COLLEGE, EASTON, PENN.

ON a recent piece of work embodying some 4,000 cu. yds. of concrete, of which the writer had charge, the cement specifications

— Result of Tensile Tests on the same sample of Cement —

— Made by different persons in accordance with their understanding of the method proposed by Committee of ".

Am. Soc. C.E.

One part cement to three parts sand. Briquettes one —

No.	Laboratory Name	Date	No.1	No.2	No.3	No.4	No.5	No.6	Mean	Rough marks in pounds	Ratio by compt. to mean	Maker %	Operator	Mixed off	Sieved in mesh	Maker gauge	Machine	Remarks
1	R. W. Hilgreth & Co. New York		68	72	74	78	82	–	75	14	111	30.4	13.4	Single	Publishing Railroad	J. Hill	Riehle Driven by hand	weights in both changed once
2	Washington University St. Louis Mo. Prof. J.B. Johnson		77	80	103	110	121	–	108	25	34.3	41.8	nor sand	Good	Man J. W. Plumen	J. Hill	Fairbanks Automatic Clip	
3	City of Easton Pa. by A. Fehr C. of E. Dept.		106	113	113	–	–	–	114	17	138	46.5	18.4	Single	Geo. Waldejoman	J. Hill	Fairbanks	
4	Columbia College New York Prof. W. H. Burr		125	126	130	137	140	144	133	15	154	34.0	15.0	Single	Man R. H. Putnam	Hill	Riehle Driven by hand	Water not changed
5	Chas. F. McKenna New York		116	132	138	144	150	153	140	37	171	34.8	8.0	Single	Geo. H. McKenna	Hill	Riehle Williams Power driven Rubber Clips	
6	Cornell University Francis Spalding		108	150	151	155	180	–	148	12	73	81.0	12.0	Single	Man Francis Spalding	Hill	Riehle driven Power driven Rubber Clips	speed 200 lbs per min. Flow of water in both slightly insufficient & cup of fresh
7	Lafayette College Easton Pa. J. M. Porter		171	172	173	176	173	–	176	8	45	7.4	11.0	Good	Man. Man.	Hill	Burn. Parker Rubber Clip	used spring on water, flowing into basket
8	Clifford Richardson Washington D.C.		220	214	214	220	210	–	217	9	35	211	10.0	Single	Man. Man.	Hill	Riehle Driven by hand Rubber Clips	speed 20 lb 60 per min.
9	Booth Garrett & Blair Philadelphia Pa.		240	240	245	240	211	–	207	12	48	100.0	12.0	Single	Both Sided Operators	J. Hill	Riehle Power driven Rubber Clip	
	Average								133	48.9	120	88.0	108					Note. All moulds and sand Am. Soc. C.E. Standard

called for, among other requirements, a tensile strength of 150 lbs. for one cement to three sand mortar at the age of seven days. The first shipment of cement received on the work was sampled and tested, and failed to fulfil the requirements for tensile strength, and the contractor was so notified. At the request of the cement manufacturers their representative tested the cement with a result about 15 per cent. below the result first obtained. The manufacturers again requested that a representative from a certain testing laboratory be allowed to make a test. This request was also granted, and the result obtained was over 50 per cent. in excess of the first test, and brought the cement beyond the requirements of the specifications. All these tests were made from the same sample of cement, using the same sand, mixed and molded in the same laboratory, and broken by the same machine. The writer knew that the " personal equation " was a more or less important factor in all testing, but had no idea of its great magnitude in cement testing.

To find what varying results different persons would obtain from the same sample of cement, the writer had ten samples taken from as many barrels of a certain brand of Portland cement. These samples were thoroughly mixed together and portioned into ten smaller samples of average quality, which were sent to ten different persons, with a request that a seven-day tensile test, one to three sand, be made according to their understanding of the method proposed by the Committee of American Society of Civil Engineers. The accompanying table gives the results obtained from nine different persons arranged according to their averages.

What value has a tensile requirement in cement specifications under the present method of testing when one person obtains 30 lbs. and another 100 lbs. as a result upon the same sample? The cement which one engineer would accept would be rejected by another under the same specifications. Where do the contractor and cement manufacturer stand in this matter? The writer knows that cement can be made to stand almost any tensile requirement within reasonable limits that would ordinarily be made by varying the method of mixing and molding, but when the mixing and molding are supposed to be done in accordance with a given method and yet the results vary widely, either the method is at fault or the results have no value unless weighed by the varying personal equation of the manipulator.

View of fractured sections of Cement Briquettes of the same composition and molded by the same method but by different persons. Numbers on right of horizontal rows indicate number of Laboratory where briquettes were made.

It may be said that when an engineer prepares his specifications for cement, he knows how much he can obtain from a good cement in the way of tensile strength. If this is the case he certainly must have had one or more brands in mind at the time of writing the specifications. Then why not specify the brands, stating chemical limits, time of setting, specific gravity, etc.? The objection to this method is that a given brand of cement will vary in tensile strength. Does any one suppose, however, that a well-established brand will drop much over 70 per cent. from the requirements that an engineer would ordinarily specify? According to the accompanying table the brand could drop that amount before it would be rejected by some other engineer under the same specifications.

The writer had two men in his employ, both equally skilled in cement testing, make a tensile test on five briquettes, one to three sand, on the same sample of cement. The tests were made in the same laboratory, the mixing and molding being done at the same time and the same bath was used, thus eliminating all atmospheric and water conditions. The results were to each other as 85 to 100; and if the lower one had been taken the cement would have fallen below requirements, while taking the higher result, the cement would have passed. The question was, which result to adopt? Again, two men employed by the same cement manufacturers, and accustomed to making cement tests for their employers, made five briquettes each from the same sample of cement. The briquettes were broken by the same machine and operator with results standing as 58 to 100. All of the before-mentioned tests were made upon a sand mixture of three to one, and it might be said that if neat tests had been made closer results would have been obtained. This brings up the question as to the relative value of sand tests *vs.* neat tests, in which the writer favors the former, as they conform more nearly to practise. A given person skilled in cement testing can obtain results from the same sample of cement under normal conditions using the present method of testing within 5 per cent. of the mean value.

The writer knows a cement inspector in one of the larger cities who is frequently compelled to go out on work, take a large number of samples, return to his laboratory with possibly 25 to 30 lbs. of cement, and then go to work and make one hundred briquettes. Does any one suppose the last briquette made received the same

View of fractured sections of Cement Briquettes of the same composition and molded by the same method but by different persons. Numbers on right of horizontal rows indicate number of Laboratory where briquettes were made.

work as the first one, or the first one the treatment that would have been given it if a fewer number of briquettes had been required? This is probably an extreme case, but, nevertheless, cements stand or fall upon this inspector's report.

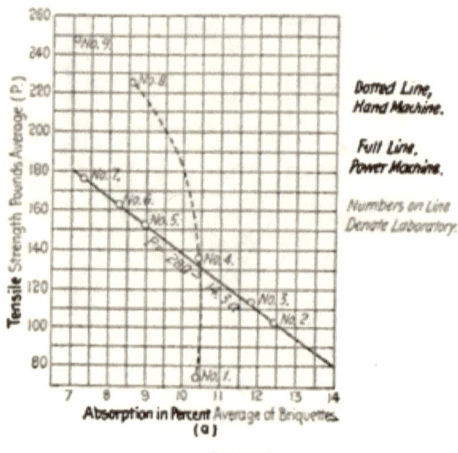

Accompanying the table is a diagram (Fig. 1) showing the relation between the percentage of absorption of the broken briquettes and their tensile strength. The relation of the briquettes broken by power-driven machines is rather striking. The term

FIG. 1.

Diagram showing relation between absorption and tensile strength of cement briquettes broken by automatic and hand machines.

" power-driven " is applied to any testing machine which applies the load other than by hand.

Upon examination of the broken briquettes, all of which had been returned, it was noticed that they had varied greatly in density In a letter accompanying the report from one of the laboratories, it was stated : —

FIG. 2.

Difference in density of two cement briquettes of the same composition and molded by the same method but by different persons.

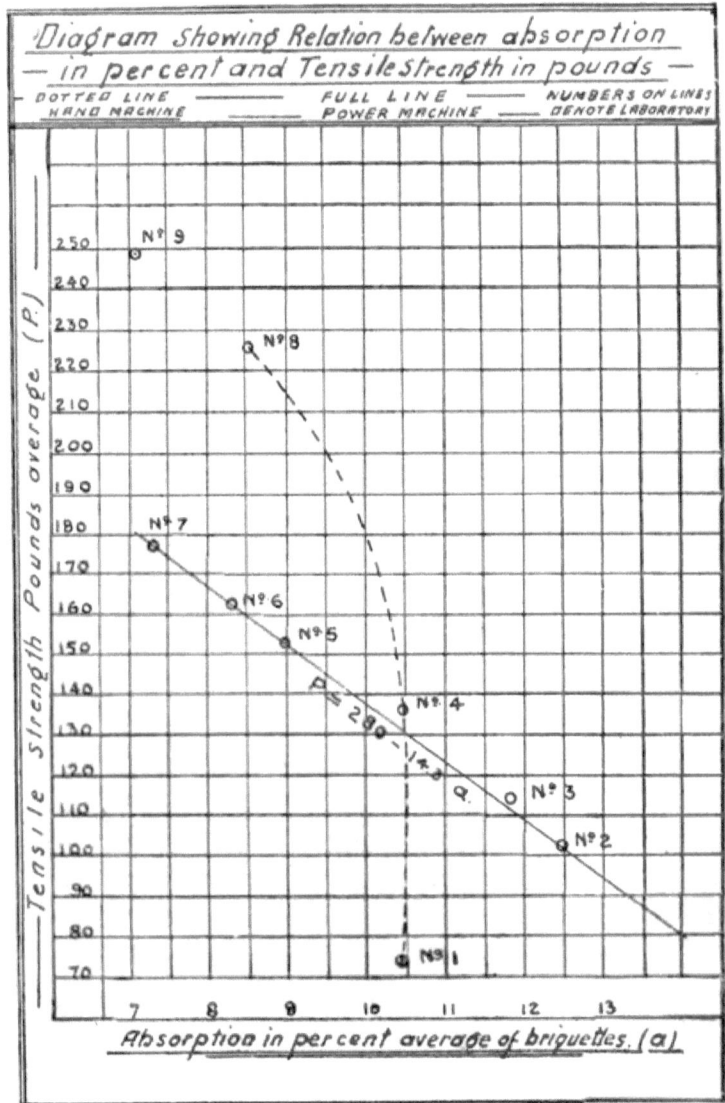

Diagram Showing Relation between absorption
— in percent and Tensile Strength in pounds —

DOTTED LINE ——————— FULL LINE ——————— NUMBERS ON LINES
HAND MACHINE   ————————   POWER MACHINE   ———— DENOTE LABORATORY

The quartz grains are so nearly of one size that the volume of voids left to be filled by the cement is excessive. If the sand (or quartz) were of graduated sizes the cement would be used wholly for coating the grains and not for filling relatively larger voids. In this case the broken briquettes show clearly that the cement was quite insufficient to fill the voids, as the briquettes are quite open and porous.

The briquettes mentioned were extremely porous, while others were quite dense.

Fig. 2, reproduced directly from a photograph showing a very dense and a very porous briquette, illustrates the point brought out above quite clearly. The most porous briquette is shown at the right, and is from laboratory No. 1. The left-hand briquette is from laboratory No. 7.

The percentage of absorption of the broken briquettes was assumed as a measure of their density, and was obtained by allowing the briquettes to remain in a dry room for two weeks or more, then placing them in an oven having a temperature of 100 degs. C. They were taken out of the oven at the end of two hours and carefully weighed, then placed in water for 48 hours, removed and again carefully weighed. The absorption was computed in per cent. of the original weight and averaged.

The tensile strength of the briquettes broken by power-driven machines, with one exception, follows very closely $P = 280 - 14.3\,a$, where P is the tensile strength in pounds and a the percentage of absorption, obtained as above stated. From this relation, it would seem, if percentage of absorption is any measure of density, that the mortar for these briquettes received about the same mixing, and that the variance in tensile strength is due to the molding alone. While this may be true for the briquettes in question, the writer does not believe it true in general, as the mixing of mortar for briquettes is too important a factor to be decided one way or another by so few comparisons.

The percentage of water used by the different manipulators in making the briquettes varied 33⅓ per cent., due to the operators' varying understanding of the term " stiff and plastic " in connection with temperature. In one case a decrease of 20 per cent. in water gave an increase in tensile strength of 5.2 per cent.

Single molds were decidedly in favor, only two out of nine per-

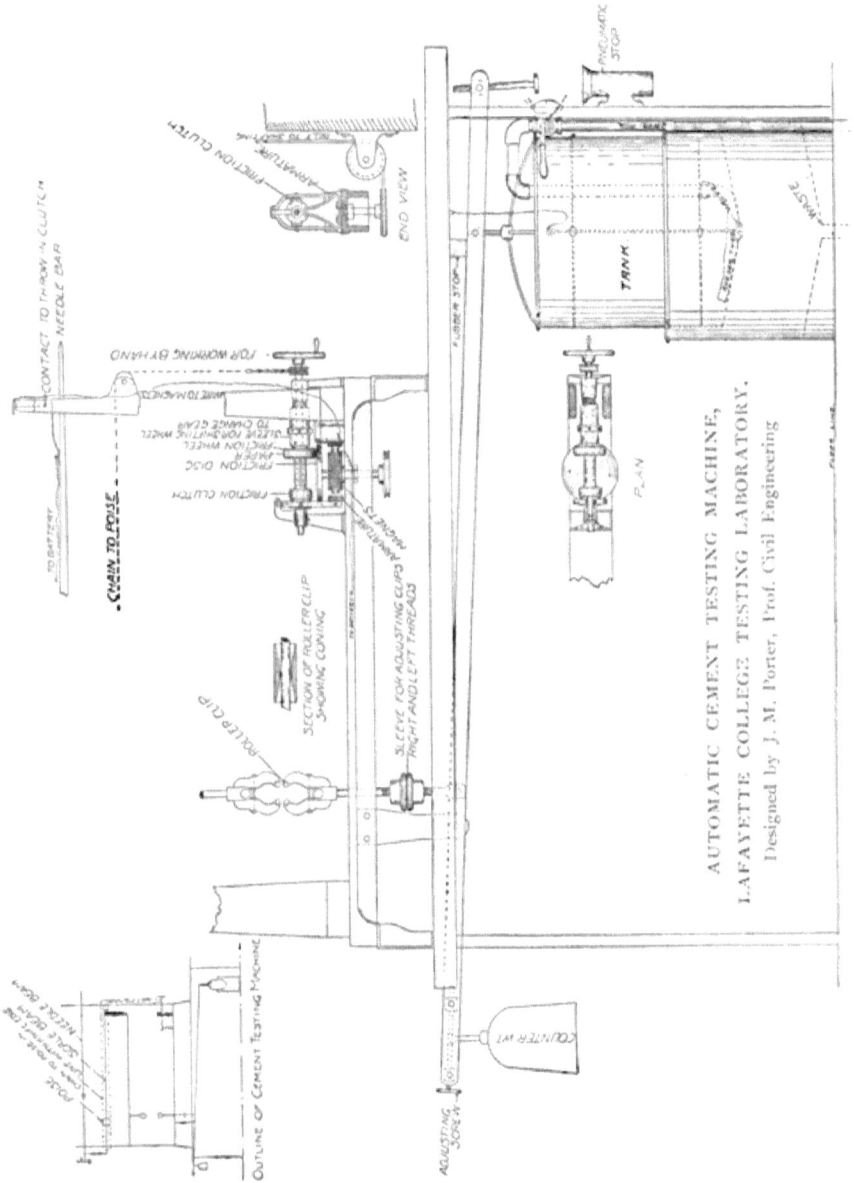

AUTOMATIC CEMENT TESTING MACHINE,
LAFAYETTE COLLEGE TESTING LABORATORY.

Designed by J. M. Porter, Prof. Civil Engineering

sons using gang molds. The writer believes it possible to obtain higher results from single than from gang molds, but if both were to be treated the same, the results would differ but slightly. A letter from one of the laboratories stated that results were about the same whichever molds were used. A person having a large number of briquettes to make will find, without doubt, that gang molds are preferable.

The term " struck off " seems to mean that both sides of the briquette are to receive that treatment ; at least, two out of every three operators so interpret it. There is not much doubt but that a given amount of work distributed equally over two sides will give a denser briquette than if one side only received the whole of it. Working both sides of a briquette gives a more homogeneous cross-section, which is as important as uniformity of the several briquettes, particularly when it is remembered that the load in testing is applied at four points.

The placing of the briquette in water flatwise seems to be the favored position. The writer, however, prefers placing them in water on edge, as more surface is exposed to the direct action of the water. The objection to this method is the danger of the briquette changing form under the action of its own weight. The writer never has had any trouble from this cause, nor does he know of any one else who has had any.

Still water for the bath seems to be in almost general use. This is probably due to the difficulty and expense of having running water, which no doubt would be preferred if a choice were given. The practise of using the same still-water bath over and over again cannot be too strongly condemned. The writer knows of laboratories where this is common practise, and where fresh water is added in quantities sufficient only to replace that lost by evaporation. In running-water baths, the supply should be so arranged as not to come directly upon the immersed briquettes. This latter point is also often overlooked.

Power-driven testing machines are decidedly in the majority. The writer believes that hand-driven machines should be entirely abandoned, as it is about all an ordinary mortal can do to handle one crank without being compelled to take care of two. In power-driven machines the writer prefers those applying the load by the weight of water or shot to those applying the load by means of a screw driven by gearing and belts, as he believes the former to give a more uniform rate of increase. Fig. 3 shows the construction of the machine designed by the writer.

The load is applied by water flowing into a tank suspended from the long arm of a very sensitive 15 to 1 lever. The weight of the lever and tank is counterbalanced by an adjustable weight shown on the left. Water is admitted to the tank from a large reservoir on the roof under a practically constant head of 90 ft., so there is no sensible variation of pressure in the stream admitted through a carefully fitted gate valve in the supply pipe. The position of this valve at " on," " off," and all intermediate points is shown by an index attached to the stem of the valve and registering on a dial marked off with the number of pounds per minute applied to the specimen as determined and verified by previous experiment.

When the briquettes break the lever drops a few inches, then the plunger at the right end of the lever enters the pneumatic stop, and the lever and tank are gradually brought to rest. During the fall of the tank and before it comes to rest, a chain attached to the end of the valve stem in the tank is brought into tension and arrests the descent of the valve before its seat stops descending. The opening of this valve allows the contents of the tank to be quickly discharged into a hopper placed upon the floor, and is then carried off through a waste pipe to the sewer. As soon as the tank has discharged its contents, the weight on the left end of the lever brings the lever and tank into the position shown in the illustration, the valve taking its seat during this movement and the machine is ready for another break. The actual load can be applied at from 0 to 80 lbs. per minute, thus giving an increase of stress of from 0 to 1,200 lbs. per minute. The speed generally used is 400 lbs. per minute, and with the valve set for this speed the needle beam will float every time within $\frac{1}{5}$ second of the proper time.

The stress on the specimen is measured by a poise traveling on a graduated scale beam, which can be read by means of a vernier to 1 lb. and can be moved automatically or by hand at the wish of the operator. The automatic movement is accomplished by the following described device : —

The horizontal disk and its engaged friction wheel are driven continuously by the pulley placed at the lower end of the vertical shaft and belted to overhead shafting. This friction wheel is feathered to a sleeve that runs loose on its shaft and carries a coned clutch that is nominally disengaged from its cone, which is also feathered to the shaft, and can be moved slightly longitudinally on the shaft into contact with the clutch by the action of the vertical lever.

When the needle beam rises, it makes contact through a vertical pin in the top of the frame, which completes an electric circuit and sends a current through the electro-magnet and causes it to attract its armature at the lower end of the vertical lever, which, moving to the right, engages the friction clutch and causes the shaft to revolve. This shaft operates the sprocket wheel and chain, which draw out the poise on the scale beam until the needle beam drops, breaking the electric circuit. Breaking the electric circuit releases the armature and allows the friction clutch to disengage and the poise comes to rest. The friction wheel may be set at a greater or less distance from the center of the disk by turning the capstan head nut, and the chain is overhauled faster or slower, causing the poise to move accordingly. If desired, the poise may be operated by the hand wheel without interfering with the automatic device other than cutting out the circuit. The chain is attached to the poise in line with the three knife-edges of the scale beam, hence the tension in the chain has no tendency to lift up or pull down the poise. This point is often overlooked in designing this detail, not only in cement machines but in testing machines in general. The writer has a cement machine in which the error due to this cause is over 15 lbs.

This machine, as described, has been in almost constant use for eighteen months and has given entire satisfaction. The operator has simply to place the briquette in the clips, open the supply valve, wait until the briquette breaks, and then note the reading on the scale beam. The objection to this machine is the space it occupies, requiring a floor area of 7 by 2 ft., and the necessity of a constant head of water.

From the figures given in the table it is evident that the personal equation is a decidedly important factor in cement testing, and before tensile requirements in specifications can have any meaning, a method must be adopted that will considerably reduce or entirely eliminate this factor. With this in view, the following requirements are suggested : —

1. Mixing and tempering by machinery, using enough mixture to make a given number of briquettes.

2. Molding under a given pressure.

3. Regulation in regard to the bath and manner of placing briquettes in the same.

4. Abolishing the use of all testing machines applying the load by hand.

THE FAIRBANKS CEMENT TESTING MACHINE.

The great necessity and importance that all cement used in any given work should be of a uniform quality and strength are facts well understood by all contractors and builders.

It was not, however, until the introduction of the Fairbanks Testing Machine, some twelve years ago, that it became an easy and convenient matter to quickly and accurately test any sample of cement required, the machine being automatic in its operation, and so compact that it may be placed on a small table, or shelf, in any office. In the machine as shown in the accompanying illustration are embodied some recent patents, the most important of which are the adjustable clamps, N. N., hung on steel points and ball bearings. Their bearing surfaces are free to adjust themselves quickly and accurately in any direction to the slight inequalities of the briquette, without any lost motion, so that the briquette, under tension, will be broken fairly in its smallest section.

In the illustration S. represents the mold in which the sample briquette is made, the mold being laid on a smooth board or glass plate and filled with mixed cement, when the top is struck off even with the top of the mold. After the cement has set sufficiently, the fastenings at the ends are loosened, and the mold is carefully taken away from the specimen. To make the test, the cup, F., is hung on the beam, D., as shown; the poise R., placed at the zero mark; the beam balanced by turning the ball, L., and a hopper, B., at the top, filled with fine shot. The molded sample of cement, U., is then placed in the clamps, and the hand-wheel, P., is adjusted, so that the graduated beam, D., rises nearly to the stop K. A valve, J., is then opened to allow the shot to run into the cup, F., through the pipe, I., the shot continuing to run until the specimen is broken by the drawing down of the graduated beam, when the flow is automatically cut off by the valve. The valve itself forms one of the recent improvements of the machine, as it may be adjusted to permit of a larger or a smaller flow of shot, and the point of cut-off is arranged

THE FAIRBANKS CEMENT TESTING MACHINE.

at the discharge end of the pipe, making the weight of shot delivered to the cup correspond more closely to the movement of the beam. After the specimen is broken, the cup, F., is hung on the hook under the large ball, E., and the shot is weighed in the regular way, using the poise R., on the graduated beam, and the weights

H., on the counter-poise weight, G., the result showing the number of pounds required to break the specimen.

The briquette molds form the samples to be tested of the exact size and dimensions called for by the American Society of Civil Engineers, having 1 sq. in. as their smallest section. The briquettes are about 2 ins. wide at each end, and, with very slightly rounding outer surfaces, taper inward toward the middle, with a form admirably adapted to be firmly engaged by the clamps without the binding of the latter on any special line. The improved clamps hold the briquettes in a manner superior to cushioned clamps, and the action of the machine is strictly automatic while the test is being made, there being no parts of the machine to be moved, thereby avoiding danger from sudden jarring, which might break the sample before reaching the limit of its strength. The machines have no springs or hydraulic appliances to get out of order, but are constructed with levers, steel pivots, and bearings strictly on the principle of the most improved weighing apparatus.

The Fairbanks Company make machines in two sizes, one to test up to 600 lbs., and the one shown in our illustration, in which tests are made up to 1,000 lbs. A mold is furnished with each machine.

THE RIEHLE U. S. STANDARD CEMENT TESTING MACHINE.

The cement tester represented is one of 1,000 lbs. capacity. It resembles, in many respects, a similar type machine of 2,000 lbs. capacity. The general appearance is the same, but the beam and corresponding parts of the larger capacity machine are heavier and slightly larger. The extreme length of this machine is 6 ft. 2½ ins.; extreme height, 5 ft.; extreme width, 2 ft. The 1,000 lb. machine is capable of testing cement briquettes with reduced section of 1 in. area. The molds are adapted to the A. S. C. E. standard. All the weight of this machine is on *one beam*. The poise is propelled the entire length of beam by a hand wheel shown at the extreme left — at the butt end of the beam. The power is applied by a crank, worm, and gear, shown to the extreme left of the machine. The specimen being in position, the power being applied, the beam raises, and the indicator point shown also at the extreme left of the machine at upper part, falls. The experimenter can operate the machine with his left hand on the crank, and his right propelling the poise. After a little practise, the operator can become sufficiently

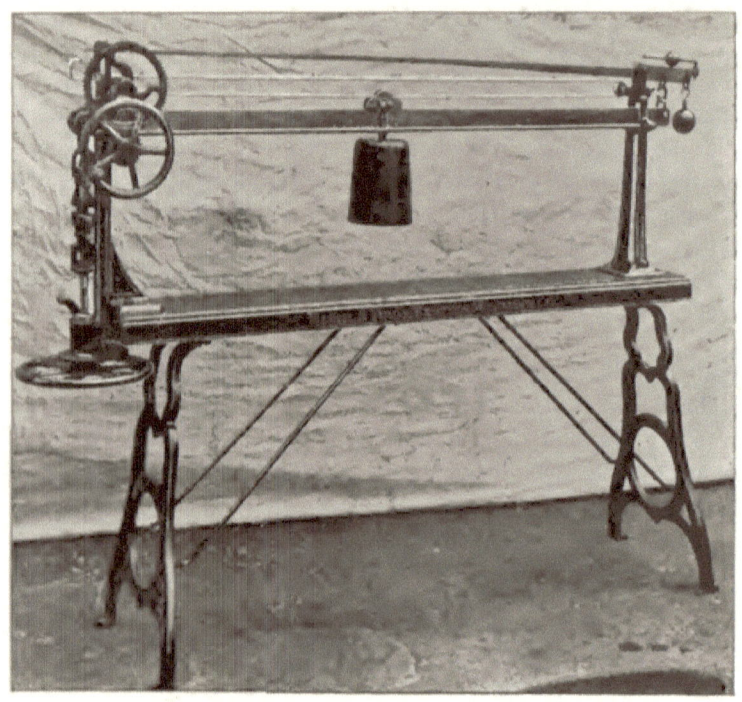

THE RIEHLE UNITED STATES STANDARD CEMENT TESTING
MACHINE.

expert to keep the beam in exact equipoise. The top indicating beam is about on a level with the eye of the operator, and he can quickly see whether the strain applied to specimen, and the weighing of the same are progressing in harmony.

This machine was designed after a thorough examination of the most approved forms of cement testers in use in this country and in Europe, with additions and improvements introduced by us to suit the requirements of American engineers and manufacturers.

The marks on the beam run up to the full capacity without having to move the poise back and add additional weights.

To make the machine more compact than the standard necessitates the use of a complication of leverage, which tends to effect the accuracy of the machine. All appliances of this kind have been studiously avoided by us, as the nature of the material to be tested does not admit of a sacrifice of accuracy to possible convenience. This machine is not automatic, but responds to every call made upon it up to full capacity, with an accuracy that does not admit of adverse criticism. The arrangement of the grips on this machine, "swinging them on pin points," is used only on this machine, and requires no explanation or comments, as the advantages are perfectly apparent to any one who knows the inaccurate results consequent upon gripping a briquette of cement otherwise than on a "dead straight line," which is impossible with "pin point grips."

This machine can be arranged to make crushing tests, but we do not recommend the 1,000 lb. machine for that purpose, as it is not heavy enough. By proper appliances one can make transverse tests, also torsional tests. These latter tests have not been receiving as much attention as the former, but are now demanding attention, and will shortly be universally considered and required.

THE CUMMINGS HYDROSTATIC CEMENT TESTING MACHINE.

The Cummings Hydrostatic Cement Testing Machine was devised by the author, and is represented in two styles of construction.

The vertical machine is provided with two pistons, while the horizontal machine contains but one.

It is evident that the capacity of these machines is governed by the area of the piston or pistons which impel the movable jaw or clamp.

The dimensions of the vertical machine are: Length, 6 ins.; breadth, 4¼ ins., and height, 6 ins. Capacity, 300 lbs. Total weight, 13 lbs.

The dimensions of the horizontal machine are: Length, 9½ ins.; breadth, 4¾ ins., and height, 4⅜ ins. Capacity, 1,500 lbs. Total weight, 20 lbs.

These machines are nickel plated, and are an ornament in any office.

The liquid used in these machines is glycerin, which insures against injury by exposure in freezing weather.

The hights given are exclusive of the gages.

The pressure on the pistons is produced by turning the crank,

CUMMINGS HYDROSTATIC CEMENT TESTER, CAPACITY 300 POUNDS.

which is attached to a screw-threaded stem, to which is attached a piston of smaller area than those which impel the movable jaw.

The pressure is registered by a gage, the accuracy of the latter being confirmed by a column of mercury.

The stem of the gage is provided with a valve which prevents a too rapid return of the indicator hand to zero upon release of the breaking strain, and each gage has a maximum registering hand.

The strain applied in the breaking of the briquettes is exactly at right angles to the one-inch cross section.

This is an important feature, as usually the direction of the breaking strain is left to accidental adjustment in the machines having the jaws or clamps secured by links.

A briquette which, by reason of its having been removed from the mold before it has hardened sufficiently to maintain its perfect shape, cannot be accurately tested in any known testing machine,

CUMMINGS HYDROSTATIC CEMENT TESTER, CAPACITY 1,500 POUNDS.

whether the jaws be rigid or held by links or points, and such briquettes should always be rejected.

The supposition that in the construction of the hydrostatic testing machines they would be subject to a certain amount of friction, due to the contact of the pistons on the inner surfaces of the cylinders, for which allowance would have to be made, was disproved in actual practise, by the breakings of many thousands of briquettes, made from the same cement, by the same **person, in the same room,** and running through a term of years.

The briquettes were broken alternately on the Fairbanks, the Riehlé and the Cummings machines, and the variation in average results was surprisingly slight, proving conclusively that the factor of friction could not obtain, as there could be no friction **without** motion, and **no motion is** possible until after the **fracture** of the briquette.

At **all events, the records of breakings** showed no higher results **for the hydrostatic** machines than for either of the other **two machines named. ***

Although the utilization of natural cement rock for Portland purposes is not **practised to any great extent in Europe, owing, no doubt,** to the uneven quality of such rocks, yet in this country **more than** two thirds of the Portland **cement** produced is from this source.

Limestone to the extent of 10 to 15 per cent. is added to the cement rock, which, in the section where such Portlands are manufactured, contains an **excess of clay.**

Portland cements **produced** in this manner are fully equal in quality to those which **are** compounded by an **artificial admixture of** clay and carbonate **of lime,** and it may be said, in passing, that there are no Portland cements in **the world superior to those produced in** this country.

The consumer who uses imported brands in preference **does so** at his own risk, for no manufacturer in Europe guarantees the quality **of his cement after it is delivered into** this country. The Portland producers here guarantee their product, as do the Rock cement **manu-**facturers, and they are here on the **ground ready at** all times to make good any damage which may be caused by the **failure of their** cements.

And yet, at **the** present **time, there are** three barrels of imported Portland used in this country to one of our home production. Such **is** prejudice. Still, it is pleasing to note that it is gradually dying out, and it **is to be** hoped that the time is not far distant when American Portlands will be used in preference to those from other **countries.**

---

* The foregoing descriptions of cement testing machines were prepared by those who control the respective inventions.

If we take a few pounds of correctly proportioned cement rock in one piece, and divide it into two equal parts, and designate them as samples No. 1 and No. 2, and take No. 1 and calcine it, and then grind it to powder, we have converted it into a natural hydraulic cement.

If we take sample No. 2 and first grind it to powder, and then calcine it, and again reduce it to powder, we have converted it into a Portland cement. This comprises all the difference in the manufacture of the Rock and Portland cements.

Now if we mold these samples separately into briquettes and submit them to a tensile strain test per square inch of cross section, treating them alike as to time in air and in water, it is probable that when tabulated they would appear about as shown in the following table, provided, of course, that both samples had been calcined in accordance with the methods now in vogue by the manufacturers of each class.

TABLE A.

Time.	Lbs. 1 Day.	Lbs. 1 Week.	Lbs. 1 Month.	Lbs. 6 Months.	Lbs. 1 Year.
No. 1	65	175	175	350	500
No. 2	125	400	500	750	1,000

Granting that this table is approximately correct, and we have a large collection of tables gathered from many sources which substantially verify the figures given, what are the conclusions to be drawn therefrom ?

If the actual values are to be measured by the pounds in tensile strength which the briquettes are capable of sustaining, and this is the prevailing belief at the present time, and has prevailed during the past thirty-five years, it would seem indisputable that up to one year No. 1 had but one half the value of No. 2.

It is safe to assert that not one engineer or architect in a thousand carries his tests beyond one year.

It is equally safe to assert that not one in a hundred carries tests beyond three months.

It is not difficult then to understand, in the light of the table given, how the prevailing opinion became so firmly established.

The idea that the higher the test the greater the value has come to be firmly fixed in the public opinion as being sound beyond question.

The manufacturer whose cement tests higher than that of his neighbor in a one or thirty day test, wears an air of superiority which is simply indescribable.

It is settled in his mind that his cement is better than that of his neighbor.

And the neighbor who is defeated in the test is correspondingly depressed. He has a feeling akin to that of the speculator in Buffalo, N. Y., who walked across the road to bestow a kick on a certain sleeping omniverous mammal lying in the gutter, because pork had taken a drop in the market that day.

And well may the defeated cement maker feel somewhat depressed, for the chances are ten to one that the engineer who made the tests believes the higher testing brand the better of the two.

It does not follow that the lower testing cement is the better, although it is not impossible, by any means. Neither does it follow that the same results would obtain had some other engineer tested the same brands from the same packages.

But in the table we have another problem to deal with. Here the two classes are made from identically the same material, and the differences in the testing can only be attributable to the different modes of manufacture.

The Portland cement has set much more rapidly than the other during the first year, and it is this fact alone that has brought almost, if not quite, all the cement-making and cement-using world to believe that Portland cement is vastly superior to the Rock cement.

The question arises as to whether or not the prevailing opinion is founded on fact. If the answer is confined to the one year's showing, then it must be said that the opinion is sound.

But if the public could be brought to realize that one year is but the beginning of the test, that the real trial is but fairly started, and is on, so long as the work endures in which the cement is used; if it were understood that after five years not one engineer in a hundred can tell either by simply looking at a wall laid in cement, or by the use of the hammer, whether the cement used was Rock or Portland cement, and if it were known that it is a fact, that when we have occasion to blast out old concrete laid in Rock cement twenty-five years before, we find it as hard as any rock ; and if it were possible for the public to become as familiar with three to five year tests as they are with the prevailing tests, then there would be a remarkable overturning of preconceived notions in regard to cement values, and thinking men would undertake a readjustment of their opinions, for nothing is more certain than that if the samples Nos. 1 and 2 of the table given were carried along in the tests yearly from one year to five, the table A continued, would appear substantially as follows : —

TABLE B.

Time.	2 Years.	3 Years.	4 Years.	5 Years.
No. 1	700	800	900	1,000
No. 2	1,000	800	750	600

The following table of tests was made by C. E. Richards, cement tester on the new Croton Aqueduct at Brewster, N. Y., from American Rock cement manufactured by the author.

Briquettes one square inch in cross section, one hour in air, balance of time in water.

No. of Briquette.	Time when Made.	Time when Broken.	Tensile Strength lbs.
1	Oct. 4, 1886.	Nov. 18, 1889.	910
2	Oct. 11, 1886.	Nov. 18, 1889.	860
3	Oct. 11, 1886.	Nov. 18, 1889.	960
4	Nov. 29, 1886.	Nov. 18, 1889.	960
5	Nov. 21, 1886.	Nov. 18, 1889.	Unbroken at 1,000 pounds.
6	Nov. 30, 1886.	Nov. 18, 1889.	Unbroken at 1,000 pounds.

The Riehlé 1,000 pound testing machine used.

The following is an extract from " Records of Tests of Cement," made for the Boston Main Drainage Works, 1878–1884, by Eliot C. Clarke, M. Am. Soc. C. E., page 160 : —

" The following series of tests may be of interest on account of the age of the specimens. The mortars were made with an English Portland cement, both unsifted as taken from the cask, and also after it had been sifted through the No. 120 sieve, by which process about 35 per cent. of coarse particles were eliminated.

TABLE NO. 12.

BRIQUETTES I SQUARE INCH CROSS SECTION.

Kind of Cement.	Neat Cement.		Cement 1. Sand 2.		Cement 1. Sand 5.	
	2 Years.	4 Years.	2 Years.	4 Years.	2 Years.	4 Years.
Ordinary cement unsifted.	603	387	339	491	182	202
Cement which passed No. 120 sieve.	374	211	478	580	250	284

" This table also shows that fine cements do not give as high results, tested neat, as do cements containing coarse particles, even coarse particles of sand. It also shows (what is often noticed) that neat cements become brittle with age, and are apt to fly into pieces under comparatively light loads."

It cannot be denied that at five years artificial cements are extremely brittle, and briquettes made from this class of cements, if let fall on a stone floor, after they are four or five years old, will fly into as many pieces as would a glass bottle falling from the same hight, and this is not true of the better quality of Rock cements.

But engineers tell us that they cannot wait five years, or five months even, to learn whether a cement is good or bad, which is true enough, but does not alter the facts in the case ; and the facts are that very high short-time tests are unfailing evidences of subsequent weakness.

These facts are demonstrated in every table wherein the tests have been carried from one day to five years, that has ever come under the observation of the author.

The following is an extract from a lecture delivered by the author before the Society of Arts of the Massachusetts Institute of Technology, Boston, November, 1887 : —

" The testing machine reveals many curious freaks, and taken on the principle that " everything is for the best," it may yet reveal to us that a cement may test too high, that this modern demand for high-testing cement, and the tremendous struggle on the part of the Portland cement manufacturers to supply it, striving by every conceivable means to beat the record, is all wrong.

" This may sound strangely at first, but a study of the tables of

long-time tests of Portland cements, as compiled by such engineers as
Clarke, of Boston, and MacClay, of New York, and others eminent
in the profession, reveals the rather startling fact that briquettes of
neat Portland do not test as high at three or four years as they do at
one or two years old.   Clarke says : —

"' They become brittle with age and are apt to fly into pieces under
comparatively light loads.'

" If this is the result with neat cement at that age, what is to prevent
the same results with sand mixtures at fifteen to twenty years or so?

"The ten years' tests of Portland cement, made by Dr.
Michaelis, of Berlin, show that the maximum strength was reached
at the end of two years, and this point held fairly well until the end
of the seventh year; but from that time until the end of the tenth
year there was a remarkable falling off in values.   We do not recol-
lect ever having seen any table of long-time tests of Portland cement
that did not exhibit similar results, and it is more than probable that
it may yet be shown that our best natural, slow-setting American
cements may, in ten to twelve years' tests, surpass any artificial
cements.   The excellent condition of some of our old work, done
many years ago with American cements, would seem to indicate as
much.

" At all events, we have no proof that the Portland is superior
in the matter of durability, and we do not believe that clay and lime
can be suddenly thrown together, and kept there by any skill of man,
that can, in any manner, compare with the staying qualities as found
in first-class natural cements, where the clay and lime have existed in
the most intimate contact for countless ages."

It is now over nine years since the foregoing was written, and
in the meantime the only changes in the views of the author on this
subject have been to strengthen rather than to weaken the proposition then advanced.

Years of close observation as to the changes constantly occurring in a cement subsequent to its use in masonry or concrete leads
to the inevitable conclusion that a cement which hardens too rapidly
in its early stages, whether it may be a natural rock or an artificial
cement, should be looked upon with suspicion rather than with
approval.

It is patent to every observer who has had occasion to examine briquettes made from both classes, and broken at three to five years, that those which by the records are shown to have tested high in their early stages are at a later period extremely brittle and glassy, and are entirely devoid of that peculiar toughness which characterizes the slower setting varieties.

A cement which attains its limit of tensile strength rapidly will, the moment that limit is reached, commence to become brittle, and from that time on there will be a continual loss in cohesive strength in direct ratio with its increasing brittleness.

Brittleness and weakness are synonymous.

Mr. C. H. Brinsmaid, city cement inspector, City Engineer Department, Minneapolis, Minn., has had twelve years' experience in cement testing in the department named, and has compiled some valuable tables of tests, some brands of Portland running as high as nine years.

In a correspondence with the author, he remarks incidentally : — " Lacking experience, nothing would surprise me more than to see how very brittle these old Portland samples become, and how they snap and fly into fragments by a blow of trowel or hammer. There is no question but that old Portlands are more brittle than Rock cements of the same age, however difficult it may be to note the proper comparison."

In Mr. Brinsmaid's tables of neat Portland tests, the figures disclose that three of the leading German and five of the English Portlands reach their limit of strength at one year, after which time they begin to deteriorate, at seven years the German falling to 476 lbs., and the English to 592 lbs.

Referring to the table (A) continued, it is pertinent to repeat the question, " What are the conclusions to be drawn ? "

Both No. 1 and No. 2 are produced from identically the same materials and in the same proportions, but No. 1 being a solid rock, and No. 2 a porous mass, they are not affected equally by the same amount of heat, and it is from this cause alone that one hardens much more rapidly than the other, and consequently tests higher in its early stages. But that is no evidence of superiority, notwithstanding public opinion to the contrary.

There are certain classes of work wherein it may be necessary to use the higher testing varieties, such, for example, as sidewalks and similar work, but for heavy foundations and massive masonry, to use the higher priced cement, simply because it tests higher in short time tests, is expensive folly, for the slower setting variety, or, in other words, the natural rock cements, have been successfully used in the heaviest masonry in the world.

It is well understood that the process of hardening of a cement is simply the crystallization of the silicates, which commences shortly after they have become hydrated by the application of water. Some hydrated silicates crystallize much more rapidly than others.

Rapid crystallization means imperfect crystallization, uneven in size, shape, and texture. In fact, a mere jumble of irregular crystals, and the very rapidity of their formation insures subsequent brittleness and weakness, while those silicates which crystallize slowly form crystals perfect in shape, size, and texture.

Dana, in his " Manual of Geology," page 627, in speaking of the texture of rocks, says: " The grains are coarser the slower the crystallization, or, in other words, the slower the rate of cooling during crystallization ; and with rapid cooling, they sometimes disappear altogether, and the material comes out glass instead of stone."

So in the crystallization of the silicates in a cement. If it tests high in its early stages, the breakings of the briquettes disclose the glassy texture, which is quite unlike the stone-like texture exhibited in the slower varieties.

It is possible, then, that the testing machine may yet be the means of convincing the public that a cement may test too high, as stated in the quotation of nine years ago.

The author does not consider it wild or extravagant to assert it as his deliberate opinion that the specifications drawn by the engineer of the future will stipulate that the cement to be used shall not exceed nor fall below a given number of pounds in tensile strength per square inch in cross section at one, seven, thirty, and ninety days.

When that day arrives there will cease this unseemly scramble for high short-time tests. Reason and common sense will prevail, guided by a practical knowledge of the chemistry of cements.

It is not the purpose of the author to disparage or discredit Portland cements, but rather to point out their defects, in the hope that in so doing, more consideration may be given to the subject, and juster conclusions reached.

Unquestionably an ideal hydraulic cement can be produced by what is known as the Portland process, and there is but little doubt it would have been much in use at the present time, had it not been for the unfortunate misinterpretation of the readings of the tensile strain-testing machine in the early stages of its existence.

At the time of its first introduction into England, Portland cements were selling at one shilling per bushel, and rock cements were selling at eighteen pence per bushel.

Such was the public opinion as to the relative values of the two classes of cements sixty-two years after Parker had brought out his Roman (Rock) cement, and thirty-four years after Aspdin had produced his artificial (Portland) cement.

Even at the difference in prices, the Roman cement had by far the larger share of the market, and the only means of ascertaining the relative values was by the behavior of the cements in actual work, and making such tests as placing balls of the cement under water.

Then came the tensile strain-testing machine, and it was soon ascertained that the Portland brands tested higher than the Roman cements.

It must have been an important event, an epoch, in fact, in the lives of those engineers, to be confronted with the revelations disclosed by the testing machine.

They had been using both classes of cements, and the Rock cements stood, if the price is any criterion, 50 per cent. higher in their estimation than the Portland cements. And yet the testing machine showed them that the Portland cements were the stronger, and so, they reasoned, that if stronger, they must be better. Therefore they had been laboring under a hallucination for, lo, these many years.

Judging by their experience in the use of both classes, the cement which had seemed to them to be the best, that had given them the least trouble, was not the best, after all.

They never questioned the soundness, or rather unsoundness, of their new-found scheme for determining values.

It did not occur to them that the higher testing cement was not necessarily the better cement, and they accepted the result as indisputable.

With their former teachings and experience on the one hand, and the testing machine on the other, the question was not long in doubt. The machine was victorious, and thenceforward all judgment founded on experience was laid aside, and they became blind believers in the tensile strain tests.

What matter though they were continually befogged by the frequent, unreasonable, and capricious pranks of the machine, they had found a god, and were determined to worship it.

And so it came to be established as a fixed belief among engineers and architects that the best cement was the one which tested the highest, and the manufacturer had no alternative but to strive to make his product test as high as possible.

The next step was in the direction of forcing higher tests by using an excess of carbonate of lime, or by adulterations.

Henry Reid in his work on " Portland Cement," London 1877, page 315, says: " The presence of free lime thus unconverted is now frequently due to an over-dose of carbonate of lime in the cement mixture to enable it to pass successfully the modern onerous tests."

From that time until to-day the demand for higher tests has been continuous and more burdensome, and the manufacturer has not scrupled to employ any and every means within his power to accomplish the required results. He has to do it or retire from the field.

And thus, by an unfortunate misinterpretation of the readings of the tensile-strain testing machine, in the early days of its existence, the opinions then formed have passed current as sound and unquestioned through all the subsequent years.

So strong and deep seated is the belief to-day in the reliability of the testing machine, that a person who cares to be considered as " up to date " must express no doubt as to its infallibility.

An ideal hydraulic cement, as already stated, can be produced by what is known as the Portland process.

It would consist in a selection of the raw materials which were found to be best adapted for the purpose (special care being taken, at least, as to the quality of the clay), and these to be thoroughly and finely commingled in correct proportions, then calcined to a mild clinker, sufficiently vitrified to produce a medium weight, and then ground exceedingly fine.

Such a cement would test only about half as high as the present so-called Portlands, yet it would be an ideal cement.

It could not be excelled, and could be equaled only by a rock cement having its constituent parts present in exact chemical proportions.

It is only through the engineer that any improvement may be expected. He alone is entitled to the doubtful distinction of bringing about the change from the slow-setting pasty Portlands of twenty-five or thirty years ago to the harsh, high short-time testing Portlands of to-day.

It is neither pertinent nor sound to reason that because the Portlands used twenty-five or more years ago may be in good condition to-day, the Portlands of the present are worthy of the utmost confidence, for every person at all conversant with the facts knows that those earlier Portland cements tested but about half as high in one, seven, thirty, and ninety day tests as do the Portlands now on the market.

If an artificial cement of a pasty consistency should test 80 lbs. in one day, and 175 lbs. at seven days, 300 lbs. at six months, 600 lbs. at one year, 1,000 lbs. at two years, and 1,200 lbs. at five years, and should be found at that age to be tough and stone-like in its character, can any one for a moment doubt that such a cement would be infinitely superior to the harsh, high short-time testing cements of to-day?

Is it not worth while to reflect that for every one year that harsh cements have been in use, those of a pasty character have been in use fifty years?

Is it difficult to understand that it is only the pasty cements that eventually assume a stone-like character, while those that are harsh inevitably become glassy?

It is well known to every manufacturer that the latter class is much more expensive to produce, but the manufacturer has no alternative. He must produce such grades of cement as the engineers demand.

It is to the engineers, therefore, as has already been stated, that any improvement may be looked for, and the only improvement needed, with respect to artificial cements, is to get back to the sensible Portlands of thirty years ago.

Let the engineer stipulate that cements shall not test below or above certain fixed limits, and there will be an end to this doctoring and drugging of the artificial cements, which is resorted to simply and solely for the purpose of meeting arbitrary and unreasonable requirements.

The following table of tests of English Portland Cements by Reginald Empson Middleton, M. Inst. C. E., was printed in *Engineer*, London, Vol. 65, p. 279, April 6, 1888.

The figures given represent the average strength in pounds per square inch, in tensile strain, and the ages in days of the briquettes when broken.

No.	Days.	Pounds.	Days.	Pounds.	Days.	Pounds.	Per cent. of Loss or Gain.	
1	7	258	942	440	1325	550	Gain.	113.
2	7	320	900	635	1283	577	Gain.	75.
3	7	371	982	560	1365	500	Gain.	61.
4	7	419	1040	435	1423	492	Gain.	18.
5	7	479	1088	542	1471	551	Gain.	15
6	7	534	858	545	1241	520	Loss.	1.5

This table discloses the fact that artificial cements which at seven days test from 250 to 350 lbs. show higher ultimate results than those which at seven days test 400 to 600 lbs.

The following quotation from the " Transactions of the German Association of Cement Makers " discloses either a deplorable lack of common honesty or a desperate attempt at fulfilling the severe requirements of engineers. " In order to obtain the best results (?) the amount of plaster of Paris used must be proportionately increased in accordance with the quantity of ground slag employed." Presuming it to be a case of necessity rather than a lack of common honesty, what a commentary on the straits to which the producers are reduced to meet the requirements of engineers, knowing, as all manufacturers do know, that plaster of Paris is in no sense hydraulic, although it tests neat as high as 250 lbs. per square inch in tensile strain in twenty-four hours.

The time must surely come when it will be well understood that any and all schemes of hot-house forcing, for the purpose of obtaining high seven-day tests, constitute an unnatural interference with the crystallization of true silicates, and are therefore a serious damage to their most desirable qualities of endurance.

Verily it is the pace that kills, and even when applied to hydraulic cements, there is, if we may be permitted to employ it, no truer saying than " Soon ripe, soon rotten."

For hydraulic purposes there is no known substance that can in any way aid or improve the quality of pure unadulterated hydraulic silicates, when left to crystallize in their own natural way.

THE BOILING TEST.

During the past few years it has become quite the fashion to boil samples of cement in order to test their qualities.

If one brand sustains the test without serious results it is considered superior to others which fall down during the boiling. This is about as wise and logical a conclusion as that arrived at by some of our good old Puritan fathers during the witchcraft craze.

The witch, being thrown into a pond, if she went to the bottom and stayed there, was considered innocent. But if she managed to float, she was deemed to be possessed of the devil, and was then forced to the bottom on general principles.

By the boiling test, many of our very best brands of cement are condemned.

It is safe to assert that of the more than one hundred and fifty million barrels of American Rock cements used in all the great engineering works throughout the country during the past fifty years, and with no evidences of failure, not 1 per cent. would have sustained the boiling test.

A cement, whether natural or artificial, that will crystallize so rapidly as to sustain the boiling test, ought to be looked upon with suspicion, as it is either naturally too quick setting, or is too fresh and lacking in proper seasoning.

FREEZING TEST.

The many experiments that have been made by different authorities in the freezing of green cement samples would seem to indicate that Portland cement mortar will sustain severe freezing without appreciable disturbance of the exposed surfaces, but it suffers in loss of strength in some cases as much as 50 per cent.

While the Rock cement mortars will show disintegration to the extent of ¼ to ½ in. on the exposed surfaces, yet the portions not disintegrated are shown to have sustained no loss in strength, and in some instances the strength is above the normal.

A series of tests made by the author, the results of which are herewith tabulated, differ somewhat from those of other writers, resulting, no doubt, from having experimented with different brands of cement.

All of the briquettes were given one day in air and six days in water, those in the second column being placed in water and set outside, where they were soon frozen, and so remained in solid ice, until thawed out and broken at the end of the seventh day.

All of the briquettes represented in the second column, after

TABLE OF TESTS OF THE RELATIVE STRENGTH OF FROZEN AND UNFROZEN SAMPLES OF THE SAME CEMENT.

No. of Column.	1	2	3	4	5	
Kinds of Cement.	Not Frozen.	Frozen.	Per cent. of loss by freezing.	Per square inch of the frozen samples.	Per cent. of loss or gain by freezing, of equal areas.	
Medium Burned Rock Cement.	138	135	2.17	194	Gain.	40
Hard Burned Rock Cement.	226	225	0.44	323	Gain.	43
Slow Setting Portland.	388	280	27.83	402	Gain.	04
Medium Setting Portland.	419	292	30.31	419	Gain.	00
Quick Setting Portland.	433	255	41.11	366	Loss.	15

being thawed out, were shown to have lost equally in area, by scale and disintegration to the depth of ⅛ in. on all sides.

There was no appreciable difference in the losses, the Portlands having suffered equally, in that respect, with the Rock cements.

The figures in the second column show the actual breaking strain of the frozen briquettes, but it will be borne in mind that the areas of these briquettes were greatly lessened by freezing; therefore the percentage of loss in strength, as shown in the third column, represents the loss without regard to actual areas.

The fourth column represents the strength of the samples in

the second column when **calculated at** 1 full square inch, **or equal in area to** the samples in the first column.

The fifth column represents gain or loss in strength of **the frozen** samples, with equal areas of the unfrozen ones.

All of the briquettes were gaged neat by the same person, and were treated alike as to plasticity and temperature.

There is a surprising gain in strength of the Rock cements by freezing. With the Portlands, the slow and medium setting samples held their own, while the higher testing Portland, under ordinary rules lost 15 per cent. in strength of equal areas by freezing.

It is not good practise to use any kind of cement in cold weather, especially when it freezes during the night and thaws during the day, and should be avoided whenever possible.

COLOR.

There is no one feature connected with **the subject of cements** which exerts a stronger influence in the building up of opinions **concerning** the qualities of a cement than that of color.

The belief is almost universal that a good **dark color is a sure** indication of a good strong cement.

The tester is an exception who does not express surprise when he finds a light-colored cement testing higher than a dark one; and he almost invariably attributes the cause to some defect in his dark briquettes.

If he should be told that the way it came to be discovered that **the world was** round, and revolved on its axis, was by observing that people **who did** much walking **in easterly** and westerly **directions** invariably ran the heels of their shoes down at the back, while those who wore theirs off at the sides were found **to** do most of their walking in northerly and southerly directions, he would feel that his intelligence had been called in **question;** but it would not occur to him **that** his own theory in regard to the color of a cement was equally **as** whimsical. It is remarkable how strong a hold some absurd prejudices have upon the general public. It was not so very many years ago **that** any brand **of** Western flour, to obtain a market in the **Eastern** States, had to be put up in round-hooped barrels.

For more **than** a **third of a** century **it has been** repeatedly **stated that the color in a cement** was due to the presence of a small amount of oxide of iron, and that in no manner did its presence affect the quality of a cement.

General Gillmore so stated it in his treatise on " Limes, Cements, and Mortars," issued thirty-five years ago ; and the same statement has been made by various writers during all the subsequent years. Yet the belief prevails that color has to do with the quality.

So strong is this prejudice, that manufacturers of Portland cements, when they find that their available clay does not carry sufficient oxide of iron to give the requisite color to their product, resort to the use of artificial coloring matter, on account of the difficulty experienced in finding a market for light-colored Portland.

Any coloring matter, whether in a natural or an artificial cement, is an adulteration, and is inherent in the Rock cements, while it may or may not be so in the artificial product.

In the Rock cements the oxide of iron is closely associated with the clay, and its quantity, as a rule, governs the shade of coloring given to the cement.

If the amount is small and the calcination is light, the color of the cement will be a pale yellow. But with a higher degree of calcination, the color becomes a deeper yellow, or a light or a dark drab, dependent upon the intensity and duration of the heat.

If the amount is large, the cement will be light to dark brown, according to the intensity and duration of the heat.

Whatever may be the color of a cement, its quality is in no way affected thereby, unless the amount of coloring matter is excessive.

The quality of a cement is governed by three important requirements, no one of which can safely be dispensed with, namely : —

First, a proper proportion of the essential ingredients, *i. e.*, silica, lime, magnesia, and alumina.

Second, a proper calcination, which must be varied to suit the requirements of varying proportions of the constituent parts.

Third, fine grinding.

It will be seen, then, that a cement may be either light or dark, and yet be of good quality, while a very poor quality of cement may be accompanied by the most taking shade of colors.

And yet, inasmuch as the constituent parts named, when free from impurities, are white, it cannot but be clear that an absolutely pure cement cannot be otherwise than white.

The Rock cements are never colored artificially, and so we find as many variations in color as there are different manufacturing centers, each having its own peculiar shade or tint, while the different brands of the same locality are usually of the same color, yet they may vary considerably in quality.

With the artificial cements, the natural coloring matter is to be found in the clay, the same as with the Rock cements, and, as has been stated, when this is insufficient to suit the prevailing taste (?) resort is had to artificial coloring by the use of some form of carbon, or pigments.

Though the appearance of Portland cement, unadulterated with extraneous coloring matter, is an indication of its merits, it is clear that if artificial coloring matter is employed, the appearance of the cement is no criterion of its quality.

TENSILE TESTS.

The system of arriving at the value of a cement by means of the tensile-strain testing machine has grown to such proportions, and is so universally relied upon, believed in, and so seriously regarded as the Ultima Thule of all the knowledge necessary to determine values, and make or unmake a cement in the public opinion, that it seems almost sacrilegious to disturb the serenity of the faithful followers of this modern Juggernaut, who, metaphorically, throw themselves under its sacred wheels.

And yet the system is so permeated with inaccuracies, inconsistencies, and absurdities, that the temptation to puncture the venerable humbug is well-nigh irresistible.

The system contains many features in common with the alleged virtues of the divining rod.

And, although the comparison may seem odious to a large majority of the champions of the tensile test system, yet the author feels measurably assured that a few, at least, of the undoubted facts which he may present will be recognized at sight by many engineers and architects whose experiences with the system have led them into labyrinths of uncertainty and doubt.

The following from a paper on " The Divining Rod," presented by R. W. Raymond at the Boston meeting of the American Institute of Mining Engineers, in February, 1883, is sufficient to illustrate the parallel : —

"First. The immense literature of the divining rod shows nothing more clearly than the boundless confusions and contradictions of its advocates and professors.

"Second. Of the dozen different schools of practise, each is necessarily obliged to reject half of the asserted principles and certified facts put forward by the rest.

"Third. It will be remembered that the Egyptian sorcerers confronted by Moses carried rods, as Moses and Aaron also did.

"Fourth. Cicero, who had himself been an augur, says, in his treatise on divination, that he does not see how two augurs, meeting in the street, could look each other in the face without laughing.

"Fifth. The following formula, cited by Gaetzschmann, may serve as an example : —

"'In the name of the Father, and the Son, and of the Holy Ghost, I adjure thee, Augusta Carolina, that thou tell me how many fathoms is it from here to the ore.'"

One has but to consider that if a package of any brand of cement is divided among fifty expert testers, to be made up into briquettes, all the testers being governed by one set of rules, as to time, temperatures, percentage of water to be used, and the other ordinary requirements, the breakings, when tabulated, will show fifty tables of tests, no two of which will be alike. In fact, they will vary from each other all the way from 1 to 300 per cent., and so, if in the first paragraph of the quotation we insert "tensile tests" in the place of "divining rod," we come near to describing the present chaotic state of the art of briquette making, and, in the fourth paragraph, in the place of "two augurs" read "two testers," after they have stood side by side at the same table, and have each made and tested five briquettes from the same sample of cement, and find the results from 50 to 200 lbs. apart.

And as to the fifth paragraph, let us read it thus, "In the name of the American Society of Civil Engineers, and all the other societies under the sun, whose members practise the art of cement testing by tensile strain, I adjure thee, O thou testing machine, to tell me whether it is thy fault that I am thus befuddled, or am I drifting into incipient idiocy."

A tester makes up briquettes and tests them from a given brand of cement, and reports to his superior that "the cement runs very uneven." The fact that it is his briquettes and not the cement which "runs very uneven " never occurs to this knight of the testing machine.

When Don Quixote made his famous charge on the windmills and was unceremoniously overthrown, he had the courage to beat a rather undignified retreat.

But not so with our knight of the testing machine. He may be overthrown day after day, but he does not know it, and with an assurance bordering on the sublime he will tell you that such and such a brand of cement is not first class, for he has tested it, and the cement is not up to the requirements, for it "runs very uneven."

It is useless to confront him with the fact that other expert testers have found that the brand in question tests above the requirements, for, lacking the prudence of Don Quixote, he is overthrown, but does not realize it, when he says he " can get now and then a briquette to come up to or even go beyond the requirements, but it will not average (?) more than as shown in his tables."

It is probable that we are indebted to the engineers of a past generation for that altogether brilliant idea of giving a brand of cement a record based on its average (?) breakings. And for some unaccountable reason its utter absurdity seems to have escaped the notice of the ablest engineers of to-day.

If a trotting horse should be sent to the track, on a trial of three one-mile heats, for the express purpose of making a record, and the three trials should result as follows : —

min. sec.

1st heat, 2.15

2d „   2.20

3d „   2.10

total time   6.45

would we calculate the time thus, 6.45 ÷ 3 = average time 2.15, and seriously contend that the horse takes a record of 2.15 ?

Should this be done, the whole trotting world would smile, and yet it would be no more absurd than it is to give a cement a record based on the average (?) result of breaking strains of three or five briquettes, made from the same sample of cement.

The tester makes three briquettes from a single small sample of cement, and no one will deny that it is precisely the same in all its parts, and to the best of the tester's knowledge and belief, he has made the briquettes precisely alike. He has treated them alike as to every known detail, and yet one breaks at 100 lbs., while the others fall off 30 and 60 lbs. respectively, and the engineer, while knowing these results, from habit or custom, permits the cement to be deprived of its just record, which in this instance is none other than 100 lbs., and the record is fixed at 70 lbs.

If one portion of the sample tested 100 lbs., surely it is not the fault of the cement that the balance did not, and the conclusion is inevitable that it is the tester who is at fault. But the fault is laid to the cement, and so this inanimate though wonder-working material suffers in reputation by the carelessness and blunders of the average knight of the testing machine.

During the construction of the new Croton Aqueduct at New York, a certain brand of Rock cement was tested in one-day neat tests by two sets of testers, —

835 briquettes made by one set of three testers averaged $62 \frac{3}{10}$ lbs.
2434 „ „ „ „ ten „ „ $85 \frac{2}{10}$ „
a difference of nearly 35 per cent., and yet one set of rules governed all the testers, and the tests were made daily from the same consignments of cement.

From the table of tests of Mr. Thompson, City Engineer, Peoria, Ill., as shown in connection with his specifications as herein given, the following are selected from a large number, as a fair example of one-day neat tests of Rock cement.

No.	No. of Samples.	Highest.	Lowest.	Average	Per Cent. Variation.
1	8	118	45	77	162
2	6	138	80	109	72½
3	6	104	65	79	60
4	10	103	47	65	119
5	5	142	50	79	184
6	8	143	48	70	193
7	9	141	57	122	145
8	8	167	80	140	108

Mr. Thompson's tables contain the unusual merit of showing the highest and lowest breakings.

The absurdity of giving a cement a record on the average (?) system is well demonstrated in No. 6 of the table.

The eight samples were made from the same cement. One of the briquettes happened to be well made, and it tested 143 lbs., and yet it takes a record of barely one half that figure. It is deprived of its just and true record presumably because the briquette maker, when he made the one which tested only 48 lbs., was either very tired, or careless, or was unduly hurried.

The table given is not an exceptional one. Tables as uneven as this are to be found in nearly every cement-testing establishment in the country, and it has always been so since the tensile test mania began, over a third of a century ago.

The prevailing practise in the making of briquettes is to apply sufficient water to produce the proper degree of plasticity, thereby enabling the operator to press the material into the molds with the thumbs or a trowel.

This method is supposed to attain medium results, and is advocated by engineers generally, under the impression that the breakings of such briquettes indicate quite closely the actual strength of the cement in the masonry in which it is used.

However true this theory may be, it opens the door to a wide diversity of results, as each briquette maker is a law unto himself as to what constitutes the proper degree of plasticity of the material; and herein lies the chief cause of the surprising difference in the strength of briquettes made up from a single sample of cement.

The author has for many years been firm in the belief that the only correct way to test a cement by tensile strain is to use just enough water to properly hydrate the silicates, then pack the material into the molds, making the briquettes as dense and solid as is possible, by tamping or ramming, the object being at all times to make the briquettes test to the utmost limit of the strength of the cement. We would then know the capabilities of each brand tested.

There is a satisfaction in knowing the full strength of a cement whether or not it is ever called into practise in masonry.

Once the full strength of a cement is known, it becomes an easy matter to estimate the strength values of different degrees of plasticity.

. By this method we avoid the contradictory and unsatisfactory variations which continually arise among different testers of the same brand, which will always obtain so long as moderate results only are aimed at.

So long as the qualities of our cements are to be measured by tensile strain tests, there is no good reason why the system should not be open to improvement.

If it is self-evident that to the system of aiming at moderate or medium results is due the variations which are often so wide as to be really grotesque, why not abolish such a system and adopt that which will give us without question a full knowledge of the highest limit of strength in the cement, and at the same time reveal to us all its capabilities?   And, instead of giving a cement a record based on the average breakings of five briquettes, a most absurd and indefensible system, let the highest testing briquette of the five make the record of the cement.

It is only by the employment of this system that the question of the relative strength of different brands of cement can ever be settled.

It is the only system that is fair to all brands of cement.   This is shown by the wonderful uniformity of breakings of briquettes made from any brand of cement where the aim has been to get the highest possible results.

In nearly all the tables of tests that are published where the records of several brands of cement have been carried along for any length of time, it will be observed that one or more of the brands will fall off in a most inexplicable manner.

Perhaps the records are higher at three months than they are at six, or even nine months, and yet at twelve months they may have recovered all the lost ground, or even have made a substantial gain; and so we often notice in long-time tests that a cement may show a strength of, say, 500 lbs. at one year, and 400 lbs. at two years, while the three years' column will show 600 lbs.

This uncomfortable feature is common to the Rock and Portland cements alike.

Should such an uneven showing of one brand be recorded in a table among other brands which show a steady gain, the comparison is naturally unfavorable to the one with the unsteady record.

In fact, it is not at all unusual to meet with those in authority who will unequivocally express a preference for the cement showing the more steady record, even though the brand which has fallen off may have surpassed all the others at the final closing of the table.

The explanation for this curious phase of the subject is found in the deep-seated and profound faith in the infallibility of the testing machine.

If three briquettes are made from a single sample of cement by one person and they are treated alike until broken at six, nine, and twelve months, and the breakings are 500, 400, and 600 lbs. respectively, nothing is more certain than that the briquette which was broken at nine months was not as well made as the others.

If a cement is really weaker at nine months than it is at six months, it is simply impossible for it to show any gain in the twelve months' test.

The absurdity of a cement gaining and losing in strength alternately must be apparent to any person who will study the cause of its setting and hardening.

In the testing of cements by tensile strain the engineer meets with many conditions which seem to puzzle and confuse, among which may be noted that it oftentimes happens in the testing of two or more brands of cement neat, and in sand mixtures, that although the brands may be equal in fineness, the same quality of sand used for all, and all the briquettes made by the same person, yet the cement which tests the highest neat tests the lowest in the sand mixtures.

Rarely more than one set of tests is made, and so the tables are made up, and it is recorded against the highest testing cement that it "tests high in neat tests, but cannot carry sand equal to the lower testing brands."

This is a condition which often confronts the engineer, and, strangely enough, the opinion formed is almost invariably adverse to the brand testing the lowest with sand mixtures, although showing the highest in the neat tests.

In ninety-nine cases in every one hundred the opinion would be corrected by further tests, for it is certain that all conditions being equal, the cement testing the highest in neat tests will also test highest in sand mixtures, and the failure to do so may be looked for in the imperfect manner of making the briquettes.

The only possible exception to the rule will be found in the fact that a cement containing an excess of clay may test high in neat tests, yet will not carry sand equal to one that is correctly proportioned.

But such cements are so exceedingly rare in this country that the rule may be said to hold good, that the fault is in the making of the briquettes.

There are thousands of masons and contractors throughout the country who buy and use cements, in the construction of cisterns, cellar floors, sidewalks, milldams, foundation walls, and for various other purposes, who have no mechanical means for testing the cements they are using.

To such we suggest the following method.

Although the process is very simple and easy to practise, yet it involves a principle which embraces the chief and most valuable features of all other tests.

In fact, it may be said that there are no known methods for testing the hydraulicity of a cement which for effectiveness and reliability can compare with it.

The author has employed this method, whenever occasion has arisen, during the past thirty years, and he has never known it to fail to detect and expose weaknesses or imperfections, if they exist in the cement.

In the practise of this method it is only necessary to make a mold with which to form bars of cement.

All that is necessary for this purpose is a piece of hardwood plank 3 ins. wide, 2 ins. thick, and 12 ins. long.

Mortise into one side of this bit of wood a cavity 1½ ins. wide, 1 in. deep, and 8 ins. long, making the sides and ends slightly beveled, which, with the bottom, should be made smooth, and then the cavity should be well oiled, after which it is ready for use.

Wet up a sample of the cement to be tested into a stiff paste, and with a trowel press it in firmly, and smooth it off level with the face of the mold.

After the cement has hardened, which will occur in from twenty minutes to two hours, turn the mold bottom up, and let it rest on supports ½ in. thick under each end.

By careful jarring the cement bar will drop out of the mold.

Place the bar on the broad side in a pan or box, with the ends resting on supports in such manner that at least 6 ins. of the length of the bar shall be free and clear underneath, with a vertical clearance of 1 to 2 ins.

Next, fill the receptacle with water until the cement bar is completely submerged.

If the cement is strong in hydraulicity, the bar will maintain its shape indefinitely; but if it is lacking in this quality, or is weak, or defective in its composition or manufacture, it is sure to give way between the supports.

The author has known of rare cases where the bar maintained its shape ten days and then collapsed, but the ordinary defects in a cement will be made manifest within twenty-four hours.

Bars made with sand mixtures, of course, require a longer time to harden than those made from neat cements, and, therefore, should be given a full opportunity to crystallize before submersion.

In closing our chapter on the testing of cements, the thought arises, which, although somewhat tinged with impertinence, will not be dismissed without expression.

In our first chapter we quoted from " Hydraulic Mortars," by Dr. Michaelis, Leipzig, 1869, as follows: " The Eddystone Lighthouse is the foundation upon which our knowledge of hydraulic mortars has been erected, and it is the chief pillar of our architecture."

This sentence covers a great deal of ground, and is worthy of much thought and consideration; and granting that it is true, we are lost in conjecture as to what John Smeaton would have done when he built the Eddystone Lighthouse, had the cement which he used in the construction of that famous tower been passed upon by a British government engineer, with a tensile strain testing machine as his guide, and governed by the absurd rules and specifications, for this cement could not possibly have tested 25 lbs. per square inch in a seven-day neat test.

What would be thought of the manufacturer of to-day who would have the temerity to offer such a quality of cement for the construction of a lighthouse in this country or in Europe?

Everybody knows he would be ridiculed, for it is a question if Rock cement testing 150 lbs. in seven days would be considered strong enough, and it is more than likely that a Portland testing 400 lbs. in a seven-day neat test would be required.

Yet the Eddystone Lighthouse stood in good condition over one hundred and twenty years, until taken down to make way for a larger structure; and the mortar was found all that could be desired.

This being true, what becomes of our boasted advance in the art of cement making?

Where can we find a more trying place for a cement mortar than in the stone walls of a lighthouse standing out in the open sea?

Wherein lies the benefit of using a high-testing cement for such work, when a cement of the quality of the Aberthaw hydraulic lime used by Smeaton in the walls of the Eddystone Lighthouse can be supplied in this country for less than one fourth the cost of the high-testing cement?

If we care to build for all time, we must remember that that which causes a cement to set promptly in water also causes its comparatively early disintegration when exposed to the atmosphere.

A cement, therefore, which requires sixty or ninety days to harden in exposed masonry will be found in perfect condition ages after the mortar made from quick-setting cements has crumbled out and disappeared.

The investigations of Professor Tetmajer, of the Federal Polytechnical School, at Zurich, developed the fact that some German Portland cements, when used in work exposed for several years to the air, lose their consistency and crumble.

So serious had this danger become that, only a few years ago, the German Minister of Public Works issued a circular restricting within narrow limits the use of Portland cement in work exposed to the air.

Professor Tetmajer found, after careful examination, that the cause of the disintegration of Portland cement exposed to the air is found in a want of proper preparation of the materials, particularly in the lack of sufficient grinding together of the chalk and clay to insure the complete silification of the lime during the process of calcination.

He also found that the best brands of German Portland cement which had withstood the action of water for several years became soft on exposure to air.

He says, also, that " air especially attacks sharply (hard) burnt cements, which imbibe a great deal of carbonic acid, and the decay in water is caused by an excess of matters which undergo an increase in volume by oxidation and imbibing of water."

What, then, can justly be claimed as an advance in the art of cement fabrication since the days of Smeaton, one hundred and forty years ago?

We have managed to make a cement which will set hard in much less time now than then, but at the expense of endurance and this is, practically, all that has been learned.

The cement world of to-day is wrought to a high pitch in the matter of high short-time tests. The pendulum has swung in that direction without let or hindrance. But it will start on its return as soon as sufficient time has elapsed to prove beyond question that a cement may test too high, that all tests above the medium are developed at the expense of endurance.

And so there are those living to-day who will witness the passing of the high-test craze, and who will smile when they read of the conditions surrounding the testing of cements during the latter half of the nineteenth century.

CHAPTER VIII.

The Manufacture of Rock Cement in the United States
— Value of Properties — Geological Ages of the Cement Rocks in Europe and the United States — Kinds
of Cement Packages in Use — The Sturtevant Crushers
and Emery Millstones Illustrated — Typical Rock Cement and Portland Cement Works Illustrated.

There are seventy-one Rock cement manufactories in this country, which are distributed throughout the several States in the following order : —

STATE.	Number of works.
Georgia	1
Illinois	2
Indiana and Kentucky	15
Kansas	2
Maryland and West Virginia	5
Minnesota	2
New Mexico	1
New York	29
Ohio	3
Pennsylvania	6
Texas	1
Virginia	3
Wisconsin	1
Total	71

These properties, together with the known undeveloped cement
rock deposits, at a conservative estimate, are worth about ten millions
of dollars.

To describe in detail all these cement works would require

many **pages.** In fact, an entire volume could be written with **very** interesting details, especially **in regard to** the geological **ages** in which the several cement rock deposits occur in this country.

And **it** may be said in passing that **it is** the intention of the author, in the preparation of a future edition, to take up this question in detail.

For the **purposes of this** work, however, it will be briefly **noted** **that all** of the cement rock formations that **are** worked in this country occur in the Silurian (both Lower and Upper), the Devonian, and the Carboniferous ages.

The author attaches great significance to this fact, which **will** be more apparent to the reader if he will recall the matter found on **pages 23 and 24** of this work, a thorough understanding of which will explain why the cement rocks **of** this country are so superior to those of Europe, and especially those in England, where all the Rock **cement** produced has **been taken** from the Upper **and Lower Lias** **subdivisions of the** Jurassic period.

We have already stated the uneven character of those cement **rocks,** and in closing the subject it may be pertinent to add **that in** the Jura-Triassic rocks of this country, and notably in the State of Connecticut, commencing at New Haven, on Long Island Sound, **and** extending to Northern Massachusetts, having a length of 110 miles **and an** average **width of 20** miles, these deposits contain cement rock formations which have the same unfavorable characteristics mentioned in **connection with those of** England.

Three **attempts have been made** to utilize **these rocks for** cement purposes.

In West River Valley, **near New Haven, two works were erected** and operated for a brief period, but owing to **the uneven character** of the cement rock the enterprises had to be abandoned.

The plant at Kensington (noted **on page** 19) was **one of the** earliest in this country.

It was learned by the **author, on a recent** visit to this picturesque locality, that the chief incentive to the erection of a cement works at **this point** was **the fact** that the only hydraulic cement then known **was produced in England from the Jurassic rocks, as** stated, and the **corresponding rocks in this country were expected** to furnish the **cement for New England, at least.**

The little factories started in 1818, at Fayetteville, Onondaga County, and at Williamsville, in Erie County, N. Y., in 1824, taking their cement rock from the Lower Helderberg formation, were at that time "away out West," unheard of and unknown.

The Kensington works had a fitful existence. The cement rock was found only in pockets or in broken fragments, distorted by upheavals. The works were operated spasmodically until the cement from the Lower Helderberg, at Rosendale, Ulster County, N. Y., came into prominence, and, owing to its even quality and general excellence, it soon supplanted the Kensington cement.

Next came the operations near New Haven, as already stated, and this was the last of the attempts to produce hydraulic cement from the Jurassic rocks of this country.

And, as previously stated, all the Rock cement manufactured in this country is derived from the earlier rocks, that were laid down in times of comparative quiet, as is evidenced by their even and uniform character, their large and extended bodies, which furnish, year after year, the same quality of cement, so even, in fact, that the brands of all the seventy-one factories have each their own unchanging characteristics, familiar to all large consumers, each and every brand representing a good, reliable cement.

Were this not so, it could not be sold; and a brand which is offered on the markets year after year is evidence of the most convincing kind that the quality is good, for if it is not good it must inevitably disappear from the markets within two or three years from the time of its first appearance.

European writers on the subject of cements have but little to say relative to the Rock cements of those countries, except in terms of disparagement.

In this country there are writers who gather up the European magazine articles on the subject of Rock cements in those countries, and by vamping them up, seem to expect them to pass as sound American literature.

These writers, after making a few laboratory tests, stand forth as full-fledged authorities on the subject.

It is amusing to note their studied attempts to instruct the American people as to the relative values of Rock and Portland cements.

Every line displays the fact that their entire knowledge of the subject is gathered from foreign sources.

Therefore, as the foreign writers treat the subject of Rock cements in those countries, so also do their American imitators treat the subject of American Rock cements.

Lacking utterly in technical knowledge and practical experience, it never occurs to these writers that it is possible for the cement rocks of Europe and America to be quite unlike.

And so pages are filled with meaningless platitudes concerning the uneven qualities of Rock cements in general, with the probabilities more than likely that the writers never saw an American cement rock deposit, or a plant for its manufacture.

KINDS OF PACKAGES IN USE.

Nearly all the cement works of this country are located on the lines of railroads, and by reason of car shipments, the expensive wood packages are fast being supplanted by cloth and paper sacks, the author being the original introducer of paper sacks as a substitute for wood packages, about twenty years ago.

This innovation proved successful, as is evidenced by the fact that about 4,000,000 barrels of cement are sold annually in paper sacks, resulting in a saving to the consumer about $650,000 annually, this sum representing the difference in the cost between paper and wood packages.

The use of cloth sacks is confined mostly to contract work, where the contractors in many instances own their sacks, and buy the cement in bulk at mills, sending their empty sacks to mills to be filled.

In cases where the manufacturers own the cloth sacks, they charge a slight advance over the bulk price to cover wear and loss.

Nearly all the domestic cement trade in Europe is done in sacks, at an enormous saving in cost in the packages; but for the export trade wood packages thus far seem indispensable, and so we find in this country that all imported cement is sold in wood packages, which, if calculated to cost twenty-two cents each, the American people paid for the wood packages containing the Portland cement imported during 1896, the sum of $657,711.34.

CRUSHING AND MILLING MACHINERY.

The Sturtevant Mill Company, of Boston, Mass., manufactures cement-grinding machinery of such undoubted merit that the author feels assured a brief illustrated description of these most modern methods of cement reduction will prove of especial interest to all cement manufacturers, and perhaps of general interest to many others.

STURTEVANT ROLL JAW ROCK BREAKER AND
FINE CRUSHER.

The Sturtevant Roll Jaw Crusher is a peculiar machine, and is capable of fine work; it takes in rocks of large size and reduces them at once to gravel and sand, thus doing the work of a large jaw crusher and one or two sets of rolls without any auxiliary machinery.

The cut shows a 6 by 16 roll jaw crusher; the toggles are like those of other crushers, but the long lever roll jaw gives immense power, and as its curved jaw face makes a perfect roll, it crushes without any rubbing action whatever.

The roll jaw passes over the rock being crushed, which then drops out without any tendency to clog. The product is as regular in size as that from rolls.

This machine crushes Portland clinker, or any hard rock, to such fineness as may be suitable for fine reduction in mills or millstones.

The Roll Jaw Crusher requires little power, and is a solid, well-made, and durable machine.

This crusher will take Portland Cement clinker just as it comes from the kiln and at a single operation will reduce it fine enough for milling.

The 6 by 16 breaker weighs about 7 tons; the heaviest piece weighs less than 3,000 lbs. and the machine will run with 10 h. p. under ordinary conditions. It will crush 3 tons per hour of Portland clinker, or any hard, dry material, such as granite, limestone, etc., when set to ¼ in. opening, and about half of such product is ⅛ in. and finer.

These machines are made in larger and smaller sizes. The crushing motion is a true roll without any grinding action whatever, and this ensures great durability to the jaws and the minimum cost of running.

Rock Emery Millstones may be seen running in many of the Rock and Portland cement works of this country and England.

They are made in all sizes and to fit any mill frame. As is shown clearly in the cut, the skirt of this millstone is formed of large blocks of emery, set in a metal filling that holds them with ample strength. The center of the millstone is made from a single block of Esopus stone, and the furrows are of sandstone set on edge.

This combination of materials forms a grinder that is not injured by heat, and consequently, Rock Emery Millstones may be run at high speed.

The extraordinary hardness and cutting properties of emery are so well known that it would be surprising if it did not form the hardest, strongest, and most abrasive millstone face that can be made.

Emery millstones are capable of doing fine work, and they are rapid grinders. They require to be fed with finely crushed material, if it is hard, and it should not be larger than grains of wheat.

The Emery face should be dressed occasionally. In careful hands these millstones grind fast and fine, and last long.

The Sturtevant Emery 42 in. Complete Mills are grinding, on an average, 5 to 6 bbls. of finished Portland cement per hour, when working on properly crushed clinker, 93 to 95 per cent. of the product passing 100 mesh.

The same machines are grinding steadily from 18 to 20 bbls. per hour of Rock cement 95 per cent. fine, and are also turning out from 1 ½ to 2 tons per hour of raw Portland material.

Emery stones often wear from three to five years on Portland cement, and will average to grind under the same conditions at least one third more than the best French buhrs. They will run from

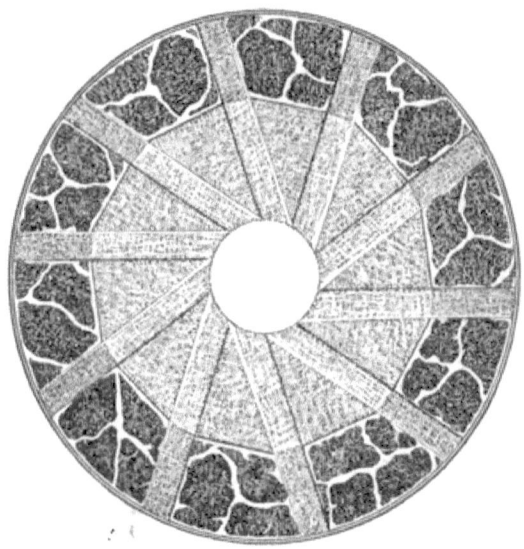

STURTEVANT ROCK EMERY MILL STONE.
Trade Mark.

3 to 4 weeks on Portland cement without being taken up for dressing, and the dressing which they require at the end of that time is of the simplest character.

These machines take about 15 to 18 h. p. to drive, and will run smoothly and without vibration on a good mill floor, thus requiring no expensive foundation.

These 42 in. mills are heavy and substantial, weighing fully 6,000 lbs. complete, and are constructed to run at high speed (which does not injure emery stones) and with the least possible vibration, thus being able to do the very finest grinding.

The bedstone is bolted in place, and cannot be got in wrong, and the hand-wheel adjustment raises and lowers this stone with absolute accuracy upon the runner, against which it presses elastically (with as much force as may be desired), and is thus able to release quickly bolts, nuts, or any hard foreign material that may, by accident, get between the stones.

The running stone is rigidly fixed to the very short and large shaft, and has no adjustments. By this arrangement the stones are

STURTEVANT ROCK EMERY MILL.

always together in perfect alignment, and cannot be carelessly set or run; i. e., it requires no expert to keep the mill in running balance, as is the case with cock-head mills, and these mills are much finer grinders. Indeed, there is no mill made that can compete with this for fine or rapid work.

The frame is built to run at high speed, and, if provided with emery stones (which do not crack when hot), can do more work than other mills, and reduce materials heretofore supposed to be ungrindable. The bearings are bronze, and all run in oil. The remarkable simplicity of this horizontal mill, and its great solidity, is shown in the cut. It is made to last, and to give no trouble. With Rock Emery Millstones it can grind rapidly and economically a long list of substances that would rapidly dull the best French buhrs.

CEMENT MANUFACTORIES.

While in these pages we cannot undertake to describe all the existing cement works, we have selected a few which may be considered as fairly representative.

They are typical works, and embody about all the most advanced methods employed in manufacture.

They are chosen with a view to representing the types which are prevalent in the leading districts of Rock cement production.

The Portland cement works represented may be said to stand in the front rank of that class of manufactories in this country, and is given that our readers may get a clear idea of the prevailing methods employed in the production of high grade artificial cements.

THE MANUFACTURE OF UTICA CEMENT.

The works of the Utica Hydraulic Cement Company, of Utica, Ill., consist of a plant capable of producing 2,000 barrels of finished cement per day.

The company owns 1,500 acres of land, containing the cement rock, the latter being about 7 ft. in thickness, which belongs in the calciferous epoch of the Lower Silurian age.

The company usually mines the cement rock, although having open quarries as well.

The drilling is done with power drills, driven by compressed air.

The chambers in the mine are about 40 ft. square, 26 in number, all connecting with a main gallery.

The kilns are of the iron type, and in operation are continuous.

The mill is equipped with a double Corliss engine of 300 H. P., which drives all the machinery.

The material as it comes from the kilns is deposited into a No. 5 Gates crusher, which crushes it to the size of a walnut, and from the crusher it passes into two roller or pan pulverizers, from which the cement is elevated, coming down over three sliding screens, from which is obtained 60 per cent. of finished cement.

THE CLARK MILLS, UTICA, ILL.

PACKING ROOM

GRINDING ROOM

THE CLARK MILLS, UTICA, ILL.

The tailings from the sliding screens are carried to a battery of millstones consisting of four run of 30 in. vertical buhrs, and two run of 42 in. horizontal emery stones, where the grinding is completed.

The finished cement from the rollers and the millstones meet in a general conveyor, where a thorough mixing takes place before the cement reaches the packing room or storage rooms.

The company enjoys most excellent facilities for shipping by rail, and has an immense storage capacity in warehouses adjoining the railroad tracks.

On page 20 a brief history of these works will be found.

This company has recently come into possession of the large and important Rock cement works at La Salle, Ill., where the " Black Ball " brand of Utica cement is manufactured. A notice of these works will be found on page 22.

CUMMINGS CEMENT, ITS MANUFACTURE.

The works of The Cummings Cement Company are situated at Cummingston, New York, on the Batavia and Tonawanda branch of the New York Central and Hudson River Railroad at its intersection with the West Shore Railroad, twenty miles northeast of Buffalo, N. Y. Post-office, Akron, N. Y.

The cement rock of this locality belongs to the Lower Helderberg period of the Upper Silurian age. The color of the rock is a dark blue, the fracture conchoidal, and the texture exceedingly fine and uniform, showing the clay and carbonate of lime to be intimately commingled in the rock.

The company owns 575 acres of land containing this material, which is sufficient to produce 63,500,000 barrels of the manufactured cement.

The deposit is from 7 to 8 ft. in thickness, and the strata, which are remarkably uniform in character, lie horizontally underneath a rock capping of about 60 ft. in thickness, the lower 15 ft. of which consists of hydraulic limestone, the rock above this being black flint.

The cement rock is mined by drifts which widen into chambers from 80 to 150 ft. in width, pillars of cement rock being left occasionally for the support of the roof.

The drifts are started in the perpendicular ledge facing the plant, and are nearly on a level with the tops of the kilns, which stand about 75 ft. away from the face of the ledge.

Power drills are used in the mine and are driven by compressed air, and the working face of the cement rock strata is three fourths of a mile in extent.

After the rock is blasted out, it is broken into suitable sizes, and is then loaded into tram cars and hauled to the mouth of the tunnel facing the plant, where the cars are attached to cables and are drawn upon the kilns.

Layers of coal are spread over the cement rock in the cupolas of the kilns, and the rock in the cars is dumped thereon, when another layer of coal is applied; and thus the kilns are kept filled during the day, while the calcined cement rock is removed from the base of the kilns, where it is shoveled directly into cars, and thence hauled by cable into the second story of the mill on an incline track.

The calcining department consists of 8 kilns, the cupolas of which measure 9 by 22 ft. in surface area, and 9 kilns with round cupolas 9 ft. in diameter, all being 34 ft. in height.

The total surface area of the cupolas in the 17 kilns is equivalent to 34 kilns with round cupolas 9 ft. in diameter, or 28 kilns having round cupolas 10 ft. in diameter.

During the calcination, which is done at a white heat, a considerable proportion of the cement rock becomes clinkered, and the latter is exceedingly hard and heavy, and is very difficult to reduce to powder; but as it possesses hydraulic properties to a remarkable degree, it is not rejected, as is customary at manufactories where the clinkered portion is light and friable.

But the machinery in common use throughout the country for grinding ordinary Rock cement was found entirely inadequate. In fact, such machinery could not handle this material without being soon broken and destroyed.

It was necessary, therefore, owing to the extreme difficulty experienced in reducing the product to a fine powder, to devise special machinery for the purpose of overcoming the extraordinarily abrasive character of this material.

To that end a general system of gradual reduction was employed, which finally proved adequate.

It consists of four different systems. First, Sturtevant crushers;

THE CUMMINGS CEMENT COMPANY, AKRON, N. Y.

ENTRANCE TO MINE.

second, Cummings pulverizers; third, ten run of 42 in. underrunner millstones faced with chilled iron plates; fourth, ten run of 42 in. hard Esopus underrunner millstones.

The material, as it is conveyed from one to another of these systems, is made to pass over screens whereby such material as has been reduced to proper fineness is separated from the mass and is spouted to a general conveyor, which finally receives the product from all of the systems and conveys it to the packing house.

Each system, while it finishes a portion of the material, reduces the sizes of the unground portion to such a degree that the material which is fed to the fourth system is broken and worn down to the size of kernels of wheat, and is exceedingly hard to reduce.

The power necessary to drive this machinery consists of a battery of seven tubular boilers 5 ft. in diameter and 16 ft. long, and a pair of engines whose cylinders are 24 by 48 ins., connected to a single shaft which carries a balance wheel 20 ft. in diameter, with a face suitable for a 36 in. heavy belt, which, at a speed of 3,900 ft. per minute, drives the entire machinery.

There is also an auxiliary plant joining the main mill, consisting of two boilers of 6 ft. diameter and 18 ft. long, and an 18 by 24 in. engine, and two roller pulverizers with the necessary equipment for use in emergencies. This power is also used for handling coal cars on the trestles and dumps.

The cooper shop is connected to the works by a covered inclined track 400 ft. long, by which the empty barrels are rolled into the packing department.

There are 5,400 ft. of railroad track in and about the works, the latter covering $3\frac{6}{10}$ acres of ground, and thirty cars can be loaded from the spacious warehouses without the necessity of moving a car.

In the mines there are 8,000 ft. of tramway track, to which constant additions are being made as the tunnel is extended by the removal of the rock.

The testing department is equipped with the most approved machinery for the purpose, and test sheets are furnished with each shipment of cement, and are mailed to the purchaser. These test sheets show the quality of the cement as guaranteed by the company.

The " Cummings " brand of cement was established in 1854 by

H. Cummings & Sons, at Akron, N. Y.; the head of this firm being the father of the president, and treasurer of the present company, and grandfather of the secretary and vice-president.

From the date given until Jan. 1, 1898, the number of barrels of cement bearing the name of "Cummings" has reached the total of 8,000,000 barrels.

This company also manufactures Portland cement in large quantities, which is sold under the following brands, namely: —

"Storm King," "Uncle Sam," and "Roman Rock." The natural rock cement produced by this company bears the "Obelisk" brand. These brands are shipped to nearly every State in the Union.

The Western Union Telegraph wires enter the office of the company at the works, Akron, New York; main office, Buffalo, New York; New England office, Stamford, Conn.

Its officers are: Uriah Cummings, president; Ray P. Cummings, vice-president; Homer S. Cummings, secretary; and Palmer Cummings, treasurer and general manager.

THE MANUFACTURE OF LOUISVILLE CEMENT.

The discoverer of the Argillo magnesian limestone formation under the falls of the Ohio River, from which Louisville cement was first made, is unknown. John Hulme & Co. operated a grain mill on the banks of the Ohio, in which cement was manufactured in limited quantities, prior to 1829. Fragments of stone in the river exposed in low water were collected, burned in improvised kilns, then cracked in small pieces and ground in the Hulme Mill, between stones driven by a water wheel in the river. "All was grist" that came to Hulme & Co. Persons desiring cement took their turn at the mill with farmers having grain to grind.

To supply cement for use on the locks of the Louisville and Portland Canal, in process of construction by the United States Government in 1829, the first permanent kilns for calcining cement stone were built. From this time the manufacture of Louisville cement has continuously increased. For many years the mills located on the Ohio River enjoyed a monopoly of the cement business, the impression generally prevailing that cement stone was to be found only in the bed of the Ohio River, and, therefore, inaccessible except in the shallow water of the rapids. Increasing demand and large profit

LOADING CARS IN MINE

ROCK DRILLING IN MINE

LOADING CALCINED CEMENT

THE CUMMINGS CEMENT COMPANY, AKRON, N. Y.

THE CUMMINGS CEMENT COMPANY, AKRON, N. Y.

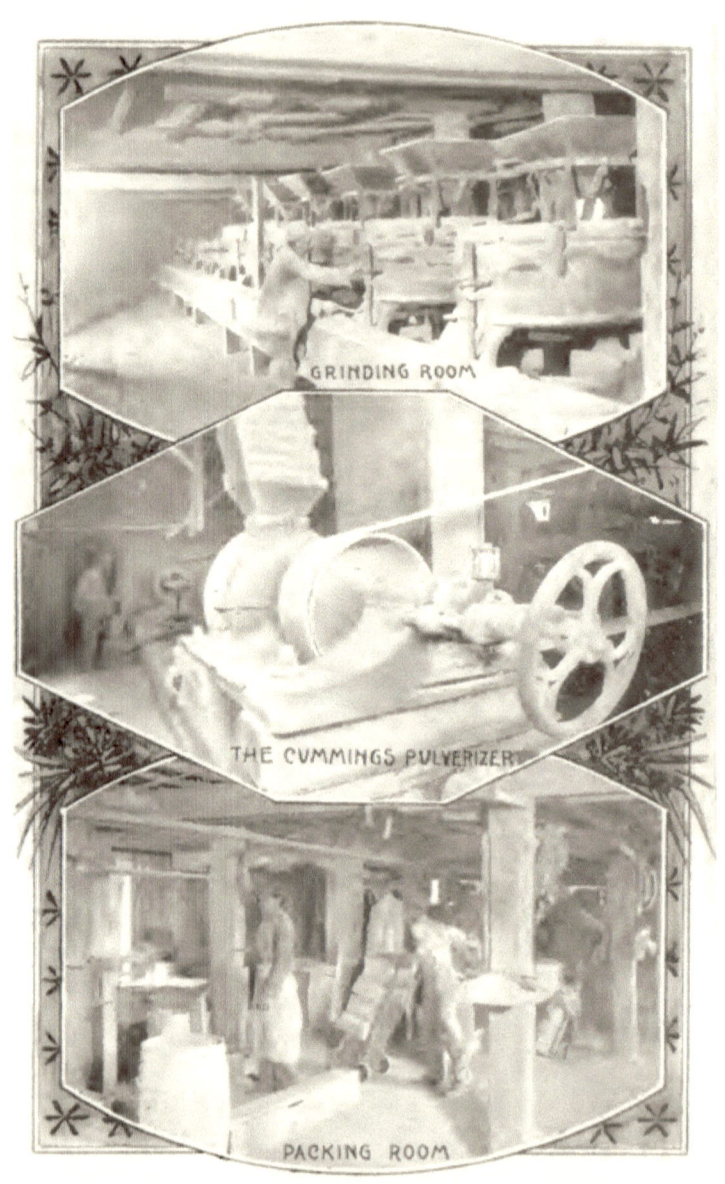

GRINDING ROOM

THE CUMMINGS PULVERIZER

PACKING ROOM

THE CUMMINGS CEMENT COMPANY, AKRON, N. Y.

realized from the mills on the river stimulated investigation on the part of others, who, carefully tracing the strata of rock, then exposed to view only in the Ohio River, for some miles north of the river, in 1866 located a small plant, with a daily capacity of 200 barrels, on the line of the J. M. & I. R. R., in Indiana. The advantages of railroad transportation and economical quarries, which could be operated without the interruption and consequent expense to which the river quarries were subjected by high water, were too great to be long enjoyed by the pioneer inland mill without competition under normal conditions.

The destruction in the South, incident to the Civil War, to be repaired, the extension of old and the projection of new railroads, and other enterprises in the North and West, created a demand in excess of the capacity of the then existing mills. Others followed at intervals, until the works in the Louisville group, devoted exclusively to the manufacture of Louisville cement, consisting of thirteen mills, have a combined capacity of 15,000 barrels per day, and are now the largest and best-equipped works in the world for the production of natural cement. From a few thousand barrels produced by the original mill on the river for local consumption, the annual production of the thirteen mills has exceeded 2,100,000 barrels, or about one fourth of the natural cement manufactured in the United States, and if necessary could be increased without enlargement of the present plants, the capacity now being greatly in excess of any consumption of cement which may reasonably be expected for many years to come.

The stone from which Louisville cement is made is peculiar to a small area, only a few miles wide, extending north of the Ohio River about fifteen miles, and is not found elsewhere. It is generally covered with earth, but occasionally a stratum of limestone intervenes between the earth and cement stone. Where this occurs the stone is mined; where covered by a few feet of earth only it is obtained by open quarrying. The illustrations, given on another page, of the entrance to the tunnel and the open mine are typical, and show the two methods of obtaining supplies of stone for the manufacture of cement at all of the mills in the Louisville district.

The formation of cement stone is generally in horizontal strata, dipping slightly to the southwest, nearly uniform in size and color, and varies from 10 to 16 ft. in depth. The open mine shown is about 900 ft. long, with a face of 16 ft., and furnishes material for 3,500 barrels of cement daily.

In the preparation of stone for the manufacture of Louisville cement, no admixture of the different strata is necessary, the formation being uniform in all essential characteristics. The liability of an inferior product, due to an improper mixture, is eliminated; there being no material to be obtained more cheaply than the best, there is no incentive to the manufacturer, in seasons of great demand, to increase his product at the expense of quality.

The process of manufacture, from the removal of the stone from its bed to the finished product, being substantially the same in all of the works in the Louisville district, a description of the process at one of the thirteen plants will suffice for all.

At the works described, stone is obtained from the open quarry in the usual manner, by means of steam or compressed air drills and high explosives. It is loaded in boxes of about 3 tons capacity, which are hoisted by a 10 ton locomotive crane, and deposited on the trucks of the quarry train. The trains of stone are hauled by a locomotive to the crusher house, there the stone is reduced by a Blake crusher of 400 barrels per hour capacity into pieces of three uniform sizes for calcination. By means of screens and chutes, each size is discharged into cars in which it is hauled to the kilns.

The kilns are of the usual pattern, cylindrical in shape, about 45 ft. high and 16 ft. in diameter, made of iron, lined with fire-brick. The stone is charged into the kilns from bottom dumping cars on the track which surmounts the kilns. By means of a coaling machine the proper amount of coal is accurately measured and charged into the kilns in alternate layers with stone. By the use of this machinery the personal factor is eliminated, and a more evenly calcined product secured, than is possible by the old method of leaving the amount of coal necessary to the judgment of the burner. The kilns are continuous, after being kindled in the spring, until operations cease for the winter.

The calcined stone is drawn from openings near the base of the kilns, from which it falls by gravity over iron aprons into cars on a track below. These cars are hoisted into the mill, and dumped upon an inclined platform, on which the material descends automatically

THE LOUISVILLE CEMENT COMPANY, LOUISVILLE, KY.

to the coarse crushers. While upon this platform, the imperfectly burned material is carefully culled out, thrown aside to be reburned; in this connection it may be interesting to note that overburning does not impair the quality of Louisville cement, the effect of overburning being to diminish its activity only, without impairing its hydraulic energy.

A battery of three 250 H. P. Babcock & Wilcox boilers supply steam to two Corliss engines, which furnish motive power to the grinding machinery in the mill proper, consisting of seven cast-iron coarse crushers, twelve fine crushers, and ten pairs of emery stones 54 ins. in diameter.

The process of reducing the calcined stone, as it comes from the kilns, to powder begins in the coarse crushers, from which it passes in pieces about the size of a hazelnut to the fine crushers, which reduce it in varying degrees from particles about the size of wheat to fine powder, the coarser particles passing on to the emery stones.

By means of a system of elevators and screens the material is screened as it comes from each crusher, and the various streams of finished product from the crushers and buhrs are carried through a common spiral conveyor to the packing room. By this arrangement a thorough mixture of them all is effected, and each package of cement contains material from 6 to 12 kilns, thus securing uniformity of product not otherwise obtainable.

The entire process of manufacture from the quarry to the packing room, where the cement is packed for shipment, is under the supervision of competent men. Samples are taken at frequent intervals during the day, which are carefully tested for fineness, time of setting, and tensile strength.

In the transportation of the stone from the quarry, and of the daily product of 3,500 barrels of 265 lbs. net from the mill to the tracks of the P. C. C. & St. L. R. R., several locomotives and a large number of cars are employed.

In connection with this work is a machine shop, a cooper shop, a store, 88 residences for operatives, and storehouses capable of storing 80,000 barrels of cement.

In the machine shop are facilities for making repairs and building new machinery. As an indication of the completeness of this shop, may mention one of the large Corliss engines used in this works was built here.

The cooper shop is fitted with the latest trussing, setting up, and crozing machinery, capable of producing 2,000 barrels per day, when operated to its full capacity. In connection with this shop are ample storehouses for staves, heading, and other supplies. Here, as in every department of this works, nothing is done by hand that can be done as well by machinery.

Methods of manufacture being substantially the same in all of the works in the Louisville district, the variation from a uniform product is reduced to a minimum, as the stone varies only slightly, either in its physical properties or chemical constituents. The widest variation is in color, chiefly due to the presence, in varying quantities, of oxide of iron, which has no effect other than to deepen the color of the cement.

The consumption of Louisville cement is not confined to restricted territory. It is shipped from Ontario to Florida, and from the Atlantic coast to the Rocky Mountains. It is employed in piers of railroad bridges spanning our great waterways; in reservoirs containing water supply of our Western cities; modern city roadways and pavements are supported on concrete foundations made of it; currency and valuables are secured in safes and vaults rendered fire-proof by the use of it. For building purposes it has largely superseded lime, and its worth as a building material is receiving the attention it has long deserved.

A brief notice of Louisville cement is given on page 19.

THE LAWRENCE CEMENT COMPANY.

In 1823, while building the Delaware & Hudson Canal near the village of Rosendale, Ulster County, N. Y., the fact was discovered that the dark-blue limestone rock through which the canal was being excavated possessed hydraulic properties, and, upon proper calcination, would produce a powerful hydraulic cement. About ten years later, or in 1832, Watson E. Lawrence built a few small kilns, opened a mill, and began the manufacture of the "Lawrence" brand of Rosendale cement on the banks of Rondout Creek, not far from the village of Rosendale. This mill, which has long since been closed, was operated by water power from the creek, and

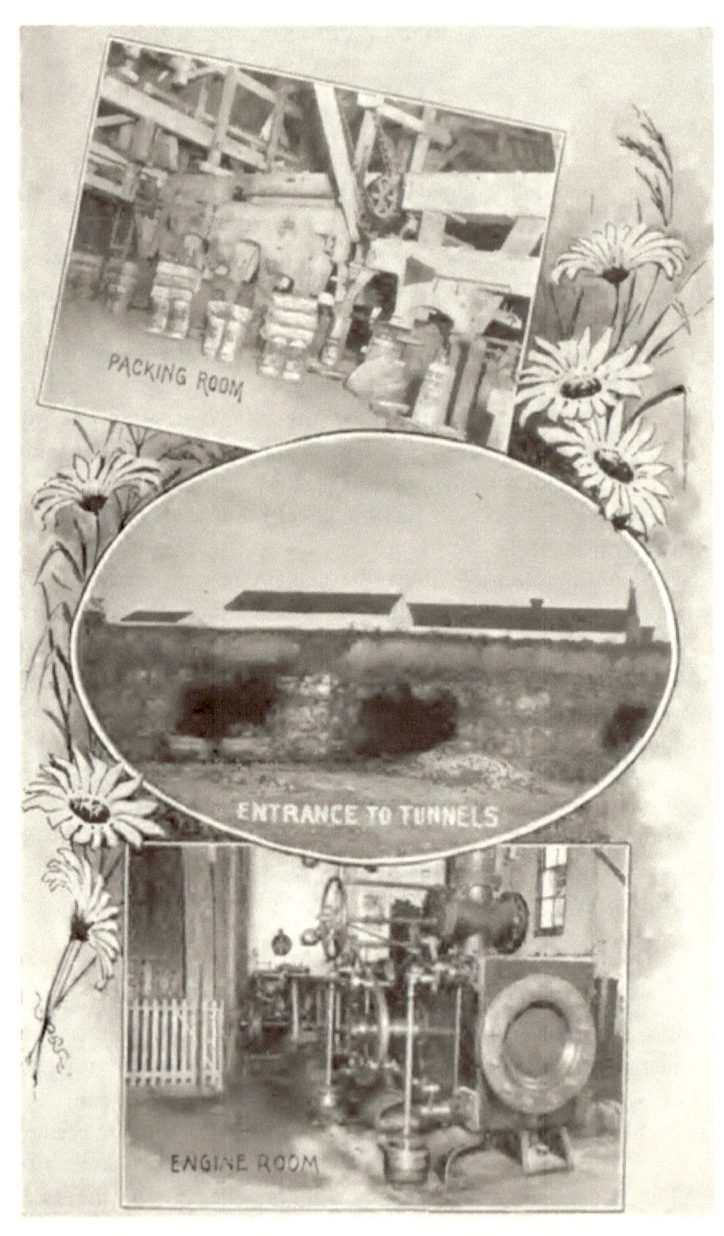

PACKING ROOM

ENTRANCE TO TUNNELS

ENGINE ROOM

THE LOUISVILLE CEMENT COMPANY, LOUISVILLE, KY.

was capable of producing 20 barrels of cement per day. The growth of the company's works since the opening of the first mill has been in proportion to the enormous growth of the Rosendale cement industry in this country. The present mills of the Lawrence Cement Company can produce 5,300 barrels of cement per day and about 1,166,000 barrels per year, or about one third of the Rosendale cement manufactured in Ulster County, and about one eighth of the total amount manufactured in the United States.

Briefly summarized, the company's works consist of three mills, located at Binnewater, Eddyville, and Esopus. The mill at Esopus, although in full working order, is not being operated, but the other two are grinding the rock from 66 kilns, and producing, as before stated, 5,300 barrels of cement per day. The respective capacities of the two mills in operation are, 2,500 barrels and 2,800 barrels of cement per day. In connection with each of the cement mills proper are storehouses, cooper-shops, repair shops, power houses, and offices, and, in addition, all the cableways, tramways, and hoisting apparatus necessary in handling both the cement rock and the barrels and bags of manufactured cement.

The source from which the Lawrence Cement Company derives its supply of cement rock is the well-known tentaculate of water limestone belonging to the great natural cement rock formation extending along the Appalachian Mountains from Vermont to Virginia. In Ulster County the deposits are mostly found within the limits of a narrow belt, scarcely a mile wide, skirting the base of the Shawangunk Mountains, along the line of the Delaware & Hudson Canal, in the valley of Rondout Creek. Owing to a succession of upheavals, of which the whole region exhibits remarkable evidences, the bed, or strata, of cement rock is found in almost every conceivable inclination to the horizon, but ordinarily dipping in a greater or less degree to the northwest or southeast. The useful effect of these upheavals has been to raise into accessible and convenient positions the cement rock which would otherwise have been buried beyond practicable reach for manufacture. As it is, the outcropping strata are worked by open quarrying.

The rock used in the manufacture of " Hoffman " Rosendale cement is taken from two beds separated by a sandstone rock known as the " middle rock." The upper of these beds is known

as the " light rock," and the lower as the " dark rock," and the two
are mixed together in the proportion found to give the best results.
These quarries are carried into the hills to various depths, following always the layer of cement rock. In the quarrying, power drills
are used, and the explosives employed are dynamite and black powder. After blasting, the rock is broken into pieces varying from the
size of an orange to that of a football, loaded into tram cars and
taken to the kilns for burning.   The appearance of a quarry after
the excavation of the cement rock is very clearly shown in the illustration given on page 249, titled " Hoffman" Rosendale. Here it
will be seen that all of the cement rock in sight, excepting the pillars left to support the roof, has been excavated, and quarrying operations are now being carried on further in to the left of the view.

In describing the process of manufacture of " Hoffman" Rosendale cement, from the blasting of the rock to the labeling of the
barrels of cement ready for shipment, the works at Binnewater have
been selected for illustration. This may be taken as a typical plant,
and a description of the process of manufacture as carried out here
will apply equally well, except in minor details, to any of the company's other plants. At the Binnewater plant the quarries are located
in the ridge directly to the rear of the mills. This location is un-
usually favorable, however, and for the other mills the rock has for
the most part to be transported a considerable distance by tramway. In several instances, also, the kilns are located at some distance from the mills, and the burned rock has to be conveyed to the
mills in tram cars. After the excavation and breaking of the rock it
is conveyed to the kilns, and, by means of a track passing over their
tops, is dumped directly from the cars to convenient points for charging them. In the view, showing the Binnewater plant, the location
of the kilns to the rear of the mills is shown, and in another view
are shown the kilns at Hickory Bush supplying the Eddyville mill.

The process of calcination is very simple, in as far as not
requiring an elaborate apparatus is concerned, but it requires constant watchfulness and care, a thorough knowledge of the effects of
the temperature and of the velocity and direction of the wind, and
perfect familiarity with the characteristics of the different classes of
rock. In other words, the personal element enters largely into the
process, and, as the quality of the cement depends in a great degree

GRINDING ROOM.

KILNS AT HICKRY BUSH.

BINNEWATER MILL.

THE LAWRENCE CEMENT COMPANY, ROSENDALE, N. Y.

upon the care taken in the calcination, it is important that only men of experience and skill should be employed as burners. The kilns are built of stone and lined with brick. In these kilns a fire is built, the calcination being carried on by placing on the wood used for lighting a thin layer of coal, over which a layer of stone from 6 to 8 ins. thick is placed, then a thin layer of coal, repeating the process as often as the removal of the calcined rock at the bottom requires it. The coal used is anthracite, usually of pea or buckwheat size, and is placed on the rock in very thin layers, scarcely covering it. Each morning the previous day's burning is removed from the bottom of the kilns, as by this time the rock has become sufficiently cool to be handled. In drawing the kilns it is always found that some of the rock has been much overburned, in fact, having reached a stage of incipient vitrification, while another portion, consisting usually of the larger fragments, is underburned and perhaps partially raw inside. The overburned stone is, of course, quite worthless, and is carted away to the dumps, but the underburned stone is conveyed to the tops of the kilns, and again subjected to calcination.

From the bottoms of the kilns the stone, which has been properly calcined, is taken directly to the cracker room. In the view, showing the draw pits of the kilns at Binnewater, this cracker room is just across the tramway tracks, and is partly shown at the right hand. In the cracker room the rock is crushed to a fineness varying from dust to lumps of the size of a hickory nut, by what are known as crackers. These are made of cast iron, and consist essentially of a frustrum of a solid cone called the core, working concentrically within the inverted frustrum of a hollow cone, both being provided on their adjacent surfaces with suitable grooves and flanges for breaking the stone as it passes down between them. The elements of the lower portions of both cones make a smaller angle with the common axis than those pertaining to the upper portions, with a view to lessen the strain and the effects of sudden shocks upon the machinery, by securing a more gradual reduction of the stone to the required size. These lower portions, being subject to very rapid wearing, are made of chilled iron, and are, moreover, cast in separate pieces in order that they may be replaced by new ones, as the occasion requires. At the Binnewater mill there are eight of these crackers driven by steam power, which, it may be stated here, is used in all of the company's mills, both for driving the mill machinery proper, and for running the various hoisting engines.

After leaving the crackers all the cracked cement or burned stone goes to an elevator boot which is located two stories, or about 22 or 23 ft. below the crackers, from which place it is elevated by the elevator referred to about 33 ft. perpendicularly, and there it is thrown into a conveyor. This conveyor carries it along for distribution to the different mills or grinders, there being spouts opposite each mill leading from the conveyor to them, and as the cracked stone passes through the different spouts it runs over a sieve or screen made of steel wire cloth. This sieve is about 11 ft. long by 10 ins. in width, and is fastened into a box or portion of the spout referred to above, which is about 12 ins. wide and 6 ins. deep, so that 25 to 27% of the cracked cement passes through this sieve, which would give an average fineness of 96 to 97% when tested through a sieve of 2,500 meshes to the square inch.

After being crushed in the crackers all of the cracked cement which fails to pass through the sieve is conveyed by chutes directly to the grinders, which look as nearly as possible like the stones of an ordinary grist mill, as will be seen from the illustration of the grinding room. In fact, the grinding of cement is exactly like the grinding of corn. The Shawangunk conglomerate, or grit, which is found in large quantities in Ulster County, is used for the millstones. At Binnewater there are 16 grinders, or, in other words, 16 pairs of millstones, and they grind sufficient rock to make 2,500 barrels per day. The grinders are placed in a single row, and discharge into boxes containing screw conveyors which run from each end to the center. The ground cement is thus conveyed from each grinder to a central reservoir, from which it is taken by a bucket conveyor to the mixers. By means of the mixers the cement coming from the separate grinders is thoroughly mixed, and uniformity of quality secured. To remove the cement dust, which rises thickly from the grinders and is both disagreeable and unwholesome for the workmen, a powerful ventilating fan is used. This fan draws the dust through the pipes shown with funnel-shaped openings for each grinder in view of the grinding room and conveys it to the floor above, where it is separated from the atmosphere and deposited to be put in barrels and

PACKING ROOM

HOFFMAN

DRAW PIT AT BASE OF KILNS

THE LAWRENCE CEMENT COMPANY, ROSENDALE, N. Y.

sold. About one and one half barrels of this cement dust are collected every day at the Binnewater mill.

From the mixers the cement passes by chutes to the barrels in the packing room (see illustration). The metal pipes in the right foreground connect directly with the mixer, and, as will be seen, discharge into the barrels underneath. To settle the cement thoroughly in the barrels, each is placed on a circular iron disk or table which is capable of a vertical movement. This disk is connected with suitable machinery which lifts it vertically a few inches, then suddenly releases it, allowing it to fall with a concussion which settles the cement in the barrel. As each barrel is filled it is removed to the scales, where a man removes or adds sufficient cement to bring the weight exactly to 300 lbs. The barrels then pass to men who put in the heads and label and stamp them ready for storage or shipment.

As stated before, steam power is used for operating the mills. At Binnewater five boilers supply steam to a pair of Corliss compound engines, with the high pressure and low pressure cylinders mounted tandem, driving a single shaft. The cylinders are 24 by 48 ins., and 44 by 48 ins. At the Eddyville works the Wm. Wright engines are used. In order to bring the equipment of the two mills into convenient position for comparison, the principal details are given in the following tables: —

	Binnewater.	Eddyville.
No. of kilns	30	36
No. of crackers	8	8
No. of grinders	16	16
No. of packers	12	20
Daily capacity	2,500 barrels.	2,800 barrels.
Storage capacity	15,000 barrels.	25,000 barrels.

Hickory Bush warehouses storage capacity 60,000 barrels.

In addition there are at the Esopus mills two crackers, four grinders, and four packers with a daily capacity of from 600 to 800 barrels. The production of the three mills in operation in 1896 was 1,120,769 barrels of cement.

As an indication of the conscientious care displayed by the company in the manufacture of its cement may be mentioned the thorough system of tests carried out. The daily product is subjected to an examination as regards fineness, setting qualities, and strength. Not only is this done every half hour of the day before the cement leaves the mills, but in the New York office laboratory tests are made of each day's grinding.

In this brief statement of the manufacture of cement by the Lawrence Cement Company, it will be noticed that the manufacture of supplies for the mills forms industries of very respectable magnitude in themselves. The most noteworthy of these is the manufacture of the barrels in which the cement is packed. This is all done by the company, cooper shops being located at each of the mills. At these shops are facilities for manufacturing the barrels complete, lining them with paper and storing them for use. The raw materials, hoops, staves, heads, etc., are stored in and about the mills. At Eddyville the company has a large boat yard, where repairs are made to its fleet of boats, about fifteen of which are used to transport the cement on the canal and down the Hudson River. In addition, at each mill blacksmith and carpenter shops are located, where repairs are made to the drills, tram cars, and tools used in the quarries and about the mills.

A very prominent factor in an industry requiring frequent shipments of cargoes of large bulk and weight is, of course, the proximity of transportation lines in the center of production. It is a somewhat curious, and, withal, very important fact that nearly all of the present cement rock quarries were discovered while constructing the great waterways in the early part of the century, and the first use of the cement manufactured was in the masonry of the locks, walls, and bridges of these canals. The constructions of the Delaware and Hudson Canal first disclosed the cement rock of Ulster County, and, until recently, furnished the means of transportation for the greater part of the cement manufactured by the Lawrence Cement Company from the quarries brought to light in its construction. The company has two shipping points, viz., at Binnewater and Eddyville. At Binnewater the works are located within a few rods of the Wallkill Valley Railroad, and all of the cement manufactured here is shipped by railway. The works at Eddyville are located on Rondout Creek, and here are built extensive docks for the boats used in the transportation of cement to all points reached by the canal and river. The production of the Eddyville mill, 2,800 barrels daily, is shipped at this point.

The Lawrence Cement Company, like many other large companies, has undergone many changes in its organization and personnel. Taking its name originally from Mr. W. E. Lawrence, who made the first cement in 1832, the company in 1853 reorganized under its present title. At the same time the works were enlarged and the name of the brand of cement changed to "Hoffman" Rosendale Cement, of which more than twelve millions of barrels have been manufactured since and used in the construction of important buildings and municipal, railroad, and government work.

DESCRIPTION OF THE WORKS OF THE EMPIRE PORTLAND CEMENT COMPANY, WARNERS, N. Y.

MARL AND CLAY DEPOSIT.— The marl consists of carbonate of lime, varying in depth from 3 to 18 ft. The blue clay is immediately under the marl. Following is the analysis of the marl and clay:—

BLUE CLAY.		MARL.	
Silica	40.48	Silica	.26
Alumina and iron oxide .	20.95	Alumina and iron oxide .	.10
Carbonate of lime . . .	25.80	Carbonate of lime . . .	94.39
Magnesia	.99	Magnesia	.38
Potash	3.14	Organic matter	1.54
Water and organic matter	8.50	Water	3.10
	99.86		99.77

There is from 6 to 12 ins. of muck overlying the marl deposit. The marl and clay is excavated with a revolving derrick, with clamshell digger, which lifts a yard and one half each dip; the marl and clay is loaded separately on cars having a capacity of 3 yds. each. The cars of marl and clay are delivered to the works, which are one mile distant, by means of a narrow gauge railroad.

MIXING DEPARTMENT.— The cars of marl and clay are hauled up an inclined track, by means of steel cable and hoisting drum, onto the second floor of the mixing department. The clay is delivered to two large rotary drying cylinders, where the moisture is driven off; the dried clay then passes through steel elevators and conveyors, the heat being carried off with suction fans as the material passes through the conveyors; it is then delivered into large steel bins, and from there passes into under-runner emery mill stones, where it is ground to an impalpable powder; it is then delivered into large steel storage bins over the mixing pans.

The marl is delivered direct from the cars to the mixing pans; the dry ground clay is drawn from the storage bin and delivered into scale hopper, where the proper proportion is weighed and discharged into the mixing pan on top of the marl; this constitutes one charge of 3 cu. yds. of marl with proper amount of clay. The material is thoroughly mixed, sample of the mixed material is taken to the laboratory, where proper tests are made, to determine if the mixture is correct; this being done, the material is discharged into brick machines, and from there delivered onto iron or wood pallets which are 5 ins. wide by 48 ins. long; 52 of these loaded pallets are placed on each iron car.

The cars of brick are passed into hot-air drying tunnels, where the moisture is entirely driven off. The brick carry about 35 per cent. of moisture as they go to the drying tunnels. The drying tunnels are 100 ft. long, 4 ft. 4 ins. wide, and 5 ft. 6 ins. high; each tunnel will accommodate 17 of the cars of brick, there are in all 29 tunnels. It requires from 30 to 36 hours to thoroughly dry the brick.

The burning kilns are the ordinary type of dome kilns, with added improvements to facilitate the filling and for the utilization of the waste heat. 20 of these kilns are used, 10 on each side.

The dry brick are elevated with power elevator to the different floors of the burning kilns. The kilns are filled with alternate layers of the dry brick and coke. About 60 cars of the dry brick are put in each kiln with about 4½ tons of coke. After the kiln is filled with the alternate layers of coke and dry brick, the doors are sealed and the fire is started below. The temperature gradually rises to a white heat and slowly rises to the top; while the kiln is burning no attention is necessary. When the fire has reached the top the stack of the kiln is covered and the heat is drawn off by a system of suction fans, and utilized for drying the wet brick. As soon as the clinker is sufficiently cool it is removed from the lower part of the kiln, where it is carefully selected and delivered to the crushing machinery.

The time required for charging, burning, and emptying a kiln is from 5 to 6 days. Each kiln produces from 20 to 22 tons of clinker.

EMPIRE PORTLAND CEMENT COMPANY, WARNERS, N. Y.

MARL BED.

MIXING DEPT.

DELIVERY OF MARLAND CLAY AT WORKS.

EMPIRE PORTLAND CEMENT COMPANY, WARNERS, N. Y.

EMPIRE PORTLAND CEMENT COMPANY, WARNERS, N. Y.

CORLISS ENGINE

DRYING TUNNELS

CLINKER ROOM OF BURNING KILNS

EMPIRE PORTLAND CEMENT COMPANY, WARNERS, N. Y.

The clinker passes through crushers and rolls until it is reduced fine enough so that the coarsest particles will pass a No. 8 sieve; it is then delivered to emery millstones, where it is finely ground.

From the millstones it passes through a vacuum separator, the coarse particles being returned for further reduction. The finished product is so finely ground that 95 per cent. will pass a 10,000 mesh sieve.

The finished product is conveyed to the storehouse, which is arranged with a system of bins having a capacity of 25,000 barrels.

From the storage bins the cement is conveyed to a barrel packer, which is adapted for filling in either barrels or sacks.

One barrel of the Portland cement weighs 400 lbs. gross, 380 lbs. net.

The laboratory and testing department is under the supervision of experts, and is equipped with the most modern chemical and mechanical appliances.

By continuous chemical analyses of the marl and clay the composition of the mixture is kept absolutely correct, thus insuring a uniform quality. In addition to this, frequent analyses are made of the finished product. The cement manufactured each day is tested to determine the tensile strength, both neat and with sand, for periods ranging from 48 hours to 12 months; tensile test for 48 hours and 7 days is also made of each shipment, so at any time tests can be furnished on any particular lot. These tests, together with important engineering works which have been constructed with Empire Portland cement, demonstrate beyond a doubt that it has no superior.

The high standard attained by the Empire Portland cement has only been secured by the expenditure of over half a million dollars, and the devising of improved machinery, in the erection of large and commodious buildings, and the employment of skilled help in the manufacturing departments.

Possessing a practically inexhaustible supply of the very best of raw material, and aided by the employment of all the appliances that money can command, it is the steadfast purpose of the Empire Portland Cement Company to produce a Portland cement which shall be to-day, to-morrow, and for the years to come, always the same, always reliable.

CHAPTER IX.

The Uses of Cement — Increasing Use per Capita — Concrete Growing in Favor — Sand Cement — Discrepancies in the Proportions of Sand by Measure or Weight — Table of Weights and Measures — Volume vs. Weight — Ultimate Strength of Both Classes of Cements — Machine vs. Hand-made Mortar and Concrete — Disastrous Results from Poorly Made Cement Mortar — Ancient Mortar Scientifically Made — The Author's Collection of Ancient Mortars and Concretes — The Formation of Stone by Natural Infiltration — By Artificial Infiltration as Practised by the Mound-Builders — The Natural Process in the Formation of Hydraulic Cement Rocks — Statistics of the Rock Cement Industry in the United States — Imports and Domestic Portland Table of Statistics — Notable Structures Laid in Rock Cement — A Wonderful Record.

The use of cement is largely on the increase in this country, as may be seen by the following table showing the number of pounds of Rock cement consumed per capita at the dates given : —

1850	pounds per capita	. . . .	6.46
1860	,, ,, ,,	. . . .	10.49
1870	,, ,, ,,	. . . .	12.77
1880	,, ,, ,,	. . . .	13.04
1890	,, ,, ,,	. . . .	33.93

The older States consume more cement per capita than do the younger States.

In the larger cities the brick and stone buildings are being laid in cement, whereas in former years quicklime was used for the purpose.

The use of concrete is rapidly increasing. It is being adopted in places where not many years ago it was considered unsafe to use anything but heavy stone masonry.

The new $4,000,000 Federal building in Chicago will stand on a series of points instead of resting on a foundation extending evenly along the entire wall line. The weight of the huge structure will be so adjusted that it will rest on concrete columns 32 ft. apart, these columns going down to bed rock 72 ft. below the surface of the earth. This is the plan adopted in modern bridge building, and represents the most advanced progress in that field of construction. The mode of excavating for the foundation is very interesting and simplicity itself. A section of a wrought-iron tube of the desired diameter is set upon the ground on its rim, and as the earth within the circle is removed the tube sinks. When the top of the first section settles down to the level of the earth's surface a second section is placed above it and the digging process is continued. One section after another disappears, and bed rock is eventually reached without the slightest disturbance occurring to the surrounding material. There is no settling of neighboring foundations, no tottering walls, no alarm or disquiet of any sort.

When the excavation is completed there is a clean iron-walled hole into which the concrete is poured and subjected to the necessary pressure. When the iron tube is filled the job is finished, the iron casing being allowed to remain. The columns which will constitute the foundation for the Chicago building will vary in diameter from 12 to 15 ft. Through the wear and tear of ages they will support all the weight that they will be called upon to bear.

By this plan it will not be necessary to drive piling down to bed rock or to resort to any of the methods for making broad bases for foundations to rest upon, so familiar to Chicago builders of lofty edifices and heavy business blocks. The element of uncertainty will be entirely eliminated. Concrete columns have been tried in the construction of all the great iron and steel bridges built in recent years and found to be wholly satisfactory. There is no guesswork, no speculation as to the precise weight a concrete column of certain dimensions standing on solid rock will sustain. It is a simple mathe-matical and engineering proposition.

The concrete will be composed of American Portland cement one part, sand two parts, and five parts of broken stone.

The foregoing description is derived from Chicago journals and private correspondence.

For concrete sidewalks for the Federal building at Mankato, Minn., in 1896, the following specifications were drawn by William M. Aikin, United States Supervising Architect, Washington, D. C.: —

" The bed for sidewalk to be excavated to the required depth, and the sidewalk constructed as follows ": —

" A 6 in. thick layer of broken stone, same as hereinafter specified for concrete, thoroughly rolled solid ; on this lay a 6 in. thick layer of concrete and a 2 in. thick finish coat.   The concrete to be composed of five parts sound hard stone, broken to a size to pass through a 2 in. diameter ring ; two parts clean, sharp sand, and one part of approved hydraulic cement. Sand and cement to be mixed dry.   Water added to make a mortar of proper consistency, and the broken stone, drenched and drained, to be stirred in until each piece is thoroughly coated.

" The concrete to be laid and tamped until free mortar appears on the surface.

" The concrete to be laid in blocks, and as near 4 ft. square as may conform to width of sidewalk.

" These blocks to be cut clear through, down to broken stone base.

" The finish coat to be composed of two parts approved Portland cement, and three parts of clean crushed granite, all thoroughly mixed, tempered, laid in place and properly tamped with wooden tamps, and have a dry coat of two parts cement and one part sharp white sand floated on, troweled down to a smooth, hard finish, and the surface slightly indented for foothold.

" The finish coat to be cut through on lines corresponding with the concrete blocks below.   The finish surface of the sidewalk to be graded as shown and noted on the drawing.

QUALITY OF CEMENT.

" The Portland cement, herein called for, to have a tensile strength of not less than 350 lbs. to square inch.

"That for hydraulic cement to be 90 lbs.

"Samples of the cement, proposed to be used for the work, must be submitted by the contractor for test, about 2 qts. of each kind. (It is presumed that 7 day tests are meant. — AUTHOR.)

"Samples of the cement delivered on the premises for use in actual construction will be subject to test; and all cement found to be unsatisfactory will be rejected, and the same must be immediately removed from the premises.

"The names and brands of cements proposed to be used must be stated in the bid; and all cements must be of uniform quality; not damaged; satisfactory to the supervising architect; delivered on the site, in the original packages, with the brand and makers' name plainly printed or stenciled thereon, and kept dry until used."

A. S. Cooper, in *Journal Franklin Institute*, November, 1895, writes as follows in regard to fine *vs.* coarse sand for a cement mortar: —

"During the construction of a mining casemate at Fort Pulaski last year the question arose as to the advisability of using fine beach sand instead of coarse river sand, on account of the greater cost of obtaining the latter. The writer took the position that fine sand would be nearly as good, and as it was estimated to save nearly $1,000 in the total cost, experiments were made which proved the fine sand to be slightly stronger than the coarse. These results are opposed to those obtained by all previous experimenters. Generally speaking, the coarser the sand the stronger the mortar made from it; but the difference between the grades below 30–40 are so slight that, as far as sizes are concerned, they might be considered in one class. There seemed to be a tendency toward an increase in strength with grades below 100–120, but so few samples of these grades were obtained that this slight increase may be put down as accidental. There is an unmistakable indication of weakness in the upper grade, 8–12. It is apparent that the specific gravity of all of the various kinds and grades of sand tried are not materially different, and that therefore the difference found between the weights of different volumes are principally due to the different percentages of voids. It is further apparent that the smaller the grade, the greater percentage of voids in loose sand, and *vice versa*; while in well-packed sand there is practically no difference in percentage of voids. These results indicate that uniformity of mortar briquettes for tests can be obtained only by either measuring the sand while well packed or by weighing. Other things being equal, coarse sands are better than fine sands for cement mortar up to the grade 12-16, or about one twelfth of an inch in diameter. Below the grade 40-50, or about one sixtieth of an inch in diameter, there is no practical difference in the value of the different sands, as far as the size is concerned. The shape and condition of the surfaces of the grains of different sands has as much to do with the value of cement mortar as the size."

In the selection of sand for cement mortar or concrete it is important to know that the amount which may safely be used depends largely on its purity.

It is by no means an easy matter to find pure sand. A portion of a handful dropped into a glass of clear water will demonstrate quite accurately its condition.

If absolutely pure, the sand will settle, leaving the water clear.

If it contains clay or loam, those impurities will cloud or discolor the water.

The impurities named are by no means fatal to a mortar or concrete, but the sand containing them cannot be used as freely as one that is pure.

Either one of the impurities named, if present, will retard the setting of the cement, the degree of retardation being in direct ratio with the percentage of impurities present.

It is understood that ordinary clean sand contains voids amounting usually to about one third of the total volume. It will be seen, then, that with three barrels of sand the voids may be replaced by a barrel of cement without an increase in volume.

It will also be apparent that, if more than three parts of sand to one of cement are used, whether the latter is Rock cement or Portland, there will be voids amounting to one third of the volume of sand used in excess.

If one barrel of cement and three barrels of sand are mixed together, and the latter contains loam or clay, the voids, instead of being filled with pure cement, will be filled with cement which, by reason of its being mixed with the impurities named, will be greatly retarded in setting.

Within the past few years there has been placed upon the market a cement known as "sand" cement. It is produced by grinding together to a fine condition a mixture of Portland cement and sand, usually in the proportions of one barrel of cement and three barrels of sand.

It is claimed by the advocates of this kind of cement that it will test equally as high, when mixed with three parts of sand, as will the pure Portland when mixed with the same amount.

In other words, by reason of the fine trituration of the cement and three parts of sand, the original one part of cement will carry six parts of sand, and test equally as high as the one part of cement and three parts of sand mixed in the ordinary manner.

However true it may be in regard to the tests being equal, it can readily be seen, if three parts of ordinary sand are mixed with one part of the "sand" cement, that the voids are filled with a mortar instead of being filled with pure cement.

And as but one fourth of this mortar is cement, and as it is a fact that it is only the cement in the mortar which has any setting properties whatever, it would seem, if there is any benefit to be derived from the use of the so-called "sand" cement, it must follow that a cement mortar can be made to equal the pure cement in strength, a proposition which on its face appears to be unsound, notwithstanding the results as claimed to be shown by the testing machine.

The report of the committee on a "Uniform System for Tests of Cement," to the American Society of Civil Engineers, states that "the proportions of cement, sand, and water should be carefully determined by weight."

This practise of determining proportions by weight in the making of briquettes for testing purposes is quite rigidly adhered to, but whenever cement mortar is made for masonry work there is a wide departure from the rules observed in testing.

In the mixing of cement mortar, it is customary throughout the country to use an empty cement barrel for measuring the sand that is to be mixed with the cement.

There are, in this country, three distinct standards of weight for a barrel of cement.

The standard weight throughout the Eastern and Atlantic States is known as the "Eastern" weight for Rock cement, while the "Western" weight is prevalent through the Middle and Western States.

The Portland weight is the same throughout the country.

TABLE OF STANDARD WEIGHTS PER BARREL.

Net weight of a barrel of **Eastern** cement is 300 lbs.
Net weight of a barrel of Western cement is 265 lbs.
Net weight of a barrel of Portland cement is 380 lbs.
Net weight of a barrel of sand is 300 lbs.

It is customary in the use of Rock cements to spread out two barrels of sand in a mortar box, and over this spread one barrel of cement, and these are mixed together while dry, and water is then applied.

If Portland cement is to be used, it is customary to employ three barrels of sand to one barrel of cement.

This manner of measuring is practised throughout the entire country, and while it is a convenient system, it results in a disparity of proportions when weights are considered, which militates against the Rock cements, and correspondingly favors the Portland cements.

It also favors the Eastern as against the Western cements, as will be seen by the following : —

TABLE : —

RATIOS OF CEMENT AND SAND BY WEIGHT AND MEASURE, AND
PER CENT. BY WEIGHT.

	Ratio by measure.	Ratio by weight.	Per cent. by weight.
	Cement 1	1.00	56
	Sand 1	.79	44
	Cement 1	1.00	39
PORTLAND	Sand 2	1.58	61
CEMENT.	Cement 1	1.00	30
	Sand 3	2.37	70
	Cement 1	1.00	24
	Sand 4	3.36	76
	Cement 1	1.00	20
	Sand 5	3.95	80
	Cement 1	1.00	17
	Sand 6	4.74	83

	Ratio by measure.	Ratio by weight.	Per cent. by weight.
Cement 1	1.00	50
Sand 1	1.00	50
Cement 1	1.00	33
Sand 2	2.00	67
"EASTERN" ROCK — Cement 1	1.00	25
Sand 3	3.00	75
CEMENT. — Cement 1	1.00	20
Sand 4	4.00	80
Cement 1	1.00	17
Sand 5	5.00	83
Cement 1	1.00	14
Sand 6	6.00	86
Cement 1	1.00	47
Sand 1	1.13	53
Cement 1	1.00	31
Sand 2	2.26	69
"WESTERN" ROCK — Cement 1	1.00	23
Sand 3	3.39	77
CEMENT. — Cement 1	1.00	18
Sand 4	4.53	82
Cement 1	1.00	15
Sand 5	5.66	85
Cement 1	1.00	13
Sand 6	6.79	87

It will be seen in all the mixtures of cement and sand by measure throughout the entire table, that by weight, the Eastern Rock cement is carrying 26 per cent., and the Western 43 per cent. more sand than is the Portland.

It will also be seen that with Rock cements at 1 to 2, and the Portland at 1 to 3 by measure, the difference in the percentages of sand by weight is but a trifle, while the percentages of sand in the Rock cement at 1 to 3 and the Portland at 1 to 4 are practically the same.

By weight, there is 15 per cent. more sand in Western cement mixed 1 to 4 by measure, than there is in Portland mixed 1 to 5; while with Eastern cement mixed 1 to 4, the percentage of sand is precisely the same as with Portland mixed 1 to 5.

So long as it remains the prevailing custom to mix cement and sand by measure rather than by weight, it is not strange that people are deluded into a belief that Portland cement will carry 50 per cent. more sand than will the Rock cements.

It is due to the unfortunate establishment of the different standards of weight per barrel that has led to many errors in judgment concerning the relative values of the two classes of cements.

There is a very large question involved in the matter of bulk as between the two classes of cements.

The volume of a given number of pounds of Rock cement is 25 per cent. greater than is that of the same number of pounds of Portland cement.

In the production of concrete, when the surfaces of the sand, gravel, and broken stone are fairly coated with cement, and the sizes of the gang are selected with a view to the prevention of voids, and the mass is properly rammed, it is generally understood and admitted that all has been done that is possible toward the production of a first quality of concrete.

If, therefore, the volume of 100 lbs. of Rock cement is 25 per cent. greater than is that of 100 lbs. of Portland cement, and assuming that both classes are ground equally fine, it is difficult to disprove that 100 lbs. of Rock cement will not coat over the surfaces of 25 per cent. more sand and gravel than the 100 lbs. of Portland.

In any event, it must be clear that, pound for pound, the Rock cement will coat over an equal amount of sand and gravel more thoroughly than the Portland cement.

Herein undoubtedly is to be found the solution of a problem which has puzzled the cement world since the foundation of the present system of cement testing; namely, that as the proportion of sand is increased, the difference in the relative strength of the two classes of cements decreases.

This fact would seem to indicate that the Rock cement, by having the greater volume, has a greater capacity for coating over the surfaces of the gang in mortar or concrete.

May we not find here the cause for the unexpected results that were met with by Mr. Smith when he tested the two classes of cements by shearing strain and by compression? He used twice as much sand with the Portland as he did with the Rock cement, and in the tests the latter named cement tested more than 100 per cent. higher than the Portland, a result so surprising as to bring out the comments by the author of the tests, on pages 143, 146, and 147, which will well repay careful perusal.

It is a popular delusion concerning Portland cement, that there is hardly a limit to its sand-carrying capacity, and oftentimes it is overloaded, producing a weak, dangerous mortar, which can in no manner compare, either in cost or quality, with a mortar made of Rock cement and a lower admixture of sand.

The ultimate strength of neat Portland cement is reached in one year, and one half of its strength is reached in seven days; while with a mixture of one part of cement and three parts of sand, it reaches its ultimate strength in four years.

The ultimate strength of neat Rock cement is reached in five years, and at seven days it has attained but one eighth of its ultimate strength; while with one part of cement and three parts of sand its ultimate strength is not known to the author beyond ten years, but it is certain that there is a gradual increase in strength during the period named.

MACHINE vs. HAND MADE MORTARS AND CONCRETES.

One of the most approved forms of concrete mixing machines is shown in the following illustration.

In these machines the feed and discharge are continuous, the capacity being 30 cu. yds. of well-mixed concrete per hour.

They are largely used where extensive work is to be done, such as in the construction of reservoirs, bridge-piers, sea-walls, jetties, and heavy foundations for business blocks, and wherever concrete is to be used in large quantities.

It is claimed that by the use of these machines the cost of mixing is reduced to at least one half below that of hand-mixed concrete.

It is beyond question that machine-made concrete is vastly superior to the hand mixed, as it is next to impossible to perform such work as thoroughly by hand, except at the expense of much

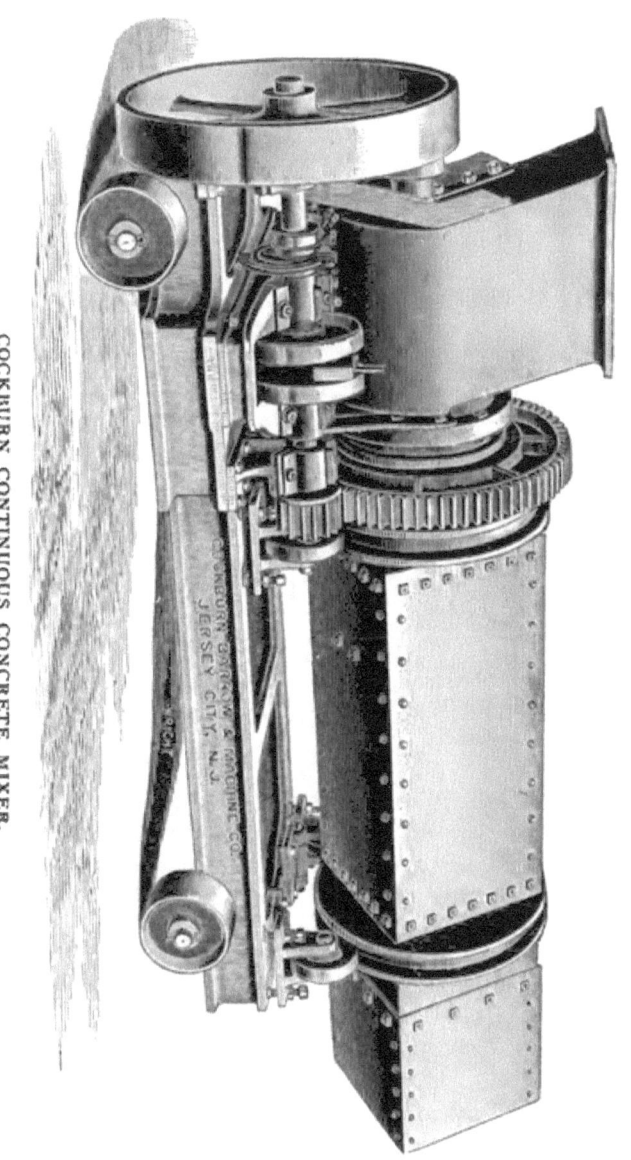

COCKBURN CONTINUOUS CONCRETE MIXER.

longer time, and even then **there is** the constant **factor of human weakness.**

In the making of concrete by hand, it is doubtful if one set of **hands can produce** two batches of equal merit. In the mixing by **hand of ordinary** cement mortar, where the specifications call for cement one and sand two parts, the amount of mixing the material receives depends largely upon circumstances, and it is strange that **the** masonry work throughout the country stands as well as it does, **for on** many works of importance the quality of the mortar as regards **mixing, is simply wretched.**

During the past summer the stone piers for a railroad bridge over a small river near the home of the author were under construction.

The specifications governing the quality of **the** mortar called for a mixture of one part first quality **of natural hydraulic cement,** and two parts of clean, coarse, sharp sand.

The quality of the materials furnished **was excellent, a** good quality of Rosendale cement being **used, and the sand, though of a** dark-reddish cast, was all that could reasonably be desired.

The number of hands employed to prepare **the mortar was dis**tressingly inadequate.

A " batch " of the mortar consisted of one barrel of cement and **two barrels of sand.** An empty barrel minus both heads was used **for measuring the sand.**

This was placed upright in **the** mortar box by one man, while two others with shovels commenced to toss sand from a pile about ten feet away, presumably with the intention of having it land inside of the barrel; **and at** this they were fairly successful, as the barrel was soon filled, and heaped up by the time the sand which did not land **inside** the barrel had accumulated **around** on the outside nearly half **as high as** the barrel itself. In the meantime the man who handled the headless barrel was wringing and twisting in a desperate effort to empty the barrel and set it again, during which time there **was no let up** by the sand tossers.

They worked away **for dear life, without** deigning to cast even **a** glance at the man, whom the author expected to see buried alive.

How the man did it is a mystery, but certain it is that the barrel **was finally set for** the second time, and the man emerged from **behind the sand storm** looking not very much the worse for wear.

In a twinkling the barrel was again heaped up and running over. Interest in the project now became absorbing, and the author walked around on the opposite side to get a better view.

The instant the sand tossers had dropped their shovels, what before had appeared to be unseemly haste had become a whirlwind, but the author was not left long in doubt as to the cause for it.

The barrel handler had learned from experience that he had no time to waste in meditation, and he clasped his arms around the barrel and swayed it from side to side, and back and forth, working with all his might to free the barrel and get clear of the mortar box.

And well he might, for the sand tossers were upon him.

With a barrel of cement between them, they cast it upon the pile of sand in the mortar box, and almost before it had landed one had knocked a head in with the edge of a shovel, while the other had up-set it, and the flying cement was close upon the heels of the retreating barrel handler.

But his turn had now come, and quick as a flash he had grasped a hose and was turning water upon the pile of sand, cement, and men in the mortar box.

The stream struck the heap of sand and cement just as the heels of the sand tossers were seen emerging from it.

Now came the mixing. No hoes were used. The sand tossers simply turned up the edge of the sand with shovels, while the barrel handler held the hose on the cement in the center of the pile until the mass was saturated.

That ended the mixing, which had consumed possibly forty-five seconds of time, and the sand tossers quickly deposited the alleged mortar in another box which was swung away by derrick to the masons on the piers, and the comedy began again.

Occasionally when some of the masons happened to be engaged in setting a large face stone, the mortar would be fairly mixed, but when the work on the piers was mostly backing, then indeed were the mortar mixers called upon.

With so small a mortar crew, for so many masons, it was simply out of the question to produce good mortar.

The color of the sand and cement being so nearly alike, it was easy to imagine, by those who wished so to do, that the materials were fairly well mixed; while the facts are that about one half of the sand which was used in the mortar was as innocent of a coating of cement as when it laid in its native bed.

Later in the season the author noted the pointing of the finished piers with Portland cement, and thus was hidden from sight another instance of the almost criminal folly of giving out such work by contract to the lowest bidder.

No more pernicious system was ever devised.

Several years ago the author, who manufactured the Rock cement used, had occasion to witness the construction of some stone-masonry piers for a railroad bridge across a river where the water was from 40 to 50 ft. deep, and the current was very strong.

The masonry was constructed in wooden caissons, which were built up a little in advance of the masonry work, the caissons being gradually sunk to their foundations by the weight of the masonry.

It would seem that if there ever was need of mortar being well made, it was in such a structure as the one under consideration; but as a layer of stone was completed, sand was sprinkled over it, and on top of this was sprinkled some cement, and a hose was then turned on for awhile, whereupon another layer of stone followed.

There was not the slightest pretense of mixing the cement and sand together, and yet the cost of this bridge was over one million dollars, and, strange to relate, it still stands.

There is scarcely a year passing that spring freshets do not carry away many bridges, and when the stone piers are broken and destroyed, it is invariably found that the bedding of the stones is practically clear of cement mortar.

There is but one cause for this — the cement and sand were never properly mixed together.

Had they been, and the mixture rendered quite plastic, the stones could never have separated from the mortar.

As well pull the stones apart in their center lines as at the joints.

With poorly mixed mortar, the weight of the superstructure and the stones themselves is all that prevents the bridge from moving down stream at flood time.

Up to the time when setting commences, cement and sand cannot be too well mixed.

In short, if the mortar is treated properly, there will be fewer bridges moving from their foundations at flood time, for nothing is more certain than that when good cement is used, and the mortar is worked as it should be, a bridge pier will become monolithic in character, and immovable unless carried away bodily.

As an instance of the result of a proper manipulation of natural hydraulic cement mortar, attention is directed to page 13, in which reference is made to an aqueduct built by the Carthaginians over 2,500 years ago.

From the top of this aqueduct, probably through scismic disturbances, an enormous body of stone masonry was dislodged, falling over 100 ft. upon the rocks below, where it still lies unbroken, a silent but powerful argument in favor of thoroughly honest work in the preparation of cement mortars.

A RARE COLLECTION.

In the author's collection of ancient mortars and concretes, a few specimens, with the probable dates of their fabrication, are noted as worthy of mention.

GERMANY.

Bonn. — Mortar from the Cathedral at Bonn on the Rhine, constructed in the fourth century. Sample exceedingly hard.

Coblenz. — Mortar from the Kaufaus overlooking the Moselle, 1688.

FRANCE.

Paris. — Mortars from the Catacombs, 1786; from the Arc de Triomphe de l'Etoile, 1806; and from the staircase in the Louvre, 1541.

Versailles. — Mortar from one of the cottages in the garden of the Petit Trianon. Time of Louis XVI.

ENGLAND.

Oxford. — Mortars from the old city walls at New College, 1370; from the Carfax Tower, 1327; from an old stone gateway leading to St. Mary's College, 1437; from St. Magdalen College, 1475; from Wadham College, 1610; from columns of Christ Church, 1180; from the battlements of New College, 1386. The latter is a fine specimen of a hard and durable concrete.

Warwick. — Mortar from the entrance gate to Warwick Castle, 915; firm and hard. Mortar from Guy's Tower, Warwick Castle, 1394.

Windermere. — Mortar from the ruins of a tower formerly occupied by monks, opposite Bowness, Lake Windermere.

Kenilworth. — Mortars from the ruins of Kenilworth Castle, and from the south side of the "Old Norman Keep," also from the interior " Norman Court," twelfth century.

London. — Mortar from the main banqueting hall in the main tower of the " Tower of London." A fine sample of mortar from one of the passageways in the " Tower of London." This tower was founded by William the Conqueror. Mortar from the stairway leading to the tomb of Henry VII., Westminster Abbey. Time of Edward I., Edward II., Edward III., and Henry VII. Mortar and stone from the monument erected by Sir Christopher Wren to commemorate the great London fire of 1666. The stones for this monument were quarried at Portland, on the south coast of England. It was the color of this stone which suggested the name for artificial cement (see page 18).

SCOTLAND.

Edinburgh. — Mortar from St. Anthony's Chapel, a ruin near Edinburgh; dark colored and exceedingly hard and firm; 1435. Mortar from an old chapel situated at Edinburgh Castle. Mortar from a room in which the seventh Duke of Argyle was imprisoned at Edinburgh Castle. Mortar from the abbey at Holywood Palace, 1128.

Dunkeld. — A piece of stone and mortar from the walls of the partially ruined cathedral at Dunkeld, taken from a point near which rests a carved figure of the " Wolf of Badenoch " recumbent and in full armor. This figure is one of the few which survived the destruction of the ruin. The " Wolf of Badenoch " belonged to the " Clan of Cumin." Time, twelfth century.

Fort William. — Exceedingly hard and firm concrete from the ruins of Inverlochy Castle. Formerly the property of " The Black Cumin " of the " Cumin Clan." Time, thirteenth century.

Kingussie. — Mortar from the ruins of Ruthven Castle. Formerly the property of the " Red Cumin " of the " Cumin Clan." Time, thirteenth century.

Stirling. — A hard and heavy concrete from the wall surrounding Stirling Castle. Time, James III. to James V.

ITALY.

Rome. — Mortars from the walls in the Appian Way, from the

Catacombs, from the Coliseum, and from the old Roman Forum; also a fine specimen of Pozzuolana.

UNITED STATES.

Nebraska. — Mortar from a prehistoric stone wall surrounding several acres of level land on a prominence about twenty miles southwest of Chadron. This mortar is somewhat friable, but it is well calculated to resist the effects of the extremes of temperature prevalent in that climate, as it bears no evidences of disintegration.

Indiana. — Samples of artificial stone produced in Posey County, by the prehistoric race known as the "Mound-Builders," in the manner described on pages 44 to 49, also in this chapter.

THOUGHTS ON STONE-MAKING.

And this our life, exempt from public haunt,
Finds tongues in trees, books in the running brooks,
Sermons in stones, and good in everything. — *Shakespeare.*

He builded better than he knew;
The conscious stone to beauty grew. — *Emerson.*

On the desk at which the author is sitting while he pens these lines there rests three fine specimens of stones. They are very similar in composition, yet wholly unlike in the manner of their creation; and as they either directly or indirectly relate to hydraulic cement, we venture upon a brief dissertation, trusting that it may not prove entirely devoid of interest.

Taking down the first specimen, we examine it as we have done many times before, yet always with curious interest, for it seems impossible to hold it in one's hand for examination without wondering what can be its true history. It is but one of hundreds of this kind of stones in the collection of the author. Its hardness was caused by natural infiltration and subsequent evaporation of water charged with calcium carbonate in solution, through clay beds which had become cracked in all directions by shrinkage due to exposure to the direct rays of the sun. The seams thus produced became filled with nearly pure calcium carbonate much darker in color than the main body of the stones.

These stones represent, then, what was at one time a single sheet of petrified mud, which was broken up by the ice floe, the resultant blocks becoming rounded by abrasion, or attrition caused by moving waters or ice, or by surface decomposition. They were carried along and deposited during one of the glacial periods, and are now found in a drift of shale 15 to 25 ft. below the surface.

The shale occurs at a bend of a rapid stream in the town of Alden, Erie County, N. Y. During the spring freshets the stream, which at this point has an impact of at least 1,650 lbs. per square foot, undermines the shale and deposits the specimens along the river bed. In the summer the water falls, and specimens varying in weight from 3 to 100 lbs. may be readily secured.

This beautiful specimen, then, which we now hold in our hand, did not assume its present form and comeliness when the world was young. Ages may have elapsed during the time when it was in a state of mud. It may have lain for countless centuries in this condition at the bottom of some vast inland sea, and ages upon ages must have passed before the slow uplifting of the land exposed the mud to the direct rays of the sun. Then came the almost interminable length of time when the mud would be exposed alternately to water and sunshine. Finally there came the complete drying out with the resultant checks and cracks. Next there was required a body of water charged with calcium carbonate in solution, and the mud had to be alternately saturated with this " hard " water and subjected to the sun's rays. Thus slowly the mud became petrified. Then, how much time must have elapsed after this before it was disturbed and broken up, and how far did it travel before it found its resting place in the shale bank? And how long did it lie there before it was again disturbed by the stream which disclosed it to the author? Thus the world was not young when this specimen finally assumed its present form. But long as the time may seem since the mud was deposited on the bottom of the sea, it was but a day as compared with its existence previous to that time.

Let us go back to the time when this mud was part and parcel of some lofty granite cliff, perhaps forming the crown to some vast mountain peak. Who can tell how long it stood thus under the full rays of the sun, or the pitiless rain beating down upon it, bearing the great rock destroyer as well as maker, carbon dioxide gas, which sought out its interstices and inaugurated the work of decay and disintegration, which never rested, until finally the granite crumbled, decomposed, and was carried down by the rains to the streams and rivers, the feldspar giving up its potash, soda, or lime to the great destroyer, leaving behind only mud? The quartz, in the meantime, had succumbed and turned to sand, while the mica, following the fate of the feldspar, gave up its potash, oxides of iron, or magnesia, as the case may be, thus leaving the silica and alumina to become clay mud.

And now let us take one more look backward, and imagine, if we can, the existence of this material before it became granite.

Was it thrown up in the manner of igneous rocks, in a molten or plastic state? And when the rain fell upon it, thus providing the water of crystallization, the latter taking place as soon as the material was sufficiently cooled? And if so, how long was the material held in a molten or plastic state? What was its condition before it became molten or plastic? Or, was the material a bed of clay or mud, which became subject to metamorphic action, and thus became slowly converted into granite?

How many times have the rocks in the hills beside the roadways, which we see daily, but upon which we scarcely bestow a thought, been converted from rocks to mud, and from mud to rocks, since the days when the world was young?

And now we reluctantly return this most interesting bit of stone to its accustomed place, and with a feeling of awe and veneration we take the next specimen into our hands.

My fingers press the places that once were pressed by the fingers of the Mound-Builder, who formed it and molded it, and turned the plastic clay into stone.

On a summer's day, under wide-spreading branches, by the bank of a stream, with his wife and children about him, the Mound-Builder sits and "finds tongues in trees, and books in the running brooks," as he molds the plastic clay into the forms then prevalent for domestic use.

Now he arises, and with a stone pail of his own creation in his hand, goes down to the spring of "hard" water, and returning, he gently sprinkles the molded vessels which, by a retention of the calcium carbonate, gradually becomes hardened, as the process is repeated day after day.

Was this really the first lesson in the art of hydraulic cement fabrication? or was the process an old one handed down for hundreds or thousands of years?

At all events, it is quite true that "it is not alone in Europe that we find a well-founded claim of high antiquity for the art of making hard and durable stone by a mixture of clay, lime, and sand."

It seems hardly credible that the Mound-Builders could have been possessed of the knowledge necessary to have enabled them to observe the processes of nature in the conversion of mud flats into hard and durable stones as already described.

Admitting, however, as we are forced to do, that they did observe and did understand this transformation, how are we to withhold our profound admiration for their truly scientific attainments as shown in their ability to produce, artificially, the same results?

Truly there must have been men of ability in those days long dead, and artists as well, for who among us of to-day can excel them in the construction of vessels one eighth of an inch thick, and able to withstand heat as described on page 45? or the construction of such vessels 5 or 6 ft. in diameter as described on page 44?

Indeed, the principle involved in the operation is practically unknown to the people of to-day.

When we think of the people "who inhabited this continent at a period so remote that neither tradition nor history can furnish any account of them," we are led to reflect that it may be only a question of time when people, in speaking of the present age, will refer to us as a race of half-civilized tombstone-builders.

These people are known to us only as a race of "mound-builders," when the mounds they built were simply the graves of their dead over which the earth was raised to mark the place of burial, while we at the present time place a stone to mark the spot.

And it is clearly evident, if we are to judge by the appearance of the latter in the old burial places throughout New England, that the mounds, if left undisturbed, will far outlast any stone that may be raised for the purpose.

Therefore, in so far as relates to the permanency of burial marks, we are a long way behind the unknown race who occupied this continent long before the advent of the red man. How long before is unknown. It is even unknown as to the time when the race of Mound-Builders became extinct. It is not altogether improbable that some of the blood of the Mound-Builders may still be coursing in the veins of the red man.

The system of government established and maintained by the Five Nations of the State of New York, and which was known to have been in existence over one hundred years, and how much longer is unknown, before the landing of the Pilgrims at Plymouth Rock, measured by its utility was not inferior to any system established by the Puritans, or any known system of government in Europe at that time.

Those who study the history and lives of the races which once occupied our land do not readily fall into the common error of believing that all was ignorance and barbarism which preceded the advent of the Puritan.

Reverently we lay down this piece of stone, this relic of days long gone by, with a feeling akin to the warmest admiration and kindliest friendship for the man whose hands fashioned and held it up for approval.

The centuries which have elapsed since he held it as I now hold it seem as but a day. His workmanship proves that he was every inch a man, and I hold out my hand to grasp his across the abyss of time.

We come now to our third specimen. It is merely a fragment of hydraulic cement stone, yet it contains within its mysterious body many a long, and ofttimes tedious sermon.

As we take it down and examine it, perhaps for the hundredth time, under a strong glass, we can never restore it to its place without a thought as to its wonderful construction.

It is but a limestone, called by geologists an "impure limestone," which expression can be and is used to cover numberless variations in the percentages of impurities which it may contain.

Absolutely pure limestone is practically unknown. It is a very pure limestone which does not contain more than 3 to 5 per cent. of impurities.

The specimen before us contains about 30 per cent. of impurities, and it is this amount which determines its classification under the head of hydraulic cement stones. With one half the impurities named present, it would have been classed as an hydraulic limestone.

It is to be understood that the impurities in this case consist principally of clay.

How does it come about that a limestone may contain 30 per cent. of clay? We will find, if we take the limestones as a mass, that not one cubic yard in ten thousand will contain clay to the extent of 30 per cent.

Hydraulic cement rock, then, is not so common a mineral as many would suppose. The beds of limestone, which fall below the requisite amount of clay to constitute a good cement rock, are practically limitless.

It will be observed by those who take an interest in the study of rocks, that in a majority of cases, where cement rocks occur, they are found to lie underneath several layers of limestone which vary from practically pure strata at the top to hydraulic limestone as we approach the cement rock in the descending order.

It is a rule that in a deposit of impure limestone, while the lower layer may contain a percentage of clay which renders it eminently hydraulic, the next layer above may contain a trifle less clay, and so on to the upper layer, which may be practically a pure limestone.

How are we to account for these facts? There is but one way that is at all clear or conclusive to the author, and it may be said in passing, that his conclusions are not in full accord with the higher authorities on this subject.

The question is, then, in what manner are the calcium carbonate and the clay intermingled in an hydraulic cement rock?

The process of intermingling these two ingredients in the first specimen has been shown to be by infiltration; but that process will not satisfy the conditions in a cement rock, for it must be clear that by the process of infiltration the amount of carbonate of lime must be limited to the voids or interstices in the clay, which do not form one fourth of its volume; whereas, in a cement rock, the amount of carbonate of lime must reach as high as 70 to 75 per cent. of the entire volume.

It is well known that limestones are always deposited in water, and in a vast majority of cases, in sea water. Clay beds also are deposited in water, but are subject to subsequent drift.

Now if we take a lump of clay and drop it in a glass of water, leaving it undisturbed for a few days, it will be found, if the clay is pure, that it will have become settled in the bottom of the glass, leaving the water practically clear.

But should the clay contain a small percentage of soda or potash, it will not settle down so readily. In fact, it will be held more or less in solution, the water remaining in a muddy condition.

If now we state the further fact that of the hundreds of

analyses of Rock cements and cement rocks which are familiar to the author not one thus far has been found where the clay portion did not contain a small percentage of one or the other, and in most instances both of the alkalies named, the way will have become cleared for an easy understanding of what is to follow.

It is well understood that water will hold calcium carbonate in solution indefinitely, or until it is surcharged, in which case it will be precipitated. This is noticeable when hard water is boiled in a tea-kettle, or when used as feed water for steam boilers.

In these instances the volume of water being reduced, it becomes surcharged, and the carbonate of lime falls to the bottom. The same result will follow if, instead of the volume of water being reduced, the quantity of carbonate of lime is increased.

It is the latter condition which prevails when the deposition of calcium carbonate takes place in the formation of large bodies of limestone, and when the water is pure, or practically so, the deposition will become what is called pure limestone.

But when clay is held in solution in the water, the atoms of calcium carbonate, in falling down, will become coated with the clay through which it passes, and thus we have impure limestone, the amount of the clay in solution governing the percentage of clay found in the stone and thus is determined whether the stone becomes eminently hydraulic cement stone or hydraulic limestone.

It is thus that the lower layer usually contains more clay than the layer next above; and so, as the calcium carbonate falls, carrying down the clay, the latter becomes less in quantity in the succeeding layers, until, if the deposition of calcium carbonate continues, and there is no new influx of clay, the layers will become practically pure limestone.

Instances occur where a layer of cement rock may contain a trifle more of clay than the layer next below. This is caused by a temporary influx of more clay, but it is exceptional.

There are instances where the clay is in excess in cement rock throughout the formation. In these instances the clay carries quite a large percentage of the alkalies.

Where the Lower Silurian limestone formations rest directly upon the Potsdam sandstone the lower layers usually contain sand. In some instances it is so excessive as to cause the formations to be called "calciferous sandstone"; but whenever there is found a bed of clay lying between the Potsdam and the limestone, then the lower layers of limestone are found to be hydraulic in character.

And thus it is in all the known cement rock formations, either clay or clay shale lies underneath ; and the same quality and kind of clay is found in and throughout the cement rock, thus proving conclusively, to the author at least, that first came the clay, a portion of which was deposited and a portion remaining in solution in the water, due, as we have stated, to the presence of soda or potash; then came the carbonate of lime, which in its deposition carried down a coating of clay ; and thus was provided by nature for the use of man one of his most valuable building materials.

In restoring this our third specimen to its place, we note its fineness of texture, and this suggests the thought as to the size of the atoms of calcium carbonate when held in solution, which are so small as to be invisible to the naked eye.

When we consider these minute particles as being coated with clay, and thus being formed into compact cement stone, we come to realize the difficulties encountered in the attempt to imitate the physical condition of this material in the preparation of the same ingredients for artificial cements.

STATISTICS.

From the year 1818, when the Rock cement industry was first established in this country, until 1882, no public statistics were kept to show the extent and growth of this branch of the building trade.

Since 1882, however, such records have been faithfully kept by the United States Geological Survey, Washington, D. C., and have been published yearly in *Mineral Resources of the United States*, which is issued by the Survey.

The author has prepared several of these yearly reports, and, having a natural taste in that direction, he has let no opportunity pass to add to his little storehouse of knowledge concerning the statistics of the Rock cement industry from the date of its birth in this country near the little village of Fayetteville, in Onondaga County, N. Y., in the year 1818 until the present time.

During the past thirty years the author has been adding little by little to the items bearing on this subject, either by correspondence or in conversation with the oldest persons engaged in the industry, by gathering bits of family history, and in ways too numerous and uninteresting to record.

The difficulties encountered in the compilation of these statistics during the period named have been much greater than would readily be believed by a person who has never attempted such work.

Information seemingly reliable would accumulate in the course of years, and be found at last to bear but a slight resemblance to the truth.

But by dint of persistent effort and careful gleaning and sifting, the author has been enabled to form a table covering the entire history of the industry in this country, which he feels assured will be accepted as being practically accurate, and in the entire absence of any other known effort in the same direction, authoritative.

Production of Rock cement in the United States during the time since the industry was established in 1818 to Jan. 1, 1897.

TIME.	Years.	No. of barrels.
To 1830	12	300,000
To 1840	10	1,000,000
To 1850	10	4,250,000
To 1860	10	11,000,000
To 1870	10	16,420,000
To 1880	10	22,000,000
1880	1	2,030,000
1881	1	2,440,000
1882	1	3,165,000
1883	1	4,190,000
1884	1	4,000,000
1885	1	4,100,000
1886	1	4,186,152
1887	1	6,692,744
1888	1	6,253,295
1889	1	6,531,876
1890	1	7,082,204
1891	1	7,451,535
1892	1	8,211,181
1893	1	7,411,815
1894	1	7,563,488
1895	1	7,741,077
1896	1	7,970,450
Totals	79	151,990,817

The following table gives the number of barrels of Portland cement imported into the United States, and the number of **barrels** of that class of cement manufactured in this country during the years **named.**

YEARS.	Imported.	Domestic.
1878	92,000	28,000
1879	106,000	39,000
1880	187,000	42,000
1881	221,000	60,000
1882	370,406	85,000
1883	486,418	**90,000**
1884	585,768	**100,000**
1885	554,396	150,000
1886	650,032	150,000
1887	1,070,400	250,000
1888	1,835,504	250,000
1889	1,740,356	300,000
1890	1,940,186	335,000
1891	2,988,313	**454,813**
1892	2,440,654	547,440
1893	2,674,149	590,652
1894	2,638,107	798,757
1895	2,997,395	990,324
1896	2,989,597	1,543,023
Total	26,567,681	6,804,009

PRODUCT OF ROCK CEMENT IN UNITED STATES, 1895 AND 1896.

STATE.	1895.			1896.		
	Number of works.	No. of Barrels.	Bulk Value at Mills.	Number of works.	No. of Barrels.	Bulk Value at Mills.
Georgia	1	8,050	$6,038	1	12,700	$9,525
Illinois	2	491,012	171,854	2	544,326	217,731
Ind. and Ky. . .	14	1,703,000	681,400	15	1,636,000	654,400
Kansas	2	140,000	56,000	2	125,567	50,226
Md. and W. Va. .	4	242,000	116,700	5	271,500	125,175
Minnesota . . .	2	73,772	33,621	2	83,098	38,549
New Mexico . .	1	5,000	6,000	1	idle	. . . .
New York . . .						
Erie County . .	4	556,754	269,089	4	550,851	275,426
Onondaga ⎫ Co. Schoharie ⎭	10	152,973	77,974	10	204,375	92,450
Ulster County .	15	3,230,000	1,938,031	15	3,426,692	2,056,015
Ohio	3	38,060	22,836	3	28,565	17,139
Pennsylvania . .	5	600,895	300,447	6	608,000	304,000
Texas	1	10,000	17,000	1	12,000	18,000
Virginia . . .	2	13,050	7,830	3	16,776	10,566
Wisconsin . . .	1	476,511	190,604	1	450,000	180,000
Total . .	67	7,741,077	$3,895,424	71	7,970,450	$4,049,202

The foregoing tables afford a wide field for speculation as to the uses to which this enormous amount of cement has been applied.

One can hardly realize the value of the properties which have been constructed with mortars and concretes made with this cement.

. Among those which seem most prominent to the mind may be mentioned the almost innumerable number of tunnels, bridges, culverts, and buildings connected with the 235,000 miles of railroad track in this country, the improvements made in all cities in the line of waterworks, in the construction of aqueducts, reservoirs, and dams, and in the street pavements, concrete foundations, sewers, and sidewalks.

The amount of American Rock cement which has been used in the construction of cisterns by the farmers and planters of this country, and in the villages having no waterworks, is almost inconceivable.

We append hereto a list of a few of the notable engineering and architectural structures which have been laid in American Rock cement.

It is difficult, if not impossible, to estimate the cost of these improvements, the permanence and stability of which depend so much on the cement used in their construction.

Important as these structures may be, they are absolutely insignificant when compared with the immense body of work done with American Rock cements, of which no complete record can ever be made.

STRUCTURES LAID IN AMERICAN ROCK CEMENT.

CUMBERLAND, MD., CEMENT.

Washington, D. C. — Boundary Sewer, Bureau of Engraving and Printing, New Patent Office, National Museum, New Pension Office, New Navy, State, and War Department, New Library Building, Tiber Sewer.

Federal Buildings. — Pittsburgh and Harrisburg, Penn., Baltimore, Md.

U. S. Government Work. — Kanawha River Locks, W. Va.

Bridges in Pennsylvania. — Altoona, Columbia, Harrisburg, Millersburgh, Johnstown, Williamsport.

Centennial Buildings in Philadelphia, Penn., and Johns Hopkins Hospital Building, Baltimore, Md.

ROUND TOP CEMENT, HANCOCK, MD.

Washington, D. C. — United States Capitol, Washington Monument, War, State, and Navy Building, Washington and Potomac Tunnel, New Washington Reservoir, Boundary Sewer 2½ miles long, 20 ft. internal diameter, Long Bridge over the Potomac River, and Cabin John Bridge, which is the largest stone arch in existence. It was built by General Meigs in 1866, and has one span of 220 ft., with a rise of 57 ft. 3 ins., and is 20 ft. wide. This bridge is only exceeded in the world's history by a bridge built in 1377 by Barnabo Visconti over the Adda at Frezzo, Italy, which was destroyed in a local war in 1416. It was a segmental arch, with a span of 237 ft. and a rise of 68 ft.

Baltimore, Md. — Gunpowder Waterworks, City Hall Building, Gas Works.

HOWARD CEMENT, CEMENT, GA.

Two bridges across **Tennessee** River at Chattanooga, Tenn.; **Kimball House**, Atlanta, Ga.; Georgia Central Railroad Bridge at Columbus, Ga.; Fulton County Jail and Seaboard Air Line Depot, **Atlanta**, Ga.; Times Building, Chattanooga, Tenn.; the Vanderbilt **residence**, Biltmore, Asheville, **N. C.**

JAMES RIVER CEMENT, GLASGOW, VA.

Waterworks in Virginia.— Richmond, Lynchburgh, **Staunton**, Charlottesville, Liberty, Lexington, Danville, also in Durham, N. C.

Richmond, Va.— New City Hall, Church Hill Tunnel, bridges across James River at Snowden and Joshua Falls, high bridge at Farmville, Va., Washington Monument foundations, Capitol Square, Richmond, Va.

HOWE'S CAVE, N. Y., CEMENT.

State Capitol Building, Albany, N. Y.; Federal Building, Albany, N. Y. *Waterworks* at Albany, N. Y., at Plattsburgh, N. Y., at New Milford, Conn., at Cobleskill, N. Y., at Ware, Mass. County Court House, Scranton, Penn. Used exclusively in the walls of the Hotel Holland, Fifth Avenue and 30th Street, New York City, and in the Postal Telegraph Building, New York City.

BUFFALO, N. Y., CEMENT.

In City of Buffalo. — Iroquois **Hotel, Niagara Hotel, Buffalo Library**, St. Louis Church, Church of the **Seven Dolors**, Board of Trade Building, Bank of Buffalo, Bank of Commerce, German **Insurance Building, Erie County** Penitentiary, Erie and Niagara Elevators, **Trunk Sewer, and Hertel Avenue Sewer, both 8 ft. diameter, New** York **State Asylum, Inlet** Pier and Waterworks **tunnel under the** Niagara **River, one of the most** difficult under-water **constructions in** the world ; **Buffalo General** Hospital, **Erie County** Almshouse, Buffalo Medical College.

Towers of Suspension Bridge, Minneapolis, Minn.; Kokomo Gas

Works, Kokomo, Ind.; **Court** House, Dansville, Ill.; Court **House, Hamilton, Ont., State House** of Correction, Ionia, Mich.; piers **of** Erie Railway Bridge, Portage, N. Y.; Soldiers' Home, Bath, N. Y.

Federal Buildings. — Post-offices, Buffalo, N. Y.; Cleveland, Ohio, Pittsburgh and Alleghany, Penn.

U. S. Government Work. — Falls of St. Anthony; Mississippi River, Minn.; Rock Island Arsenal, Rock Island, Ill.

The dams in the Missouri River at Great Falls, Mont.

AKRON, N. Y., CEMENT.

Bridges. — Railroad bridge **over the** Hudson River at Pough-**keepsie**; cantilever and suspension at Niagara Falls, N. Y.; Connecticut River, Windsor Locks, Conn.; Mississippi River at Burlington, **Iowa, at St. Louis,** Mo.; Red River at Fulton, Ark.; great viaduct **over the Cuyahoga** River at Cleveland, Ohio; waterworks tunnel under **Lake Michigan at Chicago,** Ill.; elevated tracks and bridge over the **Genesee River at Rochester,** N. Y.; waterworks reservoir, Buffalo, **N. Y.; City and County Hall,** Buffalo, **N. Y.;** Grand Central **Depot, New York, N. Y.**

UTICA, ILL., CEMENT.

Chicago Buildings. — Armour & Dole Elevators, Central **Elevators** A and B, Hough & Galena Elevators, Chicago Board of **Trade,** Pullman Works, Rialto Office Building, Pullman Office Building, Rookery Office Building, Home Insurance Building, Chicago Public Library Building, Woman's Temple, Illinois Steel Company, South Chicago.

Indianapolis, Ind. — Big **Four Round House,** Home Brewing Company Building, Park Theatre, **New** Hospital, Indiana State Prison, Michigan City, Ind.

Kansas City, Mo. — Y. M. C. A. Building, Keith & Perry Building.

Saint Joseph, Mo. — United States Government Building.

Omaha, Neb. — New York Life Insurance Building, City Hall, Paxton House, **Murry** House, Millard House.

Denver, Col. — **State House,** Union Depot, The Windsor, The **Albany, The** Equitable Insurance Company Building.

Pueblo, Col. — Opera House, Board **of** Trade Building, Union Depot.

Des Moines, Iowa.— State Capitol, Y. M. C. A. Building, Dam in Des Moines River.

St. Paul, Minn.— Ryan Hotel, New York Life and Germania Life Insurance Company Buildings, Manhattan Building, Pioneer Press Building, Globe Building, Lowery Arcade, Union Depot, Gas Works, Endicott Arcade, Germania Bank Building.

Minneapolis, Minn.— Union Depot, New York Life Insurance Building.

Duluth, Minn.— Hotel Saint Louis, Spalding House, Board of Trade Building, Court House and Jail.

MANKATO, MINN., CEMENT.

Federal Buildings at Duluth, St. Paul, and Mankato, Minn.; Ashland, Wis.; Fort Dodge, Cedar Rapids, and Sioux City, Iowa; Fremont, Neb.; Sioux Falls, So. Dak.; Fargo, No. Dak. Bridge across Mississippi River at Redwing, Minn.; across the Blue Earth River at Mankato, Minn. State Insane Asylum, Independence, Iowa, and at Fergus Falls, Minn. Railroad Bridge crossing the Mississippi River at Plattsmouth, Neb. Waterworks, Minneapolis, Minn. Irrigation Canals at San Bernardino and Riverside, Cal., and State Capitol Building at St. Paul, Minn.

CUMMINGS CEMENT, AKRON, N. Y.

Federal Buildings.— Jackson, Tenn.; Macon, Ga.; Aberdeen, Miss.; Waco, Tex.; Port Royal, S. C.; Clarksburg, W. Va.; Harrisonburg, Va.; Detroit, Mich.; Youngstown, Ohio.

United States Government Work.— Sacket's Harbor, N. Y., and Buffalo Harbor, Buffalo, N. Y.

Trumbull County Court House, Warren, Ohio; Dana's Music Hall, Warren, Ohio; Otis Steel Company and Cleveland Rolling Mill Company Buildings, Cleveland, Ohio; New City Hall, Goodale Block, Burdick Block, Flower Block, Watertown, N. Y.; Herrin & Sons Paper Mills and Dam, Great Bend, N. Y.; Dexter Paper Company Buildings and stone arch raceway, Dexter, N. Y.; Globe Paper Mills, Brownville, N. Y.; Bridge at Black River, N. Y.; Ursuline Convent of the Sacred Heart Buildings, and the Episcopal Church Building, Youngstown, Ohio; the Great Eads Bridge, St. Louis,

Mo.; County Alms House, Rome, N. Y.; Diamond Match Company Buildings, Oswego, N. Y.; Faxton Hospital, Utica, N. Y.; Hoosac Tunnel, Mass.; Niagara Falls Paper Company Buildings, Niagara Falls, N. Y.; Erie County Savings Bank Building, Buffalo, N. Y.; City and County Hall, Buffalo, N. Y.; waterworks standpipe at Delphos, Ohio, and Akron, N. Y.; reservoir waterworks, Fredonia, N. Y.; Atlanta Brewing Company, Atlanta, Ga.; Chattanooga Brewing Company, Chattanooga, Tenn.; Sebald Brewing Company, Middletown, Ohio; Gerst Brewing Company, Nashville, Tenn.; Brenner Brewing Company, Covington, Ky.; old and new Croton Aqueducts, New York (613,000 barrels); Grand Central Depot, New York, N. Y.; N. Y. C. & H. R. R. bridge over the Hudson River at Albany, N. Y Waterworks dam at Willimantic, Conn.; the great International bridge crossing the Niagara River at Buffalo, N. Y., and the suspension and cantilever bridges at Suspension Bridge, N. Y.

Buildings in New Castle, Penn. — The New Castle Steel and Tin Plate Company (largest tin mill in the world), the New Castle Wire Nail Company, Shenango Valley Steel Company, New Castle Tube Company, Arethusa Iron Works, Atlantic Iron and Steel Company, Shenango Glass Company, Lawrence Glass Company, New Castle Water Company, Pearson Building, Boyles' Block, St. Cloud Hotel.

Heavy stone masonry on the new Erie Canal improvements, and for concrete pavement work, over 125,000 barrels yearly.

FORT SCOTT, KAN., CEMENT.

Federal Buildings. — Kansas City, Mo.; Atchison, Fort Scott, Salina, Fort Leavenworth, Fort Riley, Kan.; Camden, Ark.; Pueblo, Col.; Fort Crook, Neb.

Buildings in Kansas City, Mo. — New England Life, New York Life, Insurance Buildings, Union Depot, Kansas City Journal, Board of Trade, American National Bank, Hotel Brunswick, Coates House, Public Library, Gibraltar, Massachusetts, Nelson, Bayard, Baird, Peet Bros., Kansas City Star, and Waterworks Buildings. The Dold, Fowler, Allcutt, and Armour Packing Company Buildings.

State Capitol Buildings at Topeka, Kan., and Austin, Tex., County Court Houses, Fort Worth and Dallas, Tex.; Warrensburg,

Chillicothe, and Clinton, Mo.; National Soldiers' Home, Leavenworth, Kan.; Union Depot, Omaha, Neb.

Waterworks. — Lamar, Boonville, and Kansas City, Mo.; Parsons, Coffeyville, St. Mary's, and Horton, Kan.; Yocum and Cisco, Tex.; Missouri River Bridge, Jefferson City, Mo.

MILWAUKEE, WIS., CEMENT.

Minneapolis, Minn. — Stone arch bridge over Mississippi River, Hennepin County Court House and City Hall, dams and retaining walls of the St. Anthony's Falls Water Power Company, the Exposition Building, Guaranty Loan and Trust Building, Union Depot.

St. Paul, Minn. — Ramsey County Court House and City Hall, Robert Street Bridge, and the Chicago and Great Western Railway Bridge over the Mississippi River, Globe Building.

United States Government Locks at Sault Ste. Marie, Mich.

Milwaukee, Wis. — City Hall, City Library, Pabst Building.

Omaha, Neb. — Bee Building, City Hall, American Waterworks' Basins.

Duluth, Minn. — Masonic Temple, Lyceum Building, Union Depot.

Chicago, Ill. — Chamber of Commerce, Rookery Building, Home Insurance Building, C. B. & Q. General Office Building.

Federal Buildings. — Milwaukee, Wis.; Omaha, Neb.; and Duluth, Minn.

LOUISVILLE, KY., CEMENT.

UNITED STATES GOVERNMENT WORK.

Locks and Dams. — On Muskingum River; Muscle Shoals, Tennessee River; Warrior River; Kentucky River; Kanawha River; Big Sandy River; Illinois River; Ohio River below Pittsburgh; Monongahela River, Pittsburgh; Sault Ste. Marie; Canal around Falls of the Ohio at Louisville.

Custom Houses. — Cincinnati, Ohio; St. Louis, Mo.; Louisville, Ky.; Memphis, Tenn.; Chattanooga, Tenn.

Bridges. — P. H. R. R. connecting bridge over the Ohio at Pittsburgh; B. & O. R. R. bridge over the Monongahela above Pittsburgh; P. H. R. R. at Steubenville, Ohio; N. & W. R. R. at

Kenova, W. Va.; L. & N. R. R. at Cincinnati, Ohio; C. & O. **R. R.** at Cincinnati, Ohio; Suspension Bridge at Cincinnati, Ohio; **Cincin-** nati & Newport Bridge at Cincinnati; Pennsylvania R. R. Bridge at Louisville, Ky.; Kentucky & Indiana Bridge at Louisville, Ky.; Louisville & Jeffersonville Bridge at Louisville, Ky.; L. & N. R. R. at Henderson, Ky.; **I. C. R. R.** at Cairo, Ill.; K. C. & M. R. R. **at** Memphis, Tenn.; Tennessee River Bridge at Chattanooga; Eads Bridge at St. Louis; Merchants Bridge at St. Louis; C. B. & Q. R. R. Bridge at Alton, Ill.; C. B. & Q. R. R. Bridge at Bellefontaine, Mo.; C. B. **&** Q. R. R. Bridge at Leavenworth, Kan.; Illinois Central R. R. Bridge at Yazoo River, Miss.; Northern Pacific R. R. Bridge **at** Minneapolis, Minn.; N. C. & St. L. R. R. Bridge at Bridgeport, Tenn.; Bridge over Missouri River at Sioux City, Iowa; Railroad Bridges at Dubuque, **Davenport,** Clinton, Fort Madison, **Burlington,** and Keokuk, **Iowa.**

Waterworks, Dams, etc.—Chattahoochee River Dam, **Colum-** bus, **Ga.;** **Hot Springs Waterworks** Dam, Hot Springs, **Ark.;** Little Rock, **Ark., Dam;** Covington, Ky., Reservoir; Nashville, Tenn., Reservoir; Minneapolis, **Minn., Waterworks;** St. **Anthony** Falls Tunnel; St. Louis, Mo., Waterworks; Little Falls, Minn., Dam.

Public Buildings.—State House, Indianapolis, Ind.; State House, Springfield, Ill.; **State** House, Lansing, Mich.; State House, **Atlanta,** Ga.; State House, Austin, Texas.

Tunnels.—Tunnel under Chicago River, Chicago, Ill.; Cleveland Waterworks Tunnel; Sanitary Drainage Canal, Chicago, Ill.; **Sea Wall** Foundation Lincoln Park, Chicago, Ill.; Lake Shore Drive **Sea Wall,** Chicago, Ill.; Palmer House Gas Receiver, Chicago, Ill.; Farwell Block, Chicago, Ill.; Dock, San Diego, **Cal.**

ROSENDALE, N. Y., CEMENT.

New York, N. Y.—High Bridge, Harlem River; New York & Brooklyn **Bridge;** Washington Bridge, Harlem River; Madison Avenue Bridge, **Harlem River; Second** Avenue Bridge, Harlem **River;** American Museum **of** Natural History; Astoria Hotel— Largest in the World; Washington Life Insurance Building; **Co-** lumbia College—New Buildings; New Park Row Office Building— Thirty Stories; New York University Buildings; Astor's New Exchange **Court** Building; Post-Office; **Custom** House; Equitable

Building; Mutual Life Insurance Building; Public School Buildings; New York Athletic Club Building.

Boston, Mass. — Subway; State House, Bulfinch Front; Tremont Temple; Parker House Extension; Suffolk Bank Building; Austen & Doten Warehouse; Brookline Sewer Work; Metropolitan Sewerage Extension; Metropolitan Water Board — Nashua Aqueduct; Sewer Department; Water Board Department; Paving Department; Sudbury Building; Warren Chambers; Metropolitan Warehouse Company; Conduit Work by West End Street Railway Company; Boston Electric Light Company; Edison Electric Company; West End Power Station, Charlestown; Edison Power Station, Atlantic Avenue; Union Terminal Station.

Pittsburgh, Penn. — Post-Office; Court House; Carnegie Mills; Davis Island Dam; Monongahela Bridge.

Washington, D. C. — Capitol; Bureau of Engraving and Printing; New Patent Office; New Pension Building; Navy, War, and State Department Building; Washington Waterworks; Treasury Building.

United States Government Work. — Fortifications: Fort Delaware; Fort Montgomery; Fort Jackson; Fort Adams; Fort Sumter; Fort Trumbull; Fort Taylor; Fort Warren; Fort Jefferson; Fort Wadsworth; Fort Preble; Fort Monroe; Fort Hamilton; Fort Washington; Fort Knox; Fort Morgan; Governor's Island; Tybee Island; Amelia Island; Fisher's Island; Garden Keys; Hawkins' Point; Pensacola; North Point; San Francisco; Gull Island; Sandy Hook; Newport Harbor; Plattsburgh; Portland, Me.; Key West; Finn's Point.

Navy Yards. — Brooklyn; Norfolk.

Rivers. — Allegheny; Ohio; Kanawha.

Dams and Waterworks. — New Haven, Conn.; Holyoke, Mass.; Mechanicsville, N. Y.; Rochester, N. Y.; Pottstown, Penn.; Pen Yan, N. Y.; Canandaigua, N. Y.; Dunnings, Penn.; Kittanning Point, Penn.; New Milford, Conn.; New York City, Jerome Park Reservoir; Boston, Mass.

South Carolina Cotton Mills. — Spartan Mills, Spartansburgh; Pacolet Mills, Pacolet; Pelzer Mills, Pelzer; Clifton Mills, Clifton; Columbia Mills, Columbia; Reedy River Mills, Mauldins; D. E. Converse Mills, Glendale; Union Mills, Union; Pelham Mills, Mauldins; Fingerville Manufacturing Co., Fingerville.

This is indeed a wonderful record, and it is but the culmination of four thousand years of successful usage of Rock cements.

It is the refutation of all the baseless theories, false reasoning, and untenable analogies which have been evolved from the high short-time tests of Portland brands.

This marvelous record is the final justification of American Rock cements, which, setting slowly at first, nevertheless, owing to their smooth and pasty consistency and greater volume per pound, attain in time a stone-like durability impossible to the brittle, quick-setting, and glassy Portlands.

The latter are an experiment begun seventy-three years ago, and the history of it is strewn with failures.

The former have been made through centuries which disclose no recorded failure, and time but adds to the proof of merit.

If long experience is to be a guide, the conclusion is irresistible that for substantially all the manifold purposes for which a cement is used, none has yet been produced equal to the AMERICAN ROCK CEMENTS.